Mexico, 1689. Lured by the imagined grandeur and adventure of the viceroyal Court, Josefina, a sheltered landowner's wife, accepts an invitation from the Marquesa to come and socialize with the cultural elite. She is overwhelmed by the intensity of the Court's complicated world. While fighting off aggressive advances from the Marquesa's husband, she finds her marriage vows tested by the unexpected passion of the Bishop of Puebla.

Amidst this drama, Josefina finds herself inexorably drawn to the nuns who study and write poetry at the risk of persecution by the Spanish Inquisition. One nun in particular, Sor Juana Inés de la Cruz, teaches Josefina about poetry, power, and the nature and consequences of love, all in the shadow of the Holy Office. She is Josefina's mentor and lynchpin during her tumultuous passage from grounded wife and mother to woman of this treacherous, confusing, and ultimately physically and intellectually fulfilling world.

JOSEFINA'S SIN

JOSEFINA'S SIN

A Novel

CLAUDIA H. LONG

ATRIA PAPERBACK

New York   London   Toronto   Sydney

ATRIA PAPERBACK

A Division of Simon & Schuster, Inc.
1230 Avenue of the Americas
New York, NY 10020

The author gratefully acknowledges permission from Princeton University Press
to reprint the poems on pages 13 and 14 from *The Dream of the Poem,*
translated, edited, and with an introduction by Peter Cole, © 2007 by
Princeton University Press.

First Atria Paperback edition August 2011

ATRIA PAPERBACK and colophon are trademarks
of Simon & Schuster, Inc.

For information about special discounts for bulk purchases,
please contact Simon & Schuster Special Sales at
1-866-506-1949 or business@simonandschuster.com.

The Simon & Schuster Speakers Bureau can bring authors
to your live event. For more information or to book an event,
contact the Simon & Schuster Speakers Bureau at
1-866-248-3049 or visit our website at www.simonspeakers.com.

Designed by Esther Paradelo

Manufactured in the United States of America

10   9   8   7   6   5   4   3   2   1

Library of Congress Cataloging-in-Publication Data
 Long, Claudia H.
 Josefina's sin : a novel / Claudia H. Long.
 p.   cm.
 1. Wives—Fiction. 2. Inquisition—Fiction. 3. Mexico—History—Spanish colony,
 1540–1810—Fiction. I. Title.
 PS3612.O4925J67   2011
 813'.6—dc22   2010037890

ISBN 978-1-4516-1067-3
ISBN 978-1-4516-1068-0 (ebook)

To Clyde

PROLOGUE

I am twenty-seven years old today. My husband, the Honorable Don Manuel Castillo Coronado, has immured me in a convent, with his mistress, Doña Angélica, to tend to me. She can only hope that my palsy, which first rendered me mute, and now lame, will soon be fatal, and that Don Manuel will then marry her. Poor deluded fool that she is—but her ambition could well hasten my demise.

The rustle of nuns' habits, the whispers of their cautious voices, these are the musical accompaniments to my restless hours. My mind spins forbidden, dangerous verses, though my hands are idled, one by palsy and the other by my husband's command. Only in secret, safe from the sorrowing eyes of the nuns and the pitiless glare of the Inquisition, are these pages of my story penned, destined only for the pyre.

My breasts are hard as bricks. The new milk goes unsuckled and my infant Juan Carlos finds his nutrition at the pap of a wet nurse; his early cries are heard by another. It has been ten days now, and the ache is diminishing. But the after-birth pains between my legs are still sharp reminders of my sin. Angélica will bring the warm cloths for my breasts. Angélica will part my thighs and lay poultices where my husband has not been for almost two years. I will be forced to bear her mocking smile as she opens and closes my legs, knowing that at night, Manuel lies between her thighs.

Tend to me indeed.

PART ONE

*O*NE

*I*N THE SPRING OF the year of Our Lord 1683, on the high and
dusty plain of the City of Mexico, in the land of New Spain, I,
Josefina María del Carmen Asturias, became Doña Josefina María del
Carmen Asturias de Castillo. I knelt trembling before the Bishop, my
eyes cast down in maidenly modesty, my new husband at my side. My
lace mantilla covered my face, but I felt myself so conspicuously flushed
that I imagined light gleaming through the lace and casting an intricate
pattern on the altar cloth.

Don Manuel's large hand covered mine. "I do take her to be my wife,"
he said. The warmth of his hand traveled up my arm, reassured me.

"Yes," I whispered when the Monsignor asked me to accept my vow.
The beautiful words of the Mass were intoned, the Latin flowing over me.
Though I had only, at that time, read simple psalms, and did not often
write more than my Christian name, I was a quick learner of language. I
knew and understood every word, including my vow to honor, cherish,
and obey, keeping to him, and none other. Perhaps Don Manuel's Latin
was not as good as mine.

I had heard of romantic love through whispered poems read to me
long before, but for myself, I held no such illusions of love. Marriage
was the desired state for a woman, and to make a home and fill it with
children was her duty and her highest goal. My father had concluded this
most advantageous deal with Don Manuel. He had a nineteen-year-old
daughter to marry off, one who was intelligent, serious, and, though not
pretty, certainly virtuous. I had managed my father's household since my
mother had died in a late childbirth when I was fifteen, and I was capable

and industrious. Manuel had land, and a need for sons. Though he could have chosen another, he and my father had reached an understanding quickly.

"Is she pure?" Don Manuel had asked. My father had not taken offense.

"Of course," he had answered, "look at her." He could have meant that my chastity glowed from my virgin brow. Or he could have meant that I was ugly. Given that I was already nineteen, if I had not been seduced yet, I had to be plain.

My virginity had been the deciding factor. Don Manuel's lands were vast, and he did not want a false heir. We were married as soon as the banns had been posted.

MY HUSBAND GAVE A *charreada* to celebrate our wedding. We rode from the church together, and arrived at the Coronado hacienda in the midday. I was shown to the room that would be mine forevermore. My family was given lodgings elsewhere in the hacienda, for though the distance from my home was but an hour, the fiesta would go long into the night.

My wedding dress had been my mother's, and my two sisters had worn it as well. I had lengthened it a bit, as I was taller than they were, and slimmer as well. My curves had increased somewhat with time, but I was not lavishly gifted as my mother had been, or as my sisters were, and the alterations had taken the better part of two weeks. To cover where I had taken in the skirt, I had embroidered climbing roses in red and pink, and the vibrant colors were repeated where I had gathered the low neckline as well. The glow of my warm complexion and chestnut hair was deepened by the white blouse, and the lace mantilla now draped over my shoulders completed my ensemble.

The wedding feast was sumptuous. My husband's home was large, and the entire front of the hacienda and the great room within had been decorated with flowers and bright cloths. There were tables set with food and drink, and there were many servants to attend to the guests. A small table in the center had been laid with plates for two, and there, side by side, he and I would sit and enjoy our first meal as man and wife. Though I had been horribly nervous before the ceremony, in terror that Don Manuel would somehow change his mind and leave me at the altar, I had no fear of my wedding night. I was a woman of the land. I was ravenous.

I sat beside my new husband and watched him eat. He cut into the soft green chile, and the filling of nuts and cream oozed out from within. He put some of the luscious cream on a tortilla, rolled it, and took a bite. Then he turned to me and offered me a taste. The bite of the chile played with the unctuous filling and the dry wrapping, and I licked my lips. He smiled at me, his green-brown eyes looking into my coffee-dark ones. I did not look away.

We went out to the back of the hacienda, where a great fence encircled a corral. There was a stable with horses, and beyond, sheds for cattle. Past the sheds lay fields for grazing, and my husband's extensive landholdings. Our rancho at home, where I had always felt wealthy, was more modest in contrast.

Servants brought some tables from the feasting area and set them up around the corral. Men pulled riding pants over their wedding clothes; spurs were attached to boots, and horses brought out. The musicians struck up country tunes, lively and loud. More food was brought, and wine poured for the men.

My sisters and their children sat with me as the men saddled up. My father, advancing in years, smiled at me as he mounted his own horse. He would ride, but not with the young men. Other older rancheros joined him as they circled the corral.

Then I saw Manuel, my new master, ride out. He rode bareback, urging his horse all around the corral. As he passed before me he removed his hat and tossed it to me. I caught it, laughing, and placed it on my own head. Now hatless, he sped around the corral, as a bull calf, nearly grown, was released into the corral. The calf pranced and bucked wildly.

Everyone shouted and clapped as Manuel's lasso whirled through the air once, twice, and landed squarely around the neck of the bull calf. Manuel quickly circled the calf, and, twisting his rope, brought it around the young animal, hobbling it. With another twist, he brought the calf to the ground. Cheers erupted, and Manuel, still riding with one hand, holding the lasso with the other, bowed to me.

Then he dismounted in a great jump and unbound the calf. With only the rope around the calf's neck, Manuel led the now-docile animal back to the cattle pen.

I clapped and laughed, enjoying his skill. He was tall and strong, and his lands stretched forever.

Soon other men entered the corral. Some rode the bucking bulls, others roped steers. All were skilled and daring, but in my eyes none was more daring, more dashing than the newly wed Manuel.

Dusty and smiling, he joined me at the table, raising another glass of wine. I raised my glass as well, though after the first glass of wine, it had been filled with *jamaica,* the sweet-tart hibiscus water. "To my bride!" he called out. Light glinted off his silver-encrusted belt, and from his hazel-dark eyes, as he smiled down at me.

A wedding anticipates a deflowering. At the end of the feast, as the musicians shifted to the tender songs of Old Spain, the maid led me away from the party. The rest stayed to revel, but I was taken to my new room, where my belongings had already been placed. The maid, an Indian perhaps twenty years my senior named Cayetana, had been given charge of me, and she had laid out two basins of warm water and a thick towel.

"Wash yourself, señora," Cayetana said, "all over." I had done so before the wedding, but I complied. The water in the rinsing basin had been scented with geranium, and I liked the smell. I put on a soft white gown with flowing sleeves, and nothing underneath. I lay down on the soft blankets and Cayetana trimmed the wick on the lamp. "Are you scared?" she asked.

"No. I'm happy."

Cayetana grinned at me. "Like an Indian," she said, and left.

Though virginal, I was no stranger to the mating act. I had witnessed it enough on our small farm, and I knew enough from the Psalms to recognize desire. And there had been the visit from Father Alonso, when I was sixteen. He had come to console the family, give my father strength after my mother died. I had never seen a person with hair the color of fire, and at first I had trouble believing that he was a man of God, not of the Devil, but he made it his mission to disabuse me of my backward superstitions. He spent long hours praying with my father in our study, and longer hours with me. His visit had awakened in me a longing for something I couldn't name, but I sensed, in my innocence, that it could only be filled by marriage.

Father Alonso had traveled the world. He had seen the pyramids of Egypt, and our own heathen pyramids in Teotihuacán. He had taken the waters in the land of the Teutons, and had dipped in the healing fountains outside Guadalajara. He read to me of faraway places, mythical beings, and the bloody sacrifices of our indigenous predecessors, and, most of all, he read to me of love. Though he was a priest, sworn to abjure the pleasures of the flesh, he had not recoiled from the bursting flora of the works of Calderón de la Barca, or the earthy delights of the *villancicos,* songs of the people, sung by slaves, Gypsies, and the Portuguese.

He was always slightly furtive in his readings. This gave both him and the poems he read an air of mystery and danger. There were powerful men within the Church who would punish anyone who strayed from the purity of Rome's doctrine, he whispered, and our explorations had to be kept securely within our thick stone walls. Of course, it was God's love he was talking about. I smiled at the memory. It was my one secret.

I lay in the broad bed in my new room, waiting in the golden light of the lamp until I heard the door open. I smelled him before I saw him, for I kept my eyes closed. I did not want to seem immodest. The leather of his jacket, the sweat from the long day, the aroma was as mouthwatering as the feast itself.

He stroked the side of my face and I opened my eyes. Again he smiled, and I felt any resistance melt. "I will be quick with the first time," he said. "Don't be afraid." I didn't answer. That suited him, for he took off his jacket, his shirt, and his boots, and through barely open eyes I watched it all. Then he unbuckled his pants, letting the heavy silver-trimmed belt fall to the floor. That is the sound of my wedding night, and the nights thereafter. He lifted my gown. I shut my eyes tight.

After the first painful penetration I found my husband entirely to my liking: attentive, skilled, and passionate. More than the act of procreation, his attentions opened my eyes to the possible meanings of the Psalms. What words had hinted at, his hands conveyed. Under his demanding tutelage, I became as skilled and passionate as he.

Not surprisingly, our first son, Joaquín, was born ten months after our nuptials. He was, and remains, a large and healthy boy, as active and rambunctious as I could hope. His riding and roping, at a mere seven years old, presage the talents of a man, and his appetite is in keeping with his energies. Nonetheless, his birth left me unfit for connubial activity for quite some time.

The consequence, naturally, was that Don Manuel sought consolation elsewhere. This in and of itself was not disturbing to me, as I knew of my own father's wanderings when my mother was recovering from childbed. No woman of any intelligence would ever expect a man to be faithful. A man's needs are so great. As long as his dalliances were kept from my open eyes they did not trouble me. In some sense, I now realize, I welcomed the help, in that Joaquín's birth not only tore me inside, but also was the occasion of my first complete love.

When I arose in the morning, it was to the sweet milky breath of my newborn son. I had placed his cradle near my bed, and so lay awake listening to him breathe until his hunger woke him. My days were filled with his gurgles and demands, and my nights, disturbed by his cries, were devoted to his care. I held him in my arms, rocking gently against my pillows, while his eager mouth clamped onto my engorged and tender nipples. The initial pain of the connection quickly merged into a rhythmic and joyful suckling. I watched my life-sustenance fill him, and I became my full self in my new role. I could look into his darkening eyes for hours. I could rock him, sing to him, dandle him without cease.

Poor Don Manuel had to take a second chair to the magnificence of his son. His own pride in his son was merely in his creation. He would grow in his love for this boy who was so much like him, but that was not until years to come. For now, Manuel accepted the tiny usurper, and his attentions were thus diverted.

Was that the beginning of his liaison with Angélica? Not in the actual sense, but rather, I think there were other ladies who were eager to warm his bed for a night, in exchange for, well, I wonder. In exchange for what?

Don Manuel, for all his tall, swarthy good looks, is no conversationalist. He is generous, of course, with both his money and his manly charms. He gave me a large allowance for my clothing, and our household did not need to be run on the last centavo. Though he was not extravagant, he expected that his lands would furnish a pleasant household, and I enjoyed fulfilling that expectation. One lovely woman who graced our table many a night, Doña Carolina, remarked that the quality of our evening meals made New Spain rival the finest that Paris or Vienna could offer.

Though I have never been to either place, I like to think that it was in part my careful management, along with my husband's wealth, that allowed it to be so. Words could create pictures, and words could also inspire flavors, aromas, even a quality of light. When a fine dish was described, I somehow imagined the tastes, the smells, and the textures, and could translate the dream to the table. I remember a time that Doña Carolina told us of a French dish called a soufflé. "It's a pouffed dish, dear," she said, in that affected tone she took with me. "It seems the cheese is melted within, and the eggs grow up around it."

I knew right away, somehow, that it would be the egg whites that made the dish light, and a bit of herb, our oregano, would bring the cheese to the fore. Manuel had favored me with his tender smile the night I served it to the two of us. "It's a food for love," he'd said, again covering my hand with his large brown one. The melting smoothness had proven to be as sensual as a caress, as golden as a sonnet. He had kissed me, there, at the table.

But again, Manuel could only offer his physical attributes. In conversation with men, he could talk land, horses, crops with the toughest of them. With the ladies, though, he merely smiled that unbearably irresistible smile and narrowed his eyes in concentration on their beauty. Our dinners, when we had guests at our table, gave Manuel beauties to gaze upon but filled my head with pictures and dreams that I never thought to give voice to.

Talk of foreign lands, the marvels of Seville or Salamanca, would wash over him as he gazed in rapt delight upon the speaker. Women, eager to keep his attention, would spin tales of such wonders that I would never have believed possible, but for my memories of Father Alonso. Ships on the water, crossing oceans for a month; works of sculpture in marble that almost looked alive; cathedrals with spires that touched the heavens—such fantasies they invented to amuse him. I, of course, had nothing to add to these visions, having traveled no further than my father's hacienda, an hour's ride. But I dreamed of them at night.

In truth, Manuel and I never talked more than a phrase or two, for me to satisfy him that all was running smoothly, or for him to answer a question that I had. But with the new challenges of wifedom, followed by the rich rewards of motherhood, I had little need for his words.

When my body was healed, he returned to my bed, adding refinements to our passions. I was happy he was back, and grateful that I did not immediately conceive again. It took a full year before I found myself with child a second time. This time my confinement was easier, and I was able to weather the birth of Ernesto Manuel with less damage to myself. My period of chastity was short, and Manuel eagerly resumed his marital duties.

It was around that time that Angélica came into my life. She did not come into Manuel's bed then, but it was a progression that in retrospect I see was both inevitable and obvious.

It had long been the custom for cattle ranchers of high standing to be asked to stay in a hacienda where they had been conducting business. Before his death, Angélica's husband had been a frequent visitor to Don Manuel's, to their mutual profit. In their brief marriage, Angélica had accompanied her husband once before, and though they had stayed at a neighboring hacienda that time, she clearly had liked what she saw here. As the sales season approached, her note prettily asking for an invitation was met by Don Manuel, and hence by me, with approval.

I admired her pure northern Spanish blood, blood that gave her the golden hair and creamy skin that set my chestnut hair in shadow. I felt at a disadvantage with her somehow, even though I was entertaining her in my own home.

"Josefina, you can't spend all your time doting on those boys. You've got to get out of this backwater, into the life!" Angélica said over our cups of hot chocolate one rainy afternoon. Angélica shook her pretty golden curls, and they danced on her widow's black dress like jewelry. Her earrings glimmered in the firelight, and her eyes, auburn, if that were possible, reflected the flames wherever they burned.

I secretly thought that her wearing of diamond earrings so soon after being widowed was in terrible taste, but as she said, I was a girl of the backwater who doted on her sons, not a highborn lady of criollo nobility.

"Of course," I mused, "it must be terrible for you. To be widowed when you are barely eighteen, with no sons to keep you company." Two dots of red appeared on her cheeks. I am certain I regretted my words. I had not meant to gloat, only to express Christian pity. I begged her forgiveness.

Angélica's face softened. My remorse was so genuine, the tears in my eyes a clear sign that my dart had been unintentional, that she had to forgive me.

Perhaps as penance for my cruel words, I invited her for the evening meal, knowing how much Manuel would like such a lively and charming addition to our table. This proved to be the case. She led the conversation through tales of her youth and brief marriage, her travels to Puebla, Xochimilco, and San Miguel.

"They are building a cathedral in San Miguel. The windows are as high as, well, twice the height of your ceiling," she said, raising her golden eyes and stretching her lovely neck to look at the imaginary soaring of the arches. Manuel's eyes followed her form, arching back, and not her glance. "The windows are outlined in lead and filled with colored glass. They show the passion of Christ in glowing colors in the sunlight."

I closed my eyes, and for a moment I, too, could see the light coming through colored glass and painting a scene of Christ's glory on the kneeling faithful. To see that would be a revelation.

I brought my attention back to the table, where Angélica had left the cathedral of San Miguel and was telling Manuel of her visits to the Marquesa de Condera's Court, where she was a lady-in-waiting to the Marquesa herself.

"There was a reception held in the library," Angélica was saying. "There were dozens in attendance, and the silks of the gowns made a fine contrast to the dusty hundreds of books lining the walls."

I felt a swelling of desire, whether for the silks or the books, I did not know. And so it was that she issued her invitation that night at dinner.

"Come with me, Josefina, for the upcoming season. You will see things you never thought could exist!"

"Do you want to go to Court?" Manuel asked me then.

What could I say? To say no, that I wanted to stay with my darling sons, would seem ungrateful. But to see the Court, the highborn ladies, the finery, to listen to the educated talk of the priests who had seen the world, was a temptation that stirred me in the mysterious area of my soul that Manuel left untouched. To say yes would be to give in to temptation. To say no would be to lie. Like any good wife, I chose the lie.

"I need no more than your hacienda," I said. "I would not wish to leave our sons," I added softly, truthfully.

"Well, you would be a great success at Court," he answered, his eyes never leaving Angélica. "There would be so much for you to learn."

"Oh, you'll love it!" Angélica cried. "The dresses are so beautiful, and the men, oh, well, of course you would not be interested in any of that. But there are parties, and the nuns who attend the Marquesa organize such lovely events, musical evenings, poetry readings. Surely you enjoy poetry?"

It was my turn to flush. She knew I was not widely read. I could do numbers, in my head and on paper, but my father had no literary interests, and his library had consisted of a Bible and a ledger book. My only adventures in literature had been read to me in secret by Father Alonso.

"I find the spiritual beauty of the Psalms uplifting," I said. My mind filled with the memory of Father Alonso and I hoped not to blush.

"There is a great deal of poetry being read at the Court, and not all of it is holy!" Angélica said, with a twinkle at Manuel.

"Such distractions are unnecessary for a wife," Manuel said, rescuing me. "She has all the wifely virtues and abilities I could desire."

He and Angélica both laughed. I felt my face go crimson. I thought of our most recent exercise of some of those wifely abilities. How could he mention such private matters in front of our guest?

I failed to notice at the time that he had said more in that one evening than he would normally have said in a week of dinners.

THE FOLLOWING DAY WAS market day, and Cayetana and I lifted our skirts a bit to keep them out of the muddy road as we carried our baskets from the cart to the stalls. Angélica's conversation had given me a longing for something spicy, something different to eat. I looked over the *canela* sticks, the cloves, the long, dark-green chiles. Spring was wonderful, and the fresh sprigs of herbs—epazote, chamomile, yerba buena—perfumed the air. Sapotes, dark and lush, were just coming into season, their sweet, fruity flesh perfect for a pudding. I put some in my basket and handed over a coin to the campesina tending the stall. She took it with a dry, wrinkled hand and smiled. Her four remaining teeth gleamed, giving her the look of a *calavera* sugar skull on All Souls' Day.

We stopped while Cayetana admired the embroidery on a black shawl. "Look at this stitching," she said to me. "How fine, how delicate."

"You have the eye for it," I answered. "I like its soft feel, too."

"How much?" Cayetana asked the woman who sat cross-legged on the ground on a reed mat, embroidering her next ware.

"Two pesos," she replied, her eyes teary from the close work.

"Not a very fair price," Cayetana responded, letting the shawl drop back onto the mat. "Perhaps one peso, it may be worth that."

I turned away. The shawl would easily command four or five pesos at the central market, but that was another day's walk from here, and the embroidering woman could not afford to waste a day.

"A peso and fifty centavos," she said, bending her head back to her work. I watched her sew. The tiny stitches were exactly the same size, precise and regular, and the colors were ethereal.

"What do you make your dyes from?" I asked. Cayetana shot me an exasperated look. Flattering the seller would keep her from lowering her price.

"Señora, I am so sorry," she said, starting to rise. "I did not know it was for you. Forgive me."

I shook my head no. "It is not for me, I was simply curious." I stepped away, to let Cayetana conclude her negotiations without my interference.

I walked out from under the awnings into the warm spring sunlight. Trees were leafing, and the sun dappled the stones paving the center of the square and the benches that brought rest to weary feet. A large fountain marked the middle, with three steps leading up to a wall, reaching higher than my head, that formed the basin of the fountain. An obelisk in the center cascaded water from the top, into the stone cauldron. A man stood on the third step, leaning against the basin wall. He was holding a piece of foolscap similar, I saw, to one nailed on a tree near me. I went to the tree and read:

Who soars through air with being stricken
is a fly soon crushed in a net or prison;
and the ant raising its leg is a sign:

its doom is nigh, for an arrow will pierce him.
My songs, friend, sought to rise—
but fell to Hell like a stillborn child.

I shivered. I felt my destiny nailed to that tree, and turned away.

My path was blocked as a small crowd of people had gathered behind me, and they were pressing forward, nearing the man at the fountain. They seemed to gather force as people from the market joined them, forming a wall of humanity. I moved unwillingly with them. I was at the forefront, and soon was but five paces from the fountain and its strange occupant.

The man was not taller than most, nor was he thinner or fatter, but he looked like no one I had ever seen. His face was brown, but not like an Indian's. It was the shade of the skin of an unpeeled almond, dull and lined. His eyes, a liquid brown, were huge, and his hair, black streaked with gray, fell in greasy ringlets past his shoulders. His beard, his most notable feature, was as long as his hair, and of the same color, but coarse and matted. His nose hooked over his full-lipped mouth. He wore a small hat, richly embroidered, and had wrapped an enormous, equally elaborate shawl around his narrow shoulders. He looked like a hawk with peacock's plumage.

As the crowd neared, he pressed back against the fountain basin, but his eyes did not show fear. He kept his gaze steady, looking everyone over. At some internal signal of his own, he cleared his throat. "Señores and señoras," he began, "I thank you from my heart, my beating heart, for your ears." His Spanish was strangely flowery and bore an odd, lilting accent. I leaned forward to hear more.

"My words are just words, to bring you beauty and joy. Harken to me, and allow your souls to meld with mine, in grandeur. Some are my own words, some are of my ancestors, but they are my gift to you.

"In my lap—a doe,
and in her lap—a harp;
she plays it with her fingers,
and kills me with her heart."

The crowd applauded. It was a beautiful image. I let the music of his voice play over me, and he began another. He was concluding, "Among the wise, however, love covers nearly all transgressions," when a voice rang out from the back.

"*Judío!*"

Jew.

I turned, as the people did, to see who had shouted the epithet. "*Judío!*" hollered the voice, and I could see now that it came from a young man, well dressed, a stranger. He stood on one of the benches that lined the square. I looked back at the speaker. He seemed unimpressed. He cleared his throat and began again.

"She trapped me with temptation's bread." His voice was strong, but the crowd had begun to murmur and shift. "She held me," he continued, but it was harder to hear.

A soft sapote splattered against the man's breast. He clutched at his chest. Another fruit hit his shoulder. "*Judío! Judío!*" The crowd took up the chant. "Get the Jew!" My heart knew I should leave, but my mind urged me to stay. I wanted to hear the rest of the verse, and in some dark recess of my soul, I was in thrall to the building excitement.

I felt the people crowding in on me, pushing me toward the fountain, as the poet tried to slide around to the other side. I could not hear more than the shouting, and bodies were pushing me harder. I came to my senses, finally, and I tried to flee. I held my basket to my chest and struggled to keep my feet as we moved in a wave to the steps leading to the fountain. The basin loomed above me. I felt the stones of the basin against my hands, the basket shielding me, for the moment, from being crushed against the fountain.

When I could hold on no longer, I allowed the motion of the mob to push me sideways, in the same direction as the Jew, if such he was. I had no thought for his poetry now, but only for my safety. As I came around the side of the basin, I registered that though I was terrified, the Jew stood there, erect and proud. "Men!" he shouted. "Desist a moment! Hear my words of beauty!"

"Burn him!" the original voice said. But beside the Jew, our town priest had appeared, his long brown robe so unlike the strange and colorful garb of the poet. He held up his hand as in benediction.

"Brothers," he said. I glanced quickly around. Indeed, I was the only woman visible in the crowd. I made myself as inconspicuous as possible. "Brothers. We are not savages. This is the New World, in a new time. We do not rush to kill a stranger in our midst. Wait, while I inquire of this man. He may be a Jew, or he may be a madman. Let us see."

I shrank against the basin. I had never seen a Jew, though I knew of their existence. Some had come to the New World hidden in wine casks, with the explorers, and made their secret homelands in New Spain. Others had come from our trading with the Moors, in Madagascar, in Gibraltar, or so the history said. I also knew that the Inquisition, the Holy Office that kept our doctrines pure, had found them to be heretics of the worst sort, who deserved to die.

This man seemed more of a harmless poet. A man of beautiful words. Our priest, usually a simple, kindly, and unlearned man, gleamed with glory. For here, I could see, was a chance for him to show that he was more than just a town priest.

"Sir," he said to the strange poet, "are you a Jew?"

A couple of men tittered. I held my breath, knowing that it was impossible to lie to a priest. "I am a man of the Lord," the poet replied.

"So you say. But are you a Christian?"

"We are all descendants of David."

"But do you believe in Jesus Christ, Our Lord and Savior?"

"Kill the Jew!" the shouts rang out. A sapote splattered above the poet's head, dripping onto his face. I held my breath.

"Jesus Christ is a man of my people," the poet replied.

I exhaled. "You see," said the priest, "he is a person of Christ. A madman, perhaps, but not a Jew. Disperse," he said, "go on. Go."

I said a prayer under my breath to the sweet Virgin of Guadalupe, and I inched forward. With a trembling hand I took a cloth from my basket and handed it to the poet. He nodded, wiped his face, and handed back the cloth.

"Doña Josefina! What are you doing in this crowd?" asked the priest.

"I was at the market, and stopped in the square to rest. I was caught up in the crowd," I added. I quelled the tremor in my voice, as my own mind marveled at my boldness.

"Well, you'd best be gone now, señora. It is safe now. And you, Jew," he said, turning to the poet, "you had best be gone, too, before you are burned at the stake."

The Jew bowed lightly to the priest. "You are a man of God."

The priest shrugged. "I am who I am. Come, you will be safe walking with me to the edge of town."

"Wait!" I cried. "Wait! Sir," I said, not knowing how to address a Jew, "are you the writer of the poems you read?"

"No, madam," he answered, his accent giving the words an exotic allure. "They are the words of poets of yore, of José, son of Eli, and of Moisés, son of Habib. They were learned men. They spoke truth, two hundred years ago."

"How did you learn those words?"

"My people carried them in their hearts."

"Señora, it is not seemly for you to be seen conversing with a Jew. And you, sir, have trod on this town's soil too long. Come," the priest said, motioning with his head. I realized he did not wish to touch the Jew. He had saved his life, but would not sully himself with his touch.

The Jew seemed not to mind. He bowed to me. "Señora, remember, please. Beyond the truth, our first duty is to survive." He turned, rolled up the sheaf of papers he had in his hand, and followed the priest out of the square.

I looked for and saw the other paper, now torn, hanging from the tree. I reached up to take it. "Leave it, señora," came Cayetana's voice. "Do not bring such trials on our house."

Two

It was decided faster than I thought possible. Although I struggled with my longing, I was pulled hard home with my duties. Ultimately, and to my surprise, Manuel almost pressed me to accompany Angélica to the Court of the Marquesa when she returned for the spring season.

I sought Manuel's company, but he declined. In the weeks preceding my entry into noble society, livestock prices began to rise due to the additional ventures our Spanish King's army had undertaken. Spain was, and is, the most magnificent of lands, and Rey Carlos, in his mercy, had undertaken to increase the bounty of our wealth and the discipline and joyous worship of Our Lord Jesus Christ as far as he could. In his quest to aggrandize Spain, many men had to be conscripted, and men must be fed.

"Should I stay?" I asked. "The children, would they be too much to manage with just a nursemaid? And the accounts? The accounts will need to be kept, and visitors will come to price the cattle."

"I can keep accounts, too." He smiled. "You will be a day's horse-ride away. I can fetch you if I need to. And I will join you when I can. I would not want my wife to be lonely."

I had to smile. Angélica had assured me that I would not be lonely, that there were parties, picnics, and musical evenings, as well as the famed poetry readings, constantly. I was torn between the anticipation of seeing, finally, the noble world I had only heard of, and the fear of being so countrified that I would be mocked.

Do you like secular poetry? Angélica had asked. *Are you musical? Do you sing?* Angélica sang us a song she said was popular at the Court, filled with complicated trills, pulling and stretching the words of Scripture it quoted beyond their meanings in the service of her musical art. My heart beat faster listening. I looked at Manuel, who gazed worshipfully at this nightingale among us. I blushed each time I thought of my failings, in anticipation of humiliations to come.

But Manuel reassured me there, too. "I have seen your eyes light up when those chattering ladies tell their stories. You have every grace they have. You are virtuous and pure of blood. You will bring honor to my name in your weeks at Court."

What I dreaded more than being put to shame for my lack of culture was leaving my sons. Joaquín, even then, was well on his way to being a man. When he returned from the cattle barns he smelled like his father. But under the manure and leather odors the milky aroma of childhood still lingered.

I wandered out to the barn to watch him. Before he saw me, he pulled a rope attached to a bleating calf, hauling it into its stall. A farmhand took the rope from him to tie it. "I'll do it!" insisted my boy, overturning a bucket. He climbed up and grabbed the rope. With his little hands he wrapped the cord around the post. Then he leaped down, tumbling, laughing in the dung and hay. And he caught sight of me, sitting on a stool at the barn's entrance.

"You should have seen the one I roped in, Mama!" he exclaimed, and, like the five-year-old that he was, he jumped heedlessly into my lap. He threw his dirty arms around my neck and nuzzled into me. "He was huge and big and tough, and I got him myself!" I could hardly bear to leave that tender man-boy.

"I'm sure you were magnificent," I said. He was already climbing down, stepping on me with his little boots.

"Look!" he crowed. "Look how you do it!" He grabbed another length of rope and artfully turned it into a noose. I watched, amazed, as he whirled it over his head. "Olé!" came his cry as the noose flew through the air and landed squarely around the fence post. He laughed as he ran up to grab the rope. "You try it, Mama!"

"Silly boy," I said, but I twirled the rope around as he had done. It slipped out of my hands and landed on the ground. Joaquín was delighted. I took his hand as we walked back, a privilege I knew would not last much longer.

"Can I go with you to the big Court?" he asked.

"Of course not, my untamed boy," I said, pulling him back to me. "You would hate it. You have to sit inside all day, and read books and listen to music." This was surely how a five-year-old boy would see it. For me, I imagined it as a banquet spread before me—one I was not sure I was grand enough to enjoy.

"Then why are you going, Mama? Don't you want to stay with me?"

"You are going to give a wife a very hard life," I said. "Now go get washed."

"You didn't say why you were going," he pointed out, but being a good boy, or maybe being less interested in the answer than in asking the question, he went off to get some water to wash in.

I shook my head. Why *was* I going?

I followed him into the house and sat down in the study. It was a small room, set up just for me. My account books, paper, and quill were neatly set upon my worktable. It was still light enough that I did not light the lamp, but I straightened the rug that covered the red tile floor, and I adjusted the cushions that were spread before the unlit hearth. The afternoon sun made dust motes glitter. It was a safe, peaceful room, and not one I was eager to leave.

Cayetana brought little Ernesto in. Compared to his brother, Ernesto was plumper and quieter. He was not yet three, and he still wore the little dresses of infants. Cayetana set him down on the rug, and he toddled toward me. I scooped him up, and he gurgled.

"How's my Neto?" I asked.

"Good, Mama," he answered. "And Mama?" Though he wasn't yet the chatterbox his brother was, he had talked at six months, and he took the job of communicating seriously.

"I am fine, Neto," I said, equally seriously.

"There are birds in the nursery," he said. I raised my eyebrows at Cayetana. She shrugged. There were always birds flying in and out of the house here, and I had tried hard to get used to it. In my father's house, birds stayed in the sky or in the trees where they belonged.

"Maybe we can keep the shutters closed," I said. Though the rains were tapering off, the heat of the dry season was a long way away, and we could still close the house without suffocating.

"But then it will be dark, Mama. I don't like the dark."

"Then we must have birds," I said.

Ernesto smiled at me. He didn't wriggle or try to get down. "Then we must have birds," he echoed.

"Your dresses are all but complete," Cayetana said. I put Neto down.

"My dresses. Yes. I will have to make the final preparations. I can't believe that Angélica is right, that I will need so many!"

I had ordered four, the least number that Angélica had insisted on. My own wardrobe would have to suit for the remainder.

"Don Manuel is not displeased at your expenditure, is he?" Cayetana asked, although doubtless she knew the answer.

"Of course not!" I laughed. "I doubt he even knows. After all, he stopped looking at the accounts as soon as he married me." I wondered mildly what her real question was.

"You have a most unwomanly head for numbers," Cayetana remarked. I didn't answer. Many felt that such learning was unsexing. Some went as far as to believe that reading was the tool of the Devil, and a woman who read, never mind did numbers, was on the road to harlotry, if not directly to Hell.

Although I had never heard that the Holy Office forbade such learning, I had no doubt, from the days with Father Alonso, that taken too far erudition could bring about the unwanted attention of the Church. I was certain that I was nowhere near the edge of that abyss, with my accounts and my reading of the Psalms, but the specter was enough to keep one from brazenly trumpeting those skills.

Though Cayetana was my servant, and an Indian, she did not hold learning in such low esteem. She had been in Manuel's household since she was five, and knew more about him, and men in general, than I felt I ever would. She knew that Manuel both appreciated my accounting and trusted it completely, and that he was generous with me and the household without stinting. I still awaited the reason for her comment.

"While you are gone, who will keep the books?"

I thought for a bit. I had arranged for the care of the boys, though it wrenched my heart to do so. I had ordered the dresses as Angélica had advised, and I had planned for all of the household needs, but I had left the accounts for my husband. "I think Don Manuel will manage fine without me for such a short period," I said.

"But he will be out with the cattle," Cayetana replied.

"He handled it all himself before me, and I do not believe that in five years he will have forgotten how."

It gave me pause to realize that we had been married for almost six years. Even stranger, I had not been away from the hacienda overnight in all those years.

Manuel would not have prohibited a long visit home to see my father, but there was no reason to go. My brother lived in the North, and my two sisters, both married long before I came of age, had their own households to look after, so only my father kept up his tie with me.

My visits to my father, though monthly at first, had tapered off, and even then I had returned to the hacienda before bedtime. Our family home was but an hour away in the carriage, and at first, though I was taken up with learning the hacienda ways, I was eager to see my father. He and I had been each other's strength after my mother's death, and we had established a smooth, well-oiled way of existing together day by day. I would direct the meal preparation, keep his accounts, and manage the daily work of the household. I would pray quietly, read the Psalms, and dream of the exotic worlds the words created. He would ride out to the land, to the markets and exchanges, and return with stories to tell me over our dinner. Those days of peace seemed endless then, and my dreams, existing in their own self-sufficient unreality, were enough to fill my quiet hours.

I had thought, on my first visit home, that all would be the same, and indeed he had tried to make it so. But though he was the same, I was not. My first month of marriage had introduced me to the joys of an independent household, and to the mysteries of a married woman. I had felt, to my shame, an eagerness to get back to Manuel.

My father had sensed this, and he, too, began to look elsewhere for the quiet companionship he had lost by my marriage. He remarried shortly after my wedding, and his new wife, María Marta, was soon less than enthusiastic about my visits. She had been delivered of a daughter within weeks of my first son's birth. The birth had left her querulous, and my father, I believed, regretted his decision to wed. Now, with the children, my father visited me more than I visited him. Each time, I rejoiced that I had my own world, where I was the lady of the house. The exotic images of the Psalms and of Father Alonso's poems had been buried under the pleasures of my new daily life.

"He will manage somehow," I said to Cayetana, breaking the silence and finally answering her question. "And if not, I will come home." Cayetana looked mollified, but I sensed that her disapproval remained.

OUR LAST DINNER ALONE together before I left, Manuel and I were at the table, with no visiting hacienda owners or their wives. Angélica was not due to arrive until the next morning to spend the day with us before accompanying me to Court.

"Of course I will manage without you," Manuel said. He was not dismissive of my concern, just sure, and so I was relieved.

"Send for me if you need me," I said.

He nodded. "I will need you even if I don't send for you. And you send for me if you want to come home." I looked at my plate. Such sentimentality was unlike him. But he ate his dinner without further comment, so I did not pursue it.

"Angélica will be here tomorrow by mid-morning," I said. "We are to leave the next day, at dawn. I have all my dresses." Manuel nodded. I wanted to talk. I wanted him to know that although I was going away, I didn't want to leave him. I wanted him to understand that if I didn't go, I would regret it forever. And yet, he had not said once that I should not go. In fact, it had been his idea, his desire, that had allowed me even to consider this adventure. My argument, therefore, was with myself, and was silent.

When he came to my bed, I had already anticipated him. I had washed, put jasmine flowers in my rinsing water, and was wearing my softest gown. As I heard the silver-encrusted belt hit the floor, my body responded as if he had started to stroke me.

He began tenderly, with feathery touches and long, warm caresses. I responded, mirroring his methods, and enjoyed the feel of his work-hardened muscles under my touch. He wrapped his arms around me and held me so tight it hurt.

Then he dropped his lips to mine, and his kisses became urgent and his tongue demanding. He slid down to my breasts, and both his hands and his mouth got rougher. He led where I could not follow, except by being swept up in his wake, and he drove into me as if he wanted to press his seed into my very womb. His passion was not quickly spent. He rode long and hard, and with the help of his knowing hands, I crested in my pleasure before he finished pounding into my body. When he finally rested, sweating and breathing hoarsely, neither of us was in any state to talk.

Two days later, I left for the Marquesa's Court.

THREE

No words could have prepared me for my first sight of the castle where the Marqués and Marquesa made their home in the New World. The journey had been long, with our carriage bumping over the rutted roads. Cayetana, along with Angélica's maid, followed behind us in a cart with the luggage. We had left just before dawn so as to make the trip in a single day and spare ourselves a night in a roadside inn.

I sat next to Angélica. I was dressed for travel in a gray muslin dress with sleeves open at the cuffs for ease of movement, and a soft serape to keep the dust off my hair and dress. Angélica wore a Spanish cape in light blue, having left off her mourning at the year's anniversary of her husband's death. The sun beat down, but the sky was reflected in Angélica's cloak.

I was attuned to these matters of dress most unwillingly, as Angélica had scrutinized every aspect of my traveling wardrobe the night before. "We must make an entrance, even if no one sees us," she had said.

The thought of such strange judgments being passed on the most minor of matters made me tight with anxiety and trepidation. I had given more thought to my wardrobe in the past month than I had in my twenty-five years of life before then. How could such venal and insignificant fixations be the warp to the woof of the intellectual brilliance I was dreaming of? I wondered, for at least the tenth time, whether really I should not go.

But the carriage clipped onward, and anticipation warred with fear and won. The road brought us past towns I had never seen, and I looked avidly at the dusty houses and farms. A church appeared on the horizon, its gray tower piercing the sky, but it was almost an hour before we passed it. It truly rose high enough to touch Heaven.

I was an uncomplaining traveler, and our groom was considerate in his stops. We stopped at an inn to rest and water the horses. Angélica conducted me to a small private room, with a table, chairs, and a small curtained alcove with the necessary basins. "There," she said, indicating the alcove. "Take advantage of the amenities, for there is but one other inn along the way, and it is more than two hours before we reach it."

The landlady of the inn brought us some cold meats and hot tortillas, and glasses of tamarind water. Nerves made it hard to swallow more than a few bites before our driver knocked at the door. It was time to move on.

Angélica kept up an unceasing patter, telling me the rules of etiquette, the names of those I would meet, the best and worst things to say, do, or wear under various circumstances. At last, though, I begged her to stop, so I could indulge my dreams. I was more nervous than at my wedding, and I felt as if I was embarking on at least as perilous a journey.

Late in the afternoon, the castle came into view. All my dread, my eagerness, and my exhaustion vanished. Like our hacienda, it was surrounded by a high stone wall, with sharp stones on top like a frieze, but it was covered in bougainvillea, the crimson flowers softening the effect of the barrier. Above the blossoms, I could see the stone towers of the mansion, and I recognized flags in the colors of Spain, France, and others I did not know, fluttering from the turrets.

The gate was opened by a boy in a costume called a livery, with the green and gold colors of the Marquesa. He took his hat off, and his long black hair cascaded down his back. We rode into a yard alive with servants, chickens, a couple of yellow dogs. The groom took us up to the front portal before stopping the cart. The entryway was an arch of tiles leading to a huge, heavy, and intricately carved wooden double door. Another boy, perhaps twelve years old, also in green and gold, helped us from the carriage. The ground was just getting dusty, as the dry season was only beginning, but he rolled a length of carpet before us to keep our shoes from picking up the dust.

The open portal doors led us into a hall, all of stone, with thick wall hangings and carpets to soften the harshness of the element. After the bright, sunlit, and lively courtyard, the hall seemed dark and silent, and I expected to smell the waxy aroma of our village church. Angélica was evidently not made blind by the gloom. She led the way, nodding to the servants, to a little room with a desk, a candelabra, and a plain-looking nun in a gray dress—to match her hair—seated in a chair with a bell and a quill pen within easy reach. Angélica announced us, and the woman looked in her book. She made a notation with a flourish. "Welcome," she said. She rang the bell. In moments, women servants appeared, all in the green and gold colors, and with much fuss and effusion led us off to the suite of rooms that was to be our home for the next eight weeks.

Though I had wanted to linger and take in every detail of the entryway, the long halls, the incredibly long stairs that led us to the second floor of this castle, the journey had left me dazed and exhausted. The servant showed me into one of two adjacent rooms. One was mine, the other would be Angélica's, our doors only an arm's length apart. I was barely able to take in my new surroundings, noting only that my room was no larger than my dry pantry at home, and yet boasted almost as much furniture as my *sala*. There was a fireplace with a laid but unlit fire, a large armoire, two carved chairs and a bed, and the walls were hung with tapestries. At least it was light, especially after the darkness of the hall. Angélica stood in my doorway as I sank onto the bed, which was covered in a rose quilt, and lay back and closed my eyes.

"We must be ready in an hour," Angélica said.

"To meet the Marquesa?" I was appalled. I could not be at my best immediately after such a long journey. The sun was sinking into a golden haze outside my window, and I was sinking with it.

"No, you ninny. The servants will bring us supper in our rooms in an hour. But we must not seem worn out. Word will get out."

I shook my head. I had entered the world of the Court, and I was as knowledgeable about it as, well, as Neto. "I will do my best," I said as Angélica turned to go to her own room.

When we were finally free to rest, I fell into a state that could only be called a torpor, with images of the day swirling around, competing with my vague and unformed imaginings of the morrow, to the background music of the faces of my sons.

FOUR

HE NEXT DAY DAWNED clear and warm. We dressed with care. I felt my hands dampening as I struggled with the new clothing. Angélica, who displayed no such trepidation, was radiant in her blue velvet gown. Her golden hair was upswept, and her skin shone as we entered the Marquesa's antechamber. I stood a bit behind her, self-conscious in my maroon dress. Its cut was unfamiliar to me, with a square neckline surrounded by a froth of ruffles. My darker skin contrasted with the froth, and my chestnut hair gleamed with the maroon dress's reflections. The woman who looked back at me in the glass before we left our room was unfamiliar, sophisticated and graceful. She could not be me.

Angélica walked with full confidence into the room. She smiled her perfect smile, inclining her head to the ladies already present. They were numerous, and they looked us over with a mix of disdain and envy. I was sure the disdain was for me. Angélica held out her hand to me and gave me the names of those present. I forced myself not to cast my eyes to the ground. I was Doña Josefina, wife of wealthy landowner Don Manuel, and I could be as proud as anyone there. My knees, under the maroon satin, trembled.

The ladies-in-waiting had arrayed themselves in languorous splendor. One, in light green silk, reclined with her legs swung up on an upholstered settee with a long seat, like an extended chair or a couch for one. Above her, a portrait of a woman in severe black, with eyes and hair to match, glared down upon her harshly. Another lady, with more lace than neck, sat on a tiny pouf, almost on the floor. A third, with a dress that betrayed mending at the sleeves and collar, stood back, away from the others, fingering a small sculpture on a shelf arrayed with tiny figurines. The long, narrow windows let in a fresh, almost green light, and the sheer curtains billowed gently in the easy breeze.

The company was rounded out by the presence of three nuns, who, in contrast to the well-dressed ladies, were clothed in habits that could only be hideously uncomfortable. The bodices wrapped unkindly around their bosoms, and the coifs bit into their necks and chins as choking cloths before cascading with heavy drapery and veils over their shoulders. I was unsure what to make of them. Although Angélica had mentioned their presence at many of the occasions she had described, my only prior knowledge of religious sisters related to the quiet women who nursed the sick and tended to our church's altar.

One glided up to us. She offered me tiny sugar-covered sweets on a tray. I took one, biting into its tender crust, and rich lemon custard filled my mouth. Angélica narrowed her eyes at me. I looked around; no one else was eating. Had I committed some foolish social error? The sister smiled.

"I am Sor Inez. Please, the sweets are for all to enjoy." She took one herself and popped it in her mouth. "I especially like the lemon ones," she added, around the mouthful.

I smiled gratefully. "It was delicious."

"This is Sor Juana," she added, turning toward a youthful, dark-eyed nun behind her. Sor Juana had the requisite nun's habit on, black over white, with a black veil over a white cowl, but she also wore a gigantic brooch at her throat, maybe ten centimeters in diameter, with an image of the Annunciation on it. It could not have been pleasant to live with her head held high above that brooch all the time. I wondered if it was for penance or vanity.

"Enchanted," said the young nun, looking directly into my eyes. My body stirred; I blushed and looked away. When I looked up again, both Sor Juana and Sor Inez had moved off to the other occupants of the room, and Angélica was standing by me.

"Don't eat anything else until the Marquesa comes," she hissed.

"I'm sorry," I whispered back. "Why would the sisters offer the sweets if we weren't supposed to eat them?"

"Temptation," Angélica responded.

At the far end of the room, a door I had not previously noticed opened, and all fell silent. Before us stood a tall woman, almost as tall as Manuel, with lustrous black hair piled high into a complicated twist and held with glittering combs of amethyst and silver. Her huge eyes were the same eerie jet as her hair, under perfectly arched black brows. Her skin was pale, almost ghostly, and she was so thin that her skin stretched taut over her aristocratically bony nose. She had a tiny, rosebud mouth that nearly vanished under the sway of her eyes.

The women curtsied; the nuns inclined their heads. I knew what to do, Angélica having tutored me in that courtesy, at least, and I dropped into a deep curtsy before the Marquesa. "Who is this?" she asked, her voice high and thin. I looked up, knowing that she meant me. Angélica led me forward.

"Marquesa, this is Doña Josefina María del Carmen Asturias de Castillo, wife of Don Manuel Castillo. She has come to pay her respects."

"I kiss Your Grace's hands," I said.

She laughed, a reedy, almost wheezing sound. "Your Grace? That's for bishops, silly woman. Call me Your Highness, like everyone else!" Her mirthful tone belied the social disgrace of my being corrected in front of the entire room. I felt my face burning. "Didn't you instruct her properly?" the Marquesa asked Angélica. It was Angélica's turn to blush, her fairer skin betraying what was more likely annoyance at me than shame. For once, I did not envy her fair complexion.

"She did," I said, rushing to her defense, "but my awe of your presence made me forget her kind instruction." For indeed Angélica had instructed me on a million details, and they had all fled upon the Marquesa's entrance.

"Splendid!" said the Marquesa. "A lady who defends her sponsor! How refreshing!" The other women tittered, and I wondered what I had done wrong now. "Tell us all about yourself, Doña Josefina," she added, turning away.

I felt Angélica's hand on my arm, and I remembered. "Other than my gratitude that you have received me, I have nothing to tell, Your Highness. I am only visiting with Doña Angélica, who insisted that I trouble you with my greetings." But the Marquesa had already gone on to the next phase of her morning with the ladies. She helped herself to a pastry from Sor Inez's tray.

"Today we will be enjoying a poetic reading from Sor Juana, I understand," the Marquesa said. Sor Juana, of the enormous brooch, nodded. "I hope it is as moving as your last efforts."

"I believe it will be, Your Highness," said the nun, her voice clear and firm. "I wrote it with your taste in mind."

The Marquesa raised a fearsome eyebrow at the remark, but let it pass. The ladies exchanged surreptitious glances, but I did not know them well enough to discern their meanings. Indeed, I knew nothing of the perilous path Sor Juana's poetry was about to launch me on. I only knew that my breath was caught in my heart, and that that same heart beat so loudly in my breast that I barely heard the Marquesa speak. "So, let us be comfortable, while the good sister enlightens our spirits with her verse."

I tried to make myself even more invisible than I already was, to fade into the background. I had taken a few steps back when my plans were thwarted by the Marquesa herself.

"Come sit next to me, my young lovely, and enjoy the verses with me." She patted the end of the long settee, next to where she herself was seated. I had no choice but to hurry over. "Move, Doña Granada," she added to the lady in green silk. "Make space for our new guest."

Doña Granada swung her legs to the floor to make room for me, and cast a look of contempt at me as I took my seat. "Just like a good little lap dog. She will like that," Doña Granada said in my ear. "All of you must bustle like Doña Josefina," she added to the room. Her smile dripped cruelty. I cast about for Angélica's eyes to reassure me, but she shrugged and turned to another of the ladies, leaving me to swallow the acrid taste of humiliation.

Sor Inez held out the tray to me, and this time I had the sense to decline. She continued around the room, and everyone took a pastry. "Are the confections at your hacienda so superior?" the Marquesa asked me, with that wheezing laugh.

Sor Juana came to my rescue. "Now, Your Highness, shall I begin?" I felt her voice like a knife honed so sharp that it cut painlessly and perfectly until the wound began to bleed. And I realized that such a frivolous description would never have a place at the hacienda, and could only have come to me in this new, strange atmosphere. Sor Juana looked straight at the Marquesa, who, though not quailing before this young sister, clearly did not trifle with her, either. The Marquesa nodded.

Sor Juana took a piece of foolscap from the table and held it so she could see it without bending her neck forward against the brooch.

> *"If love be its source*
> *And the stream is divided*
> *Will the river rush faster*
> *To flow once more together?*
> > *What could be more natural*
> > *than the jealous heart?*
> > *How without that pain*
> > *can love be perfected?*
> *What greater sign of love*
> *Can there be but jealousy?*
> *Like the wetness of water.*
> *Fire's smoke.*
> > *For love's children are not bastards*
> > *but true heirs to their empire,*
> > *for only they can unite*
> > *both their cause and their effect."*

There was silence. I could not imagine such daring. I never dreamed that anyone, especially a nun, would write, never mind read, such dangerous poesy. I looked cautiously at the Marquesa. Her pale skin had blotched red on her cheekbones. Her wheeze had intensified. The other ladies looked at the ground, studied their fingernails intently, were suddenly obsessed by a thread on their sleeve.

Sor Juana looked around the room, expressionless. Had she achieved her desired effect? I did not know. She rose, and took a pastry from the tray. She bit into it and licked the lemon cream that flowed from its center. The Marquesa continued to stare stonily at her. "Would you like another verse?" asked the sister.

Without waiting for the obvious answer, she picked up her sheet of paper, nodded to the Marquesa, and turned to leave. She caught my eye and held it. I did not look away. A twitch of her mouth betrayed a smile, and she was gone.

In the silence that ensued, I felt the sweet pastry congeal in my stomach, and the formerly fresh air in the room sour. From under my lashes I looked at the Marquesa's face. It was far from impassive, her cheeks stained with red blotches, her eyes, under those terrifying black eyebrows, narrow and sharp. Doña Granada stirred beside me. I slid my eyes cautiously to her. To my surprise, she had a sly mien concealed behind her fan.

Angélica broke the spell. "Your Highness," she said, rising, "Sor Juana's poetry is a bit much in the early hours of the day. You should reserve her performances for the evening, when the gentlemen can appreciate her bawdy words. The morning, I think, is a time for music." My regard for Angélica soared. I would never have such courage.

"Agreed, Doña Angélica," replied the Marquesa, breathing noisily. "Sing for us, then." Angélica nodded. A nun to whom I had not been introduced produced a small lyre and plucked a few notes. Angélica arranged her skirts, clasped her hands before her, and began a song.

The notes were clear. Angélica chose wisely, a light, pleasant ode to the glory of a fresh spring rain. When she had finished, the tension had dissipated somewhat, and the Marquesa, with a nod of thanks, went on to the business of the day.

"For the evening meal, you are all invited to eat at my table. The Bishop of Puebla will be joining us, with a number of other grandees in attendance. I will not, Angélica, take up your suggestion that Sor Juana present her poetry at dinner. The Bishop would likely have her excommunicated."

A number of women giggled at that. Why was that funny? I wondered.

My mind slipped briefly back to the Jew at the fountain on market day. I had not known the dangerous power of verse.

The rest of the morning was spent in our rooms. Luncheon was served in a large, comfortable hall, with cold meats, dressed vegetables, breads, rolls, and tortillas on a sideboard. Clearly, here at Court, the tradition of a large meal mid-afternoon was not followed. Perhaps, since ladies and gentlemen did not work in the fields or with the cattle at the castle, they could make do with a lighter repast.

By mid-afternoon I was longing for home. At this hour, my sons would be clamoring for attention, Manuel would be in the foyer removing his boots, and our meal would be served. Instead, Angélica had said I was to rest, and plan my sartorial selections for the evening. I could not imagine eight entire weeks like this.

I changed into my habitual clothes, a plain dark green muslin dress with a soft white collar and full sleeves more suitable to my daily life at the hacienda, and crept out of my room. For a moment I considered asking Angélica what she thought of my taking a stroll through the castle. I stopped at her door, but I hesitated. She was used to the ways of the Court, and surely was taking the opportunity to doze. I did not want to disturb her or be more of a burden than I had already been. The memory of her flushed face when I misaddressed the Marquesa was enough to dissuade me from bothering her.

The long hallway was dark, all doors off it being closed and the lights and tapers not yet lit. I walked softly, my slippers making no noise on the stones, and traveled down the stairs to the main rooms.

Much like our hacienda, the castle appeared to be horseshoe shaped. The central courtyard was surrounded by the two wings, and it ended in the crosspiece of the public rooms, including the foyer where we had entered on our arrival. At the foot of the stairs leading down from the wing where Angélica and I had our rooms I veered right, trying to retrace my steps toward the Marquesa's receiving rooms.

In the foyer, the old gray nun still sat in her little alcove. She was dozing, her pen, her keys, and her book laid out on the desk before her. She did not stir as I walked by. I paused before entering the right wing. I was unsure of the protocol of wandering outside the guest chambers, but Angélica had not mentioned anything about staying in the rooms until summoned. I moved on.

I could hear sounds from the courtyard as I passed the open portico. The chickens squawked and a dog barked rhythmically and without purpose; men's voices carried through the warm air. These were so like the sounds of home that I lingered a moment to enjoy them.

Behind me, away from the courtyard, were large double doors, opening out into an expanse of garden. I peered out into the sunshine, noticing that there were little spurs of building branching out behind, and that paths led away from the doors onto lawns and more gardens beyond. I was tempted by the paths, the sparkling air, and the chance to emerge from within the walls, but I was only in cloth slippers and I did not want to squander my first free time returning to my room to change footwear. Instead, for my curiosity regarding the interior of the castle was as strong, I continued down the stone hallway.

The first room I came to had its doors open, and the sunlight from the windows mitigated the darkness of the hall. It appeared to be a small music room, with a harpsichord in the corner, a lyre, and a few comfortable chairs set before a massive fireplace. The windows were large, soaring almost the height of the room, and were draped in a light material of gold and green. There was no one in the room, so I entered.

I have no musical gift, but I thought of Angélica's sweet singing, and imagined her gracing the company in this room. Walking lightly and with less caution and concern, I proceeded in my explorations, and went without thought through the doorway from the little music room into what I could see was an enormous library.

My heart quickened. A library! I had heard of them, and I had seen an illustration in one of the books the traveling priest had brought to my home so many years ago, but I had never actually seen one. My hands were damp with excitement as I pushed the door wide.

Here the atmosphere was different. The doorway I had entered was in a corner of the room, and the two adjacent walls were lined, from floor to ceiling, with books. I reached out and touched one, and then pulled my hand back as if it had been burned. They were real. I was a good estimator of numbers, but I could not imagine how many there were, with their colored bindings and lettering, in those incredible, magnificent shelves. At least a thousand, I thought, multiplying the shelves I could see by what could be the books on one shelf.

I caught my breath. I was doing multiplication to keep from throwing myself at the shelves of books, or running out of the room. I made myself still and looked around. Windows filled the third wall, and though large, they did not overwhelm the room as they did in the music room, for the library was perhaps three times the size of the music room, and the draperies were heavier. The curtains were open, giving the room a warm light from the outdoors. Tables were placed

throughout, and there were small candelabras on the tables. Doubtless they gave light during the evening and the winter days, so readers
could enjoy the bounty at any time. The chairs appeared deep and
inviting.

The wall furthest from the door connecting to the music room had
a large door in its center, leading, doubtless, to the main hall. On either
side of the door was a stone archway, from which hung peculiar heavy
draperies. In front of the archways, bookshelves were arranged almost
as moats, high enough that I could not, from my position just inside
the room, see what lay behind them. My eyes were drawn back to the
huge bookshelves and I turned to them, curious and eager. As I stood
there, deeply entranced, I was startled to hear a voice from an area near
one of the arches. The sound was muffled by the draperies, but it was a
woman's voice, soft and low. I could not make out the words, but they
were followed by a deep and rumbling laugh, punctuated by the sound
of a book slamming shut.

I jumped back, embarrassed. I had not meant to intrude, to go where
I was not invited, or disturb a colloquy that thought itself private. I
looked around for a way out of the library. I could not go out by the main
door, as that would require passing the odd area from whence the voices
had come, and I knew that to remain silent would be to add stealth to my
intrusion, so I turned to flee through the music room. A voice nailed my
feet to the floor.

"Sister, your words are far too bold. The Archbishop, should he get
wind of this, would punish you most severely." Again, the rumbling laugh
followed, but I could not move. There was something familiar about that
voice.

"The verses themselves are pure, Your Grace, even if the reader is
not. I mean only to convey the most spiritual thoughts by them." I now
recognized Sor Juana, this morning's poetess. Her words were pious, but
her tone was not.

Your Grace. The Marquesa had told me that was how to address the
Bishop. But I had never known a bishop. Perhaps it was a more general
term of address, or maybe I was mistaken altogether. "The Marqués'
bastard is not a spiritual being," the man said.

"The Holy Ghost?" Sor Juana said, her low voice mocking.

My mind rejected the notion that the man she addressed could be whom I thought. My heart said otherwise. I waited to hear him speak again, to verify what could not be so: the priest of my youth, who had opened my eyes to the world of words, could not be hidden in that alcove with Sor Juana. I waited in dread, perspiration dampening my lip. I longed to flee, but my feet were in thrall to my heart.

Their silence was worse than their words. "You will read for me again tonight, Sister," he said at last. "Filotea must be satisfied."

"As you wish, Your Grace."

I unstuck my faithless feet and dashed out through the music room.

ANGÉLICA WAS WAITING FOR me in my room when I returned. Her welcome was not warm. "Do you think you can run around like you're at your hacienda?" she asked acidly. I was breathless from my run back up the stairs, and I shut the door quietly behind me and leaned against it without speaking. "You aren't in the country here."

She would never have spoken like that in my home. She was but nineteen, and I was a matron with honor and position. Yet her knowledge of this world far exceeded mine, and I could not divulge what I had just heard. I had to submit to the chastisement.

"I'm sorry, Angélica, I just wanted to see the castle," I said, most humbly. I urged her away silently, to let me marshal my thoughts. But Angélica was bent on correction.

"You should rest, Josefina. The evenings can be long here, and we just arrived yesterday. You are not used to the hours kept by the Court, and you must not be yawning when the Marqués is entertaining us with one of his stories."

"I am certain that I will not be yawning. I am eager to hear those tales." I was still hot and trembling, and the effort to sound calm was strenuous.

She looked at me closely but could find no guile or irony in me, for at the time I had none. "Why were you running, though?"

"I just wanted to get back to the room, and the stairs are steep," I said. She sighed.

"What will you wear tonight?" she asked.

"Please choose for me."

The meek request put Angélica back in a good mood, and she proceeded to attend to my toilette with fervor. By the end of her ministrations I was dressed in a silver and white gown that set off my complexion, with tight sleeves that opened at my hands in a wave of lace. My hair was dressed by a castle maid, under Cayetana's watchful eye, while Angélica returned to her room to dress herself. With the attention to my grooming so intense, I was able to convince myself that I was in error. That voice could not have been Father Alonso's. Father Alonso could not be here; the coincidence would be too great. And there was little chance that he would have been in the library, alone with Sor Juana, at the exact moment that I happened to enter the room.

Cayetana was harder to fool. As soon as the young maid left the room, she fixed me with her brown stare. "Señora, you are agitated. Is it simply nerves for your evening, or is something chewing at you?"

Her homey expression pulled me out of my reverie. "It's nothing. I'm just nervous."

"Well, it looks like you're chasing a ghost that's after your soul. I don't like it."

"I'm fine," I said irritably. Cayetana always saw clearly.

She shrugged. "Then put a pleasant expression on your face," she advised, shaking her head.

Cayetana was right. I had to put the notion from my mind and concentrate on the upcoming evening. It was a pity that we should have a command performance so soon after our arrival, with so little time for me to acclimate to the norms of Court behavior. But Angélica's fear that I would be yawning from exhaustion during the evening was sure to be unfounded. I was so nervous about meeting the Marqués, seeing the Marquesa after that morning's poetry reading, and navigating the terrifying waters of the interactions among the ladies-in-waiting that I could scarcely breathe. I would concentrate on ensuring that I did not commit any social errors that would shame me or cast Angélica in a bad light. I would forget about strange voices in alcoves and ghosts nibbling at my soul.

When she was ready, Angélica came to my room to fetch me. She was radiant in gold, her eyes and hair matching the color of her dress. Her slippers were satin, and she wore a scent that was jasmine, and rose, and something exotic that I could not name but that reminded me of a forest after the first rain. She held out her arm, and I took it. There was no need to worry, for no one would notice me, or my country ways, in the shadow of the sun.

*F*IVE

*W*E ENTERED THE GRAND parlor unannounced. When the Marqués and the Marquesa entered, Angélica explained, there would be formal introductions. Until then, we were left to fend for ourselves. Again, there were several nuns in attendance, including the gentle-looking Sor Inez, who had offered me the pastry this morning. Temptation, Angélica had said. Mine or hers? Anyone who thought that committing to a life of religious devotion included abstinence from society was sadly mistaken, I thought. The good sisters were present in all of the castle entertainment.

The room was rectangular, with portraits of frightening-looking pale men with vicious black eyebrows lining the walls. I could see the Marquesa's lineage in their glower. The green and gold draperies lightened the mood of the room, and the upholstery matched the curtains in color and richness. Light radiated from candelabras placed throughout, and lively shadows were cast by additional scented oil lights in sconces around the room. The aroma of the burning oil perfumed and weighed down the air.

The nuns maintained their severe habits, with the veils wrapped tightly against their heads and necks before flowing down their bodies. The dark tones of their apparel contrasted with the finery of the ladies who had arrived before us. There were several ladies, perhaps six or seven, but no men.

I recognized Doña Granada, her graceful form and finely drawn features concentrated in intense conversation with the nervously shabby lady who had taken the lowest position in the corner this morning. This time the unnamed lady was dressed in a dark burgundy velvet dress, over a lace petticoat that peeked from beneath the hem. It was a clever way to disguise a dress that was too short, or had been hemmed to remove the fraying of age. When she turned toward the light I could see that the side of the skirt was worn, and had been turned from back to side to prolong the life of the garment. She was speaking, and Doña Granada was listening so intently that she inadvertently snubbed Angélica when Angélica attempted to greet her.

The shabby lady was unwilling to compound the social error. "Doña Angélica, Doña Josefina, I am honored," she said.

"Doña Eustacia," Angélica said, giving her her fingertips. "You look well." Angélica turned to me. "Josefina, Doña Eustacia is the Marquesa's cousin. She has come all the way from Sevilla to pay her respects."

Doña Granada had no choice but to acknowledge us. "Lovely dress," she said to me. "Is that the rural fashion these days?"

"Oh, don't be cutting, Granada," Angélica said with a light laugh. "Josefina's husband owns hectares and hectares of land, and has sent her to learn high culture. Surely we don't want to send her home believing that we are nothing but sniping cats." Her response irked me more than Doña Granada's insult. Don Manuel had not sent me, nor did he find me lacking in culture. Then I recalled the way he gazed at Angélica, and at the other ladies who told their tales of exotic, distant travels, and wondered if perhaps he had found me inadequate.

"Well, don't expect the Marquesa to save you a seat next to her at dinner," Doña Granada said to me. "Seating is strictly by protocol, and you will likely be at the foot of the table with the impoverished cousins."

Eustacia bit her lip, but, to my surprise, Angélica laughed again. "Sometimes it is better to sit at the far end of the table, and not at the top with the grandees. I do not believe that my husband, were he still alive, would care to have my legs caressed under the table by the Marqués."

"Unless he could find some advantage in it," Doña Granada retorted. "In which case he wouldn't have minded even the Marqués caressing *his* legs."

"Well, I will yield pride of place to you, Granada," Angélica replied, "since you are more in need of it."

Eustacia took my arm. "Come, let me introduce you to the

ancestors," she said, guiding me away from the sharp words. "Granada's acid tongue is legendary," she added as we toured the room, "but she amuses the Marqués, and the Marquesa is well able to best her in any war of words. Now, tell me, what brings you to Court?"

I could not tell her that I wanted to see the world that I had previously thought existed only in my mind, or that the pictures painted by the words of a traveling priest, embellished by tales told by fine ladies at the dinner table, had drawn me away from my duties as a wife and mother. I could not give voice to that longing, or even to the counterbalance of longing I already felt for the hacienda, for my sons, for Manuel.

"My husband thought it would be a good change for me, and I agreed," I said. Perhaps Angélica had been right, or perhaps it was the answer best given when there was no better one at hand.

Eustacia nodded. "I am unmarried, and likely to remain so, and thus had no other place to go. But you are not far from home, and can return. You have no need to bear the slights of those such as Granada."

"But when we entered, you were deep in conversation with her. Surely she must not always be seeking some advantage."

"I am poor in gold, but not in everything," Eustacia said. "Now, come, no more of Granada. This towering gentleman"—she pointed to the portrait of a particularly dour grandee—"is my uncle's brother. Your father, or your uncle, too, you may say. But he is not, since he had neither the same mother nor father as my own papa."

I frowned at the riddle. "The wrong side of the sheets for both of them," Eustacia said. "He was my grandfather's mistress's son, and my father was sired by one other than his mother's husband." I shook my head at the elaborate family tangle. "Hence, my impoverished state."

"You are so frank," I said softly. Surely her family's bastardy could not be common knowledge.

"Only concealed knowledge has any force or value."

I dared not ask what she meant, but I thought back to the poetry of this morning. All that talk of love's bastards had seemed bawdy and loose, but the Marquesa's objections had not appeared to be moral. "Is that why the Marquesa was so angry this morning when the nun read her poem?" I asked.

Eustacia raised an eyebrow, giving me a glimpse of the family resemblance. "I do not know enough to say," she said. "But tell me, my dear, are you poetic, too?"

This transition from her to me signaled that the topic was closed. "Not at all," I mumbled. Even in my inexperience I sensed that an admission of my aspirations could be considered information of "force or value."

"If you are, I will insist that you take a turn and share your verses with us. After all, we are all gifted with something, and it would be selfish not to sing for our supper."

"I assure you that I am not."

Eustacia looked at me, all deference and nervousness gone. "Then you must tell me what your special gifts are. For clearly you are not the innocent that you pretend."

"I tell you, I have no such gift. I have lived on my father's estate, and now I live in my husband's hacienda. I have never been more than an hour's carriage ride from home before today. If I perceived something in this morning's poetry, it was only by chance, like the briefest opening of heavy drapery." I felt a gasp in my chest at what I had mentioned.

"Indeed," she said, unaware of the meaning of my slip. "Well, we all have something to offer, and we shall learn, soon enough, no doubt, what is yours."

Angélica approached me at that moment. "I must tear you away, Josefina. I am so sorry to interrupt, Eustacia." She practically pulled my arm. I nodded to Eustacia and hurried after Angélica.

"What were you telling her?" Angélica hissed in my ear. "That woman trades in information and she had the look of a vulture with her prey."

"I said nothing of interest. I have nothing of interest to say."

Angélica gave me an odd look. "I should hope not. Just be careful to whom you talk too freely."

I nodded. There was so much going on in every conversation; I was never going to be able to fathom the intricacies of the simplest exchange.

"Come, Josefina. Don't look so glum, or the Marquesa will hear about it and send you home. She doesn't want sad-looking ladies-in-waiting."

Across the room a curtain was pulled aside, and the room hushed. The grandees were coming in. I craned my neck to see.

First, a tall, mustachioed man in green and gold livery entered. He bowed to the ladies, and stood holding the drape aside. Then another man, round and bald, followed, talking to a man next to him, paying no attention to the room, the introductions, the ladies, or the footman. His companion was another large man, in a black jacket and a lacy white neck cloth, his florid face all the redder from the glass of what appeared to have been wine in his hand. Neither so much as glanced at the company. Instead the two continued their discussion into the room and went directly to the sideboard where decanters of sherry and red wine glistened.

A tall lady followed, with a smaller, fair one behind her. Did some of the women gather elsewhere? Of course, I realized, the Marquesa would have to be attended by some of her ladies. Those of us in the room already were thus marked as lower than those who entered. Another man entered, and then two in religious garb. I stared. One was tall, with the unmistakable waves of red-gold hair cascading thickly down to his collar. His blue eyes glittered from across the room. Father Alonso had indeed arrived.

So it had been he. He looked across the room, into my face. His eyebrows went up, and he smiled a bit in the corner of his mouth, as he had so many years ago. He bowed to me, and all heads turned. I curtsied back, barely, unable to breathe.

"You know the Bishop?" Angélica whispered. I did not answer. Father Alonso said something to the other priest, who laughed. They turned to the sideboard, with no further look at me. The Marqués and the Marquesa's entrance went by, unnoticed by me. "Curtsy," Angélica muttered. I must have complied. The noise in the room was a roar in my ears. Then a hand was at my elbow, and he was there.

$\mathscr{S}$IX

$\mathscr{A}$RE YOU REALLY A bishop?" were the first words out of my mouth.

He laughed. "Yes, Doña Josefina. I am really a bishop. And you have grown into a lovely lady." People were staring, so I lowered my eyes.

"Your Grace," I started.

"You must call me that here, yes." I glanced up, saw that he was still smiling at me. Was it that smile, or was it the blue eyes? "I learned of your arrival from the excellent Sor Juana. She spoke of you this afternoon."

"In the library?"

He looked sharply at me. "How did you know?"

"I entered by mistake. I was exploring. I overheard you talking, and could not believe it was your voice. Could not believe it was you."

Father Alonso was silent. Then, leaning down to me, so close I could smell the aroma of the lemon verbena that he still, even now, used to scent his clothes, he said softly, "Be silent about that, Josefina. Unless you have changed a great deal, you know nothing of the ways of the Court. I will talk to you later." Then he raised his voice to normal. "So, Doña Josefina, is this your first visit to the Marqués' Court?"

I understood, and strove to reply calmly, though my throat fluttered. "Yes, Your Grace. I have never ventured from my home before."

"And have you found it interesting, so far?"

I looked into his eyes, and could see the hint of mirth that I remembered from my youth. "Yes, Your Grace. Everyone has been very kind."

"Your father is well, I trust."

"He was, by God's mercy, when I saw him last."

"Then commend me to him when you see him next," he said, and offered his ring to kiss. I curtsied deeply and took the ring to my lips. His hand was warm, uncalloused, and covered with little freckles and golden hair, so different from Manuel's. He left it at my lips longer than necessary, and I felt the same stirring in my belly that I had felt so many years before, when he read to me from mysterious works in my father's study. But I was a married woman now, and I knew what that feeling was. I turned away. I could not be such a sinner as to desire a bishop.

I watched him walk back to the sideboard. A footman poured him some wine. I had to busy myself with some conversation and not stand there like a trapped animal. I looked for Angélica but she was speaking with Doña Granada, and I was not ready for more of that acid tongue.

I saw Eustacia looking directly at me. She stood alone now, as she had in the morning, keeping apart from the others. From her nervous or frightened mien then to her role as the impoverished cousin throwing herself upon the mercy of her wealthy kin, to the broker of secrets, Eustacia had shown many faces in one day. There was definitely something sly about her, as she observed the guests from the safety of her social nadir. She approached me. "So, you are the Bishop's friend, too?"

"Too?"

"So, you do not deny the friendship, just the sharing of it?"

"I am acquainted with him from my childhood. He used to come and pray with my father, when my mother, rest her soul, died." Eustacia looked disappointed. If she was looking for information to broker, I would be a poor source.

"He seemed eager to renew the acquaintance."

"He asked that I commend him to my father, nothing more. Now, tell me who everyone is, Doña Eustacia, so I do not make a fool of myself at dinner."

Eustacia gave pithy descriptions of each guest, sparing no one. "In the black doublet, with the scar, Commander Juan José Mendilla, of the Royal Army. He seeks the Marqués' favor, and his funding, for a new campaign. In black as well, but with the silver embroidery, his second in command. It's a wonder the army can spare them both at once, given their endeavors in the Netherlands. And the lady in the light green gown, with the tower of black hair, Doña María del Pilar de Suegros, well named. Her in-laws, or *suegros,* have more land than money, and more money than God. Sor Inez, you know from this morning, is the Marquesa's protégée and favorite, and brings music and pastries from the convent."

"I do not see Sor Juana, the poetess," I said.

"Do not expect to. Her verses grow more daring daily. Then again"—she paused, looking sideways at me—"given the Bishop's support, she may be here later."

I did not react. Even in my few hours at the Court of the Marquesa, I was learning to keep my own counsel. "And the lady in the magnificent black and gold gown?" I asked. She looked more regal than the Marquesa, and was beautiful as well. She was surrounded by men, who laughed at her witticisms and sallies.

"Condesa Alejandra Colmillo de Valencia, in one of her rare visits. Be careful, she bites."

"Bites?" I echoed, laughing. "How so?"

"Rumor. It is said that her husband abandoned her, his countship, and her lands, after she became a vampire."

"Such nonsense. If it were true, she would not be welcomed here."

It was Eustacia's turn to keep her own counsel. "Let us find Doña Angélica. It will be time for dinner soon, and we must not be conversing solely with one another. You are here to be companionable and sociable."

We crossed the room, but before we could reach Angélica we were interrupted by none other than the Marqués himself. "We have not been introduced," he said to me. I blushed under my dark skin. Had I committed another social error?

"Your Highness, I am Doña Josefina María del Carmen Asturias de Castillo, come to pay my respects to the Marquesa."

"I know that, lovely girl. It is I who have not introduced myself. And don't call me Your Highness. Marqués will do." He was less than my hand's breadth taller than I, and appeared substantially younger than the Marquesa. His hair was of a neutral brown, long and straight past his shoulders, and had not been dressed. His features would have been un-remarkable, with hazel eyes of no depth, a weak chin, and a portly girth, but for the large, hooked nose that sprouted between his eyebrows and curled down to his upper lip. Nonetheless, his smile, where I could see it, was friendly.

How friendly I was soon to find out. He extended his hand. I was unsure what to do with the extremity, so I took it, then released it. He slipped it around my waist. "I am delighted to meet you, Doña Josefina. I hope you enjoy your stay." His hand lingered at my waist, slipping slightly lower. I stood still for a moment, nonplussed, then pulled away, but not harshly, so as not to call attention to my awkward situation. He laughed. "I am sure you will enjoy yourself here," he added. With another smile from under his nose, he turned his attention to Eustacia. "See to it that she does," he said softly, and walked away.

Eustacia's lips pursed in a most unattractive way. "You will be the Marqués' next victim, I see," she said.

"Victim? He is our host." I feared that I knew what she implied, though perhaps not exactly what she meant.

Eustacia raised her eyebrow, Marquesa style, and looked down on me. "You will be neither the first nor the last. The Marqués makes very free with the ladies of the Court, and few refuse him."

"Every man takes his pleasure where he finds it," I said primly, "but not with ladies. Surely there are legions of women available for him to slake his lusts."

"You are a practical woman, Doña Josefina," she replied. "You have not been influenced by foolish ideas of romance. But I can see your heightened color, the sparkle in your eye. You are flattered by the attention, aren't you? Not surprising for a woman used to her husband's protection."

Eustacia had a sharp eye, even if she mistook the source of my agitation, and I was happy for the error. But her implication, while insulting to me, was far more revealing of her own state than she must realize. "Every man has needs," I said. "It is simply a question of how and where he fills them." My answer surprised even me. I looked her in the eye. "Was he pleasant, at least?"

Eustacia turned on me fiercely. "You are a countrified fool." She pulled her skirt up off her shoes to keep from tripping as she walked briskly away.

"You have made a dangerous enemy, Josefina," said a voice in my ear. The Bishop, as I must now call him, was at my side.

"I hope, then, in Your Grace to have a powerful friend."

IN THE MATTER OF dinner, Doña Granada was absolutely right. I was placed at the lower end of the table, between an ancient gentleman, whose hearing was so precarious that conversation was limited to the weather and repetitions of what had just been said, and on the other side a slim young man whose entire interest was cattle. Fortunately, I am well versed in that subject, and could carry my side of the conversation, when it was directed to me. But my eyes, and my mind, were at the lofty end of the table, where the Bishop, the Marqués, and everyone else who mattered were seated.

The table was long enough, with twenty of us, that it was not possible to converse beyond one's sphere, but not so long that we were excluded from the Marqués' stories. When he chose to address the table, we fell silent to attend his words. I found the stories he told amusing, if bawdier than I was used to. My companion to the right, however, expressed himself far too loudly on the subject. "What did he say, my dear?" he bellowed at me.

I tried to repeat the words of the anecdote loudly in his ear, but not so loudly that I distracted the table. "Oh, not that old chestnut again!" the old man shouted. I was mortified by the smiles behind hands that were directed our way, but he seemed impervious to any mockery.

After dinner, we repaired to the main room again, for music and, for the gentlemen, more wine. The ladies took small cups of bitter chocolate, and I was glad for the familiar, comforting drink. The aroma reminded me of the little room off the kitchen where my worktable, filled with account sheets, along with a trinket belonging to Joaquín or a sticky spot from Neto's drooling, waited patiently for my return to normal life. I wished myself home, where the words we spoke were few, and meant only what we expected them to mean.

Following a quick raise of her eyebrows, I sat with Angélica. "You should look and listen more," she whispered. "And speak less."

"You told me to be lively," I protested, but I knew she was right.

"Lively without rushing into every awkward or inappropriate conversation!" she hissed back. I resolved to do so. As it happened, the final entertainment of the evening came to my assistance.

Sor Inez took out the lyre, another sister produced a flute, and we were transported to a higher plane by the ethereal music they produced. Angélica was pressed to sing, and she took her place by Sor Inez. Sor Inez, to my surprise, joined her in the singing, all the while strumming her lyre, and produced a rich alto to Angélica's sweet soprano, so that their voices were woven into a heavenly tapestry.

This was why I had come to Court. To hear such music was impossible in the hacienda, where talk of cattle, prices, and babies was the height of the day. I closed my eyes and let the beauty waft over me.

"I told you you would be tired," Angélica said, slipping onto the settee next to me. "You should have slept, instead of running around all over the castle."

I smiled at her. "It's the music. It was so beautiful. You sing splendidly." Angélica smiled back. "Manuel was enchanted by your singing at our home before we left for Court."

Unbidden, the image of Manuel's big, hard hand engulfing a spoon, reaching across to me to offer me a taste of something, rushed to my mind. I sighed.

"Are you homesick?" she asked kindly. We had only been gone a few days, but it seemed an eternity.

"No, not homesick," I said. "But you were right, I am tired."

"There is nothing you can do about that," she replied. "We must stay until the Marquesa retires, and she never flags. Come, make yourself lively. Let us go and converse with Commander Mendilla. He is known for his wit and wealth. But remember, make him, not yourself, interesting."

I trailed after Angélica. I was impressed by her courage and stamina, and by the bold way she smiled into the Commander's eyes. True to her word, Angélica kept up the questioning, and he told us in detail of his campaign in the Netherlands.

"My men were deep in the woods, awaiting the enemy. They were cold and hungry. I had to lead the charge," he went on.

The story seemed endless, yet Angélica kept his words going. She laughed, a tinkling sound, and added, "Oh, yes, Commander, that must have been terrifying!" at various junctures, and "You were so brave!" at others. I privately hoped that his renowned wealth exceeded his paltry wit.

I felt a hand on my arm, and it slid low on my wrist. I wrenched my arm away before turning to see the Marqués. "Oh, Your Highness!" I said, at a loss.

"Marqués. I told you to call me Marqués," he said, with that smile.

"Yes, of course, Marqués. You startled me."

"I am so glad. A virtuous woman is a prize beyond precious stones, as our Good Book says."

My goodness, what does one say to that? I wondered. Angélica remained engrossed with her Commander, and I was on my own. But I was saved the need to reply by the Marqués himself, who was not expecting me to do so. "I am delighted to see that my wife has chosen to surround herself with such charming and honorable women. We must deepen our acquaintance, Doña Josefina. Do you agree?"

"Of course, Marqués," I replied. I was a guest in his home, be it a castle or a hovel, I could not decline a simple request to converse. His hand returned to my arm, and this time I forced myself not to shake it off. "You honor me with your attention."

"My lady, the honor is all mine," he replied. As he walked away I expected to see Eustacia, either gloating or glowering, but she was nowhere to be seen. Perhaps as a member of the family, albeit an impoverished one, she could retire early.

Mercifully, the evening soon came to a close. Sor Inez sang one more song, the Marqués told one more anecdote, and the Marquesa announced that she would now return to her chambers. The Bishop gave her his ring to kiss, the women curtsied, and she left with her chosen ladies. We were free to go. Sor Juana, and her scandalous verses, had not made an appearance that night.

EVEN

THAT NIGHT I HAD a most disturbing dream. It began with me at home. Manuel had come in from the barn, and was ready for his midday meal. I searched the kitchen, finding nothing prepared, and nothing to make the meal from. I opened cupboard after cupboard, but in each, there were only empty bowls and baskets.

Manuel, impatient, came into the kitchen. I was not surprised in my dream, though nothing could have been less likely in reality. He came up behind me and put his hands on my breasts. I could feel the heat from his palms through my blouse, and the sparks that went through my nipples as he moved his hands over them. I leaned back, into him, and his big, hard hands dropped to my waist, and then started to raise my skirt from behind.

I felt my desire for him grow, but before we could continue, he let go of my skirt and reached instead into the empty cupboard. He pulled out a handful of jewels. They fell in a stream from his hand, which turned from brown to a delicate, milky white. He laughed and his laugh was harsh and ugly. It was the laugh of the Marqués. I awoke drenched in sweat.

THE NEXT MORNING I arose troubled and confused. I drank sour lemon water to clear my mind, but the grotesque final images of my dream remained. Their only competition were the images from the previous night's party, of Father Alonso smiling down at me, and of the Marqués leering. They were, after all, the same characters of my dreams, reconstituted in their own guise.

The disgust I felt for my thoughts notwithstanding, I yearned without respite to see Father Alonso. Although I searched for him in the library, looked for him at luncheon, and thought about him almost continuously, I did not see the Bishop for the next three days. Perhaps he had gone, and I would not see him again for another eight years. The mere idea made me despondent.

I did not see Sor Juana the poetess, either. To Angélica's dismay, we were not sent for by the Marquesa for all that time. Our days were spent languorously, in false leisure, in the music room or the garden, or dressing. While I pined secretly, Angélica was openly distraught over our exclusion from whatever entertainment the Marquesa was offering. She fretted that I had made a poor impression at the grandees' dinner, and made me review every conversation I had had, heard, or observed. I complied with all except my too-brief words with the Bishop, which I summarized while leaving out what mattered most: his promise to speak to me again, about Sor Juana, the poems, and the dangerous Doña Eustacia.

On my conversations with Eustacia and with the Marqués, her questions were sharp and unrelenting. She condemned herself for not instructing me sufficiently, and condemned me for being unequal to taking care of obvious social duties without her tutoring. While I spent the quiet hours longing for Father Alonso, and tormenting myself with his promise, she searched the castle to see which ladies had been called, and which were, like ourselves, left to our own meager company. We were poor companions to one another in those days.

We were summoned to the Marquesa's antechamber on the third day, to make an appearance for the midday meal. Angélica was pointed. "Keep quiet, and do not evince any interest in anything that the poetess may read, or contradict anything that Eustacia may say. You are ignorant of Court ways, and should maintain a humble demeanor suitable to your ignorance."

I assured her I would be silent.

"No," she said, exasperated. "Do not be silent, either. Try, if you can, to be amusing, without getting into the deep waters of family relations, or sacrilegious poetry, or anything else that will offend the Marquesa. If you still have not noticed, it is her family's money that created the marquessate, and offending her is tantamount to offending the Crown."

"So the Marqués is a cipher?"

She frowned. "No. And he is dangerous, too."

"A satyr, then."

"What? What is that?"

I flushed. It was something that Father Alonso had read aloud to me, years and years ago, from the myths of the Greeks. "A half man, half goat," I said. "With all of the bad behavior of each." Father Alonso had explained the sketchiest of details, but though I was only fifteen and virginal I intuitively grasped his meaning. And I had dreamed of the satyr, with Father Alonso's face, for a week. As the shame of the memory overtook me, I longed to take back my words, but it was too late.

Angélica looked horrified. "Good heavens, Josefina. Where on earth did you hear of such things? Certainly not in Don Manuel's home?"

I looked away. "No. It is something a priest once told me, when I was a young girl. I do not know why it came to me now. It is nonsense, of course. Please forget I mentioned it."

"Happily," she said caustically. "And I suggest you keep such nonsense to yourself for as long as you are here. I shall have to keep a close watch on you, far closer than I expected."

"I assure you, I will be no trouble," I mumbled, as we made our way down the long stone corridors to the Marquesa's wing.

When we entered the chamber, it was a far different moment than that of my initial foray, just a few days before. This time, it was afternoon, the light was warmer, and the room was crowded. The ladies who had attended the Marquesa at the grandees' dinner, along with those I had met the first day, were all there, in afternoon gowns in soft colors. There were half a dozen nuns present, including both Sor Inez and Sor Juana, the latter again with her enormous brooch under her chin. In addition, there were servants, a footman, and two small boys in green and gold livery, all tending to platters of meats, potatoes, vegetables, tortillas, chiles with corn and cream, and sweet cornmeal masa stuffed into corn husks. The aromas of the culinary delights overwhelmed me and made my mouth water.

Though the food was now all laid out, and the plates awaited us, no one made a move to be served. All awaited the Marquesa, and talked quietly in groups of two or three. Eustacia sidled up to me.

"Did you hear that the Bishop has returned to Puebla?" she said, after the preliminaries of my health and the pleasures of my stay thus far.

I felt my stomach clench, and I looked at my feet. I did not want to betray any feeling at all to Eustacia, but the sun had gone behind the blackest cloud. I swallowed and said, "No, I had not heard. May the Lord preserve His Grace and grant him a safe journey." It was a bland and pious answer, but if Eustacia was disappointed, she did not show it.

"I would imagine he took leave of you before his departure," she remarked.

"That would have been a great honor," I said, "but I would never have expected it." I wracked my brain for anything that would have given away my prior longing for him, or my present despair, and could find nothing. Angélica was watching me closely.

"I imagine that Sor Juana will greatly miss his counsel and guidance," continued Eustacia, with a malicious smile on her angular face.

I forbore to answer. "Is the Marquesa, your cousin, in good health?" I asked instead, and heard Angélica exhale with relief.

"She is indeed," Eustacia answered, and turned away. I followed her movement through the group, and saw the nuns separate to allow her passage without letting her be close enough to require that they engage her in conversation. It was a maneuver I decided I should take pains to master.

When the Marquesa came in, she was paler than she had been at our first meeting, making me wonder if my question regarding her health had been more prescient than social. She gazed around the room, allowing her glance to linger on me longer than I was comfortable with. Then she crooked her finger to me, bidding me approach.

"You are looking well, Doña Josefina. Is our Court agreeing with you?"

"Of course, Your Highness," I answered. To what, I wondered, did I owe the distinction of being singled out so?

"I am glad. I would like you to attend us this evening, if you could. We have an intimate dinner planned, the Marqués and I, with only a few attendants and guests. Would you be so kind?"

I understood an order, and graciously curtsied. "Your Highness gives me great honor in allowing me to attend you so soon after my arrival. I know so little of Court behavior, but I will endeavor to do your bidding."

"See that you do so," the Marquesa replied. I would not ask for clarification, though her response left me wondering. She turned to Sor Inez. "Sister, of course you will provide us with some of your musical grace." Sor Inez bowed her head in agreement. "Please, my ladies, let us eat before we faint of hunger!"

Though unlikely to do so in such opulent surroundings, the ladies fell to and allowed their plates to be filled, proceeding to partake of the bounty.

"So, our little country newcomer is being singled out early," said Granada, easing her shapely body into a seat next to me. She was again in light green, a color that enriched her light complexion and soft brown hair, and she had a simple silver choker as her only jewelry. Beside her I indeed felt like the country cousin.

"I am honored," I replied.

"The Marqués must have been captivated by your charms the other night."

I raised my eyebrows. "The Marqués?"

"Perhaps you have been chosen as his next plaything."

"Doña Granada, how can you say such a thing?"

"Oh, don't be the prissy miss with me. Surely in the country a man takes his pleasure the same as in Court. I saw you encourage him at the grandees' dinner. And didn't your husband send you here to gain some culture and experience?"

"I think this is most uncalled for," I said, sounding exactly like the prissy miss Granada had called me.

She laughed. "I imagine that your husband would welcome your return with a few skills you did not have when you left home!" I heard Eustacia snicker behind me, and I hoped to Heaven that the Marquesa was not overhearing this scandalous talk.

ANGÉLICA WAS LIVID. "You have been asked, and I have not! What could the Marquesa possibly mean by this?" I remained silent, for I wondered the same thing myself. During the rest of the lunch I had been quiet, keeping my remarks to the minimal and the mundane. I did not want to cause Angélica pain or incite further gossip, though it appeared that nothing I did either way would still the wagging tongues.

We walked back to our rooms to rest for the afternoon. But Angélica could not rest, and she paced her room, then mine. I had learned from my earlier evening that I would indeed regret it if I did not take my siesta, and I felt a growing resentment of Angélica's intrusion. If I had to attend the Marquesa this evening, with or without Angélica, I could not afford to be sleepy, or allow my guard to drop from weariness.

"Angélica, I must sleep. You are probably being spared a dull evening, and are held in reserve for something more enticing. Please, let me sleep."

"Of course. The favorite must have her rest."

"Please."

"Very well. But I will assist you with your toilette, so at the very least you do not disgrace yourself—and, by association, me—with some foolish dress."

I acquiesced, if only to appease her, and did not respond to the comment about my clothes. After all, she could well have been right.

Once she was gone I found that I was as restless as she. I tossed and rolled in my bed, and wondered why I had been selected for this honor. I was afraid that the Marqués had somehow misinterpreted my behavior as welcoming of untoward advances. And with the thought of untoward advances came thoughts of Father Alonso.

Father Alonso never touched me in all the time he visited with me and my father. He never attempted to seduce, lure, or misguide me into his bed. Yes, he was a man of the cloth, but even in my father's house anyone knew that a priest may be a man of God, but was nonetheless a man.

It had been his words that entranced me, his reading to me, explaining, teaching, and tantalizing me with stories that made my heart pound or my blood rush, or that left me languidly dreaming of worlds far from the dust and mud and cattle and accounts that made up my life. Greek myths, psalms from King David, *villancicos* and poetry of the people, sacred verses, and biblical visions of the apocalypse and the coming of the end of the world had all been introduced by Father Alonso.

He spoke of God's love, reading from the words of King David. "You are the flower of the garden. . . . Come down to the vineyard to see if the vines have budded, and there I will give you my love." I felt my budding body come alive, as did the vineyard of my mind, while Father Alonso taught me about God's love.

When he left, my heart ached for months, but I had the Bible to console myself with. The heat I felt when I read kept his memory strong within me, but reading and dreaming slaked it as well. My father was pleased with my purity and encouraged my studies, against the maledictions of those who said reading and writing would make a woman unchaste and lead her into temptation. He said I was living proof that learning made a woman virtuous, and it was thus that when Manuel offered for my hand I could go to him a virgin.

It was only after Manuel had consummated our marriage that I began to understand that the garden could blossom here on earth, and that the fecund vineyard was mine to share with my husband. With marriage, Father Alonso receded from my mind, replaced by the real, earthy fulfillment of my vows. Manuel was the only man I knew, and his ways were the ones that now shaped my life. I had not known that the virgin's dreams still smoldered until I heard the voice in the library. And now, once again, Father Alonso was gone. My longing, intense and unquenched, burned within me.

Had the Marqués felt the burning in my core? Had he sensed, with that huge hooked nose, that I was on fire, with a fierce and unchaste desire for a bishop, a guest of great eminence in his castle? If an animal can smell the heat of desire in another, a man could doubtless do the same.

I rose from the bed and poured cool water into the basin on the sideboard. I plunged my hands into the water, then took a length of cloth and drenched it. I wrung it out and put the cooling compress on my brow. I lay down again, and fell into the fitful sleep of the unquiet mind.

$\mathcal{E}$IGHT

OW DIFFERENT THE DINNER in the Marqués' dining chamber was from the grandees' dinner. Cayetana dressed my hair personally, sweeping the chestnut locks into a twist and holding the twist together with amethyst combs. My dress was a deeper amethyst, with a lace panel at the neckline, giving a chaste aura to the daring cut. She rubbed my neck, wrists, and temples with jasmine water, and dabbed oil on my eyebrows and cheekbones. "Where did you learn such artifice?" I asked her, looking at the transformation in the glass.

"You are not the only one whose eyes are being opened here, Doña Josefina. Look at my rebozo; I bought it from a trader who frequents the servants' wing. Have you ever seen such work?" I looked at the black shawl she wore, and indeed, it had been magnificently worked with black stitching, in a climbing rose pattern of intense intricacy. It was only my self-absorption that had kept me from noticing it before.

"It's beautiful, Cayetana."

"As are you, Doña Josefina. It is a shame that Don Manuel cannot see you tonight. You glow."

I smiled at my faithful servant. She had truly become my ally in the years since I came into the Castillo household.

"Now, hurry," she said. "I doubt the Marqués takes well to being kept waiting."

I looked into Angélica's room before going, but she was not there. I wondered what she would do for her evening meal, whether she would take it in her room or join the other uninvited ladies in the dining hall. I truly wished she were going with me.

Finally, I headed to the Marquesa's wing, and was led by a footman to the Marqués' dining chamber. The footman opened the heavy wooden door and announced me. Though my heart was pounding, I lifted my head and entered with all the dignity I could muster.

I was greeted immediately by the Marqués himself. I learned later that he did not customarily wait to make an entrance after all of his guests were assembled, but rather entered when he felt like it, and stayed only as long as he wished. His guests were free to come and go, and to leave if they were tired, or remain after he retired if they wanted to continue the revelry. The Marqués bowed over my hand, and lifted it to his lips in affected courtesy as I curtsied. His nose touched my hand before his mouth did. "Doña Josefina, welcome to my chambers. You are looking even more radiant than you did last night, if that is possible."

"Thank you, Your Highness."

"Marqués."

I nodded. I did not feel ready for such familiarity. He moved aside, and I took in the rest of the room. A large fireplace filled the back wall, and a fire was lit within, despite the mildness of the evening. The walls were paneled waist high in dark wood, and the plaster above the carved chair rail was painted a deep umber, giving the room an intimate, masculine feel. A heavy table ran down the middle of the room, with four chairs on either side, and a large, carved armchair at either end. It appeared that we would be ten at dinner, with the Marqués and the Marquesa anchoring the ends of the table. I was only partly right.

Small groupings of chairs filled the corners of the room, with low tables holding wine decanters, cut crystal glasses, and silver trays of tiny pastries. I scanned the room, noting that there were several people I had not seen before, and saw that Doña Granada had been included in the gathering. She was in yellow tonight, a shade that was less becoming on her than the greens she had worn before, as it lacked a contrast with her gold-brown hair and skin. Her neckline made up for the pallid color of the dress, in its plunge between her rounded breasts, which strained against the silky material. She wore a diamond and emerald necklace, and I wondered about her circumstances. Was she married? Widowed? She seemed wealthy, and was unpleasantly witty. She was no older than I, by her appearance, but her figure proclaimed her either childless or lucky.

She raised her glass of wine to me as I caught her eye, and she smiled a tight little smile that did not enhance her beauty. She turned her attention back to the man she was conversing with, a gentleman who had been present at last night's dinner. I remembered him as Commander Mendilla, who had so bored me with his exploits. Granada, however, seemed fascinated. Angélica had acted the same last night, so I presumed that Granada was merely being courteous.

Another lady, another beauty, slender in a severe black gown with a high neck, and diamonds in her hair, in her ears, and in a long pendant that hung around her throat, was looking intensely into the eyes of the rotund gentleman who had attended last night. His companion from the previous evening, the tall man with the straight black hair, stood with them but gazed over both their heads at the fire. And Sor Juana sat in a chair to the side, reading silently from a sheet of foolscap. I was surprised to see her in this venue, and I made my way over to her. The Marquesa was not yet present.

Sor Juana looked up when I sat in the chair next to her. "Lady," she said, her cool gray eyes looking straight into mine, "welcome."

"Thank you, Sister," I replied. "Are you planning to read to us tonight?" Her own direct looks encouraged me to omit the circumlocutions I was finding so common here at Court, and come straight to the point.

"I am."

"What will the topic of your poem be?" I did not, even with her direct way, want to ask if it would be less scandalous than her previous offering.

"My theme is always God's love. But the person who commissions my work also informs it."

"Commissions?" I felt so foolish. I had no idea what she meant.

"I have only once written a work for my own pleasure. All of my work is ordered by my patrons. It is the Marquesa who bids me write a song, for example, celebrating the beauty of spring, or the glory of Easter."

"And the poem you read a few days ago, what was that to celebrate?"

Sor Juana smiled a little. "That was to rejoice in the coming of the Marquesa's son, home from Spain, in a fortnight."

I shook my head. Nothing in that poem could have been said to celebrate a son's return. I had little experience with poetry, only the lessons Father Alonso had taught me, so I could not contest her statement. But the thought of Father Alonso brought color to my cheek and fueled a desire to quiz the sister about him.

"How long ago did you make the acquaintance of the Bishop of Puebla?" I asked.

Sor Juana raised her brows. "You are bold. Did he not tell you to keep silent on that?" I nodded. "Then you should do so. It would not be beneficial for you to disobey him."

"I am sorry, I had no intention of disobeying His Grace. He told you of his admonition to me, then?"

"Yes, and we must not speak of it now. But listen to the poem carefully tonight, for there is a lesson in it for you." Her finger traced a line across the back of my hand, and I felt a shiver go deep. "You must obey the Bishop, and, by extension, you must learn at the end of my quill. Now, go. You were not invited here tonight to entertain me, but to amuse the Marqués." She smiled at my sharp intake of breath. "You may keep your virtue close, but make no mistake: your charms, and the promise of more, are what you are fed for. Not your virtue."

I stood, shocked. But the Marqués was bearing down on me. "Come, my lovely," he said. "I am sure Sor Juana has much to prepare before her recitation tonight. Come and enjoy a glass of Jerez before we dine." He poured a glass of the amber liquid and handed it to me. "Drink it, my dear. It will warm you. And we have no need of any other chilly ladies here. Sor Juana chills the air enough for all of us!"

Sor Juana merely smiled and went back to her reading. The Marqués' hand was on my waist; I had no choice but to drink the sherry. It was sweet and smooth, and it did indeed warm me as it traveled down.

The Marqués, his hand now firmly around my waist, guided me across the room to the fire. As we walked, he asked me simple questions about my home, my family. I answered, mindful of the eyes of the room on us, and turned as gracefully as I could to escape his grasp. But he was accustomed to such feints and dodges from his quarry. His hand slipped below my waist, brushing lightly across my buttocks, as he allowed me my freedom. He licked his lips, obviously well satisfied with his sortie.

"Marqués, I would guess that you are a poetry lover," I said, referring to the inclusion of Sor Juana among the guests.

"But of course, my dear. Every cultured man loves a well-turned word."

"We are not accustomed to entertain our guests at my husband's hacienda. We simply dine, and talk, and enjoy one another's stories. So you must forgive any ignorance of mine."

"It is charming, Doña Josefina. You are a welcome change from Doña Granada," he said, looking over at her. "She is most amusing, but so much work! She is well advised to seek a maintenance with the Commander. He has the means, and she is no longer young."

"A maintenance?" Could that mean what it sounded like?

The Marqués refilled my sherry glass. I drank the sherry without needing his encouragement. I felt the warmth lower now. He smiled. "Surely even you are not ignorant as to what a maintenance is? For a woman of family, whose husband is no longer interested in keeping his wife, there are few options. And she is a most amusing companion, for a man with less wit and more energy than I have. Wish her success, my dear."

"I have no doubt she will succeed. Doña Granada appears to be the type of lady who fulfills her mission, against any odds." I surprised myself with my answer. The sherry was loosening my tongue.

"And you have a sharper wit than you pretend," he answered. "Are you musical?"

"Not at all, but I do enjoy listening."

"Pity. I do like a lady who will sing for me. Your companion, Doña Angélica, has a gift of golden voice to match her hair."

"She does. I am sorry she was not included tonight. A musical selection can smooth even the rockiest of social encounters."

The Marqués raised his eyebrows. "You do not fear the competition of one so young, so beautiful, and with enough wealth to be dependent on no one?"

"Competition for what, Your Highness? Marqués. Are we vying for something greater than inclusion at your evening meal?"

He laughed, as if I had just spoken the greatest witticism of the evening. "You are either a complete country simpleton or a minx. And with your looks, your lovely shape, and your exquisite turns of phrase, I would choose the minx." His hand slid around my waist again, then rested low on my hip. He turned me toward the fire, so my back was to the room, and he brushed his other hand across my breasts. I sucked in my breath, but I could not recoil, as he held me close. "No rocky encounters need to be smoothed now, do they?"

"None, Marqués. But the evening is still young, and her gift may come in handy should you proceed further."

He laughed again and released me, stepping smoothly away to a proper and respectful distance. I congratulated myself at having extricated myself from that awkward position without calling attention to us, believing for an instant that I had caused his conscience to command his hands. But immediately afterward I realized that he had been facing into the room, and he had acted judiciously, if not at my instigation. For at that moment the inner curtain was pulled aside, and the Marquesa, attended by the Bishop of Puebla, entered the dining room.

I curtsied to the Marquesa, but my eyes fixed upon Father Alonso. He smiled at me, and for the moment there was no one else in the room. Alas, that was but an illusion, and I had to be conscious of the fact that there were, indeed, eight others, all of whom had clearly marked the Bishop's smile and were watching with delighted malevolence to see my reaction. With every nerve in my body on alert, I returned my regard back to my hostess.

The Marquesa looked more regal than I had yet seen her, and she held herself erect and aloof. The Marqués moved to her and took her arm. "Señora," he said, "our guests have been patient long enough. Let us sit down!" He smiled at her, but there was a hint of malice in his eyes.

She returned his look but not his smile. "Indeed, señor, they could have sat at your whim. Such courtesies as you extend to me are best avoided."

I frowned, not understanding the exchange, made in full voice to include us all. Father Alonso had detached himself from the pair, and had moved to the sideboard, where he poured himself a glass of sherry. Then he walked with purpose, and sat in the chair I had formerly occupied, next to Sor Juana. She smiled at him, and I realized that the veil, the wimple, and the strange and enormous brooch notwithstanding, she was beautiful. As beautiful as Doña Granada or Angélica, or more so for her lack of artifice. I did not want to imagine the scandal that must have forced her into convent life, for surely such a beauty had not lacked for suitors.

Father Alonso seemed not to care about the social consequences of his actions; he acted as one above reproach, gossip, and censure. "Sister," he said, "I am eager for your next reading tonight. Are you going to grant us audience?"

"Yes, of course, Your Grace, as I have been commanded by His Highness, the Marqués." I glanced his way, where he still stood in quiet conversation with his wife. But Sor Juana's words had carried, and the Marquesa pulled away from the Marqués, drawing herself up icily. Her thin lips pursed, and the red spots that had stained her cheeks on my first visit returned.

"I expect that we will have no need of your poetry," she said sharply to Sor Juana. Sor Juana remained cool and impassive.

The Marqués laughed. "To the contrary, we shall have great need. And great expectations. My dear," he said to his wife, "come, let us be seated. And you, my lovely," he said, turning to me, "come and sit by me at the table. I long to enjoy your conversation in a more intimate setting."

I cast my eyes to the ground, feeling pity, such an odd feeling, for the Marquesa, and terror for myself, for there was no possible good outcome of such an exchange. The Marquesa took her seat at the foot of the table, and the Marqués moved to the head. I looked at Father Alonso for guidance, but he simply nodded to me, and took a seat to the right of the Marquesa. Sor Juana joined him, and then the Commander, who held the chair for Doña Granada to sit next to him, and thus take one side of the Marqués.

In my uncertainty I had not moved quickly enough, leaving me at the Marqués' other, left side, and I hesitatingly moved to that spot. To my left was the rotund man whose name I could never get, followed by the thin widow, and then the Commander's raven-haired assistant. Footmen immediately came forward to serve the food, and wine was poured. My glass was filled, and the Marqués proposed the toast. "Let us drink to the health of the Marquesa!" he exclaimed. We all immediately raised our glasses and drank. "More wine!" he told the footman, who complied. "And again!" the Marqués said, draining his glass. I sipped cautiously this time, for the last thing I could afford was to have the wine govern my sense, instead of the reverse. I looked at the Marquesa. She did not drink.

Dinner was served, beginning with the fish course. I turned my attention to my plate, carefully avoiding the bones, and savored the delicious preparation Veracruz style. Chopped vegetables and herbs adorned the snapper fish, and its delicious flesh melted on my tongue. I spared only a little conversation for the gentleman on my left but was forgiven, for his attention was riveted on his meal.

I glanced occasionally at Father Alonso. He managed to eat his fish in an unhurried manner, and to converse normally with the Marquesa, without whispering or commanding the table. The Marquesa appeared at her most unguarded so far. Where he went, calm prevailed.

In any event, my silence was unnoticed, as the Marqués launched into an anecdote that would brook no interruption, regarding his recent travels to San Luis Potosí, where he had enjoyed a visit with the Conde de Villarreal and his charming companion, named, apparently, Dotti.

After two courses, the Marqués, whose glass had been refilled unceasingly by his attentive footman, rose to his feet. I was amazed that he did not waver, for though I had seen my father and Manuel enjoy their many glasses of wine, I had yet to see a man imbibe in such quantity and still stand.

"A verse, Sor Juana, to aid the digestion!"

"Her verses do more to curdle the digestion than aid it," Granada quipped.

The Marqués glared at her, then burst out laughing. "Your tongue could better be used otherwise, Granada, than to contradict me!" The men at the table, including Father Alonso, laughed, the widow tittered, and the Commander placed his hand on Granada's shoulder in a most proprietary way. Granada affected indignation, but was clearly enjoying the attention. I would have fled.

The Marquesa did not laugh.

The Marqués disregarded her. "Come, Sister. A verse."

"As you wish, Your Highness," she said, and reached to the little table behind her for her foolscap. Unrolling it, she read in her cool, unhurried voice.

"If coldness and anger have their satisfaction
Clothed in righteous aloofness,
Then hear me, my love, and measure my sorrows
Which to bear belief would redress.
Hear my proud protestation,
For it lives well with showy disdain
Side by side with humbled love.
Hear in my coldness the sweet beseeching
Which with logic and teaching
Says what it cannot.
And after you have heard me
Will your breast stay hardened
As bronze?
As immovable?"

The Marquesa put her glass down hard on the table and rose from her seat. Immediately all the gentlemen rose as well. I was not sure if I should rise, or what I should do, and looking to Granada's lead could be unwise. As none of the women stood, I stayed rooted to my seat, and watched. Disregarding any courtesy, the Marquesa turned away from the table and walked to the door. This required that she pass by the standing Marqués, and as she reached him, she stopped.

"Do not think you can humiliate me with your philandering," she said to him. "You are abased by your own lusts." She walked out.

The gentlemen sat down. "Bring the next course," the Marqués said nonchalantly. "And you, my dear, must have some wine." He signaled to the footman to refill my glass. "Did you enjoy the poem?"

I was still staring at the door through which the Marquesa had passed. I did not understand the actual reference in the Marquesa's comments, but her implication was unmistakable. I could not believe that conversation went on undisturbed. "I'm sorry, Your Highness?" I said. He repeated the question. "It was beautiful," I said honestly. "The idea of the haughty mien concealing the begging, longing heart was so perfectly put into the verse's words."

"The Marquesa clearly felt otherwise," said Granada. My eyes widened. This woman's tongue clearly knew no bounds. "Oh, Doña Josefina, do not pretend to be such a naïf. I am not gifted poetically, but certainly there was meaning there to offend the Marquesa. Perhaps Sor Juana could explain her work to us." She looked at Sor Juana, eager to pull her into the conversation.

Father Alonso stepped into the brewing conflict. "Doña Granada, you are most astute. Poetry can have different effects on different hearers, depending on the state of each person's soul." His voice rumbled as from the pulpit, and it drew us like the outgoing tide.

"Doña Josefina saw only the beauty of humble love," he went on. I felt the glow of his approval. His blue eyes looked deeply into mine, and then he looked again at Granada. "The Marquesa could have seen the mockery of the face that tells one story, while the heart tells another. Pain, so well masked by disdain, could cut her." Granada cast her eyes down. Then he looked around the table. "And I saw the love of Our Lord, for us, his struggling people, in the face of our sinful disregard of His suffering on the cross. Which, I might add, is the meaning intended by Sor Juana."

"Amen," said the rotund man, and the table sighed as one. The footman served the bird in almond cream, and glasses were again refilled. Conversation returned; conviviality reigned. I gazed at Father Alonso, now engaged in conversation with the Commander's assistant. His words had wooed me so long ago, and they wooed me now, in a new way. It was almost as if he had said that I, not love, was beautiful. I closed my eyes briefly, and I yearned for those words to be washing over me, around me, followed closely by his hands, his lips, where no one but Manuel had ever been. I pulled myself away sharply from the reverie. How could I have such thoughts about Father Alonso, the Bishop of Puebla?

As the plates were cleared for the sweets, I felt a hand on my thigh. I turned sharply to the Marqués, who simply raised an eyebrow. I was at a loss. His hand was not. It traveled softly back and forth, up and down my thigh, and I felt myself tremble. I tried to move discreetly away, but the chairs were close-placed and there was nowhere to go. My squirming seemed to encourage the Marqués, and his hand was becoming increasingly bold, touching me as I had just moments ago imagined Father Alonso doing. My discomfort was fiercely compounded by my recollection of my impure thoughts.

My unease did not pass Granada's sharp eye unnoticed. Her chastening from Father Alonso's sermon had been either superficial or short-lived. She snickered, and held my gaze with a mocking smile on her lips. Then she turned back to the Commander.

"Your Highness," I whispered. "You mustn't. I am a married woman!"

He laughed out loud, and fiercely squeezing high on my inner thigh, he said in a voice meant to carry, "A married woman! Of course you are, my dear. Did you think I would want a virgin?" All conversation halted, and all eyes turned to us. I did not know where to look; my face was burning. "Oh, come now!" he went on. "Do not think that modest exterior of yours conceals your burning desire. As the poetess said, your body and face betray what your heart cannot speak!"

Over the laughter generated by the Marqués' pronouncement, Father Alonso stood and proclaimed from the end of the table, "Your Highness! Our guest is not ready for such sallies. See how she blushes!" I felt the heat buzzing through the ringing in my ears. "Perhaps we should call for some musical entertainment, to calm the overtaxed humors. Or, if you prefer, we can fall on our knees in prayer. Meanwhile, let us rise from our seats and enjoy one another's company."

The Marqués chose not to contradict the Bishop, and nodded. He, too, stood, and the guests rose, and mingled again in the room. Sor Juana left her chair, picked up her sheet of poetry, and, without taking leave of anyone, quit the room. Conversation began again, and I tried to vanish into a corner near the fireplace. I wished I could simply walk out, as Sor Juana had. The Marqués was not ready to allow my escape. He stood very close to me, and his hand encircled my wrist. "Doña Josefina, that was most charming. I am delighted to pursue my game, and I much prefer an arduous chase. Well done!"

"Your Highness, I am not prey," I replied with as much hauteur as I could manage. "Your chase will be futile. I am honored to be your guest, but I must warn you that I will not be seduced."

He burst out laughing, his nose beaklike above his open mouth. "Excellent, my dear. You will not be seduced! Oh, my. You will not be seduced!" The Marqués released my wrist, and, with a swift and much-practiced movement, pinched my breast as he turned away.

THOUGH THE EVENING PARTY broke up shortly afterward, it seemed that I had spent a fortnight in the Marqués' dining chamber, not a mere few hours. Father Alonso took my elbow and offered to escort me back to the guest wing. I accepted his offer gratefully.

We walked down the empty stone hallway, he still holding my arm. "You have certainly garnered the Marqués' attention," he said.

"I did nothing to attract it."

"Your beauty attracts it without your help. You have grown into a beautiful woman, Josefina."

In my pleasure I could not answer. We walked in silence. "When were you made a bishop?" I asked. I could not get used to the notion that Father Alonso was now such an exalted figure.

"Over a year ago," he replied. "I had been groomed for the office since I took my final vows, and that was fifteen years ago."

My arithmetical mind immediately added the twenty-one years that he would have lived before making the final, unretractable vow. He was thirteen years my senior, almost exactly as was Manuel. "And Sor Juana?" I asked.

"What about Sor Juana?"

"She reads her poetry to you."

Father Alonso smiled. "Yes, Josefina. Sor Juana reads her poetry to me. And she sends it to me as well. She seeks my counsel." I looked up at him. His blue eyes sparkled. "She is a wonderful poet," he said.

I shook his hand off my arm. "I am pleased that she has such a protector," I said, and walked a few paces briskly ahead of him. He laughed, and I stopped and faced him. We were at the music room door, and he opened it and pulled me inside. He shut the door.

"The Marquesa does not like her," I said fiercely. "And it is the Marquesa's family to whom all of this"—I waved my hand around—"belongs. Don't you think that the Marquesa could find a way to harm Sor Juana, a way to stop the poetry that mocks her so? If so, the sister would have great need of your protection."

"My goodness, Josefina. You are a confusing girl. I would have sworn that you were jealous of my godly love for Juana, and now you are in fear for her."

"I am not the least bit jealous," I said. Father Alonso continued smiling. "I am disheartened by the complexity of the interactions here at Court. I had imagined a place where great intellect abounded, and music and poetry and stories of faraway places were the subjects of discourse. But I had not imagined a society where every word was freighted with meanings, where the host attempted the seduction of his guests, and where the holy women of the convent wrote poetry that scandalized and pained their gracious patron."

"Oh, my Josefina," he said, placing his large, freckled hands on my shoulders. I stared and I did not pull away. The silence of the music room was complete, and the illumination by moonlight cast shadows of the furniture throughout the room. This was beyond what I could ever have imagined. I felt the warmth of his hands through my dress. "You have grown up wonderfully. I am pleased at your disillusionment."

"Well, I am not. I do not wish to become like Granada, sharp-tongued and catty, or like Angélica, currying favor while being overlooked for that very favor, or, worst of all, to be shadowed by Eustacia, like a vulture, in search of the last morsel of information to sell. I should go home." I did not turn away. I wanted to stay in the dark silence of the music room with his hands on me forever, all the while decrying the Court and dissecting its denizens.

"Perhaps you should go home. It may be safer for you," Father Alonso replied, pulling me toward him. With his nearness I could no longer think. He bent down to me, his red hair flowing forward, and placed his forehead against mine. His blue eyes looked into my brown ones. I could taste my heartbeat, smell the lemon verbena of his clothes. We stood there, our foreheads touching, as if he were blessing me through his mind. Then he dropped his head further, and our lips met.

With that meeting of our mouths, the castle vanished. The warmth of his mouth was the only temperature, and his lips, not soft, devoured mine. His taste, of wine and cinnamon, was my appetite, and my own lips opened to his to allow him to take his sustenance as I, in turn, took mine from him.

My hands were on his chest, both holding him away and embracing him. One of his hands moved from my shoulders across my back, and down to my waist behind me. The other slid behind my head, holding me to his lips. We deepened the kiss, and my own hands stopped pressing against him and yielded into a full acceptance of him, as my breasts moved softly against his chest.

And then the kiss was over. "We must get you back to your chambers," he said quietly. I nodded. I did not want to go, but there was no other choice. "I will be here for a few more days, a week at most. Do not ask for me. I will get word to you, and we can talk."

"Like you and Sor Juana," I said perversely. I do not know why I brought her into this wonderful moment.

Father Alonso pulled away gently. "Yes, Josefina. Like Sor Juana. I talk to her, too. She provides as much consolation for me as I do for her. Now, come, let us leave this room and get you back to your quarters before someone sees us, and speaks out of turn."

We walked slowly the rest of the way to the stairs leading to the ladies' guest chambers. At the foot of the stairs we stopped again. Father Alonso made the sign of the cross over my head in blessing. "Good night, Josefina. I will send for you soon, maybe tomorrow."

"Good night, Your Grace," I said. As he watched, I turned and walked up the stairs to my room.

ℐINE

THE SUN WAS ALREADY high in the glory of spring in the high pla-
teau. The sky was its purest blue, cloudless and as yet untainted
by the dust that would choke the air as the dry season wore on. Cayetana
stood at the foot of my bed with a pitcher of water.

"You are becoming a lady of luxury," she said, pouring water into the
basin for washing. Indeed, at the hacienda I was up with the servants at
dawn. Though Manuel's household was prosperous enough by far that
I needed never lift a finger, I had not lost the ways of my father's farm,
and Manuel was happier for it. He himself worked alongside his cattle
foremen, unlike other wealthy haciendados who idled away their days in
frivolous pursuits.

I rose quickly, triggering a headache behind my eyes. Perhaps this
pain, doubtless from my unaccustomed consumption of several glasses
of wine, was compounded by guilt over my sloth and my memory of the
evening's events. The brilliance of the sun did not help.

"You have slept through Mass," Cayetana continued.

"Mass? Have you become pious in the week we have been here?" Our
household attended Sunday Mass, of course, but we did not regularly
attend the daily services.

"The Bishop celebrated the morning Mass. I was invited." She fussed
with my toiletries, few enough to have exhausted her attentions within
a moment.

My sluggish mind labored under the choice of inquiries. The Bishop?
Invited? I was to regret my choice much later. "What was the sermon?" I
was consumed by irrational jealousy. She had seen him, I had not.

"I believe it was about sacrifice. The Bishop is a very holy man. I could feel the sacrifice of Christ in my blood when he spoke." Cayetana had stopped rearranging my bottles and was looking out the window. "You will have a beautiful day for a picnic."

A picnic. I had heard that some outdoor meal was planned, but again, I had been too concerned with the immediate events to give it thought. I did not trust myself to speak. Sacrifice of Christ, indeed. I chose my dress for the outdoors, one of my regular dresses from home. I reached behind to braid my hair.

"Should I comb for you?" Cayetana asked. I shook my head, my mouth occupied with several hairpins. "You should look more . . . more dressed," she said finally.

I put the last pin in my hair. "Why? We are going into the fields."

"I don't think so. This is not a *charreada*."

"Of course not. There are no men, no cattle. I don't expect that Angélica and Granada will ride bareback, demonstrating roping skills, nor will a calf be roasting on a spit over a fire while a band plays!" We both smiled, I, for one, remembering my wedding *charreada* at our hacienda, so many years back.

"No, I don't think most of the men here are up to a *charreada*!" Cayetana turned to leave. "But however they dress, the women of this castle are more dangerous than an outraged bull."

WE WERE TO RIDE in open carriages. The ladies had gathered at the portico. I was among the last to arrive, and so I was at first unnoticed. I was handed into a chaise with two very young women whom I did not know. They nodded to me, but continued their private chatter.

I had not been out, except for my quick and surreptitious survey of the gardens. The fresh air filled me with well-being, erasing the headache and easing the strain of the past few days. We rode companionably around the back of the castle, past the gardens, and in between two enormous fields of sunflowers. The giant floral heads seemed to follow us instead of the sun.

At last we came out of the fields into a grassy clearing. At the far end was a grove of papaya trees, green fruits emerging from glossy leaves. Closer to us was a large tent of brightly striped cloth, and more cloths were laid on the grass. Red, green, and gold pillows were strewn about, and some ladies sat or reclined on the pillows.

There was no calf roasting, but there was a fire pit, and the delicious aroma of roasting meat filled the air. I stepped down from the carriage onto the grass. A knot of ladies turned to see the new arrivals. And suddenly, there was total silence.

I did not die. I managed to survive, but I am certain that my good name did not. Granada had made sure that all the ladies knew what had transpired. I had gone from newcomer to laughingstock in a week's time. The guest dining hall had been atwitter with the story of the Marqués and the silly country lady who was the newest object of his advances.

I forced myself to smile. I saw Angélica, and I walked across the cloth-covered grass to her with all the dignity I could muster.

"Is it true she said she was a virgin?" one lady asked the other when I walked past her.

"I heard she rubbed her breast up against him, then slapped him!" another said, laughing.

"She told the Marquesa that the poem was about her!"

When I reached her, Angélica was set to wring my neck. "What did you do?" she whispered harshly. "What did you say?" The sun sparkled off her hair, her dress echoed the colors of the papaya tree, and the air brought color to her cheeks. But she was beyond beauty.

I did not want to relate to her the details of the Marqués' pawing of me, or of his comments, but I knew that unless I told her she would know only what the rumors said. I drew her as far from the others as I could, and told her. She was appalled.

"Do you want us sent home? Are you unable to carry on a simple flirtation? This is one of our duties: to entertain and amuse the Marqués, without falling into adultery."

"I am so sorry, Angélica. I did not realize that we were supposed to do this. You didn't mention it."

Angélica rolled her eyes. "It was obvious. Oh, why were you invited without me?" The omission still rankled. "And now we shall have to bear the mockery of the likes of Granada. And you have incurred the dislike of Eustacia, who, though penniless, pays for her supper as a carrier pigeon and spy. And what does the Marquesa think now? I do not dare wonder. Oh, Josefina, you are unworthy of Manuel!" Angélica buried her face in her hands.

I was too stunned to answer. I was unworthy of Manuel? What in the name of Heaven was she talking about? Any contrition I felt at having caused Angélica disgrace vanished with her last remark. I could attribute it to temper, but it was intolerable nonetheless.

"You are not to mention Manuel again," I said evenly. "If I have caused you disgrace by resisting the Marqués' inappropriate advances, I am deeply sorry. But you are not Manuel's wife, and you are not to mention his name again to me in such a context. If you would like, I will go home."

"If you leave, you will be admitting all of the crazy rumors Granada has started. If you stay, you will bear the brunt of the Marquesa's anger, and Eustacia's, and the whispers of the rest of the ladies. I will suffer either way. Choose as you will." She walked a few paces, pulled a leaf off a tree.

I was sorely tempted to toss my head and summon Cayetana to prepare our bags. But I thought of Father Alonso. He would be here another week, and would summon me. I would stay for that. He could give me good counsel. And more.

As if reading my thoughts, Angélica looked up from her leaf. "And what is it about you and the Bishop? You say you know him from childhood. He is that poetess's defender, and he is your friend. A bishop would normally be a favorable connection. How is it that you had to choose one who complicates everything?"

None of this warranted an answer, which was fortunate, for I myself asked the same questions. Angélica did not pursue that line of inquiry. "Come," she said, "at least try to be sociable."

I stayed by Angélica throughout the picnic, as she finessed conversations away from me and toward the vital topics of clothing and other people. The music became more lively, and the meal was served. We sat on the ground under the tent. The breeze rustled through the tent cloths, making them flap. Sweets were brought out, and it seemed that the event was at a close. Servants began to pack up the bright cloths.

"At home, this would be a fiesta for at least three days," I said to Angélica.

"And the gentlemen would join us," she added.

"Come, let's walk back. It wasn't far, and I am not used to the immobility of this life."

"I haven't the shoes for it," Angélica replied. "But you should walk, if you want." I was surprised by her generosity of spirit, until I realized that she was tired from the burden of protecting me, and did not relish a carriage ride trapped with me and some sharp-tongued ladies.

Several of the younger women had also chosen to walk, and I joined them, keeping close enough to be part of an acceptable group, and lagging enough to avoid conversation. When we got back to the castle I rushed to my room. There was no message on my silver tray by the door.

And so the day had passed, and no summons had come from Father Alonso. Night came, and neither Angélica nor I was invited to dine with the Marquesa, the Marqués, or anyone else. We took cold meats in the guest dining hall, and later embroidered by candlelight in my room. Angélica did not mention disgrace, but it emanated from her very being.

The following day was quiet, with a garden stroll and a pleasant luncheon, and with a bit less sniping from the other ladies. Interest in my social demerits would only last if fed, and no one cared enough to add fuel to this fire. Besides, we received word that the Marqués and Marquesa were to hold a ball in a week, to celebrate the homecoming of their son. Nothing could take the collective mind of a group of ladies-in-waiting off my peccadilloes more quickly than the thought of a ball.

By the third day my anxiety level had crested. Father Alonso intruded into my thoughts constantly and unbidden. I saw his face in my embroidery, dreamed of his kisses at night. I longed to work his name into my every conversation, and yet I knew I could no more mention his name than howl at the now-full moon. And he did not summon me.

On the fourth day, Angélica was asked to attend the Marquesa at her daily reception, but I was not included. Though I was disappointed and angry, since all I had done was behave virtuously, I was relieved for Angélica. She had held her tongue after our last discussion, but I knew that she suffered from the social neglect of the lady of the castle. Angélica dressed and left, with but a word for me. "I will tell you all that I hear," she said. She voiced no regret that I was excluded, and in fact seemed more lighthearted for knowing that she would not have to keep watch over me lest I trip on the social customs again.

Alone for the first time since the Marqués' dinner, I wandered around the guest wing, lonely and longing for home. By now, I had told myself at various times that Father Alonso had left, or had been called away on urgent Church business, that he was busy with his many duties, and that he cared little enough for me that he would not summon me at all. I ranged from excusing his neglect to accepting it, to railing in my mind against it. But without his summons, I could not see him.

When my humor was cool, I chastised myself. *Fool,* I said, *kissing a bishop.* My virtue was so sacrosanct that I could bristle self-righteously when the Marqués made his sugary suggestions, and yet so flimsy that I found myself not two hours later kissing the Bishop in the darkened music room. Of course he would not call for me. He had doubtless forgotten me the moment he left me at the stair. Or perhaps he was concealed in the library with Sor Juana, laughing over her razor-sharp poetic wit.

At last I could stand it no longer. No one of any value or concern was around, and I could not amuse myself with further self-hatred or recrimination. I dressed in a new gown of gray satin, flowing yet modest, with sleeves that were gored and inset with mauve lining, and a mauve rolled neckline that showed me to advantage. I put on soft slippers, as it was a warm and dry day, and ventured out to the main rooms of the castle.

I again passed through the foyer, as I had on the first day of my explorations, and greeted the little portress. She nodded to me, and I knew that she would make a note, whether she wrote in her book or in her mind, that I had been there. The main doors were closed, but side doors, giving out onto the courtyard, were open to the warm spring air. It had been dry for a month now, and the air was clear. In another month the ground would be dusty, and in three months the air would be choked with the unbreathable heat from the dried swamplands, but now, at the peak of spring, the earth believed that anything was possible.

I went outside and walked through the open courtyard into a garden behind the main part of the house. It was lush and green from the winter rains, and watering ditches edged the planted areas, allowing the gardener to pull water to the flower beds well into the dry season. At home at the hacienda, we did the same for the cattle-watering troughs and for the vegetables.

The garden was sculpted in a formal pattern, very unlike the garden I kept at home. Here, jacaranda climbed the walls, and below it, a green hedge plant made a buffer between the earthen path and the stones of the wall. Edging of flowers decorated all of the paths. Manuel had made me a large garden in one of the corners of the grounds, where I grew herbs for the kitchen and for our health. I imagined Neto trundling around in the flowers, Joaquín picking and crushing flowers as he made a bouquet for me. I made a note in my mind to try this style of garden when I returned.

Along the path, there were benches of adobe with magnificent tile inlays, for the wanderer to rest upon. I sat down on one and closed my eyes, turning my face to the sun. Here was a pleasure denied to fair-skinned Angélica. My southern Spanish ancestors had bequeathed me a complexion that could enjoy the rays of the warming sun without reddening or blotching. The sweet scent of the herbs planted in the far corner of the garden wafted to me, and I was content for the first time since I arrived at the Court. Perhaps there was something to be enjoyed in our remaining weeks.

After a bit, I got up again and continued along the path. I was now behind the Marquesa's wing, and large doors and windows opened onto the garden from some of the rooms. I determined to turn around, so as not to venture too far. It would be ignominious to be seen parading outside the Marquesa's sitting room, with the ladies gathered within, and the uninvited, disgraced lady without.

When I felt I had gone as far as I could without nearing the rooms, I turned back. From this angle, I saw that I was now passing the little music room, and that the library must be directly ahead. The large windows were open, from the floor almost to the ceiling, and the books looked invitingly at me. I stepped off the path and entered the library.

This time, without delay, I checked the areas around the arches for anyone who might be there. I did not wish to be an interloper in someone else's private meeting. The room was empty. I looked at the bookshelves. I wondered about the Marquesa and her family. Was she a great reader, or had her father been, before her? Since I knew the marquessate came from her side, I doubted the collection had come from the Marqués.

I had no experience with books, really. Our Bible, a collection of Saint Thomas Aquinas's letters, and a few folios of sacred writings were all that our hacienda possessed. I had never seen Manuel read. The books Father Alonso had brought with him to my childhood home had been remarkable both for their content and for their very existence. Calderón's plays, Góngora's poetry, Greek myths, all had their place in his worn leather book pouch. Here, an entire shelf held poetry, and I was pleased to see the familiar name of Góngora y Argote among them. I felt literate and accomplished in this very private moment of recognition.

I took a volume from its shelf and sat down in one of the protected alcove's chairs. I opened it to a gold-leaf-embellished engraving of an angel reclining with a scroll opened on his knees. His wings were tucked beneath him, and an aura glowed around his head. Another aura glowed from the scroll itself. The beauty of the engraving overshadowed any hint of sacrilege in the implication that secular writing could be as divine as an angel.

The lettering was difficult for me to read, but I frowned and concentrated on the words. Góngora's poetry flowed with words coupled in ways that were thoroughly unexpected, and it made me see a homely situation of domestic sorrow or love with new eyes. In addition, the pages were decorated with marginalia depicting flowers and birds that I had never seen, and showed angels in repose, angels in flight, pictures that no earthly hacienda had ever contained.

These lines of Góngora's struck my humor:

Coins buy status, forsooth . . .
truth.
He loves most, who doth most sigh . . .
lie.

There it was, in the poet's words. I could not but agree. The measure of the heart was not in its ostentatious sigh, but in the chambers hidden within. I sighed.

"Such a pensive lady."

I looked up at the sound of the cool gray voice, into the gray eyes of Sor Juana. I shut the book, but she reached for it. Feeling like a fool, I handed it over. "Góngora," I said. "Admirable poet. He speaks his heart while skirting the Holy Office."

The Holy Office, the Grand Inquisition, was known to us all as the powerful arm of the Church charged with stamping out heresy and impurity of the blood. Its Inquisitors could terrify even the innocent. And I was truly innocent. I had never written a word in my life, nor had a heretic thought. That I knew of. Yet I shuddered.

"So, you fear the Holy Office. Good. Its tentacles can reach even to here."

"I am no heretic. And I am of the purest Spanish blood."

"I am delighted to hear it, my lady. Would that your confidence were contagious."

I searched and found irony in her voice. "And you, Sister? Do you fear it, too?"

"Of course," she said, and her mouth, so full and shapely, tightened. "Any thinking person would fear it."

I bristled. "I am a thinking person, Sor Juana. But I am not a heretic."

She raised a brow. "You read." I stared. "How many of the ladies waiting upon the Marquesa at this moment have read a sonnet? Many cannot even read beyond their names, and yet they are very gently bred."

"I read," I acknowledged, "and I dream."

"Of what do you dream?" Her uninflected voice inspired confidence, almost to the level of the confessional.

"To read, and maybe, someday, to write a poem like these."

"Even to dream could be considered prohibited."

"It would be far worse for you. You put your thoughts into ink, and others may read them and hold them against you. Why do you do it?"

Sor Juana looked out the window. "I do it because I must. It is the only way I can live."

"Aren't you afraid?"

"Constantly. But I have a wealthy patron, and a powerful protector."

"Father Alonso?" I asked, then bit my lip. "I mean, His Grace, the Bishop."

"Yes," she said, smiling. "I know that you knew him when you were but a young girl, and he was not a bishop. He cares a great deal for you.

But you would be best served by not speaking openly in this Court of your history with him. Or your current affection for him."

I was taken aback. Could she know of the kiss in the music room? I was mortified. "My affection is that of a dutiful daughter," I said primly.

"No doubt."

"You have a great deal more to lose if your own affection for the Bishop were discovered," I said heedlessly. I spoke from fear, not malice, but my words hit home.

"You are treading dangerous ground, my lady. I can help you, I can teach you, and I can destroy you. You may choose, but choose wisely."

I knew I was out of my depth. I expected her to gather her skirts and leave, but I was wrong. She stayed, looking calmly at my face as I squirmed in distress. She was waiting for an answer, one that I could not provide.

After a few moments, or maybe hours, I spoke. "I do not want you for an enemy, Sor Juana. You are accomplished and are to be admired. Your writings terrify and elate me at once. Please," I finished humbly, "do not turn against me."

"Good," she said firmly. "You have made the only wise choice. Come, let me show you what you should be reading." She went to the bookshelf and pulled out a folio that was not yellow with age. It looked to be fairly new. She opened it. It was a drama, called *The Household's Dilemma*. She smiled and put it back, and chose another. The author's name, Lope de Vega, was writ large across the front of the slim volume. "You may take it to your room, if you do so discreetly."

"Whose books are these? Is the Marquesa a reader, too?"

"She is, and that is one of the reasons she tolerates me. It is her family whose money and heritage provide the wealth and title to this castle, you know. But her father and her grandfather were great patrons of writers, even while risking their lives before the Holy Office. The Marquesa has a man's brain, it is said, for she does numbers and letters as fast as any university student."

"But the poems you write wound her."

"Yes. But she commissions them nonetheless. I speak her heart. For though she is lettered, she cannot find the words to express her soul."

I still did not understand. "But the two times I have been in your presence when you read your work, both times she was angry."

Sor Juana smiled, with a look that was crafty and sly. "She is not my only patron, my lady. Life at Court is very complicated. She will not dismiss me, for I have the key to her innermost thoughts. But the Marqués, and the Bishop, must also be satisfied."

The Bishop. "Is he still here?"

"Awaiting a summons, are you?"

I was humiliated. She knew. I nodded.

"You will then wait some more. When he wishes to see you, he will call for you. Until then, there is much to amuse and instruct you without him."

I stood up. I wanted to hide in my room, away from this cool, unrelenting woman who knew secrets I didn't.

"Take the book," she reminded me. "Read it while you wait. But bear in mind, any misstep you take will be laid at your doorstep, whether you were responsible for it or not."

I nodded, uncomprehending, and walked quickly, and I hoped with dignity, out through the large open windows, back onto the path around the castle.

I hurried through the main doorway, nodding to the sister portress, and concealing the book in the folds of my skirt. I was halfway to the guest chambers when I heard men's voices. I looked for a place to hide and, finding none, I stepped as far into the shadows as I could.

Rounding the corner into the hallway came two gentlemen. The first was the tall, black-haired assistant to the Commander. Alas, the second was the Marqués. Still holding the book in the folds of my skirt, I shrank back against the wall. I hoped that they would be so enmeshed in their conversation that they would pass by without noticing. It almost worked, but the assistant to the Commander, being a military man, was most aware of his surroundings. Although they passed me, the Marqués oblivious to my presence, the soldier sensed me and stopped. He peered into the corner where I was trying to blend into the pillars.

"My lady," he said, bowing. "Did we startle you?"

His noticing me certainly did.

"Ah, it is the lovely, virtuous Doña Josefina!" said the Marqués.

"Your Highness. Sir," I said, nodding to each of them.

"Why are you cowering behind a pillar?" the Marqués asked. "Come out into the light." He put his hand on my arm.

"I was exploring," I said, keeping the book hidden. "I stopped to rest and leaned against the pillar, that is all."

"I hope that the heat is not tiring you," the military gentleman said gallantly. "Perhaps we may see you safely to the ladies' guest stairs."

The Marqués laughed. "I do believe this young minx is fatigued. Come, my dear, let us escort you to a place where you can recline, and we can help you recover your energies." His hand was still on my arm, but I knew from my attendance at his soiree that his hand would eagerly travel elsewhere, and I could not defend myself against his onslaught and keep the book under wraps.

"Thank you both," I said firmly. "I am not in any need of assistance. I will go my way now, if you please."

"Oh, but I don't please," said the Marqués, with a hint of menace. "I please to accompany you to a resting chamber. Federico," he said to the Commander's assistant, "I will join you this evening."

I looked to the soldier for help, but he simply bowed to me and left. After my conversation with Sor Juana, and possessing a book from the great library, I did not want to tangle with the Marqués. But his grip on my arm tightened, and I saw that unless I was willing to make an enormous fuss, I had no choice. And really, even if I were willing to scream or try to run, it would likely be to no avail. He was, after all, the lord of the castle.

He seemed to sense that I had finally realized his power, for his smile became more wolfish under that great nose. "I feel that you are beginning to see the generosity of my offer of a secluded place for you to rest. And given that you have brought some tome to read, you may wish to follow me sooner rather than later."

He had seen the book. I had no choice.

"I will accompany you, sir, but I will not be put in a compromising situation." I sounded idiotic even to myself.

"You already are in a compromised position, my dear. A young lady who reads subversive material should not be left alone. Should word get out that you are one of those mannish types who indulge in such behavior, you may find yourself, at best, in a nunnery."

"My husband has no objection to my reading," I said, though I knew nothing of the sort. He had never addressed the issue, though he knew

I could read. But he counted on me to do his bookkeeping, without objection to my arithmetic facility. Perhaps I was not lying.

"He may not object, but he will not be pleased to have the disgrace of his wife being sent home from the Court for intellectual heresy."

My hands felt cold and wet at those words. I was trapped. My shoulders sagged, and I followed the Marqués without another word.

"Come, lady," he said. "You must not despair. I do not relish a sorry companion." We entered a small room at the side of the hall, and he shut the heavy wooden door behind us. He threw the bolt. With the door shut and locked, and the thick stone walls around us, I could scream all I wanted to. I was his prisoner.

He pushed me lightly onto a chaise longue, wide enough for two and covered in deep green satin. Curved wooden posts extended from the top of the chaise, and they were hung with tasseled cords. The dark walls were not covered in plaster; the stones looked cold and forbidding. An effort had been made to warm the room with tapestries hung from two of the walls, but with only two high casement windows, there was little light, and no heat from the sun. A small fireplace in the corner held wood, but was unlit. Two wall sconces, likewise, were ready but unkindled.

The Marqués leaned me back against the chaise. He brushed his hands across my breasts. I shivered. "You must not shiver when I touch you," he said. I shivered again. He caught my wrist and held it tight. "Do not." I nodded, and he released me. "Now, my dear, let us converse. I like light, amusing conversation to smooth my way to fulfilling my desires. Tell me, are you enjoying your stay here at Court?" Again he brushed my breasts, but I controlled my shivering.

"I am not."

"Now, that is not a ladylike answer," he said. "Do you find the food or your room unwelcoming?" He ran his finger along my collarbone.

"No."

"Doña Josefina. Perhaps I did not make myself clear. I like bright, amusing conversation, and you shall provide it. Do you understand?"

"I understand you, sir. And I understand your power over me. But I am a country-bred lady, and I am not an amusing conversationalist. If that is what you want, you must look elsewhere." I do not know where this speech or the daring to make it came from.

"You are most definitely a minx. I like your fire." With that, he grabbed my wrist again, and lifted it. From the post he pulled a cord around it, binding my hand above my head. I struggled, but it was to no avail. "Now, perhaps you will make a bit of an effort to amuse. While I amuse myself with you."

Suiting his actions to his words, he pinched my nipples through my dress. I twisted away, but he held me back. "Talk, lady," he ordered, and there was no more doubt of his intentions. He lifted my skirt as I tried with my free hand to pull it back down. He laughed, enjoying my fight, and his hands went up, under my dress, to my pantalettes. I cried out, furious and powerless, and kicked at him with my feet.

"I see I will get a different form of entertainment from you. I had expected an intellectual battle, not a physical one. But I take my amusement where I find it." He inserted his hand into my last remaining barrier of clothing.

I could take no more. With my free hand, I made a fist as I had seen little Joaquín do when he was frustrated, and swung it into that enormous nose with all my might. The Marqués roared back in pain, and I used the moment to tear at the knot that bound my other hand. He was coming back at me, this time with fury mixed into his lust, when the knot came free. With all of my force I pulled him forward and past me in the direction he was already going, and slid away as he landed where I had been on the chaise. I leaped to my feet. Scrambling, I ran the few steps for the door.

The Marqués' nose was bleeding. I pushed back the bolt as he grabbed me from behind, and I pulled the door open. Again I slapped at his nose, spraying blood on myself and him, and when he reeled, I ran.

I ran without stopping, through the foyer, up the stairs, and into my room. I slammed the door shut and threw myself on the bed. Sobbing, I lay there until I could breathe again. My God, I prayed, what do I do now?

I looked at my bloodied hand, my stained dress. I wiped away my tears and poured water from the pitcher into the basin to wash. I remembered with dismay the book Sor Juana had given me lying on the floor in the room to which I had been taken. I had to get it back. But an excursion to that strange and horrible little room was out of the question.

At the moment I dared not venture out, even in the ladies' wing, not until Angélica and the other ladies had returned from the Marquesa's chambers. It was not that I expected sympathy from Angélica, or, Heaven forbid, that I would tell any of the other ladies about my indecent troubles. But rather it was that there could be safety in the company of others, though that had not proven to be the case with the military man.

I took off my dress, stained with blood. It was then that I realized that I had not run my courses for that month. I was so exact in my monthly bleeding that the moon seemed to time its phases by me. The moon was waning, and I had not bled. I was with child.

TEN

"I MUST RETURN HOME, ANGÉLICA," I said to her when she was back from her morning visit to the Marquesa.

"Don't be absurd. There is a ball in less than a week, and just because you displeased the Marqués doesn't mean you cannot go to the ball."

My throat closed when she mentioned the Marqués, though I knew that it was his earlier displeasure she was alluding to. There had not been enough time for word of his current displeasure to spread, and from what I knew of men, he would likely not bruit about my punching him in the nose.

Nonetheless, I was keenly aware of the fact that he would make every moment of my further stay miserable. "I still must go. I am with child."

Angélica's face took on an odd look. I understood with surprise that she was jealous. "Well, you will not begin to show for a while if you have just realized your condition. Surely you will fit into your gowns for another week."

She had not borne children, so all she thought of was gowns. "I will, but I may be queasy, or swell, or be moody. I may not be fit company."

"You'll do," she said curtly.

I sighed. Of course I could return home without her permission, but I was, to a degree, her guest, and I would leave against her wishes only if the situation were dire. My encounter with the Marqués could qualify. Yet, I could not confide in her.

"I will give it some thought. Now, tell me about your morning with the Marquesa."

Angélica brightened. "It was lovely. That odd poetess was not there, but Sor Inez brought her lyre and I sang a few tunes to entertain the ladies. We spoke almost exclusively about the ball. It is to be a full, formal affair, given in honor of the Marquesa's son and heir. I understand he is quite handsome."

"And wealthy."

"Of course."

"Did my name come up?"

"Your name did come up once or twice, but no one is particularly interested in your gaffes anymore, when there are frocks and laces and sleeves to be discussed."

"What was said?"

"The Marquesa mentioned that you should accompany me when I attend her in the mornings. So, you are no longer in disgrace, it seems, provided you are with me. And Eustacia mentioned you. She asked after your health, of course, and commended herself to you. She inquired whether you were planning to attend the ball. She said she hoped you would, and implied that the Bishop of Puebla had particularly asked about your attendance."

"I sincerely doubt whether the Bishop of Puebla made any inquiry of the sort," I said, though my heart had quivered at the mention. "I did not know that bishops attended balls."

Angélica looked at the ceiling. "Yes, Josefina. Bishops attend balls. As do nuns. You are truly backward."

"In any event, I do not believe for a moment that Eustacia is telling the truth. Her motive, I am certain, was to wrangle some additional information out of you concerning my acquaintanceship with His Grace, of which there is nothing more to tell. I hope that you did not feed her inquisitiveness." It was my turn to be righteous.

Angélica looked away. "I did not tell her anything that wasn't true."

"What did you say?"

"That you were acquainted with him from childhood."

"That is acceptable." Then, acting on instinct I added, "And what else?"

"That, well, he taught you much."

There could be harm in that, but I could not yet guess what.

We were interrupted by a knock on the door, and a young page, not more than eight or nine years old, stood waiting. With a bow, he handed me a leather pouch. I held up my hand for him to wait and took a small coin from my purse and gave it to him. He smiled widely and ran off down the hall. My heart ached briefly with a thought of Joaquín.

Angélica looked at the pouch expectantly, but I did not open it. I made a show of casually tossing it into the armoire. "What else transpired?"

She detailed the clothing worn, the gossip exchanged. But as these things did not concern me, I merely nodded and made the right noise at any given pause, until she finally wound down. "I must go and rest before the midday meal," she said. "Shall I call for you before I go to dine?"

"Please," I said. I forced myself not to even glance at the pouch. "I will be here."

When at last she retired to her room I fell upon the pouch and opened it. My spirits crashed when I saw that it did not contain, as I had hoped, a summons from Father Alonso. Instead, it held the Lope de Vega book, *Sheeps' Well,* and a note: *Minx. I will possess you yet.* It was not signed, nor did it need to be. I shivered. I had to leave.

I slipped out of my room. I knew most of the ladies would be resting before the midday meal, and I hoped to find my way quickly to the servants' quarters and alert Cayetana to our need to depart by morning. I had not seen her since the night before, and she knew nothing of my condition or my worries. I looked down the stairs, and seeing the hallway empty, I dashed down and quickly turned left. Though my speed might have indicated heedlessness, I was fully on the qui vive, my senses alert to the shadow of any presence.

I made it into the kitchen unseen, and surprised the cook in the midst of scolding one of the kitchen maids. The young girl withdrew quickly, with a tearful curtsy, and the cook faced me with her wooden spoon still raised.

"And how can I serve you, my lady?" she asked, giving no hint of dismay at being interrupted.

"I am seeking my maid, Cayetana," I said.

The cook looked surprised. "Cayetana? But, lady, Cayetana is not here. She was summoned by the Marqués' valet. I understood that she was to assist him, and a number of other highly placed servants, with preparations for the ball. She was most honored, and begged him to thank you for the special commendation."

"I see," I said, not seeing.

"She was elated. I do not believe—if you will forgive me, my lady—that she has been happy here at Court. The life of a servant is most stifling, especially for one used to being in charge of a large hacienda. And I know she was extremely grateful to you for allowing her to take on this task. In fact, she and two others so selected departed for the great City of Mexico not an hour ago."

"Oh, well, I wanted to make sure she was content with the task," I said lamely.

"Most definitely, my lady. Not many are so lucky. I am sure she will express her gratitude when she returns, in two days. In the meanwhile, there is an ample supply of servants here to attend you. Shall I send someone to you?"

"Perhaps later, thank you," I said, for there could be no other answer.

"Will that be all, my lady?" the cook asked, turning her girth and her wooden spoon back to the fire.

"Yes," I said quietly. "That will be all." I was well and truly trapped.

I STALKED OUT OF the kitchen, seething. Fine, I thought, if this was how the Marqués wanted to proceed, I would not be daunted by his trickery. Or his vile suit. I had to stay, at least through the ball, but I would not be his plaything. It amazed me that he would send my book along and suggest that my anger and violent rejection of his disgusting advances were merely a move in an amorous game. I was not going to be anyone's pawn. I would draw strength from Manuel's child growing in my womb.

I did not return to my room, but rather went back to the library. If I wished to read, I would read. Let the Marqués find me. He would see a new and different face on the minx he was pursuing. Rather than sidling in from the music room, I entered the library by the front door for the first time and saw the coy arrangement of the chairs around the little cur-tained alcoves. The design abetted or, more, encouraged trysts and secret reading. I looked boldly into each alcove, pulling aside every curtain, and found them empty. I took a book randomly from the nearest shelf and sat down as if to read. I opened it, and found that it was something almost ev-eryone had heard of, *Don Quixote,* by the renowned Miguel de Cervantes. Even the sentence I glanced at made me smile, as valiant Sancho Panza entreated his master, just for a moment, to dismount and rest. That would make for fine—and irreproachable—reading.

But I had not really come for a book. Sor Juana had given me my reading assignment, *Sheeps' Well*. I had not even opened it; it lay, sullied by the Marqués' touch, on my bed in the guest wing. No, I had come in search of the Bishop, or of Sor Juana again. I would tell them about the vile treatment I had experienced at the Marqués' hands. They could counsel me and, perhaps, protect me until I could return home. And I wanted to see Father Alonso, alone. I did not want to wait for a summons from him as he had ordered, and as Sor Juana had advised. I wanted to see him now.

Alas, my wish was not the Bishop's command. The hour passed with my skimming *Don Quixote,* but I was unable to lose myself in the story. I had situated myself in such a way that I could see anyone who passed through the front door or entered one of the alcoves, but I was invisible myself. I did not wish to be encountered unaware. However, no one appeared. Frustrated by my failure to put into effect my new plan to be bold, I tossed the book onto the next chair and stood up. I drew the curtain and stepped into the main portion of the library.

I had not taken into account anyone entering through the music room, as I had done when I previously visited the library. Seated at a small table, with a taper lit for additional light, was the Marquesa, reading intently. I did not wish to startle her. I cleared my throat and she looked up, surprised. She had a monocle before her eye, and her ferocious black eyebrow held it in place, giving her the air of an astonished owl. I smiled despite my annoyance, and she dropped the monocle from her eye to nod to me.

"Your Highness," I said.

"Doña Josefina. What a surprise." Her voice was uninflected, and I surmised that what she really meant to say was *What an intrusion*.

"I was just leaving. I was reading *Don Quixote,*" I added hastily.

"Stay a moment. I would like a word with you."

I might have determined a plan of boldness, but I could not well refuse my hostess. I approached her table and sat.

From close up, without the fawning ladies-in-waiting all around her, and dressed simply, she appeared to be an aging, intelligent, and strong woman, not the terrifying witch that she seemed in her chambers, or the insulted yet haughty lady she had been at the Marqués' dinner.

"Doña Josefina," she said, "you must find your first visit to us quite odd." I was surprised she had noticed. "Generally, a lady's first weeks are not as eventful as yours have been. But then, not many are like you."

I wondered what she meant. Not many were countrified matrons with no Court experience? Not many were readers of myths and proverbs? Most were not assaulted by the Marquesa's husband?

"I do not understand, Your Highness, though I would agree that the days have been quite full."

"You are the kind of woman who becomes beautiful with age. You have sons?"

"Two, Your Highness."

"I have one living. I bore four others, and two daughters as well, all dead in my womb. One child, my one living boy, Miguel Ángel, has lived to adulthood. He returns from Spain next week, and he is the occasion for our ball." I nodded. I could not bear the thought of losing a child. I would be worse than haughty and cold, I would freeze into a stone.

She did not need my answer, which was fortunate, since I gave none. "So, you have become a beauty, but no doubt do not yet see it. Unfortunately for you, my husband, the Marqués, has seen it. He is insatiable, and will not be denied.

"No, do not answer," she said as I was about to speak. "I do not seek your sympathy, nor do I expect you to hold out against his approaches very long. Though I am pleased with what I have heard of you."

I blushed. Surely she had heard about my verbal exchange with the Marqués, or some distorted, hideous version of it, since everyone else had. I only hoped that she had not heard of our physical encounter, for if she had, no doubt the rest of the castle would know as well. Shame attached to a woman, not a man, in that situation.

"I am not disposed to sport with men who are not my husband," I said.

"I am delighted, Doña Josefina, to hear of your virtue. But beware. It will only inflame the Marqués' passions."

"What can I do?" I asked, leaning forward intently. She looked taken aback.

"It is rare that anyone speaks so directly to me. I do not know," she continued. "I know of no one who has ever successfully resisted his campaigns. Perhaps you should just give in, spoil the chase for him. He will tire of you quickly."

I stood up. I would not give in, spread my thighs for him, so he could tire of me! "I am afraid that it is best that I return to my home. My servant has been called away, by some pretext, no doubt, and it is difficult for me to leave without her, as it would be unsuitable for me to travel alone. Nevertheless, if you wish to protect me from the devastation of my reputation, you can offer one of your servants to accompany me to my hacienda. It is a single long day's carriage ride, and I can furnish the carriage and provide for the servant's return." I spoke forcefully, unthinking.

The Marquesa smiled. "I am impressed, but I want you to stay for the ball. Besides, if you ran away like that, it would look as if the rumors about you were true."

"What? What are these rumors?"

"Can't you guess? You are a reader, and as we both know, that immediately renders a woman suspect. You are friendly with the Bishop of Puebla, whose influence locally is great, but cannot compare with that of the Archbishop of Mexico, or worse, the Holy Office. You have attracted the Marqués' eye and are rumored to be writing seditious or, worse, blasphemous tracts with Sor Juana. My goodness, lady, you have created quite a fuss in the short time that you have been here." I sat down heavily. "No, Doña Josefina. You will stay for the ball. And if you want my advice, you will allow the Marqués his way sooner, rather than later. Now, take some books back to your room, so you can enjoy some of the literature of the Spains." She replaced her monocle and picked up her book. I was dismissed.

I took no care whether I was seen or not seen as I walked back to my room. I barely noticed my surroundings. I hardly knew what books I had grabbed, for even in my fury and haste, I did not let that permission pass me by. Let the Marqués find me, let the Devil take me, I thought. And his wife, encouraging adultery and rape. The Court was proving to be a venal place indeed.

I slept until the dinner hour, and when Angélica came to find me, she was outraged that I was not yet dressed. "I am not well," I said. "Perhaps it is the beginning of the breeding nausea. Go without me." I felt no nausea, and I knew it was too soon, really, for such problems, but Angélica was childless and so she would not know. Unfortunately, as much as she was ignorant, she was coldhearted.

"I don't care. Get up, get dressed, put a cool cloth on your face, and hurry. We are dining in the ladies' dining room, but there is to be entertainment after, and you have been absent too much for your own good. People are talking."

Again the rumors were stalking me. "Well, if I have been absent, it is because I have not been invited."

Angélica sighed with annoyance. "Well, you are invited to all of the matinees with the Marquesa again, so stop skulking around. It is a privilege to be here."

I would get nowhere with her. I got up and dressed.

"The virgin emerges," said Granada upon seeing me. I cut her cold. "Oh, and uppity, too, now. Perhaps as the Marqués' current toy you are too good for us." I attempted to disregard her, and seated myself at the table next to a lady I did not know. She held out her hand and gave a name I forgot as soon as I had heard it, for Eustacia came and put herself on my other side.

"I hear you have a new protector. Is the Marqués preferable to the Bishop?"

"Why?" I asked. "Do you wish to sample the Bishop next?" I had an enemy already, I would not submit to her snide innuendo.

"Only if you are quite finished with him," she answered. "Or perhaps, when the Archbishop excommunicates him, you can go and join him in sin."

"Why are you eating at the ladies' table, Eustacia?" Granada asked, sitting next to her. "Have you been banished from the family tables?"

Eustacia ignored Granada's spite, for they had a mutual interest. I was a far more enticing target for her insults. "Doña Josefina, I understand that the Marqués was seen leaving a private room with you, and that your clothing was in disarray. Is your vaunted virtue so quickly assailable?"

"Oh, come, Eustacia. Don't be so vulgar," Granada said with a smirk. "I am sure that our lady was merely adjusting her chastity belt."

I got up. I would not tolerate this any longer. "Leaving so soon?" Granada asked. "You have barely eaten. Though I hear that an assignation is more enjoyable on an empty stomach. It makes the wine go directly to the moral center, and disable it." The women laughed.

I was stopped from leaving by the entrance of the nuns. Sor Inez, two sisters I did not know, and Sor Juana all entered together. A short hush of distraction was followed by greetings and a general return to conversation. Sor Juana deftly pulled me aside. She slipped a folded-up note into my hand as she greeted me. "Do not delay," she said softly, and quickly left me. I looked around the room, wondering where I could go to read the note. Desperate, I slipped behind the privy curtain.

I unfolded the foolscap. In excellent hand was written: "Josefina, meet me in the music room after the Vespers bell. A." Father Alonso. It had to be him. The Vespers bell would be rung soon, in less than an hour. I pulled the curtain aside and reentered the room. I looked for a way to speak to Sor Juana privately, if only for a moment, but she remained surrounded by ladies. The entertainment was to consist of music, a short reading, and a little drama to be performed by the good sisters. It required much setting up of chairs and candelabras, and so it made a private audience virtually impossible.

I helped myself to a glass of sherry to steady my nerves. I then made a point of speaking to as many ladies as I could, so as not to appear cowed by the awful things that were being said to and about me. I would hold my head high, and when I slipped out as soon as the music started, no one would think I had run away.

As the Vespers bell rang I opened the music room door. It was dark outside, and no fire or candles had been lit in the room, so it was both cold and black. I hesitated. Then I remembered my plan of boldness, stepped in, and shut the door behind me. I felt, more than saw, the door from the library open, and then saw the glow of a candle being held aloft. It cast its gentle light upon the room, and on the good father behind it. My heart soared for the first time in days, and I moved toward the light.

"Josefina," he said, his voice husky. I knew, and he did, too. He placed the candle in a candleholder on one of the tables, and I went to him. He opened his arms and enveloped me. I laid my head against his shoulder, breathing in lemon verbena, my eyes shut to the temporal world and to the spinning of my own internal moral compass as well. I lifted my face, and our lips met without preamble.

"Come," he whispered, taking my hand with one of his, and the candlestick with the other. He led me through the door into the library, and to the furthest alcove. I drew aside the curtain, and we slipped into a white plaster-walled nook. He placed the candle on the little table, next to the only other piece of furniture in the small grotto. It was a long settee, covered in deep green velvet, worn a bit at the corners and at the edges of the seat and arms. Books were stacked on the floor, and several small wineglasses, now empty, had been put carelessly on the floor against the wall. On the table, a decanter of sherry, perhaps a quarter full, and two more glasses completed the furnishings.

"My private study here at the castle," he said lightly. I pulled back a bit. It was here that he had been the day I overheard him with Sor Juana. He put his arms around me again, but I was a woman divided. "What is it?" he whispered.

"I am sorry. I was just overcome. I must not lead a good man of the cloth astray."

"Facetiousness is not a trait I would like to see you develop," he replied.

"I meant none." I had spoiled the mood, and I both regretted and was thankful that I had.

"Sit," he said, and I did. He sat next to me. "This has not been a pleasant introduction to Court life, from what I hear." I shook my head. "Tell me what has happened."

"If you have already heard . . ."

"Rumors, yes. But probably only a tenth of them true. I want to know from your lips"—he paused, looked at them, and went on—"what has actually transpired. You may confess freely, for the secrets of the confessional are not revealed."

I told him. I told him about what had happened at the grandees' dinner, at which he was present; I told him about the private party with the Marqués, which he also was witness to. And then, hesitantly, I told him about the Marqués' assault upon my virtue. I could hear his breath quicken, with what I hoped was righteous anger. And at last, I told him about my interview with the Marquesa, and Cayetana's disappearance.

I lay back in the settee. The relief of being able to tell the entire tale was immeasurable, but I held my breath, awaiting his reaction. Father Alonso stroked my hand gently. "You are not to blame for inciting the Marqués' passions. You have behaved chastely, and so the fault must likely lie with him."

I sighed with relief, for most priests were loath to absolve a woman if a man lusted after her. It was the sin of our birth, the downfall of Adam, for which we were still paying centuries later.

"Sor Juana blames the Marqués outright," he added. I stiffened.

"For what? How would she know what he did? She saw none of it!" I was furious. Rumors, and more, had reached her ears, but who knew of this shame? Most would not be as forgiving as Father Alonso was, and none but Sor Juana would absolve me completely.

"Josefina, my beautiful, innocent girl. Everyone knows most of what you have told me involving our hosts, except that you bloodied the Marqués' nose. He has managed to keep that a secret. Nonetheless, you are observed everywhere you go. Perhaps someone saw you come in here."

I felt myself grow chilled at the thought. "Then why did you summon me to such a public place?"

"It is the most innocent of choices. You are known as a reader, and it is not surprising that you have chosen to take refuge in the library at odd hours. You may well have been seen, though I have timed it so as to make this unlikely. Your little strolls, to the music room, the library, the room you visited with the Marqués, all of that gets around. You must not care what others say."

"Except that my virtue would be certified if they also knew that I had hit the Marqués hard enough to draw blood."

"Or that your coquettishness knows no bounds."

I closed my eyes. Life here at Court was like walking through a cactus garden. Once in, any way out was painful, dangerous, and unavoidable. Father Alonso cradled my head in his arms. "I have been so alone," I said.

"I am here."

"So much, so quickly. I am attacked on all sides. I have no one to turn to."

"You have me." Breathing deeply, I lay against his breast. "Now, no more talking." He lifted my face, he kissed me, as he had in the music room, and I was ready to yield this time. Father Alonso was a man. I had kissed him before, and now no hesitance was acceptable. His hands hardened, as did his kiss. "Josefina," he breathed, "do not be afraid. You are here with me now, and you are safe."

I kissed him back. He smiled in my lips, and touched my mouth with his tongue. I opened my lips a bit, and he became bolder. His hands, so warm, so knowing, traveled across my neck and around my collar. He loosened the ties, and the gown opened at the back. I moved to stop him, but he caught my hand and brought it to his lips.

"Don't be afraid, Josefina. My lovely, good woman."

I looked into his blue eyes and I fell into the sky. He pulled my dress front down, and I swelled with desire. His fingers brushed my breasts lightly and I shivered.

I put my hands to his face and traced the ridge of his brow, so prominent above his reddish-gold eyebrows. Then I drew his face down to my bosom. He lowered the straps of my chemise, and my breasts, now fully exposed, were ready for him. His lips bent to their duty, and at the first brush of his teeth I shuddered and felt my legs open in response. He pushed me back, so that I lay on the settee, and he lifted my skirts. Without pause, he reached up and pulled my pantalettes down, and off.

My clothing was bunched around my middle; I was available to his eyes, his hands. He feasted, first with his eyes, then his hands. I moaned and opened, and his breath came harsher. Then he stood and pulled off his cape, and then his collar. He removed his black jacket and his black shirt with the lace-ruffled cuffs, and I saw his chest covered with copper curls. I reached up to touch the strangely colored hair, weaving my fingers into it. He removed his boots and his pants, and stood before me, naked.

He was a golden sight. I stared. I reached for him, but he gently pushed my hand away. "Not yet," he said, "or I will explode."

He ran his hands along my thighs and they quivered. Then he spread my legs open and knelt between them. I tensed. He lowered his mouth to my belly, and then moved downward. "No!" I said. Manuel had never ventured to kiss me like that. It was sinful.

"Oh, yes, Josefina. Oh, yes." And he remained. I shook with fear and mortification, but he was relentless. His hands held me still, as still as he could. Then I felt it. The heat began to rise in me, and a wave began its journey from the base of my spine. I started to writhe, and a moan escaped me. He did not stop, and my legs opened further of their own accord, then stiffened as the wave crested and broke. I cried out, and the throbbing, harder than I had ever known, began to thunder between my legs.

When I was still, he rose up and knelt between my knees. I leaned against the back of the settee, and he offered himself to my lips. Though I had not ever tasted this before, I knew what he sought. I looked up at him, and he nodded. I opened my lips. He pressed in, and I recoiled. "No," he breathed. "Open, and take it. Do it!" I opened my mouth, and he pushed in. I pulled back and gagged.

"Come, open your mouth. Receive me. Receive me," he said. I tried to obey. His hands went around my head, and he held me to him. Then, without more words, he thrust all the way in. I felt him enter my throat. He pulled my head down, and I felt myself suffocate. I had to breathe. I pulled back.

I breathed, and he thrust again, and I realized that I could do this. His hands held my head so tightly that I felt each finger making its own bruise. He pulled and pushed me faster, harder, deeper, until I thought I would swallow him entirely. He let out a tense grunt.

Father Alonso let go of my hair and wrapped his arms around me. I buried my face in his golden chest. He lay down on top of me, with my legs on either side of his, over my bunched clothes and me, covering me with his sweat-dampened chest. He put his head against mine, and rested.

THE BELLS OF THE hour rang, and I woke with Father Alonso standing over me. He was dressed, but I still lay open and exposed. I shut my legs tight and pulled down my dress. He smiled. "I'm sorry you awoke. I enjoyed watching you."

I blushed with mortification and tried to refasten my collar. "Let me help you," he said, and tied the tie. He handed me my pantalettes, and I pulled them on over his and my wetness. He poured us each a glass of sherry and sat down again next to me. "Fix your hair, or the rumors will be even worse." He was still smiling. I was not.

"We sinned," I said softly.

"We did."

"I didn't want to."

"You did. As did I. Now, speak no more of this. I absolve you."

I took this in. "Thank you. But who will absolve you?"

He looked away. Then he said, "It does not matter if I get absolution or not. And this way, you will not conceive my child."

I turned away, even more ashamed. "Do not worry about that. I am possibly, probably, already with child." And I had sinned, with Manuel's babe growing within me.

"Whose?" he said.

"How dare you?" I said furiously.

Father Alonso shrugged. "I'm sorry I offended you. I am, after all, just a man."

He was. "Because the Marqués has tried to sport with me, and because . . ." I couldn't go on.

"And because I have," he finished, "do I think you unchaste? Is that your question?"

"You are base."

"No," he said, "I am mortal. Forgive my foolish words. I have wanted you since you were fifteen. You were not beautiful then, the way you are now, but I could see the promise of both the beauty and the mind. You are coming into your own, Josefina, and I wanted you. And you wanted me."

I could not deny that. I could only regret it. "I am glad you summoned me, though. I had grown weary of waiting."

"I know. I heard."

"You talked about me with Sor Juana." It was a statement.

"Of course. She is your best, and maybe your only, true ally here."

"Except for you." He did not answer. But I did not, at the time, take up the denial in the silence. "What are you to her, or she to you?" I asked.

He chuckled. "Josefina, you are a married woman. You are in no position to be jealous of a humble priest's companionship with a nun. But I assure you, our friendship is blessed by the virtues of Our Lord."

"I am not jealous!" He put his hand on my shoulder and the warmth of it stilled me. "I am not," I said more softly. "You will not tell her about, about this?"

He shook his head. "No, I will not tell her. But she is my friend, my trusted confidante."

I wondered what kind of friend she was. Father Alonso knew how to satisfy his lusts without procreating. He took a woman the way some men took boys. "You are a sinner in a cassock."

"And you?"

I was silent. I was no better. And yet, and yet I wanted to be near him, I wanted to sit with him next to me, and drink sherry, and talk, and hold him in my arms forever. I shook my head. "You may do what you will with her, but I doubt she can be trusted."

"Why not?"

"She writes poems for the Marquesa, but then writes a sonnet for the Marqués, wounding the Marquesa. She writes a *villancico* that glorifies the Church, and stands in her holy habit with her rosary, and then defies the Holy Office. She champions women, and yet she will mock us."

"Court life does, indeed, suit you!" Father Alonso said, shaking his head. "You have become aware; and with awareness comes suspicion; and suspicion, without knowledge or depth of understanding, becomes dangerous. Will you read the book that Sor Juana gave you, now that it has been returned to you?"

"You know that too? Have I no secrets at all?"

Father Alonso put his arm around me and leaned in close. His lemon verbena scent, the flickering candle, and the warmth of our bodies together warred with my despair at the underhanded gossip of the Court. "From me? None whatsoever," he said into my ear. "None whatsoever."

I COULD ONLY PRAY that the Court spies did not see me return to my room, almost at Compline, my clothing and hair poorly arranged by a priest, not a maid. I saw no one, but I knew now that it meant nothing. I shut my door, changed into my nightgown, and crawled into bed.

The demons of well-earned guilt climbed into bed with me. I had committed adultery and sodomy, and with a bishop, no less. Though part of me found that amusing, most of me realized that if anyone were to learn of this, I would be exiled, humiliated, and quite possibly sent to a convent by Manuel, to live out my days alone. I shivered despite the thick blankets. But the cold was replaced by the heat of desire when I remembered what we had done. Then I longed to throw the blankets off, but the mere thought of uncovering brought the entire act to mind again, and I could not bear my shame.

I got out of bed, lit a candle from the embers of my dying fire, and took up the washbasin and a cloth. I washed and washed, but no amount of water would purify my soul of sin. I returned to my bed and pulled the blanket over my head to hide in the darkness of my torment. You received absolution, I reminded myself. From a sodomizing bishop.

ELEVEN

ALL THE TALK WAS about the ball. I rejoined the Marquesa's matinees, and Sor Juana absented herself. No one made any more comments about my brush with the Marqués, and he made no contact. My only tormentor was my conscience, which, I must say, was at least equal to all of my other harassers jointly.

Angélica treated me with distance and politeness, the way she had when she visited me at the hacienda. That suited me, as I did not want her confidence or her solicitude. She made no mention of my probable pregnancy, nor did I.

I spent the time, when I was not in attendance on the Marquesa or half-listening to Angélica and the other ladies prattle on about their dresses and coiffures for the ball, reading *Sheeps' Well,* the play that Sor Juana had given me. It seemed to attack the very basis of our Spanish society, raising the value of the farmworkers and diminishing that of the gentry. I was surprised that Lope de Vega had not fallen prey to the Inquisitors of the Holy Office, or had his books banned. Of course, much could go on in Spain, and we in the colony would not know for months. But if the book sat openly in the Marquesa's library, I had to believe that excommunication was not the penalty on the horizon for reading it.

My reading became a refuge, not just from the incessant gossip and jabbering about clothing, but from the endless commentary in my mind. Within a few days, I had more or less convinced myself that though I had sinned, I could go on with living. When the ugly thoughts of my base behavior crept forth, late at night, I lit my candle and read some more.

"You have black circles under your eyes, Josefina. Are you ill, or is it anticipation of the ball?" Granada asked me, the morning before the grand event.

"I suffer from sleeplessness. It is a cross I bear," I answered solemnly.

"A bad conscience makes for sleepless nights," she replied.

"Then you must sleep the slumber of the just," I said. She looked at me. She could not tell if I had developed a facetious streak, or was flattering her. I could see it made her nervous. I smiled. "I have no doubt of that."

I left her silent, and congratulated myself on being probably the first person in history to have done so. It had to be, for suddenly I had a surfeit of false allies. "Granada has met her match," Eustacia said. These were the first words she had directed specifically to me in a week.

"Will you be attending the ball?" I asked. My malice knew no bounds.

"Of course! Why wouldn't I?" she asked angrily, before she could stop herself. Her hand went to her mouth as soon as the words were out.

"Oh, I don't know. I just thought, well, with your, er, lineage, perhaps you would best absent yourself. After all, the son and heir will be there, and I would not expect you to be welcomed as the bastard cousin on charity. Unless, of course, you were hoping to catch his eye—"

"How dare you?" she said. I shook my head, a wry smile on my lips. I had burned all of my bridges, what was one more? A glance told me Granada was smiling again behind her fan.

That afternoon, I received a summons from the Marquesa herself. I attended her, alone, in her chamber. "I am honored, Your Highness. How can I serve you?"

The Marquesa, in her usual black, sat in a straight chair with a wrought-iron back. Her private chamber was done in rose and gray, a combination I had never seen before, and the strong lines of the furnishings belied the femininity of the colors.

"Dispense with the treacle. You have been spreading poison all morning. Why?"

I lowered my gaze. I could not very well tell her that my venom was the product of being eaten up from within by guilt. "I no longer wish to be the butt of every joke, and the subject of the vicious rumors that have circulated about me."

"Had you not noticed that they had ceased?"

"I had, Your Highness, but I had not thought about that. I want the ladies of this Court to know that I no longer will be trifled with."

"So you descend to their level of discourse. I thought better of you."

"I had hoped for better of myself as well."

"There. You are not like the others. Do you not wonder why they stopped talking about you?"

"I guessed it was because of the ball. Their attention is on that."

"Indeed, that plays a large part. And more than one has set her cap for my son. Not one in this Court is worthy of him. Although your friend Angélica is the best of the lot, not a single lady has the intellect and steel needed to be a *marquesa*."

I had no answer. But I had a question. "If not only the ball, then why have I been spared Eustacia's and Granada's harsh tongues of late?"

"Well, they tire quickly of old gossip, always looking for something new. But mostly it is because I ordered it."

"You ordered it? Why?"

The Marquesa raised one terrifying black brow, the thin skin across her pale face stretching taut. "Because I, too, tire of old gossip. And because the Bishop advised me to. And because you are the first lady to wait on me in years who has a touch of any backbone at all."

It was all too much to take in at once, and there was buzzing in my ears. I relied for a moment on politeness. "I thank you, Your Highness," I said, curtseying.

"You are dismissed," she said, breathing wheezily. She looked to her dresser and found a tincture, the vapors of which she inhaled, no longer even glancing my way. I curtseyed again, to her back, and left.

The Bishop had requested it, the Bishop had requested it, the Bishop had requested it. What this could mean, and to whom he had been talking, I could not guess. Had he given a reason for his order? My thoughts were wild and disordered. I could not get back to the privacy of my room fast enough.

AT LAST, THE NIGHT before the ball, Cayetana returned. She rushed to my room, her high cheekbones flushed with excitement. "Thank you, señora! I can't thank you enough for letting me go to the grand City of Mexico. I have never seen such a place!" She almost embraced me. Her gratitude certainly prevented me from telling her that I had had no part in her deployment, or from chastising her for leaving without telling me.

"The streets! They're wider than a field. And the markets where we went to provision for the ball! Oh! You cannot even begin to imagine!" I had never seen her this animated. Cayetana was among the most stolid of women, and her breathless excitement was almost comical.

I asked a few questions, but few were needed, so excited was she to tell me the details. When she appeared to have wound down most of the way, I gave her the news. "I believe I am with child, as my courses have not run this month. We will be leaving the morning after the ball, and returning home."

Poor Cayetana. "But, señora! We are to stay six more weeks! You can be pregnant here as well as at the hacienda. I will take care of you if you require care, but your last two pregnancies were without trouble, so there would be no reason to expect difficulties now."

I bit my lip, not liking to feel a superstitious, unchristian fear from her words. "It will be as God wills," I said. "But we will leave on the day following the ball, nonetheless."

Cayetana's face became an expressionless stone mask.

I sighed. "What?"

"As you wish, señora."

"Tell me, Cayetana."

"The Marqués' valet. He . . ." Her words trailed off.

"He what? He has made a play for your widow's virtue?" Cayetana had lost her husband so long before that I no longer thought of her as a woman in that way. I could not keep my incredulity from my voice.

"No." She was offended, and rightfully. "He wishes to marry me. He is a man of my own age, of my own people. We do not prolong our misery with waiting. He wishes to marry me, I have consented, and we are, for my purposes, wed."

I stared. I would lose her. I could not imagine life at the hacienda without her, nor could I bear the thought of staying at the castle. After several minutes of silence, I said, "Then you must be married by the priest as well."

"Thank you, señora. We will do so immediately. Then, I will leave with you. Neither of us has any desire to leave our service."

"I am glad, Cayetana, for I would despair of returning without you." The arrangement was not unusual, either for a servant or a lady. Not everyone had the luxury of living with his or her spouse. I was just grateful that Cayetana was willing to return to the hacienda. "Take care of the banns and the wedding quickly, for we must leave. I can't bear to be away from my sons much longer."

"I will do so, señora. Now, let us talk about what you will wear to the ball. Your condition is not yet noticeable, and if previous experience holds, will not be for months. Which of your gowns will be suitable?"

AND SO I WAS caught up in the excitement of the ball. Two weeks before, I would have seen it as the pinnacle of my Court adventure, the fulfillment of a dream. Two days ago, I would have plunged a dagger into my breast before attending. And now, on the day of the grand event, Angélica and I, attended by our maids, spent hours on our toilette.

I had a gown of deep ochre, gored with silk of the same color, and trimmed in golden lace, which I filled even more with the swelling of my breasts, the only sign of my maternity. Angélica rejected my design of having an additional panel of silk as a collar to raise the neckline, saying curtly that my décolletage was my only truly feminine feature. I added a wide velvet choker with a simple pearl pin, to cover a bit of my neck, but I still felt slightly uncovered. "It is the mode," Angélica said, turning back to the mirror.

Angélica, of course, took the mode, as she called it, a little further. A nineteen-year-old beauty, and a widow, could do that without shame, I thought, and perhaps, if she were so inclined, could use those bounteous charms to attract a husband. Or a lover, since her departed husband had left her so well set financially. Her gown was ecru with a bronze trim, deeply cut, with a lace panel in the deep V, not even two fingers' worth of coverage wide. Her jewels were almost as simple as mine, but somehow her hair, golden and gleaming, and her eyes, the color of topaz, seemed to be adornments beyond precious stones.

Cayetana dressed my dark locks as always, sweeping them up from my long neck and wrapping them into a twist. "No," Angélica said, "make the twist double back on itself, then put one of my combs in."

"That would be excessive," I said.

Cayetana and Angélica both ignored me. The effect, I had to agree, was beautiful. I had never in my life looked like this. "If only Manuel were here," I said.

"He would prohibit your attendance," Cayetana said, laughing, "and keep you in the bedroom all night." I blushed, and Angélica did, too.

"Your newfound happiness has made you bold," I said to Cayetana. But I felt a tremor in my belly as I thought of my misconduct, sin that had been temporarily banished from my conscience by the feverish preparations.

When we were ready, we sat nervously in Angélica's room, await-ing the summons from the page assigned to escort to the ballroom the ladies-in-waiting who were not in attendance on the Marquesa. I now knew, of course, that only a few of the most select attended the Marquesa before an event, whether a dinner or a ball, and neither Angélica nor I was among the select. While that suited me, in that I would have no idea where to begin my duties, Angélica had more than once railed against her exclusion.

Angélica's room was much like mine, with a comfortable bed covered in quilts, a large window that could be shuttered against the night air or opened to welcome the dawn, and a small fireplace for light and warmth. The principal difference was the number of gowns hanging in the armoire. In mine, there were the gowns I had ordered at Angélica's direction, four of them, and my three from home. In hers, there were possibly twenty. She had sleeves and collars, slippers and stockings, capes and wraps, in several trunks. I had not remembered such a disparity in our packing.

"I had them sent from home," she said, seeing my surprised look. "I will, after all, stay through the dry season."

"Angélica, I told you, I am leaving after the ball."

"You may do as you wish. I am staying."

I nodded. I did not intend for Angélica to cut her stay short on my account, and indeed I had no wish for her as a traveling companion, especially as Cayetana had returned. I longed to put miles between myself and the castle, the Bishop, the Marqués.

The thought of the Bishop once again brought a blush to my cheek. I could not think about him without a vivid recollection, and its attendant shame.

"You are flushed," Angélica said.

"It is the heat, and my condition," I replied. She nodded. It would serve to cover almost any anomaly at this point.

"I cannot imagine that the young heir will be handsome," Angélica said, "but I imagine he will be arrogant."

I was surprised. "You are thinking about the Marqués' son?"

"Well, that's the reason for the ball, isn't it? To introduce us to him. I imagine that he is thinking of selecting a wife."

I thought about the Marquesa's comment, that no one there, including Angélica, was worthy of her dear boy. "Perhaps," I said noncommittally.

There was a knock on the door. I opened it to the young page who had brought me the book I had dropped, and the Marqués' hateful missive. Angélica gathered her skirts to go. "Señora," he said to me, "I have brought you a message." He handed me a folded letter.

"Thank you," I said. "I must go to my room to get something for your trouble. Wait here." I rushed to my room. My hands were shaking as I opened the letter, making it hard to read. I took a coin out and went to my door to hand it to the boy.

"Who's it from?" Angélica asked from her door, coming toward me.

"I don't know. Just a moment, I need to adjust my chemise," I said, and shut my door. I held the letter steady.

> My dear lady,
>   Please accept my absence from the ball. Though I have longed to see you again, circumstances and circumspection make it impossible. Until another day, another time,
>
>   I Kiss Your Hands,
>   Alonso

The effort to control my face, even though I was alone, took all my strength. I felt the veil torn from my dreams. For three days I had writhed in shame, and yet for three days I had held, in the recesses of my heart, the hope that he would call for me, or be at the ball. What had been, moments earlier, an exciting anticipation now turned to cold sweat.

What had I imagined? Had I been dreaming of dancing with a bishop?

Even in this strange world where nuns did not keep to the cloisters but attended musicales and readings, and noblemen made free with ladies of the gentry, I could not have imagined that bishops danced. But they conversed, and they loved. I crumpled the note and stuffed it in the toe of one of the slippers in my armoire.

And the use of the formal "I Kiss Your Hands," mostly abbreviated as "KYH," rather than a closing that showed he shared my earth-shattering emotions, left me feeling abandoned in heart as well as body.

But he did say he longed to see me. He did say there would be another time, another place. He wasn't abandoning me completely, but being, instead, realistic about the dangers we were running.

He was, of course, right. Circumstances and reasonable caution compelled his actions, not disdain for me, or a cooling of his ardor. Of course he was right. I only wished that I had had the strength to write that note, that I had been the one to point out the dangers of our liaison. He must love me, I thought. He only left me out of concern for my reputation.

Delusional fool. Surely his concern was for my reputation, no doubt at all. And his. And he did not come and say good-bye, or attend the ball and speak to me. He was a coward. My crazed heart changed direction like a speeding pendulum.

Would I continue to delude myself, or would I accept the plain meaning of the text he had penned? I smiled an unwilling and bitter smile. As with Sor Juana's poems, I could interpret this letter exactly as written, or I could try to divine an underlying message, or I could color the words with my own pain and mortification, and invent meanings that the writer had never dreamed of.

"Josefina! Josefina, what are you doing in there? It's time to go down to the ball!" Angélica's voice came through my door.

I do not know how much time had gone by since the page had delivered his bitter missive, but however long it was, Angélica had received our summons and it did not benefit me in the least to pique her curiosity any more than the delivery of a mysterious note already had. "Coming, Angélica. My chemise was not lying smooth." I opened the door. Angélica looked at me closely.

"What was the message you received?" she asked.

"It was from the Bishop of Puebla. He knows I am leaving in a very few days, and he will of course not be at the ball." I made it seem obvious. "So he merely wrote to ask me to commend him to my father, and to suggest some devotional readings for my improvement and faith."

Angélica pursed her lips, and for a moment I could see her at thirty. "Well, your face is blotched from his recommendations, so I suggest you put your devotions out of your mind for the next several hours."

I looked away, but did not back down. "That is from twisting around to straighten this unfortunate chemise." I had become, in a week, a shockingly adept liar.

"Indeed," she replied, losing interest. "Well, come. We mustn't be late."

A page awaited us, with two other ladies. They, like us, were dressed, coiffed, and perfumed to a fare-thee-well. Our aura of sweet aromas enveloped us in a walking cloud as we lifted our unaccustomedly voluminous skirts and carefully made our way down the stone steps to the main level of the castle. We rustled along the corridors, past the doors to the music room, past the little room the Marqués favored for his hideous fondlings, and past the library. Where we normally turned to enter the Marquesa's wing, we continued straight, still in the stone-lined hall, and found ourselves in a part of the castle where I had not yet ventured.

The hallway opened up into a wide foyer, hung with tapestries in the Marqués' colors of green and gold. I could hear murmurings, and then we came to large oak double doors, guarded by liveried men. The men bowed; the page stepped aside. The men opened the double doors together, and before us was displayed a brilliant and grand hall, lit everywhere so brightly that my eyes were momentarily dazzled to blindness.

When my vision cleared, I stepped forward into the incredible room. There were at least fifty people already present, all in such finery as to make my own beautiful gown seem pedestrian. There were women in heavy brocade despite the season, luminous in gold and silver. A woman glided by in a dress of watered silk, in a color that was papaya, but so pale as to be, on a second look, cream. I stared, wondering how a dress could be two such different tones at once. Some women had their hair piled in towers above their heads, glittering with combs dripping jewels.

Others had their locks held back with high amber combs, with mantillas of intricate lace foaming down around their shoulders.

The men, in dark-colored clothing, distinguished themselves with gold braid, silver or mother-of-pearl buttons, and the level, color, and volume of the lace adornments at their cuffs and necks. Some, Hidalgos, wore swords at their hips. Their coloring ranged from the blonds of Northern Spain to the deep browns of the Portuguese, but all were arrayed in the finest of clothing.

I scanned the room for the ladies I had met, wondering where the rest of these people had come from. It would provide a topic of conversation, in any event, to ask them this.

In truth, I also scanned the room for the Bishop. In my treacherous heart, I had to admit, I harbored the hope that he had changed his mind, and had come after all.

I was jostled a moment by a footman who passed bearing a tray of delicacies, the aroma of chiles for a moment cutting through the heat and perfume of the large but crowded room. He did not stop to offer me a taste of his wares, but continued to a group of men standing together, talking and holding glasses of wine. They took from his tray without pausing in their conversation, and I watched the footman move on to the next group of men. I looked at the group carefully, knowing the Bishop was not with them, as his clerical clothing would have set him apart most obviously, but now looking to see if the Marqués was among them. For without the Bishop to protect me, I would have to be very wary of the Marqués' approach.

The windows were unshuttered, and a cooling breeze blew in at that moment, gently ruffling the finery of the guests. It cooled my heated mind as well. I had to walk forward, attend this ball fully, and not spend the evening in my own mind, with the Bishop, or mourning his absence. I squared my shoulders within my gown, and then walked purposefully toward a station where ladies were being served glasses of sherry.

"Good," said Angélica, catching up to me after I had obtained my glass. "I was afraid that you intended to spend the night standing in one place, staring at the spectacle like the countrywoman that you are. At least you will circulate and entertain the invited guests."

I did not grace her with an answer. Instead, I nodded briefly and began a tour of the room. No sooner had I detached myself from Angélica than a trumpet sounded. Two liveried footmen opened the double doors, and another two footmen again sounded the trumpets. All conversation stopped; all eyes were riveted on the entry. A trio appeared at the door. On the right, the Marquesa, glittering with jewels, her black eyebrows raised, stood in black satin edged in red, with a red mantilla covering her black hair. Her white skin was more taut than usual, and her thin lips were pressed into a firm and unyielding line.

On the left stood the Marqués. Unlike his wife, he eschewed severity of dress, and his jacket was shot with gold that made his outfit shimmer with the light. His huge nose beaked above his mouth, which stretched into a big, open grin. He wore a sword at his hip, with a jeweled hilt and filigreed scabbard.

Between them stood a young man, perhaps my age. Taller than either of his parents, thin, with shoulders as wide as eagles' wings, he had the Marquesa's ebony hair, the arched brows, and, fortunately for him, the thin, aristocratic nose. I could not see the color of his eyes from where I stood, but they looked lively and intelligent. He had the good fortune to have an open smile—wide as that of the Marqués'—and he stood at ease, in a black frock coat in what I believed to be the European style, knee breeches, and hose. He did not wear a sword, and his shirt, though flowing, had no lace or ruffles, only a black ribbon trim around the neck where the collar met the fabric of the shirt. He stepped forward and bowed.

"The heir," was the whisper that roared around the room. The higher voices wove a chorus of "How fine!" and "Isn't he handsome!" A deeper counterpoint spoke, "A fine lad" and "So grown."

"Miguel Ángel Porfirio San Geronimo, heir to the Marquessate of Condera, son of the Marqués Don Francisco Miguel Porfirio and the Marquesa Margarita San Geronimo de Porfirio," announced the principal footman. The guests bowed and curtsied. Then the trio descended the short staircase into the room, and the guests surged forward to greet their host and the guest of honor.

The food circulated. I took a small plate of chiles filled with cream, and I ate. The wine and sherry flowed, and I drank. But the evening wore on, and though I conversed, I felt the barrier of my sorrow between the other guests and me. At last the music began. I retreated to a chair in a little alcove on the side of the room where matrons who would not be dancing could rest. I leaned back and closed my eyes, and allowed the music to waft over me.

I was startled to feel a hand on my shoulder, and snapped open my eyes. The Marqués was there, looking down at me. I twitched my shoulder away and stood up. I did not wish to be immobile and thus at disadvantage. "Will you dance?" he said. I stared at him.

"No, Your Highness, I will not."

"And why is that? It is a sarabande coming up, and we will need another to make up our pairs."

"I am a married woman. I do not know the dances. And, respectfully, Your Highness, I do not wish to learn from you."

"Such arrogance must be punished!" he answered, with a leer.

"Then my husband will exercise his right to discipline me, not you. I return to him the day after tomorrow, and you may write to him and let him know how I have transgressed."

He laughed, in wine-induced good humor. "I may do that."

I felt a chill, realizing that he could well write to Manuel, and tell him the opposite of the truth. But my only choice was to brazen out the situation. "I have his complete confidence, earned by reasons of which you already are all too aware. Has your nose healed?"

He again placed his hand on my arm, gripping like iron. "Quite. Your puny fist made little impact, only a bloody mess. Are you enjoying your subversive reading?"

"I have no idea what you are talking about. The only reading I do is of the Psalms."

He continued to grip me, and continued to smile. He took a step in, pressing his body the length of mine, so I could feel his arousal against my body. "You are quite the fireball, aren't you?"

I recalled the Marquesa's quip that my virtue only inflamed the Marqués' passions, and I feared I had overplayed my hand. "I am sorry, Your Highness. You are right. I am rude, but that is my country upbringing. I am honored by your interest in me, and certainly wish I could accommodate your charming invitations. But as a country wife, I do fear my husband more than I wish to please you, and I must not, ever, give in to your alluring attentions."

He stared at me. Then he laughed so loud that others turned and stared. But, seeing the Marqués pressed against a woman, and holding her arm, they assumed he was trysting, and that I was his newest doxy. "You are a crafty minx! I was right! My dear Josefina, your conquest will be an exquisite pleasure. You will fall to me, and when I tire of you, you will beg to still be mine. See if you don't. But first, you will fall."

He bowed, and strutted away. I brushed my arm off. I decided that regardless of the social consequences, I was returning, now, to my room. I gathered up my skirts and headed for the door.

Before I could get to the stairs, my path was blocked by a tall, black-haired young man. "Your Highness," I said, wondering if that was the right address for an heir to a Marqués.

"No, señora, simply Miguel Ángel. No titles. And you? What is your name?"

"I am Doña Josefina María del Carmen Asturias de Castillo, at your service." I curtsied, and he did not object.

"Doña Josefina, it is an honor. My mother has spoken highly of you. May I get you a glass of wine?" I could not say no to the heir, much as I hated his father. I nodded, and he offered his arm. I took it.

"This is the European style," he said, laughing easily. "A gentleman offers a lady his arm, he leads her to the wine, he offers her a drink. They may dance together, not like here, where it is only the ronda and sarabande, and never a couple. And if they are so inclined, especially in the university town of Salamanca, they may talk about literature and poetry and art, without inciting the wagging tongues of gossip. Unlike here."

I looked up at him and noticed that his eyes were a greenish brown, like his father's, but the intelligence I had seen in them when he entered was even more apparent up close. "I have always wanted to see Spain, and I have heard of Salamanca," I said, with my heart clutching at the thought of Father Alonso. It was there that he had studied, and he had told me stories of intellectual freedom and adventure that I could not imagine were real. And here was this young man, who could not be more than my own twenty-five years, telling me the same thing.

"My mother tells me that you are a reader. Have you read Lope de Vega?" I started. "No, do not fear. I am not secretly spying for the Holy

Office. I, too, am a great lover of *Sheeps' Well,* and I believe that the peons will have their rights soon."

"I am relieved," I said, though my fear had not been for the Holy Office of the Inquisition. I had a terrifying vision of his father, the Marqués, holding my book in his hand, laughing. "I am astonished at Lope de Vega's bravery. Have you read Góngora's poetry?" He nodded eagerly, and I quoted the lines that had so struck me: "Coins buy status, forsooth! Truth! He loves most, who doth most sigh, lies!"

He returned my quote with one of his own. "With ducats they buy dukedoms, true! And," he went on, "if each of the seventeen hundred men in the town were to read twenty-two stanzas, we would ultimately complete the entire thirty-seven-thousand-stanza work of the great poet in no time!"

"No, Miguel Ángel, for that would be thirty-seven thousand four hundred stanzas, so some would remain without a few verses!"

"Such ciphering, and without a pen and parchment," he remarked.

"Yes, well, I manage my husband's estate, and I managed my father's before that."

"A woman of beauty with such a brilliant mind is a rare jewel," he said. A woman of beauty. Not one person, before I came to Court, had ever regarded me as other than plain. I was too overcome to protest, and instead answered with a curtsy. Miguel Ángel found that amusing. "And modest as well!"

And it was thus that Angélica found us, laughing and talking, and drinking wine. "Darling," Angélica said warmly, slipping her arm into mine, "you are enjoying yourself at last. I am so pleased."

I did not stare. I did not laugh. Even countrified, I knew what she wanted. Women had been rushing up to the heir all evening, and though he had been polite, he had not engaged anyone in conversation. She wanted an introduction. "Doña Angélica Curtola de Sandoval, please allow me the honor of introducing Don Miguel Ángel Porfirio San Geronimo."

"Your servant, madam," said Miguel Ángel, bowing. Patches of red appeared on his cheeks, as happened to the Marquesa at a surge of emotion. While Angélica curtsied I kept my eye on the heir. He tried, I must say, to take his eyes off Angélica, to acknowledge me, but nature proved stronger than manners, and he was barely able to nod in my direction when I bade them both good evening.

This time I made it to the door, and back up to my room, without any interference. I wished Angélica all the luck in the world but sensed that her beauty would hold Miguel Ángel's attention for only a short period. Perhaps that short time would be enough to garner a marriage proposal. If such a marriage became a lifetime of boredom, disappointment, or, for Miguel Ángel, philandering in his father's style, he and Angélica, both named for angels, would find themselves at that impasse in due time.

*T*WELVE

*A*ND SO IT WAS that after twenty days, I returned home. Although I sent word on ahead by horseman, the journey took two days this time. We were unable to start at dawn, the castle carriage not being mine to command, and I had to implore the driver to stop more frequently. It was a less pleasant component of my condition, but it further served to remind me of my reason for returning home.

Alone with Cayetana, without Angélica prattling on, I was able to sleep when the jostling permitted it, but I had no distraction from musing upon my stay. I felt more tired from sitting and thinking than I ever had from a day's work at the hacienda. When we arrived at the inn where Angélica and I had first stopped, it had grown dark, and we were compelled to stay the night. I could barely bring myself to walk to the shabby room I was to sleep in, and I dropped right into a dark sleep the moment I blew out my candle.

It was late morning on the second day when the familiar landmarks at last appeared. My heart pounded with mixed emotions as we approached, but the worry dissolved temporarily with the sound of my son, crowing at being the first to sight the carriage. Joaquín forgot how grown-up he was and ran out to meet us as we rolled up the long drive to the hacienda. I forgot my misery and anger and leaped from the carriage when it had barely stopped, and scooped him into my arms. I held him so tight he squealed. I put him down and wiped the tears from my face.

"I missed you so, big boy!" I said. Joaquín pressed his little face into my skirt, and his warm grip answered me in kind. He held my hand in his sweaty, small one and walked me to the door. Cayetana followed, and Joaquín turned around and held out his other hand to her. Thus surrounded by the women in his life, my firstborn led us home.

At the door, we were greeted by Anaya, the girl who had taken charge of the children in my and Cayetana's absence. She was just out of childhood herself, barely fourteen, and her childlike energy delighted me and the children. She was holding Neto in her arms. Neto, unsmiling, held his arms out to me. "Mama is back," he pronounced, looking seriously into my eyes. He buried his nose in my neck. "Mama smells like"—he paused, pulling back and thinking—"like a mama in a pretty dress." He looked again at me closely, inspecting for signs of change. I passed muster, as he finally smiled and nestled back into my arms.

"At least let your mother over the threshold," Cayetana said, and Joaquín and Anaya stepped out of my way. I entered, and breathed with gratitude the air of my own home.

My boys stayed with me, waiting outside my chamber as I changed from my dusty traveling clothes into a fresh, homely gown of dark green. I was remotely amused to notice that it had no trim of lace, or ruffle, or piping of any sort, but was simply itself. I would never have noted that before my journey, nor appreciated the gown's simplicity.

Even in my sons' company, Father Alonso managed to poison my thoughts. I looked at the boys and imagined looking at them with Father Alonso. I walked into my house and imagined walking in with him. Each experience was colored, however faintly, by a second, parallel experience, in my imagination, occurring in his presence.

During the long carriage ride from the castle, I had feigned sleep to prevent Cayetana from disturbing my sorry reverie. She in turn had fulfilled her duties completely but without animation, thinking no doubt of her own newfound mate. In my thoughts, I swung from the agony of desire to the misery of shame.

Slipped into my Book of Psalms was a sheaf of Sor Juana's poetry, which she had pressed into my hands before I departed. "You have suffered, and will suffer more," she said, "but your consolation will always be present." Whatever that meant to her, to me it meant nothing. My consolation would always be absent.

I looked at the poems she had given me, reading them over and over throughout the journey. One spoke to my bereaved heart more than others.

> *I approach; I retreat.*
> *Who but I can find*
> *The absence of the eyes I meet*
> *In the presence of the distant mind? . . .*
> *So do I love him*
> *That in the pain I bear*
> *I feel not that pain*
> *But the loss of pain I fear. . . .*
> *Alas, your disdain*
> *Wreaked as much as your love*
> *For what was not pain*
> *You could never give.*

Father Alonso had given me only pain in his love, and it was that pain that I carried home, and that I cherished. My heart had been broken, and my virtue forever tarnished in my mind, and I felt the disdain in the words of his parting letter cut my heart over and over. Yet if I healed from those cuts, the love I had discovered would cease to exist.

Now in my room, I cried briefly, but the scuffling feet outside my door recalled me to my sweet duty. I wiped my eyes and welcomed my boys back in. Their tumbling, their serious questions, and their stories of the events during my absence were heavenly reminders of the prize for virtue.

Eventually, Anaya came to take them away for their dinner. I thanked her for her service. "Do you wish to continue to take charge of the nursery?" I asked her, conscious of Cayetana's impending marriage, and the division of her attentions.

"Yes, señora, absolutely!" A relieved smile broke across Anaya's broad, flat face. "I was afraid with your return that I would go back to outdoor work. I love the boys!" Her enthusiasm lightened the room. I did not yet tell her that there would be a third charge for her in a few months. I had told Angélica, and I had told Cayetana, but I felt at this point that I owed it to Manuel to tell him before all his household knew more about his family life than he. And I hoped that with the telling of the good news, I would erase my sin from my soul. For I would never confess the unholy deed I had done, and had permitted, to anyone.

WE HAD NEVER BEEN demonstrative outside the bedroom, Manuel and I, and so I was taken aback at his reception at my return. I had come down into my little sitting room off the kitchen, where the light was full and golden with the late spring afternoon sun, and was just standing at my desk. I was looking without seeing, noting only in passing that the books did not seem to be unbearably out of order, but also internalizing the fact that I had been gone a mere twenty days, not the full eight weeks I had anticipated, and had I remained away much longer the books could well have been in shambles. I had just decided that I would take on the task of rectifying everything on the morrow, when I heard the sound of boots being scraped off in the entry.

My heart tumbled around inside me, and I felt a wave of dizziness that made me grip the edge of the desk. Manuel was back. Would he see the change in me? Would he discern my crime? I turned to him as he came through the adobe archway.

His strong, dark features lit up. He held his arms out to me, almost as Neto had done, and crossed the little room in three long strides. "Josefina! Josefina," he said, pulling me close. He wrapped his strong arms around me, holding me pressed against him. He put his hands on my hair, his lips on the top of my head. "Oh, my Josefina. I could never have imagined how much I would miss you. My wife. My love. Josefina."

It was so that finally, after all the pain and anguish, the tears, hot and unrestrained, began to flow, and I cried without sobs or moans, just with tears, into his shirt. He did not say any more, but stroked my head, my back, and stood with me as long as I needed.

When I was finished, I wiped my face with a cloth. I did not look at him yet, for fear that my face would show how little I deserved his love, how much I prized it now, and had undervalued it a week ago. "Manuel," I said finally, still looking at the ground, "I have good news. I am with child again."

He whooped as if it were his first time. He grabbed my shoulders and spun me around. "I knew it. I knew it when you left. I could feel our daughter growing inside you!" He whooped again.

Our daughter? "You believe this one will be a girl?" I asked, incredulous.

"Absolutely. I could tell when you left. I only hoped it was true."

"May God grant us this blessing," I said.

Manuel smiled. His joy was infectious, and I smiled back. "Now, I hope our dinner is ready," he said. "I did not enjoy dining so often alone while you were gone. Come, and at dinner you must tell me all of the sights, everything that you heard, each person that you met, and the wonders of the Court."

We went in to dinner, our homely, generous platters of meat, chiles, tortillas, beans, and rice all on the table awaiting us. I sat with him, spooning a bit of this and that onto my plate, and told him a severely edited version of my stay at the castle.

Not used to so much conversation with Manuel, I kept my stories short. But he wanted more, though he did not say much, and he encouraged my tales with questions and exclamations of surprise. He looked at me attentively, and, it occurred to me, with the fascination he usually reserved for the ladies whom I had previously invited to our table. I understood suddenly their captivation with Manuel, for that regard, with his black-lashed green-brown eyes fixed upon one, and his lips curled slightly at the corners as he allowed nothing to interfere with his concentration upon one's face and speech, was vastly flattering. And it did dawn on me, darkly, that perhaps he had, as Angélica had insinuated, found me boring.

"You are not eating much," he remarked.

"No, Manuel, for I have been talking." But I found that though I was hungry, I did not want to eat. That, at least, I recognized as a sign of my pregnancy. "And I am breeding, of course, which you may recall makes my appetite skittish."

"Of course, my dear," he said, that look of joy returning to his face. He reached for my hand and stroked it. "God grant you an easy time, and God grant us a daughter as beautiful, as learned, and as virtuous as her mother."

I cast my eyes down. Twenty days ago, I would have denied two of the three adjectives. Now, I could deny only one—and the only one I would have admitted to then. "Amen," he added.

Dizziness overcame me, and I rushed from the table. I got to the privy alcove in time, and threw up the little I had eaten that day. Then I sat on the little stool, cold sweat pouring from my body, and waited for the world to stop its insane spinning.

MANUEL WAS GENTLE AND solicitous, helping me into bed, sponging my face with cool water. I shivered despite the warmth of the day and crawled under the covers. Cayetana came, shooed him out, and placed a basin by the side of my bed. "It will be a strong baby, if you're that sick," she said.

"I was never sick with the boys," I said weakly.

"Don Manuel says it will be a daughter. Girls are much more trouble," she pronounced. I knew nothing, so I didn't argue. Besides, I was too weak to care.

And it was thus every morning. I could not get out of bed without vomiting. And though Cayetana prescribed dry tortillas and weak coffee for my breakfast, to be taken in bed before attempting to rise, and though I dutifully tried to keep the meager food down, the moment I swung my feet off the bed, the food came up.

"It will be over in a fortnight, or maybe a month," she said consolingly.

Once up, I was able to function for about three hours before crushing exhaustion drove me back to my bed. Neto sat sweetly with me, stroking the bedspread and crooning to himself. He patted my face, my hair, and lay next to me when I could tolerate it. He smelled so sweet. He was my constant consolation.

During my upright hours, I went over Manuel's books. He had not made too bad a mess of things, and I was able to put the accounts to rights despite my nausea. His household expenses had contracted with my absence, even such a short one, and I endeavored to find where he had cut back, so I could reorder whatever we were lacking. In the course of this inquiry, I had a long chat with Anaya.

Twisting her braids nervously, the girl sat on the edge of the chair. Her coarse black and white skirt and shawl were so different from the rich green and gold livery of the pages and *meninas,* the young ladies-in-waiting, at the castle. I myself preferred Anaya's clothing, though I wondered how she would feel about it if she ever had the opportunity for comparison. "Did the children lack for anything while I was gone?" I asked her.

She shook her head. Given the opulence of the hacienda, opulence I had never imagined could look plain before my visit, she could see no lack. "Is there anything we need? Anything Don Manuel did not know to obtain?"

"No, señora," she said. "But there is a problem." She swallowed. She did not want to be blamed for whatever she was about to disclose, and she clearly feared she would lose her newfound position if she complained.

"Tell me. It is always best to speak the truth, immediately, and not allow it to fester." My sanctimonious voice brought another wave of dizziness and nausea.

"It's Neto. He's afraid of the dark."

I relaxed. "That is not unusual. Even our bold little Joaquín was afraid of things when he was but two. Of course, at five, he fears nothing!" I laughed. My son had been given a life in which, at five, he was the king of the world. And I intended to keep it that way.

But Anaya had grown up differently. "My little brothers, they, too, are afraid of things. But with Neto it is different. He is afraid, not just of the dark, but of spirits, and terrors, and speaks in a way that a two-year-old shouldn't speak."

"He spoke at six months, Anaya. He is several years beyond his age in speech."

She nodded. "I fear he is possessed."

I shook my head. She might be loving, but she was fearfully ignorant. "Anaya, he is not possessed. He is simply imaginative. Come. Let's talk about what we need to buy."

But I was concerned. The next day, in the afternoon, when Neto was snuggled in with me, I took out a book I had brought with me from the castle. It had beautiful illustrations of angels. I opened it and showed it to him. He pondered the picture for a bit, then looked at me, big brown eyes shining. "Beautiful lady, Mama. What's that?" He pointed to the large *A,* done in gold lettering.

"It's a letter. The letter *A.* When you see that, you say 'Ah!'"

He smiled. I turned the page. He pointed to the letter *A* on that page and said, "Ah! Ah! Aaaaaah!" He smiled an enormous smile, his little teeth glistening. I hugged him to myself, overwhelmed with pride.

"That's right, my little monkey. That's right!" Not yet three, my baby was learning to read.

But at night he cried, and Anaya had to rock him back to sleep. "Neto's a baby, Neto's a baby," Joaquín sang. And when I chastised him, Joaquín just laughed. "He is, Mama. He's afraid of the dark. And afraid of the birds that fly in and out during the day. He's a baby!"

I stroked Joaquín's straight brown hair. He looked more and more like Manuel with every passing minute. "You're a big, brave boy, just like your daddy," I said. "But Neto is still small, and you have to be nice to him."

Joaquín shrugged. "I *am* nice to him, Mama. But he's a crybaby. But sometimes, you know what, Mama? He talks, when we're supposed to be asleep, and he tells me stories about spirits, and all kinds of funny things. He's afraid of spirits, too."

What did a baby know about spirits? I wondered what nonsense Anaya had been filling their heads with. "But the stories are nice, Mama. And I like them. They're like you're there with us, in our room, only it's Neto."

"You're a good boy," I said to Joaquín. He took it as his due. Everyone praised him, for his pleasant demeanor, his precocious skill with livestock, his strength.

He gave me a big, open grin. "I'm hungry, Mama. Is it dinnertime yet?"

"For you, my big hungry boy, it's always dinnertime!"

It would soon be time to eat, and for once, I was hungry. "Come, maybe you can join me and Papa at the table today." Joaquín wrapped his arms around my neck. He was growing up and didn't do that very often anymore. I cherished the moment.

THE FIRST THREE MONTHS passed, and my nausea lessened. The baby quickened within me, and I felt, with her movement, a ray of joy and hope. Manuel had not come to my bed since my return. I had been vomiting day and night, and I was thin and tired, and he was a gentle and good man. It was now the height of the hot, wet season. The summer heat blanketed us and we kept the shutters open at night to gather whatever cool breeze might spring up in the darkness.

One night, when it seemed that the worst of the stomach sickness had passed, Manuel finally approached.

I heard him open the door to my room, long after I had gone to bed. It must have been close to midnight. The moon had risen, and in its weak light I could see Manuel's form. He was carrying a glass, and I could smell the sherry. He placed the glass on my little table. I lay motionless, my eyes slightly open, and watched him undress. He fumbled with the buttons on his shirt, and I wondered just how much sherry he had drunk. I realized that I had not sat up with him at night since my return, and I had no idea whether it was now his custom to drink in the evening.

I could smell the aroma of sweat over the sherry, the scent of a day's hard work. I felt myself tremble a bit, and an icy finger of fear ran down my spine. It was almost as if Manuel were a stranger, not my husband of six years. When I heard his silver-encrusted belt hit the floor, rather than feel my legs parting of their own volition, as they had for all those years before, instead I felt them clench and tighten. When he sat down on the edge of the bed to remove his boots, the room started to spin.

I thought I smelled lemon verbena, Father Alonso's scent. No! I could not think of that. And then the sherry, strong and sour, overpowered all other odors. Manuel reached for the hem of my nightgown and lifted it slowly. "Josefina," he whispered hoarsely. I tried to make myself say his name, but instead I shivered.

He ran his fingertips up my thighs and pushed the gown above my waist. Then he moved his hands between my legs and pressed them open. I stilled myself from pushing him away, remembering my legs wide open, and a tongue, sliding down. "Open up, Josefina," he said, this time not so softly.

The room was still spinning. I made my legs soft, and he opened them. He touched me, where I had been touched. I felt a strike of fire there. He chuckled quietly. "I have missed you, wife," he said, and stroked me gently. His hands were large and dry, calloused where the reins of a horse had long made them hard. He knew what he wanted. "Wider," he said, and I complied.

I gripped the edge of the bed to keep the room from toppling over onto itself. Would he be able to tell? I tried to pray, but his hands kept my thoughts away from the divine. And what right did I have to pray, anyway?

He lifted the gown over my head, and I was naked. He stroked my breasts, tender and enlarged as they were, and when he suckled my nipples my legs opened wider of their own accord, and my back arched. He bit my breast, sharp and quick, and I moaned. I put my hands on his head, and held him.

With his hands he prepared me for entry, while his mouth sucked and nibbled. I could not think, or resist, or deny. But as he approached, I tensed and my legs slammed shut. "You'll hurt the baby!" I said.

He stopped, surprised. He tried again, but my legs would not part. "Don't want to hurt the baby," he said. And then, he raised his head. "Here, I still want something," he mumbled. And he got up on his knees. I could see his long, brown member, hard and ready, in his hand. He brought it toward my mouth. "Open your mouth," he said. My eyes went wide. He must know, I thought, terrified. I opened my mouth, but out from it came a howl of terror, not at what abomination he was requesting, but what abomination I had committed.

He pulled back, but I could not stop, in my horror of my guilt. I cried out and twisted with shame, my mind filled with tortured images of Father Alonso, Manuel, the Marqués, and Alonso again. Distorted and crazed, their faces and other parts twisted in my mind. The room spun, and before the world went black, I saw Manuel's face break into tiny pieces and shatter on the bed around me.

I DON'T KNOW IF it was the same day, or the next day, or even the same week. When I regained consciousness, I could not move my left arm. I could not speak. The pain in my head was like nothing I had ever felt, a pounding, red-and-green-sparkling pain. But between my legs, no blood was flowing. I offered a prayer, silent by need and not desire, that I had not lost the child—that she was still inside me. I tried to rise, but could not.

Cayetana sat beside me. "Señora, you are very ill."

I tried to answer. Horrible little noises came from my throat but I could not form words.

"Shhh. Don't try. Can you smile?" I tried, and with my right hand I felt my mouth. Both sides of my lips rose. Cayetana's shoulders relaxed. "Good. You can understand me, and you can smile. You cannot speak. Can you raise both arms above your head?" I could raise my right arm, but my left arm had departed my body. I could not even find it in my mind. Cayetana frowned. "We will cure you. But you must rest. You must preserve the baby's life, even at the expense of your own."

I knew that to be true, for that was the will of God. I nodded and she smiled. I could nod. I could smile. I could understand the spoken word. All was not lost.

She brought me broth, and I could eat. Soon I was sitting up, propped with pillows.

Anaya brought the boys in. "It is God's punishment," she said.

"Oh, be quiet, fool," Cayetana said to her.

"It's because of the books," Anaya said.

"Go. Surely there's work to be done elsewhere," Cayetana ordered. "I will take charge of the boys and see that they don't tire their mother. Now get."

Anaya left. Her views were commonplace and unremarkable, except they did not fit with mine. Cayetana understood. "She should not be bringing up the boys," she said. "As soon as you are well, I will send her back to the kitchen to work, and I will take over the nursery again. But for now, I must nurse you."

I nodded.

"Good," she said. "You will recover."

That afternoon, Manuel came to see me. He did not meet my eyes at first, but stood, unsure, in the doorway. Cayetana got up. "She will be well again, señor, but she must be given time." He nodded, and she left the room.

"I—" he started, then stopped. He sighed and walked into the room. His white shirt gleamed, freshly ironed, and he smelled of hay and sunshine. "Josefina—" he started again. Then he shook his head. I grunted. I could not say *Do not apologize, it was not your fault. It was my sin, my own demon that strangled me.* I could not speak to say the words—a mercy, since those words could never be said.

He reached down and stroked my hair. I leaned into his hand and accepted the comfort. The warmth permeated my skull, and the fierce headache that assailed me receded slightly. Tears flowed from my eyes; I was powerless to stop them. Manuel took a cloth and blotted them. "Josefina. Rest and get well." I nodded my limited nod, and he smiled tentatively. I smiled back, a grimace that was the uncontrolled extent of my ability. He bent and kissed my lips, and left.

A FORTNIGHT LATER, I could speak again. Haltingly, the words started to return. I had grown accustomed to the pain in my head, so unless I moved suddenly or there was a loud noise, I could bear it. And I could read. I did pray aloud this time, a prayer of thanksgiving that I could still read. The fingers of my left hand tingled, and I could move the smallest finger. Cayetana, seeing my progress, announced her fast-approaching wedding to me. "I beg your permission, as I must leave tomorrow and travel to the castle. I will be back in six days. You will be well."

"Go. Happy," I said. She smiled.

"Thank you, señora. I will bring you books, and gossip!" I squeezed her hand with my right hand. She transferred hers to my left hand. I tried to squeeze, but only partly succeeded. "Better," she said. "Continue taking your tea, and doing the tasks I have given you." I nodded, promising with my eyes to keep working on my hand, my words.

But without Cayetana, the days dragged. Manuel came in daily, sat and stroked my hair for a minute, and left. Anaya brought my medicinal tea, my food, and helped me with my cleanliness. And she brought the boys, but she would not let them stay. "It will tire your mama," she said firmly. Neto cried when he left me, and I haltingly told Anaya to leave him. "No, señora. We must preserve the life of your baby, and not risk God's greater punishment than you have already received." I vowed that as soon as Cayetana returned, I would get up, and send Anaya back to the kitchen where she belonged.

I was now at my fifth month of pregnancy, the time period when I had most enjoyed my condition with the boys. I longed to walk around, glory in the well-being and glow of pregnancy. But the headache, which had receded during the past month, was returning at night, and I found that I was having trouble eating again. I felt the nausea returning, and I feared a relapse. I did not dare risk any activity.

On the sixth day, Cayetana returned, a married woman. She was disgusted at my condition, blaming Anaya for allowing me to deteriorate, and immediately took back the reins of the sickroom. She brewed a new tea and added herbs brought from the castle's doctors and herbalists. The flavors were hideous, and I threw up the first dose, but Cayetana insisted, and I was able to take the second in tiny sips and keep it down.

In addition to the herbs, though, Cayetana brought me books. "These are from the sister, the one who writes," she said, and laid a parcel by my bed. I kept myself from grabbing at it. "And much gossip," she said, settling into her nursing chair.

I lay back on my pillow. "Tell me," I said. I wanted to see what was in the package from Sor Juana, but I was curious about the gossip. Besides, I knew that Cayetana would stay until she had had her way and told her news. "But first, tell me about your wedding."

"It was to be simple. The castle priest had posted the banns and we were simply to be wed the evening I arrived. A number of Ygnacio's friends were planning a celebration dinner for us, and we had some plans of our own for our wedding night. But we got a surprise. I, a humble Indian woman, a widow, and Ygnacio, who though a mestizo is highly educated and refined, were joined in holy wedlock by a bishop!"

I felt my heart bubble. "The Bishop of Puebla?" She nodded, pride suffusing her face. "Did you speak to him?"

Cayetana smiled. "Yes, señora, and he sends his regards. He is very sorry to hear of your illness, and assures me that he will stop in on his travels. But can you imagine such a thing? My first wedding was a two-minute event in the little shack that we used as a chapel out in the scrub, and my wedding night was under the stars. But here, in the castle chapel, with candles, and incense, and a bishop!"

I had to comment, for her sake. "You must be elated. What an honor! And your dress, what did you wear? Not your traveling dress, I hope?"

"No." She laughed. "Don't forget that I have married the Marqués' valet! I am almost a lady! Ygnacio had one of the women who tend to the Marquesa's clothing give me a dress. I have it still. The Marquesa said I was to keep it. She, too, sends her commendations." Cayetana got up from her chair, and in her excitement she seemed much younger than her more than thirty-five years. She brought forth from a traveling case a well-folded dress. She let it hang down in front of her. It was of a deep ochre, with red trim, very festive and yet suitable for Cayetana's native looks.

"It is beautiful. Perhaps tomorrow you would model it for me," I said. "Now, tell me about the Bishop."

"I have already told you, señora. But this is not what the entire castle is talking about. Not the Bishop, but of Doña Angélica. Did you hear?"

"No. I hope she is well?"

"Yes, I believe she is well. But she, too, will be visiting, and likely sooner than the Bishop ever will. But listen, for you will be scandalized. It appears that the Marqués' heir, Don Miguel Ángel, found her both attractive and lively, and was keeping company with her. Rumors spread of a possible engagement, which would have been lovely for Doña Angélica. Such a beautiful girl, and widowed so young. Though left with a fortune, of course, but no children. But before there could be an engagement, well, they say the Marqués took matters into his own hands."

"How do you mean?" I asked, but I feared the worst for Angélica. For though she was no innocent, as I had been, she, too, could be browbeaten into compliance.

"The Marqués made most unsuitable advances to her, at one of his dinners. He went much further than his regular teasing and playful behavior. This I am told personally by a friend, who waited on the table at the dinner and saw it with her own eyes. And when Doña Angélica protested, he acted as if to overcome her protests by force." I could well imagine the situation. "Of course, everyone at the dinner knew that the Marqués was simply playing with her, as he does with the ladies when he is in his cups, but Miguel Ángel was deeply offended, and knocked his father to the floor!"

"Oh, my heavens," I said. Secretly, I was delighted. "Miguel Ángel had seemed, when I met him so briefly at the ball, to be a young man of integrity. Of course, raising his hand to his father was a terrible mistake, but, nevertheless, deserved."

"Most likely, but of course Doña Angélica took the brunt of it. The heir has left for Mexico City, and Doña Angélica is the subject of gossip and ribald songs, and she cannot stay at the castle for the remainder of the season. I expect you will receive word from her soon, and that she will be here shortly after."

"She is welcome. Anyone fleeing from the Marqués is welcome."

"Ygnacio says the ladies bring the trouble on themselves, and his master only complies, but then, he, too, is a man."

"Yes, we will always be blamed when they slake their lusts with us.

If Angélica wishes to sojourn here on her way back to her lands, she is most welcome. I only wish I could do more to entertain her. My arm is almost better," I added.

"But your head is not, and I dread your getting up."

"I dread it more, for it is I who bear the pain. But I progress." Poor Angélica. I felt the pain of her distress. And my head was beginning to hurt again from all the talk, and, I was sure, from the memories that this gossip was stirring up. "I believe I will rest again, Cayetana. But one more thing. I want you to take over the care of the boys again. I do not like the ideas that young Anaya is putting in their heads."

"Certainly. I agree. But she will be sad. I will tell her that she will have principal care of the baby when she arrives." I felt my belly tighten. But it was far in the future; I still had four months to go. I closed my eyes.

As soon as Cayetana left, I tore open the package from Sor Juana. Books tumbled out, three of them, and two folded, sealed letters. One was in the precise and delicate script that I had seen on foolscap: Sor Juana's. And the other, as my heart pounded, was in the bold, flowing hand of Father Alonso. The pounding in my head took on thunderous proportions as I broke the seal on his first.

My esteemed lady,

I hope this finds you well, though reports say otherwise. Your departure has left the castle cold and the Court bereft of your beauty and your emerging wit. I, for one, regret any role I may have had in your precipitous departure, and censure myself for not having come sufficiently to your defense from certain depredations. But trust, my lady, that I in no way regret our blossoming friendship, nor the moments in which that friendship burst into the flames of spiritual and godly passion.

Your companion and sponsor has met with amorous reversals thanks to the predatory nature of my host, and is in need of your friendship more than ever. But be on guard that your trusting nature is not overwhelmed, and that your willingness to open your heart and home is not taken at advantage. For it is your openness and willingness that invariably lead you into loss.

My prayers to heaven are for your unborn babe, and for your health as well. The mood in the castle is strained by the events above described, and the tolerance by the motherland and its colonial tentacles for learning and discourse is likewise diminishing. Immorality, obfuscation, and sophistry are conquering study and rational discourse, leaving only one side of the question, theirs. I fear that I, and the good sister, may have to find shelter elsewhere. I will write anon. Please burn this letter at once.

Yours, in Our Lord,

Alonso

I read it twice. No, that would be a lie, for I must have read it a hundred times. I no longer thought of the package of books, or of Sor Juana's letter, for each word here was fraught with countless meanings. I took it apart like a Jesuit, searching for the message behind words that could, or couldn't, get past an intervening Inquisitor.

He did not close with the standard "KYH" as he had in the last note I'd had from him, on the night of the ball, so long ago. I had to recall the time Manuel had received a formal letter from the *alcalde* of our area. "I Kiss Your Hands?" Manuel had said, and laughed. "I kiss your ass is more to the point! What an effeminate way to close a letter!" He and I did not know, of course, that it was the accepted closing. Only when I had taken over the management of the hacienda completely had I learned of the usage.

Here, Alonso had closed with something more intimate, and yet he had cloaked it in godliness. All of the intimacy had been swathed in religion, in case the letter was lost. And yet, he remembered. And he did not regret. I felt the pounding in my head grow worse.

And the language against the Holy Office! That paragraph alone was enough to get us both arrested. He was a fool to write it, and yet it must have been critical for him to include it, to risk himself, and me, by its writing. Why did I need to know this?

I got up to burn the letter. The room swirled again, and I sat on the edge of the bed waiting for it to still. My belly clutched, cramping. Was I in danger of the Inquisition? Would they come for me, in my condition? Would they torture Father Alonso, and would he confess to our misdeed? Then they needn't kill me, for Manuel would. Again my stomach cramped. I must burn this letter, and decide what to do.

I reached for the package with the books and letter from Sor Juana, and shoved it under the bed. When my head was clear again, I would open the letter and look at the books. I was shaking and sweating. I had to get up, go to the fireplace, and burn the letter with the flame from the candle.

Holding the letter in one hand, and gripping the edge of the table with the other, I stood. My head roared. I wobbled to the fireplace, picked up the candle. In the heat of summer, of course, there was no fire in the hearth, but it was the only place to burn something. I read the words one last time, but the letters swam on the page, and I feared I would set the room ablaze if I fell, so I crumpled the letter into a ball. I kissed it, lit it, and tossed it into the fireplace.

It is harder to burn a letter completely than one would think. The flame went out. I had to relight the ball of paper, for I needed it to be rendered ashes, beyond ashes, so no vestige remained. The paper's clerical thickness deterred the flame, much as our skin would deter the flames of the stake. The image roiled my stomach, and I swallowed bile, bitter and noxious.

I bent to relight the remnants one last time. My hands and forehead were wet. I replaced the candle and tried to get back to my bed. I felt sweat run down my breasts, and then down my legs. The cramping increased. When I got to my bed, I sat, fearful that as soon as I lay down I would vomit. It was then that I noticed the spreading stain of red on my gown. Mixed with the running sweat was the blood of birth, birth that would be death at five months. I called for Cayetana, and called once more. Tears of fury, sorrow, despair flowed. My baby was dying, and she was dying for my sins. And I, it could be, would be going with her.

THE PAINS CONTINUED, INCREASING in frequency and severity, for a day. Blood flowed, stopped, and flowed again. Cayetana tried all of her poultices, teas, and herbs, burning sage, and crushing leaves of maguey from Guadalajara and rubbing me with their juice. She saved my life, but in the earliest hour of daylight, a night and a day and a night since I began, the babe, indeed a girl, tiny and yet complete in her minuscule perfection, emerged, dead and blue.

With her came the rush of fluid, the blanket of thick tissue that had enveloped her in my womb, and the cord that attached her heart to mine. As it emerged, it took with it the piece of my heart that it owned, to accompany her soul to heaven. Our priest from the village came and blessed her, so her soul could ascend without sin, and he blessed me, too. I turned my head away, denying his power, but he took it as grief and rubbed the holy oil into my temples. I slept.

When I awoke, my head did not hurt. I sat up, weak and depleted, and did not feel nausea. Manuel, who had waited outside my room throughout my entire ordeal, was sitting by my side. I reached for his hand, and he took mine and held it. Our daughter was dead. But I was fertile, and there would be others. He left for a moment, when Cayetana came in to change my dressings, but he returned, and again took my hand. I slept again, deep and calm, and awoke to the sun streaming into my room, and Manuel asleep in the chair beside me.

PART TWO

$\mathcal{T}$HIRTEEN

$\mathcal{I}$N A WEEK, I was up and around. The priest gave a Mass for her little soul, and Antonia was buried in the plot behind the church. The coffin was as small as a Bible, and was draped in white linen embroidered with tiny pink roses. On her grave, I put a bouquet of the same roses, with a sprig of rosemary. I leaned on Manuel's arm as the holy Mass was said, and I prayed for her, for myself, and for the peace of forgiveness. We walked from the grave silently, and I was grateful for his strength and silence. Never before had I appreciated the beauty of few words, or none.

Joaquín took the news in stride as much as a little man of six could. He mirrored his father's solemn look, his grim silence, but he was down at the stables within hours of the burial, and I was glad. Neto, whose age would have excused his absence from such sorrowful services, clung to my hand, tears coursing down his cheeks. He would not let me leave him behind, but followed us to the grave. "I can see her spirit," he whispered. "She has shining wings." I was relieved when we returned to the house for *atole* and churros, marking the end of the solemnities.

My physical improvement after the miscarriage was, to me, a sign from God. I had not been worthy of that child, and His gentle strokes, the little paralyses and the muteness that He had favored me with, had taught me a lesson. I would forbear from sin and live a just life, to be worthy of the next child He sent.

"Good morning, Manuel," I said to my husband the morning after the Mass of Christian burial. "Can I bring you your coffee?"

He was surprised and pleased to see me at breakfast, and showed it with his smile. "Would you like a sweet roll?" he asked, handing me a plate of *pan dulce*. I took one. And so it was that we returned to a gentle concourse, kindly and cautious. But my heart had a gouge where my dreams had been, and he dared not approach me at night.

As summer was drawing to a close, there was much to be done, in the fields and in the home. Now that I was up, Cayetana had taken back the nursery, and I felt that the boys were being well cared for again, their heads not being stuffed with archaic and ignorant country nonsense. Nevertheless, with all the work, Neto's reading lessons had ceased, but as he was barely three, it did not matter. When Joaquín was ready for a tutor, perhaps in another year, Neto could learn at his side. There was no hurry, for books, I knew, were a mixed blessing.

Manuel was busy, and I was meticulous in going through the accounts, making sure that the harvest and the livestock records were up-to-date. Our dinner conversation had never been lively, and now it centered only on business. Neither of us mentioned the grief of mourning for our lost daughter. At night, he did not come to my bed, perhaps respecting the traditional forty-day abstention after childbirth. And I was far from receptive to any amorous advances. My heart, my body, and my womb were too raw.

In the midst of the harvest, Angélica came. Despite Cayetana's tale of her woes and Father Alonso's allusions, she looked well. Her lovely complexion still glowed, her hair was still golden, her body slim but curvaceous. Her dress was not luxurious, for she had been traveling, but the colors, cream and copper, made the most of her many gifts. Her arrival brought diversion into our home, and an arrow of memory into my heart.

I had not opened Sor Juana's letter. It lay in the package beneath my bed, along with the books she had sent, gathering dust and cobwebs. I had pushed any thought of Father Alonso into the recesses of my mind, and had sealed the way with Antonia's birth-and-death blood. I had put away my Court dresses, and, most of all, I had not opened a book, other than my account books, since losing Antonia. But with Angélica's visit, all that I had been trying to forget came crashing down on me. For the first time in several weeks, the headache returned.

But I mustered the will to greet her and entertain her. For our dinner on the first night of her visit, I made sure that our nicest plates and cups were shined and put on the table. Our dining room, a long room with soft candlelight all around, was prepared as lovingly as for a visiting mother. Or what I imagined I would do, had Manuel or I a mother to receive. Angélica could feel the welcome, I am sure, since she ate and drank comfortably at our table.

"Tell us of the goings-on in that faraway Court of yours," Manuel said, eager, I could see, for Angélica's tales. For though I was far better read, she could tell a tale with style and interest. It occurred to me that Manuel, though he had the freedom of a wealthy man, had never been to such an exotic place. Maybe he shared the yearning that I had felt before I had ventured out.

"I was poorly used by the Marqués, and by the Marqués' heir, as well," she said bluntly. I was shocked. She was going to tell this tale at dinner, and to a man! She looked at me and arched her brow, daring me to stop her. I could not.

"How so?" Manuel asked.

"Let me begin with your wife's last evening in Court," she said. I held my breath. I had not worried much about Manuel learning of my misadventures. There was no overlap in our acquaintanceship. Except, of course, for Angélica.

"Please tell me all about Josefina's experience. Poor woman, she has been too ill, these past months, to tell me anything at all."

"Josefina! Surely you could overcome a headache to entertain such a benevolent husband, one who allowed you the freedom to go to Court, one who lets you read and write, and who buys you such beautiful gowns! Don't tell me, Manuel, that your wife is an ingrate!" She smiled as she said this, her eyes sparkling, and Manuel laughed.

"No, my dear, not an ingrate," he said, turning to me and patting my hand. "But tell on!" he said to Angélica.

As it had been before, I felt invisible, as Angélica and Manuel connected through her lively storytelling. "Josefina made quite the impression on the Marqués' heir," she said. "The night of the grand ball welcoming him home, he could barely be torn from her side. He is but twenty-five, you know, and just returned from the university at Salamanca, in Spain. He is full of big ideas, and of course he picked out the intellectual in the room to share them."

"My wife was the intellectual?"

"Oh, no, Manuel, but she was under the spell of a lettered poetess nun, who writes both sacred and scandalous poetry under the protection of the Bishop of Puebla. And so she was seen in the library, with the sister, with the Marquesa, and even"—she paused dramatically—"with the Bishop."

I shook violently, and Manuel turned to me. "Are you all right, my dear? I do not want you to suffer a relapse."

Angélica was looking too closely at me. I should have known, since so little went unnoticed, and she had the sharpest eye of all. But I had been sure that she was oblivious to my tryst.

"I am perfectly well, husband. It was just the first chill of autumn. Go on, Angélica," I forced myself to say. "We want to hear what happened to you, since I already know what I experienced."

"But I do not," Manuel broke in. "Josefina, my dear, you did not tell me you were acknowledged by the Bishop of Puebla! That's quite an honor."

"It was indeed. Had I not fallen ill, I would have told you. But let us not take the attention from Angélica, who is so recently arrived. You and I, may God will it, have a whole life to tell our tales."

"But at the ball," Angélica continued, "I had the pleasure of becoming acquainted with the heir. He was in intimate conversation with Josefina, but I could not resist pushing myself between them for an introduction." She laughed at her own self-deprecating description, calling attention to the wording.

"And did they part for your intrusion?" Manuel asked, joining in the fun.

"As if caught in a darkened doorway by the peace officer!"

I blushed. "No such thing, Angélica. We were discussing numbers and stanzas of poems, and you came up, and he could not look away from your beauty. I had no choice but to introduce you, and yield my place in the conversation, for if I had tried to maintain my primacy, I would have been talking to myself the rest of the evening."

"You did leave in a pique, immediately after," she said.

I shook my head. "Not in a pique, Angélica. I was tired, and perhaps my condition was making me weary as well."

"Since you say so," she said. "In any event, he was indeed left with me for conversation, and though I have not Josefina's sensibilities, we did find topics upon which to converse the rest of the evening. We also danced the last ronda—and, Josefina, I noticed that you did not dance at all—and we walked in the moonlight around the castle grounds thereafter.

"In the next several days, he called on me, and we spent hours together in pleasant conversation. You know, of course, that as a widow I have the freedom to converse, unchaperoned, with whomever I please, but none-theless, rumors began to fly. Manuel, you can have no idea how rumors are cultivated at the Court. In fact, Josefina, you should hear some of the rumors you incited."

"As my behavior was faultless, I am surprised there was fodder for tales," I said. Dear God, I prayed, let her shut her mouth.

"Eustacia told me some amazing stories, but then, that is what she lives by. And I came to regret the interest I took in them, for she repaid me most unkindly, with stories of my undoing which far exceeded the sorrowful facts."

"Who is Eustacia?" Manuel asked, all ears.

"She is the poor cousin of the Marquesa," I said. "She is of a side lineage, and though of the same blood she has none of the wealth or prestige of the main line, and so she barters information for her supper." Manuel raised his eyebrows at me, surprised, I suppose, by the sharpness of my answer.

"And so she is someone to be feared, and favored," I finished.

He smiled. "Josefina, I knew from the moment I laid eyes on you in your father's house that you were a rare jewel." I did not know why he said that, but I was pleased at the public praise. I smiled back, into his eyes.

Angélica intruded, and we turned our attention back to our guest. "For reasons that I do not wish to fathom, the Marqués, and the Marquesa as well, did not want to see a match between me and the heir. Perhaps they have hopes of a greater family. But my lineage is pure, I have no Jewish or Moorish taint; I have wealth from my father and my husband, may they rest in peace; and if my first marriage yielded no heir, I doubt the blame lies with me. After all, my husband was close to fifty, and he had been married for twenty years, to two other women, and had no children. I was but seventeen when he wed me, and married just a year, and the barrenness is unlikely to have been mine."

"Perhaps the Marquesa hoped for a daughter with interests more similar to her own," I said, recalling the conversation in the library.

Angélica shrugged. "It was her son's marriage, not hers. But it was not the Marquesa who scuttled it, it was the Marqués."

I recalled what I had been told. Knowing the propensities of the Marqués, it was likely.

"Tell us," Manuel said.

"It is not usually for gentle ears, or dinner conversation, but you, sir, are worldly, and Josefina has seen it with her own eyes, so I will not shock you. The Marqués is known, Manuel, for his inappropriate behavior with ladies, including ladies of quality. He cares not if they are married, or rich, or of high position. He is greedy and feels that it is his right to possess any female in his castle."

"Surely not the highborn ladies!"

"Oh, yes. Not simply the servants or the land-tenants. He was even seen pawing at your wife." Manuel looked shocked. His head spun to me. Angélica laughed. "But fear not, Don Manuel, she acquitted herself with dutiful and pious fidelity to you. You should have heard her reject the Marqués. The entire Court talked of nothing else for a day!"

Manuel's eyes still bored in at me. "Bastard! To make advances on my wife!" He slammed his hand on the table. I had never seen him so handsome. I put my hand on his shoulder, and he exhaled hard.

"It is true, Manuel," I said. "He did make lewd suggestions, but nothing more. And he did that to everyone, so please don't take it as a personal affront to you. And the ladies, they did gossip about me, for rejecting, somewhat publicly, his advances. But I could do no less." I felt a strange stirring, recalling the punishment I suffered for that rejection, not from the ladies, but from the Marqués' assault on me the next day. "I bloodied his nose," I added.

It was Angélica's turn to look surprised. "So that was true? I thought it was more of Eustacia's nonsense. Why didn't you tell me?"

"It seemed to reflect poorly on me." That, at least, was true.

Manuel shook his head, visibly slowing his breath, forcing himself to regain his composure. I had known he would be furious, and I had never intended to tell him, but under the circumstances he handled his anger well. "What a cesspool," he said. "You bloodied his nose? How, my love?"

"Like Joaquín, with my fist!" He smiled, and the mood lightened. But he was still intrigued. "So, what happened, Angélica?"

Angélica closed her eyes, a faint blush upon her cheeks. "I was in the garden, for it had become very warm inside, and there was no breeze. I was seated on a bench, in a secluded part of the garden, hidden by tall lattices of bougainvillea, and truth be told, I was waiting for Miguel Ángel. The heir. I closed my eyes against the light and, unwillingly, felt my mind wander, for I had been keeping the late Court hours, and the heat made me sleepy.

"I heard a rustling, but did not open my eyes, for Miguel Ángel had promised to meet me at this time, and I wanted to let him find me unawares. It would heighten the courtship game."

Manuel licked his lips. His eyes were locked on her. Even I was drawn in. "Then I felt a hand on the back of my neck, and I smiled, my eyes still shut. It was a perfect approach, and I knew Miguel Ángel would kiss me. I lifted my chin. I was hoping for a proposal of marriage in the garden, and I could think of no better way to begin. Before his lips touched mine, I felt his hand caress my breast." I bit back a gasp. Could such a tale be told at dinner? But it could.

"He touched it, and I shivered, forcing myself to keep from responding more. Then, again, he touched me, but this time not as gently, not at all, and when he pinched me, my eyes snapped open, in time to see the Marqués' enormous nose coming down on my face. Before I could stop him, his mouth was upon mine, with his hand in an iron hold on the back of my neck so I could not move away. He forced his tongue into my mouth, and pulled back on my hair to open my mouth further.

"His right hand had my breast in his grasp, and the kneading and pinching made me squirm away, but he leaned over me, and with his leg he trapped me and kept me on the bench. He pressed me back until I reclined, and he drove his leg between mine. I pressed against him with my hands, but I am not strong, like Josefina. I was powerless beneath him. Every time I moved it seemed to further his terrible goals, for he was now fully atop me, with my legs spread open beneath him.

"At that moment, I heard a voice: 'Father!' It was Miguel Ángel. I squirmed. But Miguel Ángel must have misinterpreted my actions, for he read them as passion, not fury. 'Get away from her!' he cried, but the Marqués simply lifted his mouth from mine and said, 'I'm not finished, son. Come back in an hour.'"

Manuel laughed.

I stared at him. "This is not a story for the dinner table," I said primly.

"Josefina, you, my dear, would have bloodied his nose again! And good for you," Manuel said. "But let Angélica finish, for this cannot be the end of the story."

I had no choice but to let this travesty play to the end.

"Miguel Ángel dragged his father off me. They stood, face-to-face, the son furious, the father laughing. I pulled myself back to sitting and tried to rearrange my clothes and hair, but their eyes were fixed on each other. 'You are despicable!' Miguel Ángel said to his father. 'No, son,' the Marqués replied, 'I am simply a man, who saw a beautiful woman enter a secluded garden. Perhaps you should be more circumspect about your assignations. Look now to your lady, who pines for your attentions.' At this further insult to my honor, Miguel Ángel could take no more, and with a swift move, threw his father to the ground. Then, with no further look at either of us, he walked away. By the time I returned to the castle, he had left for Mexico City, the Court was buzzing with my shameful story, and I was cut dead by the Marquesa."

I rose from the table. It was indeed unfair, and unfortunate, that Angélica had so suffered, but I could not help but think that she had brought her misery upon herself. Even though I, too, had been a target of the Marqués, she had put herself in a compromising position with the heir. Her regret was not for the assault on her virtue, but for the fact that it was the wrong assailant. Then again, I chided myself, I was not so different. And I wondered, too, if the Marquesa had instigated some of this, both by rejecting Angélica as a possible daughter-in-law and, perhaps, by encouraging the Marqués to attack her when he knew that his son would catch him.

The Court was indeed a venal place, I thought, as I readied myself for bed. But I realized, too, that I was stimulated, and my thoughts for the first time strayed to the books under my bed. I felt a distant longing to return to the Court, and this time, with so much greater knowledge, get more of what was there to be seen and learned.

I washed with special care. The look on Manuel's face as Angélica had told her story, and his masculine reaction to the troubles she described, could possibly be translated into action. Perhaps tonight would be the first time since before the miscarriage that he would come to my bed. Though my forty days since the unfortunate birth had not yet passed, and though I feared his coming to me, I knew that I longed for it. I perfumed the washing water, and I put on my most beautiful nightgown. I dressed my hair with care, plaiting it into soft braids on either side of my head. I aired the coverlet, lit a candle, and opened the shutters for the sweet night breeze.

I lay awake late into the night. Eventually I heard footsteps, Manuel's rhythmic walk, but he went past my door. My heart beat wildly, and tears were in my eyes. I pulled the pillow over my ears to keep from hearing his belt hit the floor. An hour later I heard him walking back, and the sound of his door closing for the night.

Fourteen

*O*F COURSE I WASN'T surprised, only hurt. And I was angry, though my condition had doubtless been the cause of this affront. I did not expect celibacy from my husband, but I certainly would not tolerate his bedding of a lady in my home.

The next morning, Angélica slept in, and Manuel was in the fields supervising the harvest by the time I emerged. The sun shone into the windows, all the shutters were open, and fresh coffee, brewed with cinnamon, steamed in the kitchen. I took a cup, mixed into it some milk newly drawn and still warm, and carried it out to the wide veranda that encircled the house. I sat on a wooden chair with a woven seat and back, and sipped at my drink.

I could hear the shouts of the men in the field. Harvesttime was a joyful period for us, especially in a year like this one, bounteous and healthy. Cattle lowed, far off, away from the house, and there was activity everywhere. I knew without seeing them that Manuel, with Joaquín jumping along at his side, was out there, instructing, directing, and helping. Later in the month, before the rains, he would be gone for weeks on end, taking this year's cattle to market, but this was the time of fields, of Cain, not Abel.

My weeks would be busy until Manuel left; books and accounts were an important part of a successful hacienda's harvest. There were men to feed, and so the kitchen staff had to be supplemented with extra women to cook the food for the additional hired men who worked the harvest. Cayetana and I would have long, full days, and I would work into the evening by candlelight these next several weeks.

But once that was done, and Manuel left with the herds, a sort of peace would descend on the hacienda. In years past, I had welcomed this peace, for it was then that I played with one son, then with two, that I sewed, and dreamed my dreams. Now a foreign thought entered my mind, polluted my soul. Maybe, once the rains came, I could return to the Court, this time to find the Bishop, if he was still there, and to seek out Sor Juana openly. No longer ignorant, I would study and read with her without shame or pretense.

For now, though, I had an untenable situation on my hands, one I was at a loss to manage. I could banish Angélica, and both she and Manuel would very well know why. But I did not want to give her the satisfaction of knowing my heart. I put a shield of stone around myself. Until I could decide my course of action, I would betray no emotion.

I put my cup down and went to my room. Kneeling and reaching, I felt under the bed for the package I had thrown there so precipitously a month before. It was way in the back, and I brushed the sticky cobwebs from it to keep from getting them on my dress.

I meant to take the package to the veranda. I would no longer cower in hiding with my books. But I heard Angélica's door open, and my nerve failed me. I sat silently, listening to her footfall on the tiled floor as she walked past my room, and then I tore open Sor Juana's letter. It was a poem in prose.

> *Josefina, the trail of blood you leave / in swift departure*
> *needs / no words to mark your cause / or songs to sing your*
> *loss. / Our sin—blameworthy are we, / in word and thought*
> *and deed— / will drive us on to more / to blacken deep our*
> *souls: For tasted of blood we have, / with eyes, and lips, and grave.*

I read it over and over, until the words were seared into my mind, as Father Alonso's had been. She knew. He had told her. For why else would she say what she said? I felt the tears of shame begin to dissolve my will. And yet, she equated us. But how could that be, when she was renowned to the point where, if Father Alonso and the gossips were to be believed, the Holy Office had taken dangerous notice of her? And I was but a country wife, with dreams of learning.

If I returned to the Court, if I put myself in Sor Juana's learned hands, would the Holy Office come after me? And what would Manuel think, if suddenly his humble wife were a target of the Inquisition? Maybe he would be intrigued, I thought bitterly, and come to my bed. But the reality of the risk overshadowed that fanciful thought. Would the Inquisitors seize his lands? His wealth? Would I be destroying him, and the livelihood of my beautiful boys, to indulge in some far-fetched dream?

"Far-fetched" was the significant word, I decided. For no matter how much I immersed myself in reading and studying, I would never be a target. I was nobody. I had never written a poem in my life, or a play about workers, or a tract on religion. All I had ever written, I reminded myself, were the accounts of a prosperous hacienda. Yet flights of fancy were perhaps more natural to me than I had suspected.

I burned Sor Juana's poem to me. I understood the message, and there was no more need to have that in my room than there had been to keep Father Alonso's letter. Despite having buried that letter in my heart for a month, I could still recite it. And I felt an unholy stirring with the memory of his importunities. Perhaps, as he had said, he would have taken refuge elsewhere. I would find out.

I gathered up the three books and left my room. I walked out to the veranda, picked up my cup, and went into the kitchen to refill it. As I was going back out to my chair I passed Angélica in the dining room, sipping chocolate. "Good morning, Angélica," I said. I would keep my pride.

"Good morning, Josefina," she answered. She looked away. Fine. Let her feel shame.

"I hope you have rested from your journey," I added, and continued to the veranda. She put her cup down and made as if to follow. "No, do not get up. I have a bit of reading to do, and then we need to get on with the work of the day. Eat your breakfast." She sat back down, looking at her cup. As she said nothing, I continued out to the veranda, and put the books down. My hands were sweating and slippery. Dignity was a difficult thing to accomplish with one's hands full.

I opened the first book. It was a collection of ten poems by Calderón. The second, a play by Lope de Vega, who wrote *Sheep's Well,* called *The Gentleman of Olmedo.* And last, unbelievably, was a play by Sor Juana herself, called *The Household's Dilemma.* I was astonished, and deeply moved, that she would send me her own work, meticulously copied in her beautiful, small, and precise hand. It was that play that I started with.

THE SUN'S POSITION, AND the bell calling the men in to eat, told me that I had read for over half the morning, and into the early afternoon. Though my head hurt, it was not the knife-driven pain that I had felt during my pregnancy, but a dull ache from the stretching of my brain to fit all of those new words inside. And my heart was keeping pace with the story, pounding in fear, in love and despair, as Leonor and Ana fought against destiny to marry the man they loved.

I was not sure how I felt about them, or their fates. I was uncomfortable with the character Leonor, whose description of herself was so unlike me, and who, after an apology for her honesty, called herself "beautiful, discreet, and so studious that I reduced to short work, the laborious studies of a week." Not so I, who was merely discreet. Leonor had fled her father's house at midnight, with her lover, and when thwarted, had spent the following pages wallowing in her shame and self-pity. I had not yet finished the play, but I hoped that she would regain her spirit before the end.

And Ana, who received Leonor after her flight, had to live with the viper in her own home, since the lover Leonor had fled with was Ana's own beloved. Her words stung me this morning. "Heavens, in what a fix I am: in love with Carlos, pursued by Juan, and with my own enemy in my home!" How had Sor Juana known?

The dinner bell snapped my reverie, and I closed the folio. A slim pamphlet fell to the ground. "Abecedario," the cover read. I opened it. Inside was a beautifully illustrated alphabet, each letter drawn in gold and black, with tiny animals, angels, flowers, and other embellishments all around it. I smiled. It would be joy to teach Neto from this. Still smiling, I was able to greet Manuel as he came in from the fields.

He, of course, being a man, felt no shame in his behavior of the night before, and smiled right back at me. "I'm starving, Josefina. I am ready to eat." He strode ahead of me into the house, and stopped to take off his boots. "Reading?" I nodded. "Where did you get the books?"

"Cayetana brought them from the Court when she went to marry Ygnacio. I had not thought of them since."

"How thoughtful," he said, and walked on, now in his stocking feet.

"Look at this alphabet book," I said, catching up to him. I showed him the lovely illustrations. "I can teach the boys with this."

"How wonderful," he said. "I know that will please you. Let's eat."

Quickly, I returned to my room and slid the books back under the bed. Manuel cared not at all if I read, but I was not going to dilute my pleasure by having Angélica remark on them. And dinner would be awkward enough.

When I got back into the dining room, Angélica and Manuel were already there. He seated me, then her. She blushed. He did not. You have a lot to learn about married men, Angélica, I thought. I filled the dinner plates in silence.

"Manuel, tell me about the crops. What are you harvesting?" Angélica asked.

"Corn," Manuel said, around his mouthful. She waited, but he said no more.

"Angélica, tell us more about your adventures at Court after I left," I said, with a hint of malice. "Were there other balls, other soirees?"

Angélica took the bait, and Manuel looked up from his plate, making me sorry I had set the hook. "The Bishop, your friend, gave a fiery sermon the Sunday before I had my contretemps with the Marqués. He spoke against using learning to question God. As if anyone would do that."

"Reading is a fine occupation for ladies," Manuel said, smiling at me. "It is a waste of time for a man, who has work to do if his family is to eat. Unless he's a cleric, devoted to reading as compensation for his celibacy!"

I thought of Father Alonso's celibacy, and wished I had never raised the subject of the Court. But Angélica had acute feminine intuition, and was determined to exploit what she could sense was my delicate friendship with the Bishop.

"Letters, he said, were meant to be servants, not ladies of the manor, and the letters, like the slaves they were, existed only to serve the Lord. And he urged women, especially, to be mindful of this stricture, and said that while reading was an acceptable occupation for a woman, provided the topic of the reading was godly, teaching was out of the question, for that led to vanity. And women, he assured us correctly, are so deeply prone to vanity!"

At this I was able to laugh. "Oh, well, if that was his concern, his audience was well chosen, for I have never met a more vain group of ladies. The fixation on the toilette was a sin!" It was Angélica's turn to blush.

"I do not believe it was that sort of vanity he was chastising, but the kind that sets oneself up as superior, thanks to the exercise of the mind."

It was a neat dodge for Father Alonso, I realized, designed to draw suspicious Inquisitorial minds away from himself and Sor Juana. But I did not let it rest. "Like Sor Juana's, perhaps?" I asked. "For he is her protector, and the Marquesa is her patron, so it is unlikely that he would be condemning the castle poetess from the pulpit, don't you think?"

Manuel put his spoon down. "Enough of this palaver. The day is too long and the sun is too hot for this nonsense. If you ladies wish to discuss the finer points of poetry after I have eaten, do so then. For now, either eat in silence or be amusing."

"I am sorry, husband," I said humbly. I poured him a tall glass of tamarind water, sweet and tart, and refreshing against the heat. I had never heard him speak that emphatically, but then again our mealtimes were usually spent either quietly or with minimal, business conversation. And besides, I took great and most vainly feminine satisfaction in his annoyance with Angélica.

She, in fact, took his rebuke to heart, and with flushed cheeks she ate in silence. When the meal was finished, I smiled at her. "Go rest, Angélica. You are not used to the ways of the hacienda, and I wouldn't want you yawning when we are at supper tonight."

She had no choice but to obey. She knew now that I knew, and that I was not going to let her lord her conquest of last night over me. As she left the room I said to Manuel, taking care that she could hear me, "When you go with the cattle next month, I would like to return to Court. There was much I could have learned. This time, I will be able to take full advantage of my experience. Would you consider permitting it?"

Manuel looked up, surprised. I could see Angélica lurking in the hallway, awaiting his answer. She could not go back in a month, as she had just left in disgrace. It was questionable if she could ever go back.

"Certainly, if it would make you happy. You have been so sad of late, and so sick, that I would permit anything that would restore you."

"I am grateful, Manuel. I am blessed with you as a husband."

For a moment he actually looked shamefaced. Then he smiled.

"Back to the fields. I will need a hot bath when I come in tonight. See to it, would you?"

"Of course. And now, let me see Joaquín. He should rest before returning to join you. He will be a grubby little man!"

Manuel kissed the top of my head, and went back to the hall to pull on his boots.

FIFTEEN

*M*Y READING HAD BECOME much slower than it had been before my illness, and I had not been quick to begin with. "You
will tire your eyes, Josefina," Manuel said when he found me reading
by candlelight. He didn't linger to stop me, but continued to the parlor
where Angélica sat with her needlepoint. I immediately stopped my
reading and joined them, taking a glass of sherry, interrupting their conversation of light laughter and stories. As on the past few nights, they fell
silent, and then took up the discussion again in stilted and uncomfortable
terms.

I did not delude myself, but I was not going to relinquish Manuel to
Angélica. "Angélica, you must grow weary of our company. Should you
go on, back to your lands?" I said.

"I do not manage my estate, as you do yours," she said. "I have over-
seers and counting-men to do that work."

"I am most proud of the work my wife does here," Manuel interjected.
Like so many men, having achieved his conquest, he was interested only
when the topics were designed to amuse him. To maintain his interest,
Angélica would have to work at it.

"Manuel, have I told you about my visit to Madrid, when I was
introduced to our young queen?" she asked him.

"You were about to, the other evening," he replied, "but you did not. I
would love to hear the story."

"It was my wedding trip. My husband, having business with the royal
family, took the trip every three years. It is a dangerous and long voyage;
the seas are treacherous, and the denizens more so. But he took it into his

head to bring his young bride with him, both imperiling me and giving me the adventure of a lifetime."

"You mentioned that you sighted pirates," he said, all senses now engaged.

"We were sighted by pirates, to be more precise. And there is nothing romantic about them. They are ruthless cutthroats, filthy and debased. And, without bringing coarse talk into this charming parlor, they are evil and cruel to women before they kill them." Her cheeks glowed.

"The experience should have well prepared you for someone as tame as the Marqués," I said.

"But fortunately for me, for if I had had any such experience I would not be here to recount it, the Lord smiled upon our ship, and we were able to evade their predatory nature with the help of a heaven-sent storm."

"A storm at sea must be an awesome sight," Manuel said. "I have been to the Veracruz port, and when the sea is riled, the waves can reach above our roof. A poor ship, tossed on such a sea, would need a miracle to survive."

"It was indeed fearsome, and though we were thanking God for sending the storm, we were also praying for its cessation. In our little stateroom, our meager belongings, those not stored in trunks below, were tossed about until we could barely find our shoes. I lay in the bunk, sick to death."

"Doubtless when calm returned, you were returned to the pink of health," I said, "for you are of an iron constitution."

Angélica looked for the insult in my words but could find none. "You are right, Josefina. For I am strongly made."

"A pity you were not blessed, then, with children. For you would bear them well." I was growing angrier by the moment, for my attempt at scuttling her stories was not going well. And yet, I felt certain, they were inventions.

"The Lord did not see fit to bless me so." She could not argue that one, but it had been a low shot, and unworthy of me. What I wanted most was to make her ridiculous, and instead I felt inadequate, and my yearning to see the world outside the hacienda returned with jealous force.

Manuel had been quiet through our exchange. Though he was not verbal, he was no fool. I was sure he caught the drift of my fury, and Angélica's attitude of superiority toward me. "I believe it would be good for you, my wife, to again adventure out to the Court. You have seen so little of the world, and unlike many women, you are not content within this narrow sphere. Will you accompany her again, Angélica?"

My heart sank. Here, with one hand, he was giving me the freedom I craved, but with the other he was tying the noose around my neck. I did not wish to be chaperoned by Angélica, and had no need of her. But a voice deep within reminded me that if Angélica were with me at Court, she could not be with Manuel. I weighed whether the freedom was worth the fear.

Angélica preempted my decision. "I cannot return, Manuel, as you surely understand. Not without an invitation from the Marquesa, which I doubt would be forthcoming."

"I will be traveling with my cattle, and so would hate to leave Josefina here without me after her illness. If she can obtain an invitation, I would like her to go, but I dislike the idea of her being there alone."

So, of course, Manuel would not be here. Angélica would have to return to her own home. "I have an invitation, should I wish it, from Sor Juana," I said. "She is a learned nun, in the service of the Marquesa, and will be suitable company for me there."

"She is an intellectual," Angélica said. I realized with a triumphant heart that she was jealous, that I could return and she could not.

"You were the one who told me about the intellectual life at Court, before we went the first time," I reminded her. "Do not despair, Angélica. I will do what I can to smooth the waters between you and the Marquesa. But do not expect a proposal from the heir. I am certain she will not permit that!" I smiled.

Angélica pursed her lips, and again I thought that she would not age well.

"Besides," I added maliciously, "the Marquesa is very forgiving of the Marqués' foibles. She understands the weakness of men, and the ultimate value of the wifely status."

In the silence that followed, I wondered if I had gone too far. But a glance at Manuel told me that he understood my comment. He was smiling a tiny smile at me, admiration in his eyes. Angélica rose without comment and went to bed. The next morning, at breakfast, she announced her departure. I wished her Godspeed, and meant it.

THE INVITATION I REQUESTED was not long in coming. The Marquesa was grieved to hear of my loss, and she welcomed me for a visit to wait upon her for a season. The temperature between Manuel and me mirrored the waning of the summer heat. We were cordial and kind, but no more than that. He did not come to my bed, and I did not expect him.

I prepared for my departure by reading, rereading, and trying to understand the books that Sor Juana had sent me. I pored over the words, looking for hidden meanings, and finding them. If I had missed the meanings so often, how much more had I missed before? The thought engendered a deep dissatisfaction in me.

I also prepared by teaching Neto and Joaquín their letters. Despite the age difference, they learned at almost the same pace, with Neto being the more serious of the two students. No two children are alike, I knew, and so I praised Joaquín all the more. By the time I was set to leave, Neto could read and write his name, and make out some of the simple words in the *abecedario*. Joaquín could read his name, but it was a much harder one to write. To my delight, though, he seemed to appreciate the poems I read to him and his brother. He said they sounded like music.

Joaquín was pleading almost without pause to accompany his father on the cattle drive.

"But he is barely six years old," I protested, when Manuel broached the subject. "He will be tired, and he will get in the way."

"He wants to go. He's heard the men talk about our adventures, and maybe it's time for him to be a part of them."

"If I were not going to Court, I would permit it, but if I go, Neto will be alone. And I would worry myself into illness."

That stopped Manuel. "I do not want you to be ill. I want you to go to Court, to recover. I want my wife home, healthy and strong again."

"I am healthy again."

He hesitated. "I want you the way you were."

We stared at each other. He had said it. "I want you, too, the way you were," I responded. *Loving me only,* I finished silently. Tears filled my eyes. I turned away so he would not see them. He had no right to them.

"Go, then. I will leave Joaquín. He can come next year." He walked away.

Joaquín kicked the bed and cried when he heard the news. "I want to go! I don't want to stay here with the big baby Neto just because you want to go away to that place where you came home sick! And I don't want nasty Anaya to take care of me. I don't need anyone to take care of me and I want to go with Papa on the adventures!"

"Anaya won't be taking care of you," I said. "And now, stop fussing. You are acting more like a baby than Neto. You will go next year, when you're bigger." How could I deny his desire to see the world, when that was what I wanted?

"Next year is never!" He had, after all, just turned six.

I comforted him as best I could.

"Will the birds come back?" Neto asked. I was sure he had forgotten them.

"I don't know, Neto, but if they do, don't be afraid of them. They are really only birds."

"Anaya says they're the spirit of my dead sister, come to haunt me."

I would make sure that Anaya was kept from the children. My selfish desire to return to the Court had ripples I had never dreamed of. My conscience pricked me. Perhaps I should not go. Like Joaquín, I could wait until next year.

My resolve returned in full force the following day, when I received a letter from Angélica.

My esteemed Josefina,

I have heard that you are returning, indeed, to the Court. I beg of you, procure my invitation, so that I may join you at Advent. After all, it was I who sponsored you, and you will enjoy the amenities of the winter season so much more with a companion. I await your response.

KYH,
Angélica

I would go. She could not go, without my beneficence. She had stolen from me, in my own home, my husband's ardor. I would go, and Hell would freeze before I would procure an invitation for her to join me. Advent was six weeks away, and if she was so bent on returning to Court, she could seek an invitation some other way.

A week later, Manuel finished loading up his saddlebags and bade us farewell. "I wish that this visit will be everything that you yearn for," he said. "I will long for your return, and I will welcome you home in ten weeks."

"I hope your drive is successful, Manuel. Be careful. I will await our reunion." We kissed lightly, and for a moment the world stood still. And then, as if torn from me, he left. I departed the following day. Cayetana would accompany me to the castle, but she would return to the hacienda after only a brief visit to her husband. She was eager and happy, and so she talked almost constantly throughout the journey, leaving me to my silent thoughts.

MY RETURN TO THE castle was like a homecoming. It was late afternoon, though the sun was still well above the horizon. The first sight of the walls was not the surprise that it had been, but rather the sight I had been craning my neck and squinting against the sunlight to see. The entry into the courtyard had the excitement of familiarity, not novelty. Here, I knew, unbelievable things happened, and outrageous ideas were commonplace. I was shown to my room, the same one as previously, and I felt as though I had broken out of chains.

It was no more than an hour after my arrival that a page came to the door with several notes. I tipped him well, thinking of my boys, and took the letters into my room to read. The first was from the Marquesa herself, inviting me to take a cup of chocolate with her that evening, after my meal. From that I discerned that I was to take my supper in the ladies' guest dining room tonight. I would face the denizens there right upon arrival.

The second note contained another, folded within. The outer note was from Sor Juana, asking me to meet her tomorrow morning in the music room, after morning Mass. And the third, concealed within Sor Juana's, was the one that set my hands to trembling.

My lady,

You have returned. Tread cautiously. I will find you when the time is right. Until then, welcome. Should we meet in company, I urge your piety and restraint.

Alonso

Upon my first reading, I was thrilled. I could feel the excitement rising. He would find me. The illicit adventure would begin. But then, I remembered the torment of the past few months. Did I want to doom myself to it again? And if not, I asked myself harshly, why had I come?

I read it again. In an unexpected reaction, I found myself furious. How dare he play me like a marionette? He would find me when the time was right? Until then, I was to wait for him? He had misjudged me. And how dare he urge my "piety and restraint"? Had it not been he who had stripped me of my piety, and acted without restraint? I would not seek him out, but when I did find him, he would learn that I might be a humble woman, but I would not be used as a plaything to be cast aside, or as a foil for his desire for intrigue.

I took several breaths. It would soon be time to go down to dinner, and I had to be encased in iron to brave that archery range of words. And then, if I was to attend the Marquesa properly, I would need to be composed.

At the very least, I thought, as I lay down upon my bed, here at Court it was far from dull. Every emotion was heightened, and every fear had the potential to be realized. And that, I knew, was really why I had come.

I WAS MERCIFULLY SPARED much companionship in the dining room. It was, as a quiet young woman in a soft green dress pointed out, the off-season. The heat and rains had ended, and as the darker, colder months approached, this in-between time had the air of suspension, or a regathering of energy. During this time, many ladies returned to their homes, I was told, only to return to celebrate Advent, and Christ's birth, and the New Year.

"So an invitation at this time of year is not much prized," she said, shrugging. "I am happy to wait upon the Marquesa during this slow time, as I have much to attend to at home during the harvest."

"So, Advent is much more crowded?" I asked, understanding now Angélica's desire for an Advent invitation.

"Oh, very much so. For there are the finest balls, and much merry-making. I truly prefer this quiet time."

I introduced myself, and she did likewise.

"Doña Blanca," I said, "it is a pleasure to meet you." I smiled at her soft, pleasant face.

"I am enchanted," she replied. "You seem like the straightforward sort that would enjoy this time, rather than the intensely backbiting, sniping time of the higher seasons." She paused, then, looking at me closely. "Forgive me, Doña Josefina. I must speak my mind. Are you the same lady who is said to have broken the Marqués' nose when he made inappropriate advances?"

I blushed. "I did not break his nose, Doña Blanca, but not for lack of trying. I merely bloodied it. That story grows larger as the time goes by."

She laughed quietly. "From what I have heard about him, he deserved it. To many, you are a heroine. Though I agree that, for some, you are simply gossip fodder."

"How they use the story is their concern. The truth is simple, and you now know it. I do not care to be anyone's heroine, or her boot scraper, either. I am simply a woman who will not be wronged."

"It will be my continued pleasure to know you," Doña Blanca said.

I thought about the difference a few months, and the loss of my daughter, had made. I was prepared to stand my ground, within reason, and without fear of the gossipmongers of the Court. Then again, I reminded myself, I had not had to face the likes of Granada or Eustacia yet, nor even the Marquesa, but only this soft-spoken, pleasant woman of the kind I could have met on a neighboring hacienda.

And thinking of the Marquesa, I excused myself to dress for my first attendance on Her Highness of my new visit.

I was surprised to find that my audience with the Marquesa was a private one. We were served chocolate in small porcelain cups so fine that I felt the handle could snap in my fingertips. The chocolate was hot and bitter, and its richness warmed me to my core. I licked my lips as genteelly as possible.

"I am sorry you miscarried your child," the Marquesa wheezed. Her voice was breathier than I remembered.

"May God's will be done," I said. "And your health, Your Highness? Are you weathering the change of the season easily?"

"I find each year the cooling weather strains my lungs. But that is of little interest, since it happens every year. You may well wonder at my summons."

"I did. I am much beholden to you for your invitation, and your welcome."

"Palaver. I wanted you here, and I wanted to speak to you. You are aware, certainly, of your friend Angélica's disgraceful behavior." She said it, she did not ask it.

"I am aware of what happened, Your Highness."

"You keep your own counsel, do you? You have grown much since your first visit last spring. She behaved unspeakably."

"Your Highness, I am not disposed to gossip. Whatever she has done, you have judged and found wanting. I am unable and unwilling to speak further on the subject."

"Doña Josefina, let me remind you that you are here to wait upon me, not to entertain yourself. I wish to hear your opinion of Angélica's behavior."

I thought for a moment. Could I defend Angélica, who had been carnally with my Manuel? Could I fault her for aspiring to the heir, or for rejecting the Marqués?

"I am loath to abuse your hospitality by my refusal. The story I know was told to me by Angélica, and so I may not know all of the truth. But your son will know his own mind, in that he is five years senior to Angélica, who is supposed to know hers. And if he attended to Angélica, that is not her fault, for you yourself admit she is beautiful. Nor is it the least bit surprising that she returned his regard, given his high birth, his intelligence, and his handsome looks." No mother could resist flattery of her son, and this was all true.

"Agreed, Doña Josefina. But I told you specifically that I would oppose such a match. Did you fail to tell Angélica?"

I was startled. "I had no idea you wished me to, madam, or I would have done so. I took your comments as confidence."

"You misjudged the situation, then. The debacle should be laid at your feet."

I could not stop myself. I burst out laughing. "Your Highness, I cannot be blamed for your son's behavior, nor for Angélica's. Nor certainly for your husband's."

"No, certainly not for the Marqués' acts. Though in truth, if I had known how vehemently Miguel Ángel would react, and that he would strike his father before leaving the castle, I would have advised the Marqués against his attempt at seduction."

"You knew he was going to approach Doña Angélica in that way?"

It was the Marquesa's turn to laugh—an unpleasant wheeze. "Who do you think told him about the assignation?"

"That is despicable!" I said angrily. Then I caught myself. I was not in my right mind, speaking that way to the Marquesa. "I am sorry, Your Highness. But I am surprised, and, well . . ." I could not finish.

"You are an uncommon woman, to speak so forthrightly to me. I don't know if I should send you home or keep you by my side. Your disdain for my actions shows you to be a virtuous fool, for you understand very little of the needs of nobility when it comes to matters of lineage. But your willingness to speak against my actions shows you to be a brave fool. Notably, you are a fool either way."

My hands shook as I sipped my chocolate. I would compose myself before going on, but there was a question I had to ask. Even if it meant risking my stay at the castle, ending my chance to see Sor Juana, and the Bishop, I would learn the truth.

"Your Highness," I said, willing my voice to be steady. "Did you suggest to the Marqués that he attack me?"

She arched her black brow, and the red spots appeared on her cheeks. It was her turn to pause. "No," she said finally. I waited, but she said no more.

I had my answer. "Thank you, Your Highness. I am grateful. Should you speak to him about me, I implore you to dissuade him from any further attentions. I will not submit, nor will I be taken easily. His nose, and more, may well be casualties of any further importunities."

"I will so advise him, if he seeks my counsel. You are, indeed, a brave fool. Now, tell me why you returned."

We talked a bit about poetry, and literature, and the unbelievable library she possessed.

"It is the largest in New Spain," she said proudly. "By many, many volumes. Some are printed, others are inked by hand, and many came from my father's and grandfather's libraries. My father and grandfather were great supporters of poets in their day. To their endangerment, at times. We are much safer here in New Spain. The Holy Office's reach is great, but its ardor cools over the water."

"I hear that some greater strictures are coming," I said, thinking of the sermon that Angélica had quoted.

"The Archbishop of Mexico is less than enamored of your friend the Bishop of Puebla and his support of our resident scribe and poetess. But I believe his protests to be ineffective, so long as the Bishop maintains a cloak of servile godliness. If we were in Spain, my lands and title would be at risk, but at this distance, I will maintain my independence from the Supreme Council."

"Madam, if I may be so bold, you exceed me in bravery."

"Or as a fool."

THE NEXT MORNING, I found Sor Juana already waiting for me in the music room. The morning was cold, and the shutters were closed to keep the warmth of the fire within. The small room was more welcoming than ever. She did not rise when I entered, but rather looked up from the comfortable chair she was sitting in, reading, and nodded. She neither gestured to me nor invited me to join her. I wondered at the cool reception, given that this was her summons to me.

"Good morning, Sister," I said. She nodded again briefly, and continued reading. "Did you wish to see me?" If she was to be discourteous, I would be brief.

"I did."

I still stood at the door. "Well, I am here."

"Please shut the door. It locks, as well, with that key on the table next to the entry." I saw a large key, black iron, and lifted it. I shut the door as ordered, and, feeling disturbed but intrigued, I locked it. She held her hand out for the key. I was loath to give it to her, but again, if I did not give myself over to the event, I might just as well have stayed home. I handed it to her and took a seat across from her.

"Welcome back," she said.

"Thank you. I received your books, and I am grateful."

"The play. *The Household's Dilemma*. Did you like it?"

She wanted my opinion! "I did. It was wonderful."

She looked at me over that huge brooch. Her thick brows arched over deep brown eyes. She was beautiful. "Anything more critical than adulation and praise?"

"If I had written it, I would want praise!"

"Well, you didn't write it. And I am well beyond seeking praise, though I cannot lie and say praise is unwelcome. Tell me your thoughts."

I pulled my thoughts together. I understood. This was my first lesson. "I was disappointed by Ana. She allowed herself to be in a rivalry for a love that wasn't worthy of her, and she submitted to her brother's order to marry Don Juan, at the end, giving up Carlos to Leonor. I had hoped for more backbone."

"You are astute. She is a foil."

"For whom?"

Sor Juana smiled for the first time that morning, and now that I thought of it, for the first time since I had met her. Her radiance was incomparable. Unvarnished, without the artifice that one like Doña Angélica brought to beauty, she still outshone them all.

"For me. Why do we women allow ourselves to be pitted against one another for love? Is that not base? And yet, other than the nunnery, what occupation is open to us?"

"So Ana had no choice," I said.

"None. So she showed her backbone, as you termed it, by submitting to the stronger will, and doing so with pride."

"Carlos was unworthy of her. And he was not quite worthy of Leonor, either."

"No, but of the two, he was more suited to Leonor."

"Leonor wallowed in self-pity and shame after she was caught running off with Carlos. I had to work not to despise her."

"Have you never given in to self-pity after sinning?" Sor Juana asked.

I blushed, remembering her poem to me. "Our sin—blameworthy are we . . . ," she had written. And I recalled that she had described Leonor as beautiful, smart, and much sought after, indeed a fine description of Sor Juana.

"I have wallowed, Sister, and suffered, and lost my baby, and repulsed my husband, and driven him into the arms of another."

"And yet you still long for the forbidden fruit, despite the blackening of our souls, the trail of blood."

Our souls. Hers and mine. I did not answer.

"That is why we write poetry, Josefina. To bare our blackened souls, so that others, suffering with us, can do so with our better, more precise words. For by confession we expiate our guilt, and by poems, we confess."

I sat silent. I had the guilt. I had the sin. I did not know whether I had the gift of words to express them, and to be cleansed. "Do you love the Bishop?" I asked. I regretted the question as it left my lips. I did not want the answer, nor would I answer the question myself. But Sor Juana, once again, surprised me.

"Of course. As do you. But trust, Josefina, that we are not rivals for his love. He loves us both, and I am married to Christ, and you to Manuel. He causes us both to be adulteresses, but for neither of us will he leave his bishopric, nor we our lawfully wedded husbands for him. And so, to verse."

WE SPENT THE ENTIRE morning together, Sor Juana and I, and the time flew. When I joined the other ladies in the dining room, I was surprised to see both Granada and Eustacia in our midst.

"Welcome back," said Eustacia. "We feared that your friend's disgrace would keep you away."

How like her to begin with an unpleasant remark. "It is all vanity," I said. Eustacia raised her eyebrow.

"Have you become holy?" she said.

"The Lord has seen fit to bless me with sorrow, and so I will bear it with His good grace." Where these words were coming from, I knew not, but instinct told me I had found a way to thwart Eustacia's malice.

"Yes, we heard about your miscarriage. Women lose babies all the time; it can hardly be considered a gift from God to do so." Granada's malice was not so easily evaded.

I smiled sweetly at her. "Doubtless you will pray for my soul, Doña Granada, as I shall pray for yours."

"On your knees before the Bishop!" Granada said, laughing. I felt the blush begin. But I rallied.

"No, before the Lord. But you, Granada, should do as you think best. Whatever will save your soul, so be it." Granada glared, but could find no response. I crowed internally.

It is well known that pride goes before a fall, and I fell.

"A message for you, madam," said a *menina*. She was all pink and white, like a sugar pastry. I took the letter, thanking her. One did not tip *meninas,* as they were the same class as ourselves, only younger. I slid the letter into my sleeve.

"Oh, no! You must open it, see who is sending you messages," said Granada loudly. The other ladies turned to look.

I felt trapped, but would not yield. "I shall open it later. I do not wish to disturb my luncheon, or yours."

"It's from the Marqués!" piped the *menina,* all smiles. "He gave it to his valet, who said I was to take it here posthaste!"

So Ygnacio had had a part in this. And this young lady had a great deal to learn about discretion.

"Run along now, surely there are other errands for you in the castle, my dear. You do not want to waste your day listening to us!"

"Oh, madam, I love listening to the ladies talk. And besides, I was told to wait for an answer, and bring it directly to the Marqués' chambers."

"Well, Doña Josefina, I fear you have no choice but to open it now," said Eustacia, gloating. "And as for you, my dear, do not go into the Marqués' chambers unescorted, for he is a man of liberal tastes." The young girl turned as pink as her ribbons. "Come now, don't get upset. He hasn't laid a hand on you, has he?" Eustacia's false sympathy was designed to obtain confidences from this poor child, only to broker the information to her advantage. If it ruined a girl's good name, it was all part of the web of castle gossip.

"Stop pestering the poor girl," I broke in. "Come, dear, let's go out of this place, and I will pen an answer for you to carry." I walked out of the dining room, and the *menina* had no choice but to follow. Once we were out, I put my hand on her shoulder. "I am a mother. If anyone, including the Marqués, behaves inappropriately with you, you come straight to me." The Marquesa might tolerate her husband's philandering with the ladies, but no one was going to touch a child.

"Yes, my lady," said the girl. From the stricken look on her face, it appeared that I may well have been too late. I opened the letter.

Minx. I will have you. Ask your friend Angélica whether or not I get my way. All her squirming was with delight, and you will squirm, too, once I have you on your back. M.

"I have no answer," I said to the girl.

Tears filled her eyes. "Please, madam. Write something. Or I will be scolded, and I am terrified of the Marqués when he is angry."

"Why does your father let you attend him? You should attend the Marquesa, not the Marqués!"

"I do, but he asked for me as a messenger, and he often does, to take letters to the ladies. The boys don't like to come into the dining room." She didn't meet my eye.

"I will write something, to spare you, then. But give the letter to the valet, and return to the Marquesa at once."

The girl curtseyed. I wrote, at the bottom of his letter: *Sir. I am disgusted by your suggestion. I will have no more conversation with you. J. Ma. de Castillo.* I folded it in three and handed it to the girl. "Now go, and take care that you stay away from the Marqués." She was gone as fast as she was able.

I was hungry, but I had no stomach for returning to the wasps' nest of a dining room. I detoured to the kitchen, where the cook with the enormous wooden spoon held her own court. She was happy to send a plate up with a servant. I returned to my room, perturbed.

After some thought, I settled upon a course of action. I took a pen and paper, and quickly wrote a short note. When the servant arrived with a tray laden with meats, fruits, and tortillas fresh from the griddle, I handed her the note.

"Take this, immediately, to the area of the castle where the nuns take their rest. Give it only to Sor Juana." I took out a coin and handed it to her. And, taking a lesson from the Marqués, I added, "Return with an answer from her, and I will add another coin to your tip."

Delighted with the unexpected chance to make two coins, the kitchen maid skipped out of my room and down the hallway. Pleased with my progress, I ate ravenously. By the time I had finished, the servant returned with an answer. I tipped her, as promised, and she took the tray away with a happy smile. Whenever I wished for a servant, she assured me, she stood ready.

It was thus that I arranged to move to the nuns' side of the castle. Here, I would eat with the sisters, pray with them, and study with Sor Juana. When called upon to attend the Marquesa, I could do so, but I would be sheltered from the Marqués' marauding, and be spared the vicious company of the ladies-in-waiting when I was not attending the Marquesa.

The days passed in gentle study, and the weather outside grew clear and cold. I wrapped myself in my warmest shawls, as the nuns' side was not as thickly draped and fires were not laid as lavishly as on the ladies' side. The food was more like what we ate at the hacienda, with less variety but with flavors that were straightforward and strong. I felt a longing for home. For the first time in our years together, I wrote a letter to Manuel. Ygnacio was leaving at the end of the week to visit Cayetana, and he agreed to carry my letter.

> *My esteemed husband:*
> *I am studying with the nuns, and I find the work joyful and inspiring. I long for the boys, and I hope that your cattle run is successful. I await eagerly the time of Advent, when I will return.*
>
> > *Your loving wife,*
> > *Josefina*

I sent it off with my prayers. Sor Juana shook her head. "Josefina, you cannot have a foot in each camp. While you are here, devote yourself to reading and writing. When you are home, you cannot."

"But I miss them so."

I hoped I had not hurt her. With my heart with my boys, I was relishing a love that could never be hers. But she did not look sad, she looked pensive. "Did you ever wonder why I entered the convent? No, do not answer, for everyone wonders. Speculation has dogged me since the day

I took my vows. But the reason was simple. I loved life, but I loved my studies more. As you have learned, even with a most indulgent husband you cannot devote yourself both as a poet and as a mother. You must choose. I chose."

"But you are so beautiful!" I exclaimed. "Surely there was a suitor who would have indulged your desire to study."

"That is where we differ, Josefina. I will not be indulged. This is my life's work, and only by devoting myself to it do I make it that, rather than an indulgence."

That was a strong distinction, one that I would never have thought of.

"But are you content?"

She smiled. "The first convent I tried to join, the Barefoot Carmelites, was woefully strict, and I had to return to my father's house after three months, emaciated and miserable. But my second choice, as you can see, permits me the freedom of a *marquesa*'s court, the pleasures of the table, and the patronage to study."

But there remained in my mind a disbelief. "What about loving a man?"

She looked away. "I have loved. And I was not jilted, nor, as some suspect, unchaste, and forced into this way of life. But my love has no place on earth."

I thought of Father Alonso. Did he love her carnally? I trembled. His "priest's act" would not father children, and was useful in those hateful ways that some said priests had with boys, but now I thought, It could be useful in loving a nun. Did I dare ask her? I did not. I could not meet her eyes.

"Enough of this nonsense," she said briskly. "You have a poem to read, and I want your interpretation of the language Góngora uses in his description of the nobleman." We returned to work, but her phrase, a love that had "no place on earth," remained in my mind.

AT THE END OF my second week at the castle, I received the summons I had been waiting for. He did not send a note, for he could enter the nuns' area without permission. He simply knocked on my door one afternoon. Not anticipating a visitor, I had not done a Court toilette, and I was simply dressed in a woolen dress with a white collar, and wrapped in a thick shawl. I opened the door. There stood Father Alonso, long red hair gleaming, perfectly turned out in a priestly cape, collar, and black pants with a satin ribbon running down the sides. His blue eyes sparkled. He smiled and held out his hand.

"Doña Josefina, welcome to the convent!"

I opened the door wider, happy beyond words to see him. "Father Alonso! I mean, Your Grace!" I wanted to throw my arms around him, but my words embraced him instead.

"Here you can be informal. We are safe." He entered my room.

"Are you sure? Can you come in here?" This would be a scandal under other circumstances.

"I can. And I have. Now, sit down here, in front of the fire where you have obviously been studying, and tell me all of your adventures since I saw you last."

I sat. Since he saw me last. The realization that he had no idea of the pain, the sorrow, and the shame I had suffered since he had seen me was overwhelming.

"Since you saw me last," I repeated. I was surprised by my feelings.

I have borne the tortures of the damned, Father, since I last saw you. My shame at our conduct burned at my soul. I could not honor my wifely obligations, and I lost my baby. The pain in my head rendered me mute for a time, and I could not care for my children properly.

"I had a miscarriage of a difficult pregnancy" was all I said.

"Josefina, I know more about your suffering than you imagine. I have prayed for you. I know that you were wracked with guilt and sorrow, but that is all over now. Though you suffered, you came out stronger."

I sighed. "What is all over now, Father?"

He did not answer at first. "We cannot be the way we were. The Archbishop of Mexico is not a kindly man, nor does he cosset poets or thinkers. He is watching me, and he is watching Sor Juana. While we are here, we are safe, but nothing we publish is sacrosanct. We must be careful."

"And how is that related to me?"

Again, a long pause. "Here, it is not. You may study."

He was avoiding what I dared not ask. I could not say that I had suffered for him. More, I could not say that I loved him. And he did not say that he loved me.

He held me in his arms, stroking my hair, then kissing it, while I cried. I felt myself melt into his kisses, inhaling his lemon verbena smell and allowing the sadness that I had so long kept inside to be rocked away by his gentle embrace. As I had been so long ago, in my father's study, I was a child, and he was my safe haven.

Sixteen

Advent was little more than a week away. The atmosphere at the castle was changing subtly with the shortening of the days. The days themselves were cool and bright. The fields had been harvested, the cattle slaughtered or driven to market. The castle followed the same agricultural rhythms our hacienda did, and the same release and turning to indoor pursuits was evident here as at home. The difference was, those inside the castle had done none of the work, and yet were set to reap the rewards of the cessation of labor for the winter. Sconces were lit earlier to dispel the darkness of the early evenings, and conclaves of chattering women planned the revelry of the season to come. For there were not only the big events, balls and dinners, to plan, but invitations to angle for, and dresses to be commissioned as well.

I was reading quietly in the library when the pink and white *menina* I had met shortly after my arrival came in with a note. She didn't meet my eyes, and I felt her embarrassment as a sharp stab. I knew then that I had been unable to shield her from the Marqués with my advice, and I was sorry that I had done nothing more, once I had replied to the Marqués' message, to ensure her maidenly safety. In fact, I had thought of her not a moment since then, and had mercifully not seen the Marqués since my arrival. I took the note and thanked her. "Must you wait for an answer?" I asked. She nodded dumbly, still flushed, with her eyes cast down. How serious had his depredations been?

I opened the note. The Marqués' scrawl, recognizable instantly, made me want to crumble the note and toss it, but its message was far more chilling.

My lovely, wanton temptress:

Isolating yourself in the nuns' quarters and hiding in the library do nothing to shield you from my eyes. I will have you, you know, when you least expect me. For now, do my friends and me the honor of attending us at our evening repast tonight, and perhaps bring one of your new verses to entertain us. If you will not amuse me now by lifting your skirts, you will amuse us all with your newfound talent in poesy.

Yours,

M.

The *menina* was watching me from under her lowered lids.

"I have no answer," I said harshly. She looked up, pitiful. "Go!" I said, and looked back down at my book. My heart knew I should try once more to save the girl, but my mind acknowledged that she would never be strong enough to heed my counsel. I would not answer this despicable note just to preserve her. After a long moment, she crept away.

I refused to think about it. I would not be dragged into the mire of the Court's social ugliness. I had come to study. I repeated this to myself, over and over, until it drowned out both my conscience and my reading. The morning was ruined, and I returned to the nuns' quarters.

But I was not to find solace there, either, for as I entered the hall, a sister motioned to me.

"Sor Juana would like a word. In her room."

I hastened to her chamber, and entered after a quick knock.

"I hear you refused to honor an invitation from the Marqués," she said softly, with no greeting or preamble. Her dark brows knitted severely. I nodded. She knew of my history with the Marqués. I was sure she would support me. "You must go. Write a note of apology, and assure him of your presence."

"Why? If you had seen the note!" I hunted in my book for it and handed it to her. Sor Juana read it, and a small smile appeared and disappeared. She handed it back to me without comment. "You want me to accept that? And apologize for not doing so quickly?" My breath came short.

"Yes," she said, and went back to her book.

"No!"

She looked back up again, right into my eyes. "Yes. You will do so, and you will do so now. That is as close to an order as I can give you. You will obey his summons, and my request. You are his guest, and my student. When your poetry is commanded by our patron, you will appear, produce it, amuse the party with charm and wit, and pay for your supper like everyone else. I do not want to be in this position again."

"I would prefer an indulgent husband and permission to study to this hateful patronage!"

"As you wish, Josefina. But for now, we have elected patronage, and you will fulfill your side of the bargain."

"Your independence is a fraud," I said viciously. My hand flew to my mouth. Red spots appeared on Sor Juana's pale cheeks. I trembled as I awaited her verbal lash, so much more cutting than mine.

"It may be," she said softly, "but let us hope that your virtue is not."

AT THE APPOINTED HOUR, I left the nuns' wing. I was dressed in a demure dark green gown, with a high lace collar and tight lacy sleeves. It was the only gown I had commissioned for this visit, believing that my earlier wardrobe would suffice. In the quiet off-season I would have fewer occasions to bedeck myself in finery than in my first sojourn. I amazed myself in this consideration, having thought more about gowns and laces and trims in one year than I had in my first twenty-four years. Still, after weeks of plain gowns and shawls, I felt as painted as a trollop.

I clutched a volume of simple poems from the library, well-accepted and uncontroversial verses to read should I be called upon to perform. My hand left damp marks where it held the pages. Stuck in between the leaves was a single poem I had written. I did not know whether I would dare read it.

I hesitated at the door of the Marqués' dining room. A page nodded to me and held the drape aside. "Señora, come in." The bright light from the many lamps and candles blinded me for an instant as I stepped forward and the chatter in the room completely stopped.

"The beautiful, erudite Doña Josefina," said the Marqués, instantly at my side. A low rumble of laughter rippled through the room. "How kind of you to grace us with your presence this evening." He lifted my hand to his lips, his eyes on mine. As he held his lips just above my hand, he smiled. "I feared you would not come," he added quietly.

"Your Highness honors me with such an invitation," I said stiffly, suppressing the urge to pull my hand away.

"Nonsense," he said, dropping my hand. "Your presence is the sole reason for tonight's party." A chill coursed through me. "We await your entertainment eagerly. Isn't that right, gentlemen?" He turned to those nearest us, and I looked around for the first time since entering.

"Of course," said a black-mustachioed gentleman with a Hidalgo's sword at his side. I recalled him from my first visit, a military man whose name eluded me. "Doña, we are honored," he said, bowing from the waist.

"Thank you, sir," I mumbled.

The room was not large, but it was well appointed with draperies and the long table at which I had dined before. There were only three other women here: Granada, Eustacia, and a woman I did not know. Granada glittered in pale green silk with diamonds. She arched a thin eyebrow at me.

"Josefina, my dear. We have missed you in the ladies' wing. No more secret messages and sudden departures to conjecture over."

My frustration with Sor Juana, combined with the humiliation of having to obey this summons, had the heady effect of wine, including the warming flush of heedless speech.

"I have not missed you, Granada, and you would be unsuited to my accommodations. The tranquillity of the nuns' wing is far more conducive to virtue."

"Is that so? Or are you more able to hide your assignations under the sisters' veils?"

All eyes were on us now. "I have no need to hide. And I am not here as a mere adornment, as you are. I have a studious purpose, not an ornamental one."

"Better adornment than unsexed poetess."

"So now I am unsexed, where a moment ago I was trysting in the gardens? You are inconsistent in your words, though not in your venom, Granada."

"Bravo!" exclaimed the Marqués. "Our demure guest has found her tongue. You see, gentlemen, the fire I spoke of? Buried, banked embers burn oh so hotly when fanned!"

I fought to quell my fury, but failed.

"Sir, you have commanded my presence. And I am here. But I will not be trifled with."

"Oh, but you will, my dear. You are here to be trifled with. Come," he added, holding out his hand, "let me refresh that spirit with a little wine." He kept his hand out, and even in my heightened state I could not be so rude as to refuse it. I took it, as minimally as possible, and followed him to the table that held the brandy decanter. He nodded to a footman, who poured generously.

I put down the book I had been clutching, and took the glass. I sipped from a trembling hand, but the liquor warmed and calmed me.

"Now, my dear, come and entertain my companions." Still holding my hand, the Marqués led me to the window, where the drapes had been drawn against the early darkness. He released my hand, but only to drop his hand behind me, on my buttock, pinching me through the material of my skirt. I stumbled, spilling wine.

"Steady, there." He laughed, pressing me into the curtains as he pretended to steady me. I tried to push his hand away, only to find his other one on my breast. He squeezed, and I cried out. The others in the room were staring, the men smiling, the three women openmouthed but transfixed. He squeezed my breast again, and I dropped the glass to the floor. It shattered, spraying glass and wine on my feet and the hem of my dress.

The Marqués nodded to the footman, who had remained rooted to his spot. "Come, bring the lady another glass of wine! And you, Josefina, see that you keep better hold of this one!" He laughed, releasing me, and turned to his guests. "Drink up, my friends. Supper will soon be served, and your minds will be fed along with your bellies." Conversation resumed, and the footman, red with embarrassment, brought another glass for me on a tray. I took it without thinking, for my mind was numb.

The woman I did not know, with dark, sleek hair and a plump, pleasant face, approached. "So you are the famous Doña Josefina," she said, extending a soft hand. "María Luz de Albanil."

"I am not famous, but I am Josefina," I replied.

"We hear of you in the ladies' wing quite often," María Luz said. "The poetess from the provinces, who broke the Marqués' nose." She smiled sweetly. "I see your fire here tonight. Will we hear your verses?"

"I have not given it much thought," I lied. "What brings you to this sordid dinner?"

"Sordid?" María Luz asked. "Why sordid? The table at the Marqués' rooms is most abundant, the entertainment enlightening, and the company pleasant. Surely you do not take the Marqués' sallies seriously? But then again, you must, if you broke his nose over them!" Her eyebrows were raised in astonishment.

"Doña Maria Luz, do not tell me that you have just come to that conclusion! Did you think this was all playacting?"

She continued to look at me wide-eyed. Then she laughed—a tinkling, bell-like sound. "Oh, you are as witty as they say you are! My, but you had me convinced, for the moment! I cannot wait to hear your verses!" She glided away, smiling enticingly at a gentleman in an embroidered coat.

I sipped my wine, still stunned by the oddness of the conversations I had had in the brief time since I had entered the Marqués' rooms. Well, if wit and fire were what they wanted, they would be obliged. I squared my shoulders, encased in the tight green velvet of my dress, and walked purposefully to retrieve my book from the sideboard. To my relief, the footman rang a small silver bell. The table was set, and we were now to dine.

"Here, next to me." The Marqués patted a chair to his left.

"That is far too exalted a position for me, Your Highness," I said. "I will take that lowly seat where I can best observe you."

The Marqués reddened, to my great satisfaction. "Madam. Your wish is my greatest pleasure," he said.

I hastened to a seat at the far end of the table. "But you are taking my seat," said Doña María Luz.

"Then you must have mine," I replied. Unsure how to handle this unexpected honor, she glanced at the Marqués.

"I will gladly take it," Eustacia chimed in, rushing to the place of honor. I could not tell if Doña Luz was disappointed or relieved. It occurred to me that I had placed her in an awkward position, and that Eustacia's greed for attention had rescued her.

The Marqués shrugged slightly, amused at the jockeying for position. "Your mere presence disorders the room, Doña Josefina," was all he said.

When we were all seated, Granada and Eustacia flanking the Marqués, the dishes were brought in. The footman served me, first hot soup, then cold viands. I ate slowly, trying to keep my conversation with the gentlemen to my left and right civil and light. But the inevitable could not be postponed forever.

"Can we have a verse, to sweeten the dessert course?" the Marqués asked, raising his glass to me. The payment for my supper was due.

"I will gladly read to you, Your Highness," I replied, taking my book from under my seat. "A few lines from Lope de Vega's popular songs will speed digestion." I found my page and read.

When I had finished, I closed the book and sipped my wine. Chatter started up immediately, for the verses had been pleasant and not especially worthy of comment. But the conversation was quickly stemmed.

"Thank you, madam. And now may we have something original, something to chew on after that frothy confection you have just offered us?" The Marqués was boring into me with his eyes.

"My verses are yet unworthy of your company," I replied.

"I will judge that. Now, come. We wish to hear your creation."

They had asked for wit and fire. And so, they would have it.

"What is the dream, that I awake in horror—
the cold hand clutching my pounding heart?
I cannot forget your unwelcome ventures,
made with stealth and cunning art
but proving base and drawing recoil,
could only make the humors boil
and call for tears to drown the hawk
that seeks to tear the soul apart."

Silence applauded my poem. Eustacia had a small smile, but the others avoided my eyes. Finally, the quiet was dispelled.

"You are right, Doña Josefina, your verses are not yet suitable for company," the Marqués spat. "I wonder that you have indulged yourself with our hospitality so long, for so little progress."

I smiled, believing my arrow had pierced the mark. "I apologize for the artless composition. I would beg your indulgence to trouble you no more tonight." I rose to leave.

"To the contrary, Josefina. Since you have proved unworthy in both conversation and art, we will seek payment for your supper with your beauty. Stay." It was a command. And since I had already offended, intentionally and in error, I knew that I must this time obey. I resettled in my seat, and forced a falsely calm expression on my face. "As you wish, Your Highness."

I sat in silence. The men at my sides made a visible effort to talk only to those seated on their other sides. The ladies, flirting shamelessly with the gentlemen, did not direct a word to me. And as I watched from under lowered lashes, the Marqués fondled Eustacia openly, laughing at her arch comments and holding her wineglass to her lips to entice her to drink often.

Believing myself unobserved, I stealthily rose from my seat.

"Sit down," the Marqués said softly, his voice nevertheless carrying across the room. I quickly sat, unnerved, and my isolated vigil resumed.

As the ostracism wore on, and the wine wore off, I saw my situation in a different light. The verse had been foolish. I had not hit my mark, but had sailed wide of even amusement, never mind satire. I squirmed uncomfortably under my own scrutiny.

At long last, the Marqués dismissed us, bidding us all a good night, and leaving with Eustacia, flushed and victorious, on his arm. I crept quietly back to the nuns' wing, the heady excitement of my daring poem long gone. I knew payment would be exacted, both by the Marqués and by Sor Juana. And worse, I knew that the Marqués' barb about the unworthiness of my verses was true. Sor Juana could offend because she made the simile sing. Mine had been heavy-handed and obvious. "The hawk": how banal a choice to vilify the large-nosed Marqués. And tears to drown a hawk? I blushed with mortification. How could I have thought to read that foolish, transparent doggerel?

Sor Juana, in addition to the disgust she would feel for my poor verse, would be furious with me for having annoyed rather than entertained our patron. As I pushed aside the draperies that shielded the wing from the hall, I realized that I had jeopardized the rights of all the women under the Marqués' patronage who were allowed to study and write in freedom, in exchange for so little in the way of amusement. And I was certain my penance would soon be exacted.

$\mathcal{S}$EVENTEEN

$\mathcal{I}$ DID NOT HAVE LONG to wait for the first blow to fall. No sooner had I taken breakfast than Sor Juana herself knocked lightly on my door. Without waiting for me to call out, she entered, moving gracefully in her habit. She carried a small porcelain cup with chocolate in one hand and a sheaf of papers in the other.

"I hear you acquitted yourself well in your maiden voyage," she said, seating herself in the only other chair in the room, near the fire.

"Hardly," I replied, feeling the warm flush beginning at my neck. I had not dared hope for such a gentle approach.

"No, do not twist in shame over your reading. It was your first attempt at entertainment. You must surely be judged as a novice."

"I hope so. It was most humbling to hear my own verses read, even by me, in front of an audience. I do not relish repeating the performance."

"On the contrary, the sooner you try again, the sooner you will improve. To that end, you are entertaining the Marquesa, along with her ladies, this afternoon, before Vespers. I have reviewed your verses," she added, as I tried to protest, "and I have chosen three of the four you will read. The fourth, you must compose this morning, for you have nothing else that will suit. I will expect you in my room after lunch."

"Please, Sister. I cannot repeat last night's performance. I will die of shame."

"Perhaps," she said, rising. "I will see you this afternoon." She put the sheets of paper on the chair she had just vacated, and smiled. "You were made bold with wine last night, I understand."

"No. I was emboldened by the Marqués' foul treatment of me. I will not tolerate it. He fondled me in front of the entire party, and then mocked my verse. The wine only gave me courage to survive the ordeal."

"Well, you shall have no such liquid fortifier today, Josefina. Doubtless you will be able to salvage a bit of your reputation." She glided out of the room.

I stared silently into the fire. I would have to bear the mockery of the women who had witnessed last night's debacle in the Marqués' rooms. Granada, if she was going to be present, and the other, newly met lady from last night, María Luz Albanil. But it was Eustacia's sneer I dreaded most. For she had seen my humiliation firsthand, and had doubtless spread the tale, amplifying it as she went, all through the ladies' wing. The ladies would be waiting for me with sharpened knives of cutting remarks and knowing glances. I could not bear it.

When I could sit no longer, I put my shawl on to walk in the garden. I had, perforce, to compose a poem in so little time, and be ready to present it to Sor Juana after lunch. I yearned to regain her approval, for it was both the comfort of my days and the source of my leave to remain in the nuns' wing. I had to come up with something wonderful.

I was met at the garden door by a young girl, not the pink and white *menina* of prior days but a sturdy, dark girl with braids and ribbons. She handed me two letters, curtseyed, and left before I could thank her. Grateful for her lack of style and manners, I watched her go. She would be safe from the Marqués' predations.

But I was not. The first letter bore his seal, and my name was written in his characteristically bold hand. Trembling, I broke the seal, to read the brief message.

> *I do not take kindly to being mocked in verse by those whose supper I provide. Your insolence has passed the point of amusement into the realm of disrespect. Your punishment will be swift in coming. M.*

I read it again, hoping to discern some nuance, some meaning other than the obvious. I returned to my room and sank into the chair. I would not allow him to terrify me. I would go to Father Alonso, show him this horrible letter. He could protect me.

I realized I was holding the other letter still unopened. The seal was my own! My heart pounded as I opened it quickly. It was from Manuel. Had something happened to Joaquín or Neto? Tears filled my eyes. I was an ungrateful wife, traveling far from my rightful place at his hacienda, my home, my sons. I began to read.

> Dear Josefina,
>
> I hope this finds you happy and in good health. The sales were good. I am coming to Court, as Angélica has secured an invitation for the Advent season, and I am accompanying her on the journey. We will arrive on the fifth day of December.
>
> Manuel

Terse, without embellishment, or even the details of the arrangements he would make to have the boys cared for, or how long he could stay, but his words were there. He was coming. I thought through the calendar. Today was Thursday, and so next Sunday was the first Sunday in Advent. He would arrive in ten days!

I shoved the two letters into my strongbox and pulled the shawl tightly around myself. Quickly, and avoiding the commonly trodden paths, I rushed out to the garden. My mind was swirling. The poems, the performance, my shame, the Marqués' threat, Father Alonso—and now Manuel was coming. I stopped short. Manuel was coming, with Angélica. The simple contemplative life of study lay unraveled at my feet. I sank to my knees before a niche of the Virgin Mary and bowed my head. Prayer, usually best left to the priests, seemed my only hope.

When my knees began to ache I arose, no more sure than when I had knelt. The Mother of God seemed so distant when my troubles were so much of the flesh. By my own doing, I was abandoned. Had the Virgin ever pictured the sainted Joseph with another? Had she longed for the caress of one she could not want, and fled from the unwanted strokes of another? Such thoughts, in themselves, were heresy.

If I was damned, then I must also be determined. I would go back to my room, compose my poem, and seek Father Alonso's advice. My approach to him would be penitent, chaste. I needed his holy guidance, and would guard against the blinding temptations of the flesh. And I needed his protection, before I became the next of the Marqués' conquests.

"A bird will wing alone
in song
And Heaven's blessings will atone
for wrongs
But, fairest one, your song is naught
And here on earth your supper is bought
with broken wings and heart of stone
denying shelter of the home
to the child of snares in which you're caught."

Sor Juana nodded. "Acceptable," she said. "Although transparent. Here," she added, handing me a book. "Quevedo. Read his metaphysical poems, see how he uses an image to convey his feeling, but at the same time to cloak it in piety. You cloak nothing. Naked verse is what you offer."

"I will try harder," I said meekly. It was acceptable. Perhaps I would return to her good graces.

"And the meter is off in the last line," she added. "Fix it before we wait upon the Marquesa."

I COULD WAIT NO longer. I took a sheet of foolscap and penned a note to Father Alonso. I sealed it quickly, and then went to the portress to seek a page to deliver my message. To send for the kitchen maid on the ladies' side of the castle would arouse suspicion and would take up precious time. I had failed to cultivate a relationship with a page or servant on the nuns' side, and had none I could trust to do my bidding. I could only hope to buy silence for a coin, which I was more than ready to pay.

A lad of nine or so was quick and eager to run my errand. "Here's a coin to get you going," I said, "and you'll have the same when you return with an answer. What's your name?"

"Toño," he said, his voice fluty.

"Well, Antonio," I said, "be quick about it. If you do well, you may be my messenger for the rest of my stay." He grinned and took off, livery glinting in the early afternoon sun. I returned to my room to dress for the afternoon events.

It was almost time for me to leave to attend the Marquesa when the page returned to my door. "I could not find the Bishop, señora, until just now. I looked everywhere, I called on everyone, I even told the other pages, 'Doña Josefina has an urgent message for the Bishop of Puebla, it must be delivered!' All looked throughout the castle, and only now did I find him coming out of the chapel."

I stared. He had told all the pages I had an urgent message for the Bishop? I had not told him to keep the mission a secret, believing that would only add intrigue where none needed to be added, but I had not expected a clarion announcement to the entire Court. Father Alonso's displeasure would at least equal mine.

"Thank you," I said briefly. "Do you have a reply?" He shook his head sadly. No extra coin for him. He had been neither speedy nor stealthy. "Thank you," I said again, and shut my door.

My resolve of earlier in the afternoon had departed, leaving the empty desolation of defeat behind. Looking in the glass, I touched my hair quickly, putting a dark strand back where it belonged. I had it in a simple chignon with a braid around the crown to reflect the social nature of the outing, and my dress, the deep burgundy one I had worn at my first visit, flattered me more because of the pallor I had acquired since my illness. I stopped at Sor Juana's door, but her room was empty, so I went alone to the Marquesa's rooms.

The tittering stopped when I entered, replaced by a stuffed silence that threatened to burst into shards of mocking laughter. I was transfixed by sixteen eyes, their knives of knowing gossip and judgment leaving bloody streams through my heart.

"Good afternoon, ladies," I said, my voice unnaturally high but unwavering. A beat, then the little nun Sor Inez came forward.

"Doña Josefina, welcome," she said, her sweet, singing voice holding no malice. She had, as always, a tray of sweets and pastries, and she held it out to me. Without Angélica to chide me, my reputation lost in any event, I took one. I sat down on a pouf, my book and papers in my lap, and ate.

The ladies had no choice but to resume their conversation. Sor Juana nodded at me, her face a mask of cold cordiality, but she did not approach. In truth, I was glad, though my solitude kept me apart and allowed me to be the object of covert scrutiny. I could not face Sor Juana and her undoubted knowledge that I had sent a page running through the Court with an urgent message for the Bishop. Finally, María Luz de Albanil, witness to my disastrous evening with the Marqués, came to my side.

"I hear you are going to read again," she said. I nodded. "I think your poem last night was lovely, and it was most unpleasant of the Marqués to reject it." I stared at her. She flushed. "Well, I admit I am no scholar myself, but it sounded lovely. Of course, you should have disguised your contempt for him a bit better, so he could have had a graceful way to enjoy your words."

From the mouths of innocents, I thought. "Thank you, Doña Luz. You are completely right. I hope I will do better today."

"I am sure you will," she replied, smiling. "I am also a country wife, and I cannot tell you how much I admire your courage in writing and studying. I am only here at Court to enjoy the season, as the wet weather where my husband's lands are can become most unhealthy."

"Do you have children, Doña Luz?" I had met no one with young children during my stay, I realized. Such a rarity in my world, childless women seemed to abound at Court.

"Oh, my! I have borne six, of which four are living. They are cared for at home when I am here, but doubtless I will be adding to my family again before long. I am breeding, you see, and so I will likely miss the next Advent season."

She spoke so calmly, and was so clearly content in her situation. "I envy you, Doña Luz."

"Why? Are you childless?"

"No, not at all. I have two sons, but I lost a daughter during this summer. I envy your calm. Do you ever long to study, or write, or even read?"

She laughed, and again I was struck by her laughter's resemblance to the tinkling of small silver bells. "Never. But I so enjoy hearing the works of you erudite ones, and the singing of the sisters. I think"—she paused, searching for words—"I think that every art needs its maker, and its audience. I am fortunate, because the audience gets all the pleasure."

"I hope you will be replete with pleasure today, then. I believe that

Sor Juana will be reading, too. A counterpoint, in her accomplishments, to my amateurish verse."

María Luz patted my hand, in a homely gesture of friendship. It was possible, I thought, to find a friend even in this rarefied and contrived place.

When the Marquesa made her entrance, I had my equanimity well in place. I rose with the others, curtsied, and went back to my seat. The Marquesa nodded to me, but did not single me out right away.

"Eustacia, come here," she said imperiously. When Eustacia approached, the Marquesa put her fingertips under Eustacia's chin and lifted it. The room watched this bizarre familiarity silently. "You do have my father's chin, you know," she said, releasing her. Eustacia frowned, as unsure as the rest of us what to make of this odd behavior. "Perhaps that explains my husband's behavior last night."

No one dared move. Eustacia's triumphant exit with the Marqués at the end of dinner had of course been remarked, but I, concentrating on my own sorrows, had failed to take heed of the extent of that transgression. The impoverished, illegitimate cousin of the Marquesa had been bedded by her husband, the Marqués, with no attempt at concealment.

Eustacia squared her narrow shoulders, lifted her bold black brows, the twins of her more fortunate cousin's, and stared back. The room held its collective breath, as neither woman conceded the moment. "You may leave, Eustacia. Your visit here is over."

"And if the Marqués wishes that I remain?" Eustacia said boldly.

"It is my castle, and my title," the Marquesa replied, her voice smooth and icy. But I could hear the wheeze of air in her aristocratic nose. "And you, for lack of a better term, are my cousin. I have tired of you, Eustacia, and your information bartering. And now you have sullied the nest you sleep in. A nest charitably given by me. Find somewhere to go, for this is no longer your home."

"I will speak with the Marqués!" Eustacia's voice no longer held the taunt of conquest.

"Speak to whom you wish. But do it quickly, for you will not be given dinner here tonight."

The Marquesa stood her ground, and Eustacia had no choice. She gathered her skirts to leave. But as she passed by me, she took a last shot.

"Madam," she said to the Marquesa, "you should look for the snake that remains in your bosom. Doña Josefina, the innocent country wife, is the cause of this disgrace."

"I am well aware of her fault," the Marquesa replied, "but it in no way lessens yours. Begone."

"You will pay for this," Eustacia hissed at me, as she swept by.

"Sor Inez, sing for us if you would," the Marquesa said, seating herself on the chaise longue. "I am in no mood for verses today." To our collective relief, the good sister took up her lyre and sang.

WHEN I RETURNED TO my room I found a note under my door. The Bishop's seal made my breath catch. I tore the note open.

> *My dear Josefina,*
>
> *What a scandal you will cause, sending me urgent missives through unsafe channels! But your impetuous summons will not be ignored. Please come to the library this evening, after your supper.*
>
> *Yours,*
> *A.*

The warmth of the note consoled me. I hurried through the evening meal, and after brief attention to my toilette, I was at the library door.

The room was dark, but for a candle in a single holder at the far end of the library, near the curtained alcove where Father Alonso and I had met, it seemed like ages ago. I approached the light tentatively. "Father?" I called out.

"Over here, Josefina," came his voice, from beyond the curtains.

"Let us light some lamps," I said, making my way in the semidarkness. The shadows flickered, the tall bookcases looming like threatening beasts ready to crash and crush me.

"No, no need for more light," he said, emerging from the curtained area. The single candle lit his face, his red-gold hair gleamed, but his robes draped only as shadows.

"You look like a specter," I said. He reached out his hand, and I took it. It was warm and dry, not hard like Manuel's, but comforting nonetheless.

"I may look ghostly," he said, "but I am flesh and blood."

He pulled me into his arms and embraced me. My heart thudded in my ears. This was not the comfort I had expected. "Father," I said.

"Hush."

But I had wanted to talk. He led me gently behind the curtain, taking the candle with him. It cast a warm glow on the tiny area, the couch where we had—what word to use I knew not—where we had been, before. His hands moved to my shoulders, my neck, and he raised my face to his. Before I could exclaim, his mouth was on mine.

He tasted of wine and smelled of incense. His lips touched my lips, and by a trick of his hands, my head tilted back and my mouth opened to receive the communion of his tongue. I let my own hands encircle him, and the warmth of his mouth, his hands, the relief of his physical presence made the knot in my bosom melt. I opened myself more to his embrace, and he felt my yielding, for he moved the top of my bodice down, knowing he would not meet resistance, and bared my breast.

His mouth traveled down, and I arched back. He backed me up to the settee and laid me gently down upon it. I needed no further encouragement, but reached for him as he removed his robe and knelt between my legs.

He raised my skirts, then, shaking his head, pulled me back up to sitting. "Turn around," he said softly, and I turned away from him. He moved with skill unbecoming a priest, quickly loosening the buttons that held my gown together. In a moment, the dress lay discarded on the floor, and he was removing my underbodice. "Stand," he said, and I stood before him, in the flickering candlelight, in my pantalettes. "Take them off," he whispered, and without knowing where the will to obey came from, I lowered them, and he took them from me.

I was naked. I had not been completely disrobed before a man for over a year, and never before another than my husband. Alonso's voice was hoarse when he said, "You are most beautiful. Come." He pulled me forward, positioning me so I was straddling his knees, standing before him as he sat on the settee. With my legs apart, held open by his, he let his hands travel my body.

Though my face burned, it was not only with shame, and I moved away from his prying to disguise the heat of want that suffused me. But there was no hiding from him, and when he had completed his explorations, I was panting with yearning. His breath was no steadier than mine, and I could barely hear his words. But his meaning was clear enough, and I lay upon the settee as he took down his pants.

No priest's act for him this time, I realized, as he placed a pillow under my buttocks and spread my legs wide. His touch brought me almost to a silent scream, and his penetration was both release and conquest. My tender flesh had not known a man since I had conceived last, and the invasion felt like a virgin's plundering. I could not contain myself, and I cried out, in both pain and pleasure.

His hand covered my mouth, but the sound had fueled his own desire, and his demands became more forceful and urgent. I could not refuse. My body arched and writhed, and a burst of exaltation and fire came crashing through my unresisting and welcoming flesh, becoming one with his.

We rested, our mingled breaths achieving a final, quiet rhythm. I closed my eyes, against both the faint candlelight and the reality of the moment. Then our bodies stiffened as one with the sound of a door closing softly in the library beyond.

"Maybe it was the wind," I whispered.

"There was a storm brewing," Father Alonso whispered back. Neither of us believed it. "No one saw us, no one knows it is we who are here."

I nodded, only to hope it was true. For a minute more neither of us moved; we were attentive to every sound, real or imagined. The words of Sor Juana's poem from the long summer came back to me: *Our sin— blameworthy are we / in word and thought and deed— / will drive us on to more / to blacken deep our souls.* Prophetic words, those.

I had come for consolation and holy advice, and had received a different sort of consummation. With free will I had fallen, and could no more blame Father Alonso for seduction than absolve myself of sin.

"Alonso," I said. He stiffened. "Alonso," I repeated, without honorific. Naked atop me, he was no holy man of God. "We must not be discovered."

He rolled off me and stood. I looked at him, his gleaming body covered in sparkling reddish hair. I held his regard with a boldness I did not feel. He looked away.

I pulled my dress over me, and pulled the pantalettes up beneath.

"Please lie for me," I said. "Add false words to our sin of adultery. Let us break two commandments, for the sake of my life." He nodded.

"Josefina," he began. I looked into his eyes, their torment clear in their blue orbs. "I love you. I have loved you since you were a young girl. It is my own fault you have sinned. I have betrayed my vows, your vows, and your good husband for your love. Forgive me."

I felt the tears in my own eyes. His words of love were words I had craved for ten years. And now, their arrival came with perdition, damnation.

"The sin will be laid at my feet, not yours," I said. "The woman pays the price for both Adam's and Eve's sins."

He nodded. "But no one will ever know, Josefina. I promise. This is"—he paused and swallowed—"this alcove is a much-used trysting spot. Most likely someone came in search of a private nook to share his love. He will be as guilty as we, if in intent only, and not in deed, though perhaps he found another cranny to use. No one will know, and no one will speak."

"And if they do? You spoke, your voice will be known."

"But yours will not be, Josefina. If the word does get out, I will lie for you. I will say . . . I don't know, I will admit to nothing. I will insist that the other is a liar. Or that the lady in question was one of easier virtue." I did not bother to wonder whose name would be tarnished for my sake.

His promises soothed me, but only enough to allow me to finish dressing sufficiently to be seen if such sorry chance occurred as I was passing from the library, randomly grabbed books in hand, and returning to the nuns' wing. "I love you, too, Alonso. But we can never be together."

"True, Josefina. But we will always be united." The weight of his words was lost on him, I was certain. I took his head in my hands, stepped up, and kissed him. His lips were still sweet, the kiss was still sustenance. I did not break off the kiss for a long time, and then only reluctantly. If this was to end the love I had so long nurtured for Father Alonso, I wanted the ending to last. And if it was to be only a stop on a road of sin and sorrow, I wanted the sweet pain to season my descent into Hell.

EIGHTEEN

I RETURNED TO MY ROOM, seemingly unnoticed. I dropped next to my bed the stack of books I had grabbed off the library shelves for my alibi, and stirred the embers of my fire. The warmth of the flames and their dancing light lulled me to a dreamless sleep.

When I awoke I did not at first recall the events of the evening before, but when I saw the pile of books the entire day came back in garish detail. I catalogued each event, forcing myself to stare uncompromisingly into the truth of every one. I had weathered the disdain of the ladies-in-waiting. I had composed a poem that Sor Juana had deemed adequate, I had received another threat from the Marqués, and a notice that Manuel was coming to Court with Angélica. And I had fallen, fallen, fallen into sin with Father Alonso. I did not permit the burning shame that reddened my face to keep me from looking squarely at the fact that I was now, and forever more, an adulteress.

What did an adulteress wear to breakfast, I wondered. How did she eat her meals, study, or write? And how did she face her husband? Manuel had shown no shame or trepidation in facing me after his night with Angélica, in our own home. Did I dare to emulate his unrepentant ease? I would have to, if my secret was to remain my own. I dressed warmly, as the storm that had threatened last night had indeed arrived. Wrapped in my thickest shawl, I went to breakfast.

The sisters greeted me with no sign of contempt, no indication that they knew of my transgression. Though Sor Juana did not make an appearance at the table, this was not unusual, and so I did not permit myself more than a tremor of concern over her absence.

I took my chocolate back to my room, and by the refurbished fire I looked at the books I had taken. They were of only moderate interest. I mused on how spoiled I had become. A year or two ago, I would never have believed the abundance of written words available here, and now I picked and chose to my personal taste. I opened one, a play by Lope de Vega, and began to read.

Time flew by, and by lunch I was tired but exhilarated. This was a man who truly understood the human condition, and could write about it as well. I was consoled by the ongoing existence of such erudition.

Away from the safe haven of my room, my trepidation returned, and again I watched the nuns' faces for any sign of knowledge. When one nun dropped a fork, I jumped as if stabbed myself. And when Sor Inez, in her quiet way, asked me if I was quite well, I was at foolish pains to reassure her, to the point where her suspicions would have been raised if she had been more of the doubting type. I fled back to my room at the earliest moment politeness allowed.

I REMEMBERED THE WARDROBE needs of my prior visit and, like an experienced Court visitor, had commissioned two gowns for Advent. The seamstress sent word that they were ready for fitting, and I left the nuns' wing to venture into the central area of the castle. I prayed that I would meet no one in the hallways, but that prayer was ignored, as my prayers for more important needs should be, by the God I had offended. The seamstress's rooms were full of ladies, of course, as Advent was approaching and the gowns were ready.

Another woman would have relished this time when the ladies all gathered to chat about slips and sleeves, laces and collars, and to compare, admiring aloud and condemning internally the selections of the others. Though I could not force gaiety, I could, and had to, feign neutrality, and so when I walked into the rooms I composed my face in a pleasant, uncommitted look.

"Señora, your dresses are ready for the first fitting," the seamstress said. "Ernesta!" she called to her assistant. "Help Doña Josefina into this one!" A thin, tired-looking young woman rushed forth to guide me into a dressing area.

As she was pinning up the hem, the seamstress kept up a chatter from around the pins in her mouth. "Are you looking forward to the balls? Will you be attending the dinners?" All questions that meant nothing, for of course every lady was looking forward to the balls, and hoped to attend as many of the dinners as possible. "You only ordered two dresses, señora. You must have brought quite a wardrobe from home."

I nodded, not wishing to engage in any detailed conversation. But I was joined behind the screen by Doña Luz, who also was to be fitted. She smiled at me as she struggled out of her brown muslin dress, to be helped into a gown of deep navy velvet.

"This dress will mask your condition yet awhile," said the seamstress to Luz, pulling the folds over Luz's just barely rounding belly.

"I should hope so, for the amount of material we put into it!" Doña Luz replied, with that silver-bell laugh. I felt my hands grow icy. Her condition. It could well become my condition, and my husband had not touched me in more than a year. I could not imagine how I had ignored that threat.

"Don't you agree, Doña Josefina?" Luz asked, and I startled.

"I'm sorry, Doña Luz, I was dreaming," I said, not mentioning that it was a nightmare.

"You poetesses! Living in a different world!" She laughed again. "But your gown is beautiful. The deep rose becomes you. You are almost radiant in it. You must be deeply joyful, though I confess I did not notice that radiance when you were at the Marqués' dinner!"

"Your gown is beautiful, too." I was at a loss for more words.

Luz smiled, and it was she who was radiant. "Come, join me for dinner. You must long to leave the nuns' wing now and then!" She took my hesitation for modesty, not terror. "No, come, you will be quite welcome."

"Perhaps tomorrow," I said. And not wanting to seem ungracious, I added, "I have yet much to read tonight, but surely tomorrow, if you will indulge me."

"Of course," she answered. "I will count on it."

I would not be able to hide for the remainder of my stay, arousing suspicion and talk. Her invitation, I decided, was most timely.

THE NEXT DAY PASSED as the first, though I still saw no sign of Sor Juana, and I received no summons to read, sup with grandees, or otherwise imperil my solitude, leaving me only with my invitation from Doña Luz to mark the end of the day. I steeled myself for a meal in the ladies' wing, and reminded myself that only I knew of my sin. I had now to add falsity to disgraced state, and brazenness to it as well.

The room was well lit, and the economies of the nuns' wing were nowhere evident in the ladies' dining room. Though of course I had dined regularly here during my first visit, that was during the summer, when the meals were all held while it was still light. Now, as darkness came well before Vespers, and the excesses of Advent were approaching, everything was sumptuously arrayed. The contrasts with my severe living conditions on the other side of the castle were highlighted.

The wall sconces were all lit, and a lovely cloth embroidered with peacocks covered the table. I sat next to Luz, with a pale, quiet woman of age to my left. I looked around the table. Although many of the faces were familiar, none of the ladies who had been the mainstays of my prior visit were present. Of course, Eustacia had been banished, and Angélica had not yet arrived. Where Granada was I did not know, though I imagined she dined frequently with the Marquesa herself, as an old favorite.

Tureens of steaming soup were brought in by servants, and we were served while seated; this was different from our more homelike service in the nuns' wing, where we circulated the dishes among ourselves at the table or brought our bowls to the sideboard for filling. We were served a fragrant, clear liquid, in which floated dumplings of corn masa, as light as clouds. Wine was poured into our glasses without our asking. I tasted the soup, and allowed the warmth to fill me. An herb I was unfamiliar with flavored the broth. For once, there was someone at the table who would not consider my question foolish.

"What is this unusual herb?" I asked Luz.

"Cilantro," she answered. "I don't use it either, but it is wholesome and good for the digestion. Flavorful, as well. Do you manage your cook, or do you cook yourself?"

Another question I could not imagine Granada or Eustacia, or even Angélica, asking.

"I manage my cook, though in my father's home I prepared most of the meals. At home"—I felt my heart catch—"at home, except for some preparations I make for my sons, my cook follows my instructions."

"And does she faithfully?"

"No," I replied with a laugh. "Not unless I lend more than my instruction, but follow it with my own hand in the seasonings."

"The same." Luz smiled.

"I miss my home," I said truthfully. "I love the time to study here, but I long for the rhythms of the hacienda."

"I do not! I miss my children, of course, but they are well cared for. I love the dry warmth here, the ease, and with four children, and one following, this is my cherished respite."

"Your husband obviously permits this," I said, wonderingly.

"Oh, you know how men are. He does his duty to me"—she patted her stomach—"and I do mine, and we live in companionable harmony ten months of the year. And then the rains start, and I start to sneeze and wheeze, and he sends me to wait on the Marquesa. It enhances his standing, and it keeps me from sneezing in his soup!"

We both laughed at that, and heads turned to see what caused the merriment. But I was troubled. I could not ask her, on such slim acquaintance, whether his duty to her extended to masculine fidelity. And, of course, there was never going to be anyone I could ask about her own duty. Ours lay clearly before us.

"Will you go home after New Year's?" Luz was asking.

I ratcheted my attention back to her. "Oh, yes, of course. But my husband comes soon, at Advent, for a visit."

Luz's eyebrows shot up. "Well, that will cause no end of consternation, won't it!"

Consternation was the word.

"Indeed. I will have no time to write or study once he arrives, I am sure. But I wonder, what shall I do then? I have never seen a woman here with her husband!"

"True!" Luz exclaimed. "Although I never thought of this before. And you will certainly not be attending any of the Marqués' soirees, once your husband arrives."

"Certainly not. I doubt I will be attending any before then, either. I believe I have offended beyond redemption."

"Well, it is to be hoped," Luz replied, and again I thought, From the mouths of the innocents is the truth spoken. "Will you write me a poem, then," she asked, "before your husband comes and puts an end to your creativity? Something to enjoy after you return to your hacienda?"

I blushed: my first commission. Though perhaps the Marqués' request for a verse qualified, here was one I welcomed.

"I am such a novice. Perhaps you would prefer one of Sor Juana's sonnets. She is honored and known throughout the land for her brilliant poetry."

"No, no! I must have yours. And in truth, I never really understand what she is saying. But your work is clear as crystal, and shines as bright. It would do me honor."

"The honor is mine, Doña Luz!" I felt a glow, new and warm. I was really a poet now; I had a commission, and a reader.

"Oh, let us dispense with the formality of our titles. We are the only hacienda wives here, we must be sisters while we enjoy this grand hospitality." She put her arm around me. "Sister?"

"Sister," I replied. I had found a friend.

EVEN SISTERS DO NOT tell each other everything, and I could certainly not tell Luz about Father Alonso. For though it was as Father that I once again thought of him, I confess that the memory brought blushes—and not just of shame. I had not been with a man carnally for so long, and though it was shameful to admit, his caresses returned to me at night, in my dreams, both waking and sleeping.

The night I had dined with Luz I dreamed again. But this time, it was Manuel who lay with me. His scent was that of leather, not lemon verbena, his hands were hard and warm. His passion aroused mine, and I awoke damp with sweat. I lay there in the darkness, yearning for him. But with that longing, which increased with each day that brought closer his arrival, my fear increased. I did not know how I would face him, how I could let him approach my body, when I had been so sullied.

It was now five days since my tryst. I had not seen Father Alonso since that fateful night, nor had I received any message from him or sent any to him. My waking dreams were most specific, and I remembered every moment of his approach, his conquest, my yielding. I could not stop myself from reliving the experience, and my unruly body felt each tremor and vibration again and again. But I had no desire to speak to him or to see him.

At first I thought it was the fire of shame that had left my heart an unfeeling cinder, and certainly that was a part of the cause. But once the initial mortification had passed I became aware of a second emotion, lurking in ugly ambush in my heart. Father Alonso was well schooled in the arts of love, and I wondered, with jealous fury, why a man of the Church should know so much.

I had not seen Sor Juana anywhere, nor heard her voice. Had she left the Court? And had Father Alonso left, too? And the final question—who had softly closed the library door that night?—joined my other thoughts in battle for what remained of my equanimity.

I recalled the first time I heard Father Alonso's voice on my earlier visit to the Court, coming from that very alcove. He was in private conversation with Sor Juana, intellectual conversation, they had assured me. I could picture now the Bishop, with his pants down and his cassock up, and Sor Juana with her enormous pin under her neck, and though tears came to my eyes, my mind would not erase the imagined image and the conflicting flames of jealousy and desire that tore my body apart.

No, I did not want to see Father Alonso, and I made no effort to seek out Sor Juana. If they had gone, and had gone together, my heart and my mind might be bereft, but my secret was safely gone, too.

IT WAS THE THURSDAY before the beginning of Advent. I returned to the seamstress for the final fittings, and sent word to Luz to meet me there. Manuel was due to arrive on Saturday, and I had but two days left of freedom. I had a poem for my friend, and a longing for the easy conversation we could have together.

"The seamstress is going to have to give me more fabric here," Luz giggled, as the assistant pulled at the waistline of the gown again. "I am growing faster with this one than the others. Perhaps it is another boy."

My gowns fit well, and the process was quick. A small tuck in the waist, and a slight lifting of the hem, and the dresses were perfect. I took Luz's arm. "Come and walk with me in the garden. It is not too cold out," I said.

She pulled her shawl around her and joined me willingly. My own rebozo that Cayetana had brought me from Mexico City was wrapped around me snugly, the elaborate embroidery making a pattern of flowers and birds across my bosom. I pulled a sheet of foolscap from inside my dress and handed it to Luz.

"You did it!" she exclaimed, her silver-bell laugh tinkling with delight. "Oh, read it to me!"

"Read it to me yourself," I said, smiling, "it belongs to you now."

"Oh," Luz said gently, "I don't read very well. I will beg you to read to me."

I blushed. I remembered my own unschooled days, when I would have been ashamed to read, too. But her embarrassment was more than that, and I wondered if she could read more than her own name. I could not ask, so I took the paper back and read.

"Your charm lies not in artifice,
Nor do you feign an innocence
Of worldly woes and practices,
Nor trade genteel for crassness.
Your bells chime sweet,
Your eyes see clear
And light pours forth
With honor dear
And fecund life will spring anew
To answer riddles—who are you?"

"Oh, I love it!" Luz said. "You wrote that for me, about me!" Her smile was wide and unrestrained. How easy it was, I thought, to please one so good.

"I was honored to have my first patron," I said, laughing.

"You see, I was right. You don't cloak what you say, so the rest of us can understand it. Too bad the Marqués didn't like to be told straight out where his virtues are!" We both laughed. I handed her the paper. She folded it carefully and tucked it into her bosom. Arm in arm we continued along the garden path.

"Did you hear that the Marqués has put Eustacia into a little villa of her own?" Luz asked. "After the Marquesa threw her out, it's a wonder that the Marqués would set her up. After all, the Court and the money are all in the Marquesa's family, not his."

"No, I had not heard, but I have not been in the ladies' wing except on the night we dined together, nor have I been asked to wait upon the Marquesa since the day she excused Eustacia."

"Then you must be terribly out of favor," said Luz, "for we have all been back and forth to and from the Marquesa in preparation for Advent. I only thought that you had been asked for times other than mine."

"Well, mercifully the Marqués has had his attention drawn away from me, for I have not heard from him since that day, either." We continued along for a bit more, until we turned the corner and found ourselves at the bench where, as Angélica had described it, the Marqués had found her, and Miguel Ángel had found them both. We sat, and I told Luz the sad tale. "Angélica came to my home after that. I had just recovered from the stillbirth of my daughter." I wondered if I dared to tell the rest.

"Seeing your friend in disgrace must have added to your sorrow," Luz said, patting my hand. "Were you able to console her?"

"Not I," I said bitterly.

Luz raised a brow, then lowered it. "I see. And so you returned to Court." I nodded. She understood without being told. "I wondered that you could resist the Marqués so vehemently, when submission would have allowed his ardor to tire. Now I understand. You will not join another on an unvirtuous path."

Her kind assessment shamed me. A more chilling thought followed.

"But then, if submission were sufficient to sate his ugly humor, why is he keeping Eustacia?"

"To humiliate his wife?" Luz offered.

"No, she is beyond such suffering. Eustacia must be giving him something more, something he really wants. And there's only one thing Eustacia trades in. Information."

As IF COMMUNICATING THROUGH thoughts, the Marquesa sent me a summons to wait upon her that very evening. I steeled myself first to go in search of Sor Juana, both to appease my nagging mind and to obtain her counsel if she would give it. I tapped at her door, but received no response. Gathering my nerve, I tapped next on Sor Inez's door, and got a quiet "In the Lord's name" greeting, bidding me enter. I pushed open the heavy door, to find Sor Inez on her knees before a votary altar. A crucifix and candles were arranged in a small nook, and she knelt on the stone floor with no carpet to lessen the hardness. She looked up at me when I entered, crossed herself, put away her rosary, and haltingly brought herself to her feet.

"Forgive me, Sister. I didn't mean to interrupt your prayers," I said. Sor Inez was well on in years, perhaps fifty or more, and I could see the pain in her eyes as she struggled to work off the soreness in her knees. "Can I bring you some chocolate?"

"I would like that," she said gently, putting her soft hand on mine. I led her to her chair before the unlit hearth, and quickly left to get a hot chocolate from the nuns' kitchen. The cook accommodated me right away when I mentioned it was for Sor Inez.

"She is almost a saint," said the cook, handing me the cup.

I had not thought of Sor Inez in any holy way, only as one who played a lyre and sang so sweetly. But now I thought more, and realized that she always had a tray of pastries to offer, always was on hand to smooth ruffled feathers. I could not be the only one who sought her consolation.

I handed her the cup, and she sipped gratefully.

"Is there something troubling you, dear?" she asked after a bit of color had returned to her cheeks.

I nodded. "I have not seen Sor Juana in days. Has she gone away?"

Sor Inez looked into the cold fireplace and did not answer. After a minute, I thought maybe she would not reply at all, and gathered my skirt to stand.

"No, don't go yet," she said, putting out a hand. "Sit. And please, Doña Josefina, listen to me.

"Sor Juana has gone away, briefly, back to the convent. She has taken shelter in our motherhouse, away from temptation. You must not write to her."

"Temptation?" I asked before I thought. Then I felt the heat as my blood rushed to my face. Sor Inez looked into my eyes until I looked away.

"Temptation. But not of the flesh. Temptation of words, of ideas, that may not please those in high positions in the Church. I was praying for her just now. She must be shielded, and the Bishop has taken her away from Court to protect her from the Holy Office's long arms. You must not trouble her now."

The Bishop had taken her away. They were both gone, and without a word to me. I realized how selfish that thought was, especially as their troubles were far more severe than mine if the Holy Office had taken offense at her works. My mere moment of adultery, the shattering of a commandment, the destruction of a marriage by a common sinner, was nothing compared to the Inquisition. But to me, waves of relief that Father Alonso was gone crashed against the rocks of jealousy, that he had gone with Sor Juana, without a moment of consideration.

I looked up to see Sor Inez watching my face closely.

"You love His Grace, the Bishop, Doña Josefina. We know that." She held up a hand to stop my protest. "But he must attend to Sor Juana, for he is protecting her life.

"Your husband comes in two days," she went on. "You must prepare to meet him. Love is holy when it is proper. Do not shirk your duty, or you will do so at your peril and to your regret."

I nodded but could not speak. Finally I rose. "Thank you, Sor Inez. I must wait upon the Marquesa this evening, and I will endeavor to begin to do my duty outside the nuns' wing. Bless you for your prayers."

"You are in them as well. You will need strength, Doña Josefina. Do not forget to pray for strength."

I crossed myself, as she did, and returned to my room to dress.

LATE ON SATURDAY AFTERNOON, I received word that Manuel had arrived. I had paced the floor of my room for an hour, after completing what I hoped was a welcoming but modest toilette, awaiting the message. It was brought by little Toño, and I felt the need to give him a small coin for his efforts. It brought a smile to his chubby cheeks, and I hoped it helped him forget his earlier indiscretion with my message to the Bishop. It would not help me to have Manuel hear about that.

I rushed to the central door, only to be met by the portress. "Your husband has gone to his rooms in the gentlemen's quarters, and Doña Angélica is in the ladies'." I nodded my thanks. The portress had seen much in her long life, and she made no comment, or any vocal fluctuation, to indicate any judgment of the fact that my wedded husband had arrived accompanied by a young and beautiful widow. I had not forgotten that he was traveling with her, but I had successfully put it out of my mind until that moment. I was faced with the ugly necessity of greeting Angélica in her rooms. I did not wish to do so without first seeing Manuel. The unfairness of this situation infuriated me.

"Toño!" I said, and he came dashing over. "Go to the gentlemen's wing and tell Don Manuel Castillo that his wife is below, and awaits him. And do not rush around crying that you have an urgent message for anyone, do you understand?"

"Yes, señora. I will run right away!" He stood there smiling.

"I will give you a coin for your efforts if you do this right," I said more gently. "I will fetch it from my room while you go." He ran off, and once again I thought of Joaquín. All this boy's energy was being wasted inside a castle, when he could be roping calves and getting muddy with men, and learning to be a real person. I shook my head. I aspired to the quiet contemplative life of study, so perhaps little Toño longed to be a gentleman in a ruffled shirt, drinking Madeira and flattering ladies.

Before I had time to get a coin from my room, Toño was back, grinning widely. "Don Manuel paid for the message!" he crowed, showing me a shiny escudo.

"I should say he did!" I replied, awed by Manuel's generosity. "Did he give a reply?"

Toño nodded. "He said he would see you as soon as he changed from his traveling clothes. He has a big, shiny belt!" I thought of the sound of his silver-encrusted belt hitting the floor and winced. Toño took no notice, dashing off to gloat over his good fortune among his fellow pages.

The reply left me unsure. Manuel had never changed his clothes to see me when he returned from the barn. Why would he do so now? Was he intimidated by the fanciness of the Court, as I had been upon my arrival? Or was he simply less eager to see me than I was to see him? I thought of the five weeks I had been gone. He had spent some of that time with Angélica. I began to tremble.

I returned to my room before the tears fell. I realized it was foolish of me to carry on so, but the thought of Manuel making love to Angélica, night after night, while I struggled with my unruly passion here at Court, undid my strength and resolve. I would not see him. I would not see her! I would not bear her smirk of triumph.

My festival of self-pity was interrupted by a soft knock. Before I could forestall admittance the door opened to let in the dark-haired *menina*.

"A message for you, señora." I took the paper.

Will your husband enjoy a bit of scandal? Or will you pay for your room and board personally? I wait, and will abide by your reply. M.

"No answer," I whispered. I was undone.

Nineteen

HE WAS WAITING FOR me at the foot of the stairs, where they joined the grand foyer. Behind him, the light from the setting sun streamed in the open door that led to the gardens, its dying red-gold rays lighting him from behind. It cast his face in shadow, but the gleam of his strong smile, his dark hair wet and brushed away from his rugged brown face, his wide shoulders, were unmistakable. My reserve and fear vanished, and I threw myself into Manuel's open arms.

He held my head against his hard, flat chest; he stroked my hair, and I breathed in his leather scent, now overlaid with that of a strange and scented soap. No amount of Court-created aroma could mask his unforgettable smell. I closed my eyes, and for the second time that day felt the tears run down my face.

"Don't cry, my Josefina. I am here now," he said, over and over, petting my head as if I were a child. Heedless of any passing gossip or grandee, I stayed in his arms. Eventually, though, I did raise my head from his embrace, and stepped back.

"Welcome, Manuel," I said simply. I looked into his green-flecked brown eyes, wondering how I could have ever been swayed away from them. Father Alonso, with his sparkling blue eyes and hell-colored hair, could never hold me like Manuel. And yet, the mere thought of Father Alonso brought back my shame, my descent into the hell that Manuel's arrival had sealed along with my fate. I shivered and turned away.

"You are looking well," Manuel said, and I recalled his chariness of language.

"As are you. Was your journey good?" I could not meet his eyes.

"Uneventful," he replied, without inflection.

The blissful moment of reunion was past. The painful specter had wormed its way into our conversation about the most banal of topics. But I was not the timid country wife who had first journeyed to Court last spring, I was a woman who had suffered. I steeled myself and said, "Angélica weathered the journey well?"

"She did."

I cursed his brevity, yet I could not have abided the verbosity of the Court-trained men I had been in company with, either. Torn, I, too, was silent.

At last the rustle of skirts broke the stalemate. Two ladies in dinner finery hurried past on their way to the Marquesa's wing. As they passed, they looked at us with malicious curiosity. Did they already know? It could not be, as Angélica had been here less than an hour, but word, of course, traveled fast when it was as gossip-laden as this story.

"Do you know the protocol for dining here?" I asked. I did not truly know whether the men acted as the women did, dining together unless they had an invitation to wait upon the Marqués or the Marquesa, but I assumed I knew more than Manuel.

"I have been told, somewhat. It seems fairly odd to be invited and yet not dine with one's host, but there are odd manners throughout. I believe that tonight I am dining with you, and others. A page will direct me, I am told."

I knew nothing of this. I had not thought to arrange dinner with my arriving husband, but someone had. I forced myself to look at Manuel. He smiled down at me, a little half smile. "I am not used to being so unsure," he added.

"You will get used to it. I am surprised Angélica did not give you a full introductory lesson on your journey out. It was one thing for her to want me to look foolish, but it would be far from her interest for you to stumble."

We were both amazed at my speech. Manuel responded with silence.

"I must dress. I will see you at dinner," I said, turning away. I moved slowly, waiting for Manuel to call me back to him, but even a snail would eventually have to arrive at its destination, and so, without looking back, I made my way uninterrupted to the nuns' wing.

I was met by a bustle in the nuns' kitchen. Sor Inez and a young nun named Sor Teresita were speaking quickly and quietly, the younger one holding the older one's hands. Their intensity, along with the rapt attention from the several other sisters in the kitchen, presaged important news.

"Doña Josefina," Sor Inez called to me. "Come, we must speak." Her normally placid face was animated, her light Spanish complexion flushed. I joined her and Sor Teresita, who nodded a modified curtsy to me. "The Bishop has been seized," Sor Inez said. "He has been taken by the Holy Office!"

I felt my throat close. "Why?" I croaked.

"His writings, no doubt."

"Is Sor Juana safe?" I asked.

"That is the question on everyone's tongue," she replied. "Teresita believes she is. Word is that Juana is at the motherhouse, but we cannot be sure."

"We want to send someone to the convent to find out," Sor Teresita said.

"If she is hiding, we must not ferret out her location," I replied. Both nuns looked at me, astonished at the unexpected note of authority in my voice.

"It is as I feared," Sor Inez said. "You must tell us what you know about this."

"I know nothing," I answered. That was true, though I surmised much.

"But I thought the Bishop was safe. He had modified his sermons to obey the Archbishop's commands. He was superbly connected. It is unthinkable that he has been taken!" Sor Inez had lost her characteristic composure.

I folded my hands as if in prayer and bowed my head. I felt the terror overcome me. My two powerful allies were gone and everything I held dear hung in the balance.

"Sor Inez, you are right," I said. "Someone should go to the convent and find out if Sor Juana is safe, but it must be someone trusted, for if Sor Juana must hide, we must not jeopardize her safety for our curiosity. As to the Bishop, he will extricate himself, no doubt, with his own resources."

"We must bow to your greater knowledge," Sor Inez said. I shook my head. I did not want to be charged with knowing what I did not know.

I went to my room to change, searching my brain to figure out what had led to this. It was clear that Sor Inez was counting on me to find the solution. I could only come up with Eustacia. Had it been she who had spied on us in the library? I had assumed it was. She was a vicious woman, used to parlaying gossip into power. Alas, what I did know was that Eustacia was ready to tear down all who had slighted her, and with the backing of the Marqués, she now had the power to do so.

If Eustacia was behind this, then it was my sin, and my foolishness, that had given her the power she now wielded so wantonly. It became my duty to stop her, as far as I could.

I DID INDEED RECEIVE word about the dinner to welcome my husband. It seemed that there were dinners in small rooms throughout the castle, but in all of my time here I had never yet been included in one. It made me wonder what else I had missed.

I had dressed carefully, in a cream-colored dress with black lace adornment that had been Luz's. The dress did not fit her properly, being too small in the waist and shoulders, and there was not sufficient material to let it out. Luz had offered it to me along with several others after our last fitting. It fit me perfectly, and the lace added an unexpected softness to my worried features. I dared not hope that Manuel would see me as more beautiful than Angélica, but only that he would recall his love for me somehow, and be turned back to me. That I deserved less was undeniable.

I approached the room not knowing what to expect. I could not imagine who would arrange this, who would host it. I pushed aside the heavy purple curtain that served as a door, and almost turned and ran. At the center, being served a glass of wine, glittered Angélica. She was in a gold and white gown, and her hair shone with the same light as the sun. As I stood in the doorway she turned to me and smiled.

"Welcome," she said, greeting me in a clearly hostess voice.

My mouth gaped, and I shut it sharply. Angélica was welcoming me to the dinner for my own husband. Angélica, on her first day back at Court with a finessed invitation despite her prior disgrace, was the hostess. She held out her hand, and before I could run, behind me a familiar woman's voice exclaimed, "Angélica, how kind of you!" I whirled, my escape blocked by Granada.

I had no choice. "Angélica, thank you for so thoughtfully arranging this soiree. Your kindness, especially when you must be so tired from your journey, is peerless." I tried to pitch my voice as if I were thanking a particularly diligent servant, although I doubt I succeeded. At the very least, my pride could be temporarily salvaged.

I turned to Granada, and before she could make some horrid comment, I added, "And you are looking lovely, Granada. Manuel will be infatuated." Angélica shot me a venomous glance, and I preened with pleasure. I had indeed learned something here.

To my relief, Luz de Albanil had been included. I took a glass of wine and moved to her side. "So this is the lady who caught Miguel Ángel's eye," Luz commented softly to me. I nodded. "Such daring, to show her face here, and to host a dinner for you and your husband, after behaving so badly."

"She traveled here with Manuel," I added in a whisper. Luz's eyes grew round. I nodded miserably.

"This is going to be a most interesting evening," she said, and turned to the curtain. Manuel had arrived.

The ladies fell silent. He looked handsomer and more manly than anyone I had seen at the Court. His shirt, which was clearly new, buttoned high into a folded collar, but he affected no lace or ruffle. His black coat was unadorned, and it fell in straight folds from his shoulders to his hips. His tight black pants had a single ribbon of black satin down each side, and his boots, like none he had ever worn at home, gleamed with polish around the elaborate stitching.

He looked around the small room, his smile instant at the sight of Angélica, but it was when he saw me that he stepped forward, his face attentively alight. I took a step toward him, drawn without will, but Angélica stepped between us.

"Don Manuel, welcome to the Court of the Marqués and Marquesa de Condera," she said, holding a glass of wine out to him. He took it, and was surrounded by Angélica, Granada, and another lovely woman, wearing a gray gown. He lifted his glass and drank, while I stood there with Luz, forgotten.

I was forced to endure. Granada's sharp eyes missed nothing, and I would not give her more satisfaction over my humiliation than she already had. I pretended that I found this arrangement most suitable: in my need to study and write, I had no time to arrange social frivolities. The company included two gentlemen I had mercifully never met, a Don Carrazo and an Honorable Señor Matanzas. Both held large estates to the north, where Luz's husband's hacienda lay, and Señor Matanzas had a remote acquaintance with my sister's husband. Though I had not seen my sister in over three years, and she was twelve years my senior, this allowed for some trivial conversation.

Though I struggled to eat the well-prepared food Angélica had ordered, I could barely swallow through the bitterness. Manuel was never left alone, and we had no chance to converse. He did occasionally look my way, but as was his wont, he spent most of the dinner admiring the ladies' beauty, and saying little. During my silence I watched his face. Knowing he had sampled Angélica's favors when I was at home, I was certain that he had enjoyed them in my absence. I wondered how in Heaven's own name this next month would pass. Though I kept my mask of neutrality, I was alert to any possible hint that Angélica or Granada knew anything at all about Father Alonso. They appeared ignorant, but with Angélica, knowledge was only impeded by lack of time.

I could not end the torment, for with the ending of dinner I would have to face the truth. Would Manuel want me, and if so, could I lie with him? Would I feel Father Alonso's hands in his place, his presence in my body where only Manuel should be? Or would Manuel choose Angélica, a choice that every lady in the entire Court would know of by morning? But dinner could not last forever, and finally Angélica raised her glass once more in welcome, and signaled the ladies to retire.

To my surprise, Manuel took my arm, escorting me out and down the stairs.

"You are still in the nuns' quarters?" he asked. I nodded. "I cannot come to you there, Josefina. You must move."

I had thought of that. "I do not know where married women stay," I said. I had put off inquiring about this, fearing the public shame of moving to more accessible rooms, only to be rejected by Manuel.

"Then you shall sleep in my room tonight," Manuel said simply. "I have a bed too small even for one, but still we shall manage. I will lock the door to the adjoining suite. Those gents I am assigned to share the rooms with shall have no part in this." He was smiling.

He had chosen me. The warmth of joy suffused me, though I knew I could not yield to my happiness tonight. I shook my head. "There are no women in your wing because all the suites are shared. I will move tomorrow. I promise you."

He embraced me again, for the second time that day, and kissed my hair. "Until tomorrow, my wife."

I WOULD LIVE TO regret that night's excessive modesty. My ignorance was the instrument of my defeat. To move from the ladies' wing to the nuns' quarters had been easily arranged. I had only to ask Sor Juana, and within two days a servant had arrived to carry my simple belongings to my new room. But with Advent upon us, the castle was more like an inn. And even more like the inns where Mary and Joseph sought shelter for the oncoming birth of Our Savior—there was no room to be had. I asked the portress, who summoned the head housekeeper, who consulted the majordomo, all to the shaking of heads.

At last, the ladies' chancellor, a pallid woman with gray hair and a perpetual frown, shrugged and said, "I can offer you only two choices. First, you could move back into the ladies' wing, but you would need to share the room with your friend Angélica de Sandoval, who has a room much larger than her station warrants. Or you may remain in the nuns' quarters and hope that someone is taken ill, and leaves."

She could not understand my mirthless laugh. To share a room with Angélica for the purpose of receiving my husband at night left me choosing laughter over tears. I returned to my simple quarters, grateful that at least Angélica was not with me.

I sent a note to Manuel, asking him to meet me in the music room before the midday meal, so we could talk. Little Toño returned to say that Don Manuel was out riding with other gentlemen, and that they were set to return late in the afternoon, but that he had left my note in his room. I had time to formulate my plans.

My first inquiry was to Sor Inez. "When was Sor Juana called away, Sister?"

"Wednesday," she replied. "A most severe-looking priest came to call for her. She was barely able to pack a small bag before she left."

I took a chance. "Did she leave you any writings?"

Sor Inez looked away, out the window of her small room. Finally she nodded. She went to her dresser, a plain wooden piece with no adornment or carving, and opened the top drawer. If the papers were important it seemed a sadly obvious place to hide them. But Sor Inez merely pulled the drawer out and emptied it on her cot. When the drawer was turned over, I could see a sheaf of papers tied to the bottom. At least some stratagem had been attempted.

She pulled out the papers and handed them to me. "Bless you, Doña Josefina. Please do not lose these." I looked at the top page: "A Letter to Sor Filotea." Innocuous enough, I thought.

"I will take good care of them. So, she left Wednesday, then?" Sor Inez nodded. That was a week after my reading for the Marqués and Eustacia's banishment. "Did she say anything at all that would allow us to help her?"

Sor Inez frowned. "She said the fault lay with her, and that she would make it right with the Holy Office. She was calm and determined. But she gave me these papers and asked that I keep them safe for her return. It was like her not to confide, and there was so little time that had she had the inclination to do so she would not have been able to."

I tried to look caring, but I was in too much of a hurry.

"Did you read the papers?" I asked. Sor Inez shook her head. "Do not worry, Sister. We must trust in Sor Juana's judgment."

"And in the Lord's mercy," Sor Inez added, crossing herself. I crossed myself as well, all the while thinking that the Lord had shown little mercy thus far to those caught in the Holy Office's web. I excused myself to return to my room.

The sheaf of papers contained two letters: one that appeared to be a first draft of a letter from Sor Juana to a Sor Filotea of Puebla, taking exception to the sermon of some distant Father Vieira, and asserting, in a postscript, that the greatest of God's gifts was not love of our fellow man, as Vieira claimed, but the taking away, as divine punishment, of the gifts God Himself had given us; and the second one, Sor Filotea's response, defending Sor Juana's right to study, learn, and write as gifts from God. The sheaf also had two poems I had not seen before. I put those aside for later.

The letter to Sor Filotea made no sense to me. If this Father Vieira, whoever he was, thought that Christ's commandment to us to love our fellow man as we loved ourselves was the greatest of God's gifts, how could Sor Juana find fault? And who was Sor Filotea, arguing that Sor Juana's greatest gifts from Our Lord were her desires to learn and to write? I shook my head, which had begun to ache from the difficulty of the reading. One thing was clear: if the Holy Office were to find these letters, both Sor Juana and Sor Filotea would suffer.

I looked at the dying fire in my hearth. A fine place for the letters, perhaps. But had Sor Juana wanted them burned, she would have done so herself. Unless she had had no time . . . I could not know what to do.

The name of Sor Filotea, of the Santisima Trinidad Convent in Puebla, was vaguely familiar. I did not know where or how I had heard the name, perhaps in one of Sor Juana's intellectual teachings to me over the past month, but I was certain that I knew of her. And her affiliation with Puebla, and therefore with Father Alonso's bishopric, was a matter of further confusion. One thing was certain, and that was where my duty lay. I must ensure that the Holy Office would never get hold of these letters.

Inspiration struck. The Inquisitors were all men. Naturally, no woman would ever affiliate herself with a cruel and life-destroying force such as the Inquisition. Our Heaven-ordained role was to be givers of life, not takers. And so, no man, especially of the priestly sort, would care to delve into the areas most feminine and mysterious. The bag where I kept the cloths to absorb my monthly courses, along with those powders so vital in soothing the cramping pains of my womanly bleeding, would be safe from prying male eyes. I folded the papers carefully, wrapped them in cloths.

I would not need any cloths for another week, and my hands ran cold at the thought that I might not need them at all. Whispering a prayer that I might not have conceived with sin, I shut the drawer tight. The bells were ringing for the midday meal by the time my prayer had ended. I sent a note to Luz, inviting her to join me in a walk to the stables when the men rode in. Until then, without Manuel to seek out, I was free to dine with the sisters, and was spared having to face Angélica for another day.

LUZ AND I WALKED together to the courtyard outside the stables. It was a masculine area, with carved wooden benches, paving stones, and small tables where the gentlemen could rest their tankards while removing spurs or other riding gear. A servant rode up ahead, alerting the grooms to the men's return and sending a boy for wine.

The sound of the horses quickened my heart as the men appeared over the crest. Evidently the activities and movements of the gentlemen were monitored by interested females. Several other ladies, mostly of the very young set, had appeared, walking casually, as if by chance happening upon the stables just at the time the men rode in.

It had not rained that day, so the air was cool and crisp, and I pulled my heavy rebozo around my shoulders. The sun was low, red and gold, casting a false warmth on the courtyard. The horses glowed, almost as in a vision, as they cantered into sight.

I saw Manuel immediately. He rode so well, with the practiced ease of the cattleman, but with the erect dignity of the haciendado. He was not in any finery, though he wore leather leggings I had never seen before over his black pants, and his hat was trimmed in silver braid. Unlike some of the men, whose coats were elaborately fur-trimmed, he wore his customary leather riding coat, unadorned by anything but use.

He dismounted, accepted a cup of warmed wine from a page, and smiled at me. He bowed lightly to Luz, who offered her hand and then thoughtfully withdrew from sight. Manuel's eyes sparkled with the light of the setting sun, and doubtless with the pleasure of being once more in his element.

He had enjoyed the ride into the forest, and had made the acquaintance of many of the men sojourning here for the Advent season. I sat on a bench, and he joined me. I finally had Manuel to myself.

"I have it on good information that we will have an even better market for the cattle next year," he said, putting his mug down and crossing his long legs.

"Have the gentlemen here been discussing business?" I asked, astonished. I had observed only frivolous communication among them.

"Of course, Josefina. What else would we talk about? The King needs money, there may be a war with France. For money, he needs taxes, but for armies, he needs food."

I was silent. The question burning in my heart—no, one of many questions—must eventually be asked. I steeled myself.

"I am grateful that you are here, Manuel, but I do not know why you came."

He looked surprised. "To see you, my dear. I am lonely without your company. When can you move?"

I had to give him the unfortunate news that it would not be tonight. Manuel took the news with reasonably good grace.

"I have waited for six weeks for you. I will wait another day and endure the gentlemen in my suite who snore like bulls. I can offer you news of home, and yet you have not asked after your beloved sons, or of Cayetana, or even of me. Has this life at Court severed you from your home?"

Tears filled my eyes. There was so much to inquire about, and yet I had not done so. What had happened to me? "The children, please, Manuel. Tell me about them."

"Joaquín spent all the days I was home with me, and he is truly going to be a great cattleman. I returned from the cattle drive only to hear Cayetana's complaints that he had spent every day at the stables, getting underfoot, trying to ride all the horses. Next year, indeed, I will bring him on the drive with me."

"And Neto?"

Manuel shook his head. "Neto clings to Cayetana. He misses you. He needs you home. He has your mind, Josefina. Perhaps he will be our priest."

"I hope not," I said without thinking.

"You hope not?" Manuel looked in my eyes.

"I do not think Neto will want to be a priest, once he grows up," I said quickly. "But it would be a great honor, of course."

Manuel smiled, his face gloriously handsome. "No, my Josefina. I also hope he will not be a priest. He must be a man!" I did not say that a priest could also be a man.

"We will return home as soon as the Christmas day is passed," I said.

"Of course, although I hear that the New Year's celebrations are not to be missed."

I knew from whom he had heard this.

"I, for one, will not stay for them," I replied. If Angélica had told him about the New Year's celebrations, then her association with them poisoned them.

"Of course I will return with you," Manuel replied.

I touched his hand in gratitude. He was too distracted to return the touch. "Have you met the Marqués yet?" I asked.

"No," he replied, "but I assume I will be summoned to dine with him eventually. Although he is my host, and I have brought a substantial tribute for the castle from this year's sales, I am looking forward to the meeting for other reasons."

"There are many reasons I can imagine, Manuel. But take care, he is not to be believed, or to be trifled with."

"Are you advising me on my actions, wife?" Manuel asked. His voice was harder than I was used to.

"Of course not," I said quickly. "But the ways of the Court are strange. He will say things, about me, or"—I whispered—"about Angélica, that are not true."

"He will not discuss my wife, with me or anyone else, if he wishes to see old age," Manuel said. He moved to rise.

"Wait. You must know something. He has made odious comments to me, but has not in any way assaulted my honor. Please, do not charge him falsely." My God, if Manuel approached the Marqués as a husband whose honor has been tarnished, I would be destroyed.

"I will charge him as he deserves. My wife will not be touched."

"No, Manuel. Manners here are very easy, and the rules that we live by are unrecognized at Court."

"I know nothing of special rules. I do not understand why you defend him."

I was on dangerous ground. "I do not. But you must see, he is powerful."

"And I am powerless?" Manuel roared.

"No! Please. But see the way the land lies before you act, I beg of you."

"I will not be ruled by you, Josefina, nor will I tolerate whatever special views the Marqués may have of his rights. If he says but a word about you, he will be unable to enjoy his own wife's favors again."

He rose and walked to the stables. The wind had come up, and his hair blew into his eyes. He put his hat back on. With his hand on the bar lock, he turned back to me.

"Josefina, you are my wife. No man may touch you, or your honor, while I live. But you will not become an unsexed harpy with these studies. I will order you home if you persist in telling me my duty. I will ensure that you return to yours."

TWENTY

I CONTINUED TO ABIDE IN the nuns' quarters. Word came that Father Alonso had been freed and Sor Juana was at the mother-house. I breathed with relief.

My days were taken up with the preparations for the first ball—the first Advent *posada*—on the sixteenth of December. I was called to wait upon the Marquesa, but was taken no notice of, with the incessant talk of gowns, balls, and finery. I did receive an occasional question from Granada or others as to whether I had written anything, but I was no longer interesting. I ate in the ladies' wing with Luz, and I dined occasionally with Manuel and others, but he found neither way nor reason to join with me alone at night. After our discussion at the stables he remained displeased with me. I would have heard, at least from the gossip of other ladies, if he had dined with the Marqués, and I had not, so at least that was not the cause of this continued estrangement.

At last, though, the fear that had taken root in my heart could no longer be ignored. I must lie with Manuel, or be damned to living hell if my sin with Father Alonso bore fruit. As Manuel did not seek me out, I had perforce to embolden myself and seek him.

At the end of our meal I followed Manuel out into the hall. "I miss you," I said. I gazed into his eyes, trying to look as seductive as I had seen the many other ladies behave.

He frowned. "Have you taken too much wine?"

I shook my head. "It is just that since you have arrived we have not been able to enjoy one another," I said. I touched his jaw. His eyes opened wide.

"Josefina, you are truly forward now. First you tell me how I should act to the Marqués in defense of my honor. Now you tell me my manly duty!"

"No! I just want to be with you," I whispered. Seduction was far more difficult than it appeared.

"Then see to your room arrangements," he replied. "It is unsuitable for a wife to be creeping around the gentlemen's apartments. It would be easy enough if you were in the ladies' wing where you belonged."

His answer told me far more than I wanted to know.

Angélica, on the other hand, was everywhere. She attended the Marquesa; it seemed her previous disgrace was forgiven. She sang prettily, looked stunning, and conversed lightly with all. The excitement of the season was growing, and the night before the first *posada,* I found myself invited to the Marqués' drawing room, along with Luz, Granada, Angélica, Manuel, and many of the other grandees, for a gala supper. The moment of confrontation would no longer be put off.

I reached into my drawer for the monthly cloths. I was due, and my courses could begin to flow any minute, so I affixed a cloth to avoid any problem. I mixed some powder into a bit of sherry, to forestall cramps. I rarely suffered excessively, but with the courses an unusual two days late I would have a rougher time. The powders made me sleepy sometimes, but were well worth it. I prayed for blood.

While I was in that drawer, I felt for the safety of Sor Juana's papers. They were still there, still in their cloth cocoon. Although I hated to take the next step, prudence, at least self-protection, demanded it. I took the bag from the drawer and brought it with my gown and my hair combs up to Luz's room. The thought of facing the Marqués, along with Angélica and Manuel, had me jittery and tense, and I needed the sweet company of my friend. We agreed to dress together for all the *posadas.*

"Will you be reading us a poem tonight as part of the entertainment?" Luz asked. I shook my head.

"Oh, why not? Don't you want your husband to see how accomplished you have become in your time here?"

"He would not find it amusing to see me perform. Though I will bring a volume of Góngora's poems to read if called upon. They can be most amusing and not the least bit controversial. Here, could you fix the neckline?"

Luz reached around my neck to button the back, so that the high velvet collar draped down in waves of forest green. It was a beautiful dress, and I felt lovely in it. "You wear this dress far better than I ever did," she said.

I was not too proud to enjoy the cast-off clothing of another, especially dresses that had been barely worn, and I was most definitely not above delighting in a compliment so freely and honestly given. I put the bag with my monthly cloths and the secret letters in a corner of the armoire in Luz's room. With that one single act I had now brought gentle Luz into my deadly conspiracy without her knowledge or consent. I prayed she would never know.

"Are you running your courses?" she asked.

"Not yet, but within any minute I will start." Maybe hope could make this the truth.

She nodded. "I have powders. I have no need of them, of course."

"Thank you, Luz, but I have already taken some, to head off any pain." It was good to have a woman I could talk to again. I sorely missed Cayetana, and in the nuns' wing, though they, too, were women, such topics never came up.

"Luz, how do you think a husband and wife can be together here at the castle?"

Luz pondered. "I truly don't know! Though many a lady in our wing has a tryst, she conducts it in her room, and the gentleman leaves by the rear stairs. I cannot imagine a lady going into the gentlemen's wing, and sneaking out before the light of dawn. But a properly married lady, well, I simply do not know."

"Ladies have trysts in their rooms?"

"Of course, Josefina! Surely you knew that!"

And so my understanding, gained at great pain from Manuel the night before, was confirmed. Perhaps it would have been better for me to accept the offer of sharing rooms with Angélica. Then at least I would prevent Manuel from going to her, even if he could not come to me.

"Have you not found a way to be with your husband since your arrival?" Luz asked.

"I am in the nuns' wing," I reminded her. "No man older than ten years can enter there, unless he's a priest." I could not tell her of my clumsy attempt at seduction, or of Manuel's disgusted reaction. "But enough. Let us not be late for this supper. I can only hope that the Marqués says nothing to incite Manuel. I am terrified."

"I am certain that he will not. After all, his desire is for you. If he angers your husband, he will never have you."

"Nor will he have another woman, if Manuel is to be believed."

Luz smiled. "You are fortunate to be loved by so many."

I HAD NOT BEEN in the Marqués' rooms since my command performance. Luz and I entered arm in arm, into a lively room filled with people. Double doors that I had not noticed on my other visits, because they had been closed and covered with tapestries, now stood wide open, allowing the guests to enjoy a second room, filled with greenery and garlands. There were at least thirty people, all talking at once, and we were able to enter without undue notice.

I spied Manuel at the far end of the room, talking with the tall black-haired man whom I recalled only as the Commander. Manuel seemed at ease, and the Commander was talking with a detached air while scanning the room from his high vantage point. I wondered that my country husband could find it so easy to join this company, while I struggled with every word, every nuance of etiquette. Men's conversations must certainly be less fraught with traps.

I took a glass of sherry from a passing servant and raised the glass to my lips. I had the warm feeling that my medicinal powder always gave me, so I reminded myself that I should indulge very lightly in any wine tonight, lest I fall asleep at dinner. Nevertheless, I was grateful for the false comfort the powder gave, for otherwise I would have collapsed from terror at the prospect of being in the same room with the Marqués, the Marquesa, Angélica, and Manuel.

I also took momentary comfort in the realization that Father Alonso would not be present to complete the dangerous mix, nor would Sor Juana be adding her cool, appraising eye and stiletto poetry to the evening. Their lives could be in danger, but at the moment I was selfish enough to be thankful that the instruments of my fall would remain mercifully absent.

With this bravura, I made my way to my husband. He greeted me with the appropriate courtesy of a husband to a wife, but without the warmth that I associated with him. I looked into his eyes, but could only see the chilly curtain that had fallen between us since our conversation out at the stables.

Luz joined us, and I made the introduction to the Commander, who graciously kissed her hand. I recalled that he had been forward with Granada at our first dinner, and wondered if he made a habit of flirting with every woman he met. It was of no consequence, as Luz made gentle and pleasant conversation but avoided the witty sallies that marked the conversation of a Granada or an Angélica.

As if thinking conjured presence, Angélica and Granada both appeared at our sides.

"Good evening, Commander," Granada said, looking up at him through her lashes. She was well turned out in emerald velvet, and though she was not as beautiful as Angélica, she exuded a lively sarcasm that obviously made her alluring to men, though distasteful to me. Luz shot me a covert glance, and I felt an alliance.

"Good evening, Doña Granada," the Commander replied. He and Manuel both smiled. Angélica chimed in a greeting. She, of course, was stunning, once again in gold and ivory, and easily the most beautiful woman in the room. Next to her, Luz, with her dark hair pulled neatly into a chignon, and her soft features, looked like a wren beside a peacock. I harbored no illusions, knowing myself to be in the wren category. And yet, I thought, Luz was right. Manuel, at least at one time, had loved me, and Father Alonso had desired me, and the Marqués was hunting me, so there had to be something in my unsophisticated and unremarkable physiognomy to attract such attention.

It did not matter that I had become lost in my own thoughts, for the conversation swirled around me without my needing to do more than smile and nod. Manuel did nothing that I noticed to indicate any extreme favoritism toward Angélica, though he smiled at her jokes and witticisms. She, in turn, behaved almost territorially in his presence, smiling and preening before him. I would have found her ridiculous, but neither Manuel nor the Commander seemed to notice.

Others joined and left our conversation, and the talk was all about the upcoming *posadas*. Tomorrow's ball would be the first of the nine evenings of celebrations, dinners, and balls, culminating in the grand ball of

Christmas Eve, ending with Midnight Mass. At home, the first night was the most modest, with neighbors visiting, singing, and asking for shelter, emulating the Blessed Virgin and her husband, Joseph, seeking shelter at an inn. It was an unvarying ritual, the words of the songs scripted and known. Homes were visited in a prearranged order, with the hosts singing the part of the unwelcoming innkeepers. Although shelter was denied until the last night, it was only a symbolic denial, and families invited neighbors in each night for chocolate, and tortillas fried in oil and dipped in cinnamon sugar. On the last night, a dinner was served, before all in the town went to Mass. We did not stay up until midnight in the country, and I wondered how that would be possible here.

I pulled my mind back to the present, as I sensed a new arrival to our group.

"Doña Josefina, you are looking flushed. Are you well?" Luz asked, putting her hand on my arm. My flush, though, had nothing to do with the warmth of the room, but rather stemmed from catching the eye of the Marqués as he joined our group.

"I have not met your gallant husband," were his first words to me, after he kissed my hand. I pulled my hand away. "Come, do not be shy. Introduce me."

"I am so sorry, Your Highness. I forget my manners. His Highness, the Marqués of Condera; my husband, Don Manuel Castillo Coronado." Manuel, his face impassive, reached across the group and shook the Marqués' hand. I offered a silent prayer for restraint.

"Your wife has been a most delightful addition to our social evenings," the Marqués said. "She has a charm and talent that few possess." Manuel's lips tightened.

"Oh, I am nothing but a beginning student," I rushed in.

"Her beauty has caught all of our eyes, and her verses will not let us go!" the Marqués went on, still addressing Manuel. I had to stop this. But I had no chance. "Her false modesty is ill-suited to her accomplishments," he added, with a sly glance at me. He was determined to punish me. Manuel was playing directly into his hands, showing his anger at every phrase.

"My wife is nothing more or less than a landholder's wife, and I hope she has been treated accordingly," Manuel said tightly.

"Fear not for your wife's behavior. She is a model of virtue," the Marqués said, and laughed. My heart pounded.

"I was not referring to *her* behavior," Manuel replied.

"Come," Angélica said, with an amused smile, "surely some women more interesting than poetesses have entertained you since I last was here."

I could not believe her daring in mentioning her prior visit, given its disgraceful ending, nor could I understand her charitable willingness to draw such unpleasant attention to herself to relieve the glare of the light on me.

"Certainly there have been none whose allure even approached yours," the Marqués replied, mercifully turning his odious wiles on her.

Rather than blush with mortification at the allusion, Angélica tossed her golden hair, drawing all male eyes to her. "I have languished in the country since my last visit, only counting the days until I could return to this magnificent Court."

I glanced at Manuel, but he remained stony-faced.

"I have no doubt there were consolations," said Granada, who had been watching the conversation silently. Now she entered the fray with her usual acidity.

"Where Doña Angélica shines, there must always be light," said the Marqués.

"Ah, but now you are a poet!" responded Angélica.

I detached myself from the group and edged toward a chair. Shortly after, Luz followed. "It is not to be borne," she said. I looked questioningly to her. "The Marqués is punishing you for your refusal of him, by poisoning your husband's mind against you. I am outraged at the attack on your virtue."

I was, too, but my virtue was of less merit than she knew. And the Marqués knew it, I was certain. "I must return to my room," I said. "I am unwell."

"No," said Luz, "you cannot. See, the Marquesa has entered. You must rise." I saw that she was right, and struggled to my feet.

"It must be the powder, and the wine," I whispered to Luz, as we curtseyed.

"Well, you must bear up under it. We will be called to eat shortly."

A moment later she added, "Your husband is a very handsome man. Angélica has merely trifled with him, though."

"How in Heaven's name do you know that?" I asked.

She shook her head softly. "She can gain nothing from a liaison with him, except entertainment. Let us hope that she has the sense not to gain anything more." I thought of the "priest's act" and blushed, but my face was already so flushed that Luz did not notice.

"The world is unfair to women," I said. Luz nodded. That truth could never be contested. "The curse of Eve is our curse." My thoughts sprang for an instant to the strange letters that Sor Juana had written and received, and to the mysterious Sor Filotea's defense of Sor Juana's need to write and study. Suddenly I remembered where I had heard the name: Sor Juana and Father Alonso had laughed about it in the alcove when I had first arrived. What could possibly be the association between this Sor Filotea and the Bishop of Puebla? What murky waters were these, that threatened to drown the writers in the black pit of the Inquisition?

Mercifully, we were called to dinner.

"ESCORT ME TO MY wing," I asked Manuel as the party broke up. With the crowd of people, I had been spared any further sallies by the Marqués until the end of the event, and had passed a pleasant enough but dull evening. One terrifying moment came over after-dinner sherry, when the Marqués lifted his glass to the Marquesa, toasting her health. She had replied in kind, but had offered a twisted version of the banal language usually employed.

"To the health of His Highness, the Marqués, may his increase decrease, but his discretion increase."

Laughter had greeted this toast, and the sherry had been drunk, but the Marqués' eyes had hardened into a pitiless glare over the rim of his cup.

It must have been his anger that fueled his final remark to me, as I bade him a polite adieu.

"Good night, Josefina. Your husband is a hard man, and you had best bear my hardness, rather than his."

"Good night, Your Highness," I replied, careful not to let my tongue slip into the pun that presented itself. "My husband's love for me, and mine for him, is all I ask."

"Then you had best look to your actions, for you imperil both. I shall see you anon, Josefina. Good night."

I turned away with dignity. His threats were now open, and I knew exactly what the risks were. I had to lure Manuel home, if nothing else.

"Manuel, I have not walked with you in days since you have come. Let us walk in the garden tonight, though it is late and cold. I do not want to part from you." I spoke gently, with no hint of forwardness to offend him.

Manuel offered me his arm, hard as oak, but gave no reply.

I turned toward the garden doors, and led him outside into the cold night air. When I shivered, he drew me close. I had to soften his heart, to find a way into his bed. "I miss our home," I said. He nodded. "Let us return early. I do not want to remain with the Marqués and his disgusting insinuations."

Manuel continued walking, keeping his pace slow enough for me to keep up, but without speaking. "Speak to me, husband!" I finally said, desperate.

"You may go home if you wish, but I will stay through New Year's."

"Why?" I cried.

"Because I will make the Marqués taste bitterness before I go. He is royalty, and I cannot challenge him with a sword, but he will be punished."

"He has only insulted me, Manuel. I have no need for vengeance. I bloodied his nose, remember?"

Manuel smiled a little at that, but remained unmoved. "He insults you, and he insults me, with his words. He has tried to do far worse to you. And worse to others." Manuel paused. "I will be avenged."

Angélica. He was referring to Angélica, and the way she had been treated. For she and the Marqués had done far more than tussle on the garden bench, I was sure, given the Marqués' lust, and Manuel had fallen in love with Angélica.

I pulled my arm away from his. "Have you made Angélica your mistress?" I asked, anger making my voice shake. A liaison I could bear, and had borne it. But a mistress—an arrangement that was more than passing—was more than my pride could endure.

"You are my wife, and your place is secure," Manuel answered. I turned and ran from him, ran from the garden, ran sobbing to my cold, bare room in the nuns' wing.

I WOKE WITH A fearsome headache. Sometimes the powder had that effect, but this was debilitating enough that I lay in bed until the noonday meal, rising only for the barest needs. My courses had not come.

Of course I knew. I knew that Manuel's liaison with Angélica had been more than that single night, so long ago, when he passed by my room to enter hers. I knew, too—I could not fool myself—that my bleeding would not come this month, that I was carrying Father Alonso's child. I knew that Manuel had not touched me in a year, and that he would as soon kill me as have me bear a bastard into his home. My only salvation lay in luring Manuel back to the marriage bed, and soon. Yet I had failed in my every attempt to do so. When he had been willing, upon his arrival, I had not been vigorous or persistent enough in my efforts to obtain a room in the ladies' wing. Now, when he was once again in Angélica's thrall, when the Marqués was tarnishing my good name with leering flattery, he was far from my reach.

I lay there, tortured by headache and despair. If I could get home, away from this hellhole of gossip, there remained a chance that Manuel would come to me, and that I could hide the time of conception from him. The headache so early presaged a painful pregnancy, but I was slim, and my condition would not be evident for a while. I had to get Manuel away from here, though, before the Marqués tired of chasing me and divulged his hideous knowledge.

I could therefore show no sign of my condition. I must rise, wash, and put on a gay face for tonight's ball, and for all of the nine nights of *posada*. Let Manuel stay through New Year's if he must, let him enjoy the glittering Angélica as he would, but let him come home to my welcoming arms, my welcoming body, in time to save my life.

Energized by the hope that a plan could generate, I rose. When the room stopped swirling, I dressed quickly. In a paradoxical quirk of fate, the new energy, and the new life brewing within me, made me want to write. I took a cup of chocolate from the nuns' kitchen, gathered my pen and a roll of foolscap, and repaired to the library.

I opened the door to the great room and caught my breath. The Marqués and the Marquesa were squared off against each other at a table. Some bookshelves lay empty, and books were strewn about the tables and floor. The curtains were open, and the eerie light of a weak winter sun made the sight all the more dismal. Before I could back out and shut the door, the Marquesa saw me and commanded, "Stop. Enter, and close the door."

I obeyed. "Your Highness," I said.

"Spare us your courtesies. You are every bit a part of this discussion," she wheezed. Her black brows were arched high, and her pinched nose was red at the tip. "Sit down."

I looked at the Marqués, and could see the start of a little smile under his hooked nose. I had once thought that his smile was the one attractive part of him, but now I could see that even that was no more than a leer. I sat.

"You can see what has been done to my beloved grandfather's library," the Marquesa said.

"You mean Sor Juana's library," the Marqués drawled.

"Hers?" I asked.

"Absolutely. My wife's family brought perhaps half the books to this castle, but everything newer than fifty years old belongs to your dear mentor. And it is those books that the Holy Office is searching."

"The Holy Office?" I echoed stupidly.

"Indeed," said the Marquesa. "A problem brought about by my husband's ungovernable lust, and your unforgivable lack of good sense. I understand that you have been seen consorting with the Bishop of Puebla."

I opened my eyes wide. "I have done no such thing."

"Ah, offended virtue!" sneered the Marqués.

"I have virtue, and it is you who have offended it," I said haughtily. "And I fail to see how that has caused this uproar." I had but one role, and I must play it without reserve.

I feared that one or the other would press the issue, but my misery was but a sideshow to their personal battle. "So, because this nonentity of a country wife has denied you access between her legs, you have set up Eustacia as your doxy?" the Marquesa demanded. "And have called down the Inquisition on our home? On *my* home!" she added, her wheeze causing her voice to squeak.

"Do not be mistaken, Josefina," she continued when she had caught her breath. "You should have yielded to my husband's despicable demands, and quickly, and saved us all a lot of trouble. But your idiotic virtue has prevented you from performing, and my wastrel of a husband has set up that bastard cousin of mine in a house of her own, and is destroying what supports him."

She was gasping for air, and I feared she would collapse. She made little sense, but what I could understand was enough. And it was enough for the Marqués, too.

"By the laws of our land and our Church, while you live the estate is as good as mine," he said. "And if it offends you that I keep your cousin, who is more willing than either of you to do her duty to me, well, suffer. And she has paid well for her abode."

"Parasite!" panted the Marquesa. "And let her whoredom pay for her home. I do not care, except to pity you your need to bed a bastard whore."

"She has paid with more than her open thighs," he replied. "She has paid with information. And deny what you will," he said, turning to me, "she knows enough to see Juana burned at the stake." He turned back to his wife, and I was surprised to hear his voice shake. "Do not call me a parasite again, wife. Or your entire castle will burn with Juana."

"Parasite!" she spat back at him. "Go, notify the Archbishop. Tell him what he has known for years, that Juana writes poems commissioned by my household. And when my family money pays any fines, which will go far in keeping my castle safe, you will be back where you were before I allowed you to marry me. You will be selling your stud services to the poor ladies who cannot conceive with their husbands. And yet, all you will produce are dead babies, as you did for me! Worthless pander!"

The Marqués rose, moving as if to strike the Marquesa. "Liar. I gave you our son!"

"Not your son, you whoremonger!" she croaked, moving away from him.

In a moment, he was around the table, his hand raised to slap his wife. Without a thought I leaped to my feet and threw myself between them. My trajectory hurled me into the Marqués' waist. He doubled over, fell against a chair, and, with the weight of my body propelling him, fell to the floor and landed hard on his buttocks.

I heard my laughter, hysterical and shocked, before I knew it was mine. Clasping my hand over my mouth, I turned to the Marquesa. Her eyes, small and angry, flashed at the Marqués. Then she turned to me. "Thank you, though I do not need your defense. You had best leave now."

I looked back at the Marqués. He had caught the breath that his fall had knocked out of him, but he did not speak.

"Your Highness," I said. I curtsied to both of them and, turning away, I allowed myself the luxury of a smile before I left.

I TOOK MY GOWN to Luz's room. She was resting, and she moved over on her bed to make room for me. "Lie down," she said. "We have another long evening ahead."

My heart was still pounding from my encounter, and I was experiencing the delayed trembling that follows rash acts of courage. I yearned to take her into my confidence, but I still feared too much. I had new information, information that could harm so many, and I did not know how to use it. I lay on the bed, the headache returning, and listened to Luz breathe. I envied her certainty, her place in the world.

I had once been sure of mine, I thought, but coming here had undone that. It had allowed me to see a whole world that I had not known existed, one of venality and immoral behavior, but also of beautiful books and the joy of reading and writing. On balance, if it were not for the possibility of a bastard babe growing inside me, it would have been a blessing to come here. But though I was not jealous by nature, I was tortured by the loss of Manuel, both to Angélica and to the damage that would certainly be caused if he learned about the child before he and I could possibly conceive one together.

WHEN LUZ AND I woke, I was relieved that the headache was gone. We dressed with each other's help, neither of us having a servant to dress our hair. Our efforts were at least as good, and when it was time to go down for the first ball of the *posada* we knew ourselves to be as beautiful as we had ever been.

I told Luz about the ball in Miguel Ángel's honor at my last visit, and about Angélica's hope for a proposal from him.

"My. She certainly does attract more than her share of glory from her admirers," Luz remarked. "Every man seems somewhat besotted with her."

It was a mild attempt to elicit confidences beyond what she already knew, and I was ready. "Manuel is no exception. I mind, but it is more my pride that is hurt than my affection." I was surprised that this was true. "I cannot bear her smugness."

"Affairs of this sort do not last long," she answered, putting her hand on my arm. "I do not doubt that my husband keeps himself warm somehow while I am here. But to have her paraded before my eyes, as you have, is more than a woman should be forced to accept. I am surprised that Manuel would be so cruel."

"I think he simply does not realize what sorrow he is causing. And he believed, at least until last night, that I did not know."

"Men are fools, aren't they?" Luz said lightly. "But lovable fools. Well, you must pretend you still do not know, and wait for her eye to wander here at Court, or for his desire to be sated to boredom."

"Alas, he knows now that I know, and I fear that he plans to keep her. But my remedy is the same," I agreed. "Tonight we must be happy, and charming, for it is the first Advent ball, and we may never be here again."

We were at the heavy oak doors, doors that had opened to a summer ball and the returning heir the last time I was here. Again, they were guarded by liveried men, but this time the men simply held the doors open to all comers. We walked into the grand room.

There were hundreds of candles burning all around the room. The heavy curtains had been opened to the black sky of night, making the contrast of the fiery glow greater in the darkness. The Noche Buena poinsettias glowed red against their green foliage, presaging the coming of Christmas. Women swirled by in luscious winter gowns, men stood proud and erect, their high white collars and ruffled shirts set off by black jackets and ribbon-trimmed pants. Musicians played softly in a corner. The excitement in the air seemed to make the candles burn brighter.

I loved the *posadas* at home, the simple search of the Holy Family for shelter, and the moving joy of the final night, when the doors were opened to the wanderers. Right now, Joaquín should be holding my hand, I should have Neto in my arms, our voices raised into the starry night, I thought. But the magnificence of the room broke through my sudden longing for my children, as I stood transfixed, eyes misting, the light and colors blurring into a swirl of pageantry. I felt Luz's hand on my arm. "It is beautiful, isn't it?" she whispered. She was as enthralled as I, and I felt less like the country fool and more like a traveler caught in a web of beauty. I nodded. "Come," she said, "let us venture forth and enjoy the spectacle." Together we moved deeper into the crowd.

I looked up, scanning the guests' heads for Manuel. At last I spied him, against a wall near a window. "Let us go greet my husband," I said to Luz.

Manuel was more dashing than I had ever seen him. He wore his best pants and jacket, unadorned and black, but he wore a white shirt with a collar that rose above his jacket collar and cascaded in thick waves, almost like cream, softening his hard chin and further widening his already broad shoulders. When we approached, he bowed at the waist, greeted Luz cordially, and took my arm.

He leaned down to my ear and whispered, "Josefina, wife, you are beautiful." I smiled up at him, warmed. Then, speaking more normally, he added, "This is quite the spectacle. Far more elaborate than the most lavish ninth night's *posada* I have ever attended, and we are but on the first night."

I agreed. "Luz, do they continue to grow more elaborate each night?"

She shook her head. "No. For the most part, they are most fancy on the first and final nights, and in between there are dinners and musicales. But, of course, every night we will reenact the *posada*."

The banal chatter helped ease the initial nervousness I felt in being with Manuel. I could not recall the last time I felt so uneasy with the man I had been wed to for over six years. It was disconcerting, and I longed for the easier times.

A servant passed with glasses of sherry, and Manuel took one for each of us. "You are absorbing the courtly ways," I said with a smile. At home I would have served him, instead of his taking the glass for me. To my surprise, he stiffened and frowned.

"But you are the seasoned, experienced one," he replied.

"Not at all. I am almost as much of a novice as you."

"I certainly hope so," he replied. We were saved further colloquy by the arrival of several gentlemen with whom Manuel had made acquaintance in his short stay. After their bows and introductions, they proceeded to a genially heated argument about the merits of certain horses, and Luz and I were left free to wander.

"Your husband dislikes his position here," Luz said quietly, taking my arm.

"How so?"

"He feels at a loss when it comes to the ways of the Court, and dislikes your having greater knowledge. He wants his wife to be innocent and inexperienced."

I nodded. He did resent my acquired comfort with the manners he still found strange. "Though the Court and its nuances continue to confound me," I said.

"Remember your first week here. And Manuel cannot openly say that he is ignorant, or unsure, as you could. It is a privilege denied their sex."

"Handsomely compensated for by the myriad privileges that they enjoy above ours."

Luz laughed, and moved to one of the chairs. "I must sit. Though my babe is scarcely quickened, I tire quickly." I apologized immediately for being thoughtless. "It is nothing," she said. "I am in my fifth pregnancy; I can hardly be surprised anymore!"

We sat together, two country matrons, watching the glorious event. Occasionally, a lady we knew stopped at our chairs to make conversation, but mostly we were able to enjoy the beauty without having to fence with verbal opponents.

"Do you think that Eustacia will make an appearance?" I asked Luz.

She shook her head. "Not since she has been banished. Even with the Marqués setting her up as his mistress, she does not dare affront to that extent."

I thought of the horrible scene in the library today. I had not told Luz about it. I realized with a chill that somewhere in this castle the envoys of the Holy Office were lurking, spying, and waiting to catch Sor Juana, or anyone, in the clutches of heresy. No one could be trusted completely.

I caught sight of the Marqués across the room, making a young lady blush. The lady was little more than a girl, at what was likely her first ball, and her mother stood near, beaming with pride. I felt my heart harden.

"See, over there. The Marqués is surely speaking freely with that girl. And her mother takes pride that her daughter is being noticed by the host, instead of protecting her virtue."

"I do not believe the Marqués is partial to virgins," Luz answered.

"Oh, but he is. He selects a *menina* to torment, and the girl has no sense to complain. Though perhaps he leaves her maidenhead intact."

"And the *menina* feels too much shame to tell her mama. But this is no *menina,* but a girl of marriageable age. Doubtless he is merely embarrassing her, not making an assignation."

"To think that this is the lot of us all, to be trifled with at the whim of a man, only to be left to face sorrow and the consequences alone."

Luz looked at me sharply but did not immediately reply. At last she said, "Let us rejoin your husband. The singing will begin momentarily."

We reached Manuel at the same time Angélica and another lovely lady did. Manuel smiled at Angélica, bowed to the new lady, and nodded to me. I was angry that Angélica would dare to join her lover in front of his wife, but I could do nothing to stop her.

"You are looking lovely," Angélica said to me sweetly, and I was forced to return the compliment. Manuel looked uncomfortable, which went a small way in comforting me. Angélica's smile was smug.

In a moment, the Marqués had joined our little group. But rather than coming up to me, he circled around and put his hand out to Angélica. She took it, and he raised her fingertips to his lips. "You are a vision from Heaven," he said to her.

"The ball is most exquisite," she replied, turning the full light of her attention on the Marqués.

"It is your presence that lights the room," the Marqués answered unctuously. I felt my stomach turn from the treacle that was being poured, and for a moment my heart fluttered in the hope that my disgust with the conversation had started the flow of my monthly courses.

"Will there be dancing after the songs?" Luz asked, interrupting the nauseating exchange.

"Certainly, Doña Luz," the Marqués replied. Then, turning back to Angélica, he asked, "May I have the honor of escorting you in the first sarabande?"

Angélica raised an eyebrow. "Surely Your Highness would prefer some other, more graceful partner for the very first round." Her lips, reddened with unnatural color, pouted prettily. I saw Manuel's arm twitch. Manuel, the Marqués, and the two men who had been conversing with Manuel were all fixed upon Angélica's face—or in any event her form. I shot a glance at Luz, but she, too, was watching Angélica.

"There is none that I could possibly want, other than you, my dear. Say you will join me!" He put his hand out to her face, tracing the line of her jaw. Even Angélica froze a moment at this brazen act. Then she laughed, breaking the spell.

"Of course, Your Highness. I would be honored! And I hope you will all form a square, too," she added to the rest of us. "I would dread being out there alone!"

"Alone with squares upon squares of sarabande-dancing ladies and gentlemen," the Marqués replied. "But of course all eyes would be on you!"

It was all I could do to keep from throwing the last of my sherry in his face, but worse was the stealthy sidelong look Angélica slid at Manuel. She was playing him for the fool, and he was more heated with passion and fury from her manipulation than mere allure could have made him. He was rigid with anger, and my bitterness at his jealousy was complete.

Angélica curtsied. The Marqués bowed to her, smiled genially at the gentlemen, and, without so much as a glance in my direction, ambled off to another part of the ballroom. As he passed the musicians, he lifted his hand in signal, and they struck up the introductory strains of the *posada* dialogue.

We moved to one side of the room, while others, seeming to know what was expected, moved closer to the Marqués. As I scanned the room, I realized that the ones with the Marqués were titled, and those of us on the other side were not. The roles had thus been differentiated: we would be the travelers, or Pilgrims; and they would be the Hosts. The introduction music continued, with the people in the different groups conversing among themselves, until at last, with the crescendo, the Marquesa entered.

She was, as usual, dressed in black, but her mantilla was shot with gold and glittered with jewels. Though her face had its normal pallor, a telltale reddening at the end of her nose recalled the fury in the library.

She looked neither right nor left, but glided haughtily to her side of the room. She spared no look for her husband, but lifted her chin and, raising her arm, told the musicians to begin the first verse.

"In the name of Heaven," we travelers sang, "we pray, give us shelter."

The hosts gave the ritual denial, and the dialogue continued in its prescribed way to the end. The music, the familiar words and melody, soothed my heart. I stood next to Manuel, whose body had slowly relaxed to a normal state, and absorbed his warmth. His deep voice carried the melody well, and I closed my eyes to enjoy it more. I knew that the crystal-clear sounds on the other side of him were produced by Angélica, who did, after all, have the voice of an angel, but even she could not destroy the peace for me.

At the end of the song, everyone rushed together to join in the celebrations of the *posada,* and the musicians sounded the first notes of a sarabande. After the joyful salutations and wishes for the joy of the season, those of us not dancing withdrew to make room for the squares forming in the center. Angélica took her place beside the Marqués. He was right, all eyes were upon her.

Manuel was at my side. "Have you learned the dance, too?"

I was careful. His pride was at stake, and I had just been witness to his humiliation by the Marqués.

"No. I have no interest in doing so. I have only come here to study and learn at the godly hand of the nuns."

"I am glad. I would not want to imagine you prancing like a pony before all of these soft, pompous fools."

I had never heard Manuel speak like this, and I knew the pain in his heart. But he must not know mine. "You are more to be admired than any man here, Manuel."

"The Marqués is odious."

"He is." I dared not advise him in any way, for fear of drawing his ire again, especially when he felt trumped by the Marqués.

"I will not permit his crassness to deny me the pleasures of this Court," Manuel said. He had become quite talkative, I noted, since I had left home. "I am told that it is his wife's castle. He is truly not a man, to be living off his wife's estate."

I allowed the idea to bolster Manuel's injured pride. "You are much

more than he is." He looked at me quizzically and I feared I had over-
stepped. "You are courageous, and accomplished, and your land is your
own," I added. I did not want Manuel to think I was comparing their
manhood.

"You are too kind, Josefina. I see that your stay here has brought out
not only your beauty but your ease with a well-turned phrase. Have you
written much?"

"Nothing worthwhile," I replied.

"I was told you wrote a poem for the Marqués." His voice was
dangerously light.

"Do not fear, husband. It was a poem that though poorly rhymed
displayed all of my contempt for him. I was almost banished for it."
He gave a small smile. "But I did write one for Doña Luz, which was
much nicer!"

"Well, your color is good and you are glowing with health, so life
here must suit you. Your children do need you, though."

"Of course. Do not think I am staying here. I know that you plan to
return at New Year's, though I will return early, at the end of *posadas,* to
be with the children. Perhaps you, too, will leave after Christmas."

His eyes strayed to Angélica. "Perhaps, though it was my intent, too,
to stay until the New Year. I would not want the Marqués to believe he
had chased me out by his ill-mannered behavior." I cast my eyes down,
and Manuel, as if by a miracle, put his hand upon my shoulder. "No.
Forgive me, Josefina. It was not my intent to hurt you. His manner to
you is what is unforgivable, and I despise him for it." I raised my eyes to
his, and tears filled mine. "I am a fool," he said. "You are right, Josefina.
Forgive me."

I took his arm. "Let us go, then. We will not be missed."

He smiled, and he looked once again like my husband, the man of the
hacienda, with the silver-encrusted belt. "Yes, we can steal away."

We made our way across the room, evading the dancers and the
waiters with trays of chiles stuffed with almonds, empanadas with
fragrant spiced-meat fillings, and glasses of sherry. I had no doubt that
our destination would be some deserted little room, or even Manuel's
room in the gentlemen's wing.

The music ended, and the sarabande stopped before we could get to the doors. Immediately the room swirled with people, and Angélica was at our side.

"You are not leaving, are you, Don Manuel?" she said, her face beautifully pink from the exertions of the dance.

"My wife was feeling tired," he said, "and I must escort her back."

I was surprised by the quickness, the smoothness of his lie. He, too, was learning fast at Court.

"Nonsense," Angélica said. "You must stay, so that I may teach you the dance steps. You could not return to your hacienda without learning at least that. And I would not want to have to dance only with the Marqués tonight!" Her words were playful, but they hit home with Manuel. I could see the Marqués watching us, a smile lurking beneath his curved nose.

Manuel seemed torn. Then he, too, caught sight of the Marqués. He stiffened. "I have no desire to learn to dance. I leave that to the fops who enjoy such things. But I will stay a bit, to keep you from such a predator."

"Manuel," I said softly. I would not beg, nor would it do me good. I refused to see Angélica's triumphant smirk.

"I will call for you shortly," he said. "I will not stay long."

I no longer wished to go to my room while the ball went on, but I could not stay after Manuel's lie. And to stay would require that I witness more of Angélica's preening.

"I will await you," I said quietly. "Send word." He nodded, and as there was nothing else I could do, I turned and left the ball.

TWENTY-ONE

HE HALLS WERE EERILY quiet once I was out of earshot of the music. It was strange to feel the castle so empty and lifeless, with all the gaiety and noise concentrated at one end. If the summer ball for the heir was an indication, the *posada* would continue for another hour or more, and then little groups would entertain one another in rooms throughout, bringing vitality back to the other parts of the Court. That would be the time when Manuel would come to me, I was sure.

My shoes, of soft calfskin, made no sound on the stone floors as I headed back to the nuns' wing. Even there, I surmised, it would be quiet. Some sisters would be attending the ball, not to dance, of course, but in their capacity as something between guests and entertainers, to sing or converse with the invitees. The rest would have long retired. I was surprised, therefore, to hear voices as I approached, and far more surprised to hear men's voices.

I quickly lifted the curtain and entered the wing. I did not think to be subtle, or to fear interrupting something that I shouldn't, but my feet were silent and the curtain was heavy, so I entered unnoticed. I did not turn to flee fast enough to avoid discovery, alas. For standing in the middle of the entry hall was Sor Teresita, tears streaming down her face, hands clasped in prayer. Behind her were two men dressed fully in black, their faces hidden by hoods and masks. Their capes bore the unmistakable red cross of the Inquisition. They were blocking the entrance to my room.

"There she is!" said the taller of the men. I backed out of the hall, but he was at my side before I could escape. He grabbed my upper arm in a grip like iron and pulled me forward into my room.

"What is this?" I exclaimed, my voice trembling with fear and outrage. My normally neat room was in shambles. Every book had been opened and left with its pages flapping. My writings were spread all over the floor; my little dresser had been emptied, with the drawers cast away. One drawer lay broken on its side. Even my severe iron bedstead had been overturned and its mattress cut open.

"Pardon the intrusion, Doña Josefina," the second man said. "We will be but a moment. Where are the writings?" His voice was smooth and his question was asked in the most sociable of tones. I was not fooled.

"I do not know what writings you mean, señor." I took a breath to keep my voice from shaking, but failed.

"Señora, do not trifle with us," he answered. He was smaller than his counterpart, and thin, but his cape did not conceal a wiry strength that I did not wish to sample. The dagger at his side was no more appealing.

"I do not, señor, I assure you. I am no fool, and would not dare to hide anything from you." My voice was stronger.

"Bring in the other nun, Brother," he said to the taller man. He reappeared shortly, not with Sor Teresita, whose sobs could still be heard in the hall, but with Sor Inez. I gasped.

Her wimple had been torn almost off, and her shaved head was bleeding. Her nose bled, too, and it was clear that she would have a black eye in the morning. But the most horrifying was her habit. It hung from her shoulders in tatters, her thin, bony arms protruding, her sagging breasts visible through the rents in the material. Though she showed no other wounds, what the men had done to her had obviously been painful. She was beyond mortification at her condition, but she was not beyond pride.

Though she staggered and could scarce keep her feet, she did not whimper when the tall man thrust her rudely into the room. "Now, Sister," said the thin one, "you are looking lovely in that habit. Your skin will be flayed just like the cloth, you know, if you insist on keeping the writings from us." He pulled his dagger from its hilt. Sor Inez did not move.

"Come, Doña Josefina. See how obstinate she is? Will you join her? For surely your young body will provide more entertainment to the secular men who will help us, how shall we say, improve your wardrobe? Or would you prefer to see this elderly sister suffer?"

I could not answer. They must be after the letters. Where were they? I recalled that I had put them in my bag of monthly cloths, and had taken that bag to Luz's room. If I told them, then Luz would be attacked, too. And if I did not, then Sor Inez and I would suffer. Sor Inez had bravely withstood a beating and humiliation, and had not spoken. Could I?

I had no time to think, for the tall man slapped poor Sor Inez, knocking her to the ground. The shreds of her habit flew around her, leaving her exposed and bleeding on the floor of my room.

"No! Don't touch her!" I screamed, hurling myself at him. He caught me easily, but I thrust my foot into his knee with all my force. His leg buckled.

The thin man laughed. "Señora, was there something you wished to tell us?" He stood waiting, dagger in hand, but his voice remained buttery smooth. I looked at Sor Incz, still silent. I could be as brave as she was.

"No, señor. Though I assure you that if I knew what you were talking about, or where any letters were, I would tell you. I am not as courageous as Sor Inez."

"Letters, you say. Indeed."

I cursed myself, for he had not said "letters," but rather "writings."

"I am glad to hear that you lack the foolhardiness to oppose the Holy Office," the thin man continued. Lithe as a dancer, he took two quick steps toward me, and before I could react he had slit the front of my gown from neck to belly. I grasped the cloth, but not before the tall man had thrust his hand into my bosom. "Brother," said the thin man, "remember your holy vows." He was answered with a grunt, but the tall man removed his hand.

"Leave the nun. She is barely breathing, and cannot confess her sins to us. We will take Doña Josefina to the parlor. Surely she will be more co-operative there," the thin man said. The tall man pushed at Sor Inez with the toe of his boot, but did as he was told. He grabbed my arm again and pulled me along beside him. As he was shutting the door to my room, the thin man said to Sor Teresita, who sat huddled on the floor of the hall, "Attend to your sister, whose soul may need cleansing." Teresita ran into my room without a word, and I choked back a cry of sorrow for the sweet-voiced nun who had welcomed me.

"Your gown is very rich for a country wife," the thin man said as he followed behind my captor and me. "You sin in the eyes of Our Lord by such ostentation." I could not imagine a reply, but was spared the need for one by his dagger. A scratching slash began at my neck, as he slit the gown from my neck down the back. When he came close to my waist he pulled me back. "Wait, Brother," he said, and he drew his knife down to the waist. Only the intact portion of the skirt kept the dress together.

I knew too well that a priest was just a man, and I shut my eyes against the shame of his viewing of me. Still the halls were empty, but now I was torn between longing for someone to come upon us, to stop what was happening to me, and the dread that I would be seen in this condition. Perhaps Manuel could save me. Or perhaps some other men, such as those who had accompanied the Marqués the first time he accosted me, would merely find the spectacle alluring.

"Have you heard of the rack, Doña Josefina?" the thin man asked. I did not answer, but then felt the dagger at the waist of my pantalettes.

"Yes, señor."

"Ah, good, she has a voice. You may address me as Father, as I am a devout man of the Lord, consecrated to cleanse our land of heresy. Though you must know, then, señora, that you are stretched on the rack naked. Of course, when your arms come loose from their sockets you no longer care about your modesty. But as we are merely going to the parlor, where there is no rack, you will still have much concern for your decency." He cut the waist, but did not proceed.

We turned down a hallway I did not recognize. It was narrow and undecorated. There were no hanging tapestries, and no doors. It was strictly a passage, and I did not know where it led. I knew that the castle was large, and that there were many hidden areas I had never explored, away from the usual rooms and halls. This knowledge only increased my terror. I thought about Manuel, coming to look for me after the ball and finding me gone, my room in disarray, and Sor Inez possibly dead. He would sound an alarm, I was certain. But who would heed it?

And what if he did not come tonight, what if he remained in Angélica's thrall? I thought of my sons, and the tears came.

MY VISION WAS BLURRED by my crying, but not so much that I could not see the room. It was completely stone, reminding me of the room the Marqués had pulled me into the time I bloodied his nose, but it was much larger. It had no windows, but did have a rug on the stone floor. An iron bar ran along the back wall, at about my waist level, but otherwise the walls were bare. Incongruously, there were several richly uphol-stered chairs, a settee for two, and a few small carved tables set about, as if in a parlor. But the single distinguishing element was a bed, covered in a red and black embroidered coverlet, strewn with many plump pillows, and set in an iron four-poster bedstead from which manacles hung. A menacing length of rope lay coiled at the foot of the bed.

"Welcome to your new room, Doña Josefina," said the thin man. The tall one let me go, and I stood clutching what was left of my gown to my chest. I shivered with cold and fear. The uses of the room were obvious. "It is appointed especially for the housing of ladies, preferably beautiful ones," he said, as if paying me a courtly compliment. "We would not waste such niceties on the old nun."

"Fernándo, let me get this dress off her," said the tall man. He was so much coarser—and much, much taller—than his superior. He, at least, was direct in his intent. "I can't wait to see you manacled to that bed!"

"Easy, Brother," said the thin one, and his voice did not disguise his annoyance that his name had been used. "Now, señora, will you kindly tell us where those letters are? Or would you prefer to be left in my brother's company?"

I knew that in either event the outcome would be the same, but I tried to think of some subterfuge that would appease them. My hesitation was enough to doom me. In a single tear the tall man had my dress on the floor. I stood before them in my torn shift and my pantalettes, the waist of which had been cut, so that they hovered above my hips, barely covering me at all.

The tall man's laugh was like hands upon my body. Then his hands were everywhere, and though I tried to fend him off, he was big and cruel and thorough. "This will teach you to step on my knee," he said, pressing his hand between my thighs.

"Tie her to the bar," commanded Fernándo, his voice husky.

The tall man pushed me to the wall and pulled my hands behind me. He grabbed the rope and made a noose, which he slipped over my wrists. When he pulled the knot tight, my hands instantly went numb.

He looped the rope once around my neck, and then ran it between my legs. Then he tied the end of the rope to the bar, leaving a length of rope as a leash. It was an odd way to truss a person, and I was unsure of their plans. All I knew was that what followed would be unpleasant.

"Now, Brother, you may enjoy her for a bit. I will return. Leave her pants on."

"No!" I cried out. I did not want to be left with that tall cretin. Father Fernándo, if indeed he was a priest, was at least in control of his impulses, even if he was as cruel as his companion.

"You will have ample time to confess, Doña Josefina. I shall return. Brother," he added, "recall your vows, as well as your promises."

"Of course," the tall man replied, but he had directed his masked visage toward me.

As soon as the door was shut, he untied his pants. He was erect and ready. "See that?" he asked. I did not reply. His slap knocked my head against the wall.

He must have repeated his question, but my ears were ringing and I could taste blood in my mouth. The rope had pulled against my throat when he hit me. I gasped for breath. I tried to move away, but when I did so the rope chafed through my pantalettes. He slapped me again. "Answer me!"

"Yes, señor," I said, not knowing what I was agreeing to, as blood ran from my lip down my chin and dripped on my bosom. He pulled on the rope, and the chafing increased. When I winced, he chuckled.

"Kneel," he said, and I struggled to obey quickly. With the complicated rope arrangement, though, every move had the effect of tightening, chafing, or binding me worse than before, so it was only after a minute that I was in the position he desired. The cold stones bit into my knees. My hands were now raised behind me, forcing me forward, and I was barely able to breathe. Where the rope passed between my legs it was pressed hard against my body. I could not imagine a more painful or undignified posture, but I would soon discover that this was preferable to any other he could dream up.

Grasping my hair, he pulled my head back. "You know what to do, whore," he said.

Every time he pulled my head back, I could breathe less and less. I knew I would die, unshriven and ashamed. The ropes pulled tight, and rubbed me until I was raw, and yet I could not cry out, or breathe, or stop the endless torment unless I opened my mouth to receive him. If I did so, my only hope would be that he would be quickly satisfied, so he would release me. I could not yield.

"Stop! Idiot!" Fernándo had returned.

"You said I could enjoy her," the tall man answered petulantly. He clenched his fists in anger. I shut my eyes, fearing a terrible blow, but it did not come.

"Stand up, madam," said Fernándo, his voice curt. But I could not. The tall man grabbed my hair and yanked me to my feet. The rope snapped back, and my head wrenched back with it. Fernándo pushed him away and loosened the choke. He appeared, through his mask, to look me over.

"Not too much harm done," he concluded. "Perhaps he will appreciate your softening her for his approach. Now," he said to me, "tell me about those letters. If you are forthcoming, we will let you live, and if you give satisfaction, we may even give you a cloak to wear back to your room. No doubt your husband would thank us for that."

"Who will appreciate your softening me?" I asked, though it was dawning upon me quickly.

"No cloak, then, since you are not helpful. Now, with only your life at stake, you will ultimately speak. It is your choice when you do so, and in what condition you will be when you do. The sooner, of course, the less damage to you, so when you crawl naked back to your room you may still be of use to your husband, if he will have you. If you delay, no man will ever touch you again. Now, Doña Josefina, answer my question. Where are Sor Juana's letters?"

I had broken the commandment against adultery. I was already doomed to burn in Hell. I would break the commandment against false witness, and possibly, if they believed me, against murder.

"Eustacia Porfirio took them when the Marquesa banished her. She plans to use them to avenge her disgrace by seeing Sor Juana, and if necessary me, burned as heretics."

"Liar," said Fernándo. "Tell us the truth this time, or I will let my brother finish his work with you."

"It is true!" I cried. "I swear, on the Blessed Virgin!"

"The oaths of whores are worthless," Fernándo said calmly. "Now, Brother, keep your pants on, but you may assist the witness."

The tall man pulled his mask up from his mouth. He grabbed my breasts, squeezing hard, and then, with unspeakable cruelty, he bit one. I screamed. He pulled away, and then bit the other.

"Doña Josefina, please do not make my brother break his vows. You will have that sin, along with all of your others, on your soul if you do. The letters?"

"I speak truthfully! Eustacia took them! I swear upon the Christ Himself!"

"Blasphemer!" said Fernándo. "You have broken the commandment against taking the name of Our Lord in vain." The tall man bent to hurt me. I tensed, but his teeth were sharp, and again I cried out. But I could not tell them the truth. They would torture Luz, and she would lose her babe, if not her life, for something she had never touched. "It's Eustacia!" I screamed.

The door was open and it was the Marqués staring at me, his mouth open below his hooked nose. The torturers stepped back.

"Your Highness," said Fernándo. "Here she is."

The Marqués made no answer, but walked to me. "At last, my dear. You have decided to submit to me. I assure you that you will enjoy it, and in fact you will beg for more." He ran his fingers over me. I had no will left to shudder. "Why is her nipple bleeding? And her mouth?" He turned to Fernándo. "I said she was not to be damaged."

"We were softening her for you, Your Highness," said the tall man.

"Shut up," the Marqués snapped, and continued to address Fernándo. "Did you leave that cretin alone with her?"

"Yes, Your Highness, but only for the time it took to get you."

"It was clearly too long. Be gone, both of you."

"Yes, Your Highness. But you must keep your half of the bargain. We want Sor Juana's letters."

Once again, I regretted my slip. "I will keep my half," said the Marqués. "We will discuss it on the morrow. Now, go!"

"With all due respect, Your Highness, you cannot order the Holy Office," said Fernándo smoothly.

For the first time I saw doubt in the Marqués' eyes. "I am not ordering you, Father, but merely begging a moment, or more, with my lady here. I assure you that the Holy Office will be well satisfied."

"I am sure we will," said Fernándo. He wrapped his cape about him and signaled to the tall man. "Come, Brother, our work here is done."

The tall man grunted in frustration, but with one more look at me, and a lecherous licking of his lips, he turned to follow his superior. "Your Highness," he said, "if I can be of any assistance, please call on me." He laughed low, and left.

The Marqués did not bother to turn around and watch them go, but stood still, in front of me, until we heard the door shut. With a quick movement, he returned to the door and dropped the heavy latch in place. Then, with all the time granted to a man on this earth, he walked back to me.

*T*wenty-two

*L*ET ME SEE HOW they have trussed you, my little chicken," the Marqués said. He investigated the rope and its twists, following it with obvious delight between my thighs, and stroking me as he went. "Oh, my, I may wager that they have rubbed you quite raw here," he said, touching me intimately. "I hope my penetrations will not be too painful. Although they say that with a fiery minx like you, a bit of pain in the act of love is as delightful to the minx as to the man." I squirmed away from his touch. "Ah, good. They have not killed your spirit, just—what did that horrible lunk say?—just softened you. Excellent.

"Your husband is a lucky man," he continued.

"Do not speak of my husband!" I spat.

"My dear, you misunderstand. I mean that most respectfully, though he does seem to have his heart, and his pants, caught on Angélica's fishing line." He flicked my raw nipple, and smiled when I flinched. "Of course, she is merely fishing. You saw how quickly she jumped into my boat, did you not? I believe your poor Manuel was quite put out by her disloyalty." He loosened the rope from the bar, immediately relieving the pressure of the hated line between my legs. I sighed with relief.

"Better, dear? Good. Now, you see, you are caught fast on my line, like your husband is on Angélica's. Fair is only fair, don't you think? I find it despicable of him to parade his mistress before you, by the way. I only do it to humiliate the Marquesa, since she is not the least hesitant to remind me of my more humble origins. As you witnessed earlier today." He jerked the rope up. "You see, it is never good to witness a man being brought down by a woman. You have to pay for what you see."

"Sor Juana would agree with you," I said through my teeth. He was right, on so many counts.

"To become the experienced philanderer that I am, I have developed a very refined understanding of women. For example," he said, touching my breast tenderly, "I know that when you have been subjected to pain here"—he moved his hand to between my legs—"and here, by a man, and then you are stroked gently, like this, it enhances your pleasure in ways that you would not have experienced if you had not been mistreated."

To my horror, he was right.

"And to force your wife to acknowledge your mistress in public is to hurt her far worse than simply having the mistress. In fact, it may be so painful that the poor wife flees into the arms of another man. Would you say that is true, my Josefina?"

I did not answer. The truth was too painful, and too obvious.

"And now, lovely lady, let me introduce you to real pleasure, with a real man." He unwound the rope so that it was only binding my wrists. "Come," he said, leading me by the rope to the bed. He fingered the manacles. "These look so inviting. So much more sturdy than this silly rope."

He pushed me back onto the bed. "Your hands are so tightly bound that I had best leave them that way for now. It is painful when they are first unbound." He turned me so my face was down on the bed, and my hands still tied behind. He grabbed one ankle and attached a manacle. I heard it snap shut, and I lost all hope. My leg was now elevated above the bed by what felt like a handbreadth. He pulled the useless pantalettes down, leaving them hanging off the manacled ankle. Then, spreading my legs wide, he attached the other manacle to my other ankle. "There. You are now truly, truly ready to experience a new form of delight."

He slipped a pillow under my belly, lifting my buttocks. My face pressed into the bed, giving me at least relief from having to face my tormentor. He began to stroke. "Let me see if that rope hurt you here, too," he said, opening my buttocks and looking where no human should. "Ah, good, you are unhurt here." He touched me, and I flinched.

"Perhaps the priests forgot to give you unction," he said, and chuckled. I smelled the churchlike aroma, then felt warm oil poured upon my bottom. The sensation was both disgusting and soothing. He used the oil to facilitate his horrible explorations. I was mortified.

"Lovely," he said, and I felt him behind me.

"Oh, no!" I cried as I understood that he meant to enter me. "That is bestial! You must not!"

"You see, Josefina, I told you you would beg me to couple with you! But alas, I now wish to sodomize you. And I shall. But do not despair. I will enter you as a husband would, after. We have until Matins, you know."

I sobbed into the bed, but it made no difference. I was helpless.

When he was fully inside me, the pain stretching and filling my body, he used his hands to rub oil into me, paying close attention to the spots that forced me to writhe, and maintaining his pressure there. His hands were as expert as Alonso's, as knowing as Manuel's, and my body could only respond with an agony of confusion. Then his thrusts began, with increasing speed and force, and the torment of pain I felt was only devastating humiliation. Finally my cries into the pillows were drowned out by the Marqués' triumphant shout of conquest.

WE LAY THERE, ON that horrible bed, one on top of the other. His body pressed my wrists painfully into my back, and my violated body ached. I tried to twist my hands, and the Marqués moved. "I am sorry, my lady," he said. He shifted his weight, easing the pressure. "Perhaps this is no longer necessary." He pulled on the knot, and the sheer pain of the blood returning to my hands made me scream. He stroked my back and rubbed some oil from his hands into my wrists.

I lay still, except for moving my hands and wrists against my body to ease the pain of the renewed circulation. "It is painful," he said, "but the welts will be pleasant reminders of our interlude in days to come." I felt a shot of anger and, with the return of my spirit, a glimmer of hope.

He was not a young man, and I imagined he would require a bit of time before he began his next assault. I was right. "Allow me to get us some sherry, my dear," he said. "Shall I ring for a servant?"

I did not answer.

"Ah, well, you are not yet tamed. On further thought, I shall get the sherry myself. I will not allow anyone who has not, by his suffering, earned the right to see you so lusciously displayed." He slipped the rope around my wrists again, not bothering to cinch the knot. I did not resist, and I lay there passively while he dressed.

When I heard the door latch, I raised my head, to ensure that he had left, then began to twist my hands in earnest. The oil that had been rubbed onto my skin when my wrists were unbound lubricated the rope, and very quickly I was free. I twisted to see the manacles. I had not heard a key, only a catch, and I saw that they were merely closed at the top. The weight of my legs kept the latch shut. If I could shift the weight, I could open the clasps.

I wriggled and writhed, but I could not change the press of my ankles on the manacles with my legs raised as they were. With dismay I realized that I must somehow rest on my knees, and only then could I open the iron circles. I bent my knees, and with a groan, spread my legs even farther than the hated chains had demanded. If the Marqués entered now and found me in this new and even more degrading position, his imagination would take him to places I dared not contemplate.

I opened my thighs until I could barely contain the cry of pain on my lips. Then, arching back, I reached for the first clasp. It slipped out of my oily hand. Tears of frustration blinded me, as I fell back upon the bed and my legs inched closer with relief.

Gritting my teeth, I splayed myself again, and again wrenched around. This time, I pulled a bit of the coverlet with me, and the cloth interfered enough with the oil that I could get a bit of purchase. Finally, it opened. I collapsed on the bed. But that was far from enough. Though the clasp was open, my ankle was still in the manacle. I had to somehow lift my foot higher, while the other was still firmly bound. Once again, I breathed deeply and forced my foot up, my back cruelly arched, until my ankle dragged against the iron and, with a painful scrape, was free.

The ragged pantalettes hung limp around my other ankle, and I used the material to grasp the clasp on the second manacle, quickly freeing myself. I had but a moment to relish the relief before I heard the latch on the heavy oak door. I flung myself back on the bed and, swallowing my pride, spread my legs wide and slipped my toes into the horrid manacles. I wrapped the rope loosely around my hands, holding the noose in my palms. Unless the Marqués looked closely right away, I would still appear helpless and available.

As I had hoped, the Marqués' vision was impaired by his lust. "You are as beautiful as I left you," he chuckled. I heard glasses on metal. He had brought us sherry on a silver tray. I turned my head to the side, and could see him place the glasses on the small table near the bed. Then he quickly untied his pants, this time removing them and his stockings completely, so he was naked from the waist down. His embroidered vest and doublet he laid aside, and left only his ruffled shirt on.

He ran his fingers down my spine, past the slack rope on my wrists, and between my buttocks. I could see him growing aroused again. "Did you enjoy our little sodomy? Was it like a priest would perform?" I shivered. He thrust his fingers hard into my body. "Here's my next home," he said. Removing his hand, he added, "But first, some refreshment." He moved away from me, and that was my moment.

If I failed, I was doomed. I could not fail. Pulling my legs free, I rose up on my knees and turned to face him. His surprise made him stop, and I pulled the noose into my hand. "How——?" he started, and moved to grab me. He was laughing, and his mirth fed my fury. As soon as he was close enough, I twirled the noose above my head, as I had seen Joaquín do in the stables so long ago, and let it come down over his head.

My son would have been proud. I lassoed the Marqués perfectly, the rope dropping over his head. But I had no time to crow. I pulled the noose tight around his neck, watching his eyes bulge. He could breathe, but he was panicky. I pulled harder. "I am a country wife. I can choke you as easily as I would choke a turkey for my dinner. Put your hands down."

He obeyed. I put my hands to his neck, as though I would ease the knot, but instead, without loosening the noose, I wrapped the rope around him, binding his hands as mine had been. Then, having learned from the most experienced torturers in the land, I emulated the minions of the Holy Office. I wrapped the rope tightly around his no-longer-erect penis and around his drooping testicles, and pulled it as hard as I could. He screamed hoarsely, and I pulled again, harder. I tied the rope tightly to the bedstead. Unlike my teachers, I was shaking when I finished, and I tasted bile.

"Your Highness," I said, "you misused me greatly. But I must know one thing." Like the Inquisitors, I needed information. Like the Inquisitors, I was unlikely to get the truth from my tortured prisoner, nor would I be able to know whether what he said was true or not, but I had to ask. "The priests from the Holy Office. What do they want?"

The Marqués shook his head.

"Oh, you can speak. The noose is not that tight."

"It was a trade," he rasped, his breath barely able to bypass the rope. "I wanted you, and they want something to bring down the Bishop of Puebla with. His little amour with you is not enough."

I made to protest, but he continued. "Untie me. I can barely breathe."

It was, against all odds, likely that he had told the truth. But I could not free him, not after he had engineered this kidnapping, torture, and violation of my body.

"They beat Sor Inez so severely she may be dead."

"Then they are damned," he croaked. "I wanted nothing but that they take you, frighten you a bit, and bring you here."

"What were you to give them in exchange?"

The Marqués was silent, and I thought I had exhausted the confessional moment that choking nearly to death had brought on, but he had no shame. His pride in his own chicanery loosened his tongue.

"Eustacia said Sor Juana had some damning papers. I offered them to Father Fernándo in exchange for his assistance with you. But apparently the crafty sister took them with her when she left. I am relieved that they brought you here even without the papers, perhaps for the pleasure of escorting you. I am certain that they will still demand that I keep my side of the bargain. I will have to find something else to appease Father Fernándo, or he will be back."

I shuddered. "They searched my room."

"Yes," the Marqués rasped, "they are aware of your unhealthy connection with that dangerous poetess. Mark my words: they will be back, and they will be back for you. Untie me, and I and my household will protect you."

"As you did tonight?"

"Josefina," he answered, his voice fading to a whisper, "untie me or I die. I did protect you, I sent them away before that idiot José could do too much harm. Untie me!" His eyes were bulging and his face was red. I knew his pain. My feminine compassion surged in me, and I moved closer. But I had one more question.

"Who else knows that we are here?"

"No one!" the Marqués said.

I stopped. He had answered too quickly, his voice was too strong.

"You must tell me the truth."

He closed his eyes, as though fading. I did not trust him, as I had withstood far more and had not collapsed. I could not release him, but if servants found him here, like this, on the morrow, would I suffer? If he did not die, what vengeance would he wreak? I could not think about that now. I would bear any punishment that was my lot, in exchange for the futile revenge of leaving him.

I took up my torn pantalettes and gown, and dressed myself as well as I could. Then I took the rich coverlet from the bed and fashioned it around myself as a flowing cape. Its smooth and elegant fabric would make a serviceable covering until I reached my room.

"Good-bye, Your Highness," I said. "I am sorry to leave you here, but we are even. You will not die, as I did not, from shame."

WHEN I EMERGED FROM the stone hallway, I saw that I was near the back of the castle, near the doors that opened onto the garden. I stepped outside, and in the cold air of the waning night, I breathed in freedom. I had suffered, I would suffer, but I had lived. In the distance the sky was lightening. I hurried back inside, and though I took several mistaken twists and turns, I reached the nuns' wing unobserved.

I entered the kitchen, relieved by the normality of the smell of rising dough. A shadowy figure of a nun stood at the hearth, breads on a pallet, ready to be baked.

"Sister," I said, and she jumped, almost upsetting the loaves. Putting them back on the table, she rushed to embrace me.

"You are alive!"

"I am. And Sor Inez?" I dreaded the answer.

"She lives, tonight. Though her pain is great, Sor Carmen's ointments and prayers are greater."

"I thank the Lord," I said. "I have need of Sor Carmen's ointments as well. And, Sister, could you prepare me several large pitchers of hot water? I would bless you for it."

"It will be my joy to do so," she answered. "I have water already heated for the morning needs." She made no comment on the strange wrap I wore.

I entered my room. To my surprise, it was not in the shambles it had been when I left it.

"Sor Teresita put it to rights," the kitchen nun said, entering with the ewers of water. "And here are herbs for healing." She crossed herself and left me.

I thanked her and closed my door. I took off the coverlet and my ruined clothing. I dipped a cloth into the warm, scented water and, for a long time, I bathed.

I could never be cleansed, but I was clean. I longed to lay my exhausted and beaten body down on my bed, but my work was not yet done. I pulled my chair to the little writing table, took out a sheet of paper, and began to write.

AFTER THE MATINS BELL had rung, I rolled my writings into a tube and tied them with a ribbon. I hid them between the mattress and the bedstead, and finally slept.

TWENTY-THREE

FOR TWO DAYS, I tossed in my bed. Headaches pummeled me, searing ones such as I had suffered at home during my pregnancy. My body, which had sustained me during the rampage, now collapsed, and I could not move. Every intimate part of me ached, and though I could not ask Sor Carmen to rub the ointments on the worst of my pains, she left me enough to minister to myself alone. It was certainly thanks to her medicines that I did survive. To my chagrin and amazement, I still did not run my monthly course; if there was a babe growing inside of me, he would not easily be dislodged.

When I was absent from Court meals, Manuel sent a note of inquiry as to my health. I responded only that I was ill with headache. I asked Sor Teresita, but she assured me that he had not come to look for me on that horrible night. I cried in sorrow that he had forgotten me, that he had chosen to remain with Angélica that night despite his promise to me. But had he tried to find me, I could not guess at how he would have responded to my situation. Perhaps it was best that he had stayed away.

On the third day after the horrors, Luz came to me. She tapped softly at my door, and then let herself in. She looked around. "Plain, but sufficient," she judged my room. "I have never been in the nuns' wing. It is very peaceful on this side of the castle."

"I am so glad that you have come," I said, sitting up in my bed. "Please, pull a chair near to the fire, and sit. I have no refreshment to offer you— unless you would like to ask the kitchen nuns for some sherry?"

Luz shook her pretty, dark head. "No, I do not need sherry. I have drunk so much sherry in the past four days that I fear I am intoxicating my baby as well as myself. You have missed some lovely dinners, with your headache. Are you better?"

I nodded, though the action was painful. Luz sat silently for a bit. Finally she spoke. "Josefina, we are sisters in this castle. A headache does not cause a swollen lip or a black eye. You are pale, your eyes are haunted. What happened?"

A wave of nausea overtook me, and I swallowed back my saliva. Luz moved to my bed. "Let me get you something. Some sherry, something."

I realized I had not eaten in almost three days. "A piece of bread, and a little sherry, thank you, Luz." I had started to shake. She rushed out.

In a moment she returned with the victuals, meager though they were. I took a sip of sherry, and spat it back, coughing. "Try again," she said. I nibbled a piece of crust, fought the nausea until it subsided, and sipped again. This time the sherry tasted sweet; it soothed me as it went down. "Now eat some more," she said gently. I did.

As I consumed the bread, I felt my hunger return. I looked at Luz gratefully. "Do you think the kitchen sisters could warm me a tortilla?" I asked. Luz quickly made the trip to the kitchen. She returned with a plate piled high with tortillas, freshly pressed, and some oil to pour on them. With trembling fingers, I moistened one, rolled it, and filled my mouth with its earthy goodness.

Luz allowed me to eat in silence. When I had finished, she took the plate from me, handed me the refilled sherry glass, and said, "Now, sister. Tell me."

I closed my eyes. "I was raped by the Marqués."

"Oh my God, Lord of Heaven!" she exclaimed. I nodded. "And he beat you?"

I had to say more. "He had servants take me and beat me, then he locked me in a room, bound me, and raped me." I started to cry. I had not cried since my escape; I had not thought, remembered, or considered what had happened. And now, with blessed release, I sobbed.

When I finally was empty of tears, I looked to see Luz's tears flowing as well. I patted her hand, and she smiled wryly. "It is not I who need comforting."

"Your tears are my comfort."

"Servants, you say?" I nodded. In a sense, it was true. "Unspeakable,

But it gives explanation to the Marqués' absence. He has not appeared at dinner for two days. I did not connect your absence with his. The Marquesa is furious."

"Manuel must not know," I said.

"Of course not. I would not be so foolish. My God, if he learns, he will kill the Marqués. And worse, you will be banished from your home, your children. Such an unfair world we live in, Josefina. Pray he did not leave you with child." To this I could give no answer.

"Well, you must not venture out until you are healed in the face," Luz concluded.

"You are right. My shame is branded upon me. But your love soothes me, Luz." I could stay in the nuns' wing, though. They knew more of the truth. "I will stay in here a few more days. Then I must attend the final *posada* ball, or rumors will slay my reputation. Can you speak to Manuel for me?"

"Of course. What shall I tell him?"

"Tell him . . . Oh, heavens, even the headaches are suspect. Tell him that I am mending, but that I became ill from some viand I ate at the ball. Tell him I thank him for not coming to me that night, as I was terribly ill, and that I feared only that he, too, was ill, and I am thankful that he was not."

"He was to come to you that night?" I nodded. "Another explanation, then. He and Angélica had a row, toward the end of the ball. The Marqués had left, and Angélica clearly was angered by the Marqués' lack of attention. But Manuel and she argued; she seemingly accused him of being less than attentive as well. I was standing in the resting alcove, finishing my supper, and I could not help but overhear them, though they spoke in harsh whispers. Your Manuel is a man of very few words."

"True. But when he speaks, it is best to listen."

"A lesson Angélica will do well to learn if she wishes to retain his affections." I winced. "I am sorry, Josefina, but we women must be practical about this. And right now, you certainly do not want Manuel chasing after you. I will give him your message, and visit you again this afternoon."

"Thank you, Luz. You are indeed a sister to me."

After Luz left, I rose from my bed and dressed. I must return to the living, I thought, even if it was just the nuns' wing. I must visit Sor Inez.

Sor Teresita was sitting outside Sor Inez's door, her young face gray with exhaustion. "Have you been here for days?" I asked.

"Yes, señora. I have kept watch. They must not touch her again."

"You are good. I will sit with her awhile. Go lie down." She looked unsure, but I urged her away. With a look at my blackened eye, she nodded and straggled to her feet. I watched the young nun shuffle away to her dormitory, where she shared the sleeping quarters with three or four others. I wished her Godspeed.

I quietly entered the room and pulled the hard wooden chair next to Sor Inez's bed. She lay on her side, curled, her head covered with a scarf spotted with blood. She, too, had a blackened, swollen eye, and ugly bruises on her cheek. She looked no larger than Joaquín in the bed, and far less sturdy. She just barely opened the swollen eye.

"Sit down, Josefina," she said, her voice soft. It did not crack, and I felt hope.

"Bless you, Sister," I said to her.

"Did they get the letters?"

"No."

"Did you suffer terribly?"

"As did you," I answered.

"Tell me everything that happened. Leave nothing out." Her soft voice was not a command, nor an entreaty, but a statement, from one who suffered but was wise.

I obeyed. Her face did not change when I told her of my torture, of the Marqués, of the sodomy. She did not smile when I told her how I roped him like a calf, and she did not chastise me for leaving him trussed. But she did raise her eyes to Heaven when I told her of the letters I had written so carefully that night, in Sor Juana's meticulous hand.

At the end of my story, she sighed. "There is so much to do. You must do it, for I cannot. I am weak and bruised, but I feel the Lord will let me survive, as He has much more for me to accomplish. For now, you must be my handmaiden."

"I am grateful, Sister, for it will help heal me."

She nodded slightly, and only then did she wince. Before I could offer her some balm, she was speaking.

"You must do many things. I have lain here for days, how many I do not know, thinking of all you must do. I guessed at the false Inquisitors' intentions with you, but did not guess at the Marqués' evil lechery. Although it all makes sense now."

"The false Inquisitors?"

"Yes. Those two are not from the Holy Office. The Inquisition loves its torturers, and is cruel in its methods, but it is meticulous in its trials and interrogations of witnesses. There would have been a scribe, a torturer, and several priestly questioners if they had taken you for questioning."

"So they weren't real priests, either?"

"Father Fernándo is indeed a priest, though not a holy man. The Holy Office is not above buying evidence, but only if its provenance can be traced. If he got Sor Juana's letters, he would gain both gold and honor. At best, he is serving two masters—the Marqués and the Church. José is a thug. He serves anyone who pays, and the Marqués must have paid them both well.

"You did well to write those false letters. You were wise, as I knew you were, and valiant to do so the very night you suffered. Sor Juana said you were learning to think, to write, quickly. Did you hide them well?"

"Between the mattress and the bedstead. They must think it possible that they missed them when they searched my room."

"Good. As soon as you are able, you must leave your room. You must publicly return to the gentry's side of the castle. No doubt they will send someone to your room, and the letters will be found. The real ones are safe?"

"Absolutely, I am certain." I thought of Luz's pure face, and hoped I was right. I would not tell Sor Inez where they were, to protect them both. Sor Inez knew not to ask. But I had another question. "Why don't I simply burn the papers? We would all be safe then."

Sor Inez shook her head. "They are Sor Juana's legacy, the words that will live on when she is gone. They are the hope of all women in our Christian land, whether they know it or not. The letters are the children Sor Juana will never have, and are worth more than my humble life." She gasped for breath. I reached for her, but she shook her head again.

"You must heal your body quickly, so that you may go out, to the dinners, to the ball. Your heart, your soul, you must heal with prayer. I will give you orations to return life to your body, for otherwise the injuries you suffered may never heal. Men will blame you where you are completely blameless, and compound your suffering. And you must be able to lie with your husband again, and soon, or you will never be able to again."

How little she knew how true that was. I was almost certainly pregnant, and with each passing day the danger that I could not fool Manuel increased. Yet the mere thought of ever, ever lying with him, or any man, again brought back the headache.

"When do you return home?" she asked.

"After Christmas."

"Take the letters with you. They are too important to lose. Sor Juana will find a way to get them from you when it is safe. Write to me, dear." Her voice faded. "I am tired."

"Sleep, Sor Inez. I will do as you say."

"It is not all," she murmured. "There is still so much to do. But the Lord will punish the Marqués for his sin, and it is not for us to measure the justice." I held her hand until she slept.

I APPLIED SOR CARMEN's ointments to my injured face, and elsewhere, as often as I could. I prayed with every ringing of the bells, as Sor Inez had instructed, praying to the Blessed Mother for intercession, as only a woman could intercede on my behalf with the Lord. By the sixth day, I could venture out. There were three more days of *posada*. I had to make the most of them.

I lunched in the ladies' wing, with Luz at my side. She was sweet and gentle, and her daily visits had been of great comfort to me, though I felt a qualm about using her as a shield. She gave me a cream to hide the remnants of my bruises. She was so pleased to be with me that she did not seem to notice that I was suddenly insistent on being her constant companion.

She alerted the Marquesa that my illness had passed, but that I was still a bit tired. In fact, I was tired, and my constant praying and reading had not helped my condition. Luz garnered me dinner invitations for each night, and, of course, I would attend the final ball.

I sent a note to Manuel and met him in the music room. Though I dreaded it, I knew I must pretend that I was well, and that I was no longer hurt by his dalliance with Angélica. My very life depended on this.

"You are pale and thin," he said to me. "There are circles under your eyes."

"I am much better now. You are looking well." Our conversation, though never abundant, had never been so forced or stilted, either. I forced gaiety into my voice. "I am eager to return to the dinners, and the ball!" I feared he would hear my falseness.

"I am glad that you will be able to attend. Being there without you at my side makes these fancy evenings dull."

A courtier's compliment from Manuel was as false as my lightness. I searched his eyes but saw nothing other than his healthy frankness. "Well, you may forget the days I was ill, for I am well." He took my hand, and I closed my eyes and let its warmth and familiarity overtake me. Then, before I could stop myself, I was in his arms, and he was holding me against his strong chest. I was enveloped in his leathery smell, his homey, husbandlike familiarity. With the embrace, the awkwardness melted and I felt once more like the wife I had been.

We separated and he smiled into my eyes. "I have missed you, Josefina. I look forward to our return home."

"As do I. I have sent word to Cayetana that I will return after Christmas. I will arrange for her husband to escort me, and they will be able to be together for New Year's. I will prepare the hacienda for your return after the start of the New Year."

"I am happy to turn the management back to your capable hands. I expect a big cattle year, and we must plan for it."

We parted on warm terms, and I returned to my room.

It was still untouched, though I had been away for more than four hours. I rested, for my exhaustion persisted, until it was time to dress for dinner. Once again I gathered my wardrobe for the evening and clothes for the next several days, and repaired to Luz's room to get ready.

"May I leave a few things here?" I asked her. "I love to dress here with you. That is one very lonely part of being in the nuns' wing."

"Of course!" Luz said happily. "I will make a space in my closet, and my maid will arrange your clothing."

"No need," I said. "There are but a few things." I placed my dresses in a corner of her armoire, and carefully checked that the bag with the letters was still tucked away in the back. It was, and now I concealed it further with some of my undergarments.

We chattered to one another as we dressed, braided each other's hair, and she applied a bit more masking cream to the bruises still visible at the décolletage of my dress. "Horrible man," she said softly. I nodded, not allowing my mind to stray to him. I added a lace panel, to further mask the marks, but refrained from covering myself further despite my shame. No one else knew, and I had to brazen out the few remaining days.

When we reached the room where the dinner was to be, I felt my stomach sink in trepidation. I had rehearsed in my mind how I would speak and act toward the Marqués, but fear had its own effect. As the sentries pulled the curtains open for us to enter, my hands were cold and sweating, and my breath was short. I hesitated, then reminded myself that I must proceed, and I took Luz's arm as we stepped forward into the beckoning room.

Our entrance was completely unremarked. In a moment we were caught up in the swirl of people, wine, and sweet music. I had not forgotten, but had closed off the part of my memory that had welcomed the magic of the luxurious dinner parties, and my senses were overwhelmed with the beauty of the pageant. I scanned the room, but the Marqués was absent. I would not have to face my tormentor just yet.

I took my glass to a corner, where I stood watching the guests chat. A pretty nun in the opposite corner strummed a lyre, and another stood near her, as if prepared to sing. I had chosen my gown well; its dusky rose color, so vivid in the summer when I had first worn it, was made suitable for winter with a deep magenta sash, and the lace I had added made it yet more festive for the season.

The curtain parted and Manuel and several other gentlemen entered. He was wearing a vest I had never seen before, with colored embroidery. Though it hurt to realize that Angélica must have had a hand in commissioning clothes for his sojourn at the Court, I still smiled at the vanity. It did look good, and the frivolousness of its decoration lent him a more urbane air. He at least had not affected the stockinged leg of the Hidalgos; he wore his black dress breeches straight to his boots. His hat was a simple leather one, with a small feather and a silk band. His companions, however, had taken advantage of the season to wear large plumes in their hats, which fanned the air when they doffed them to greet the ladies.

Manuel walked straight to me. He bowed, and took my hand to kiss it. "Silly man," I said, smiling.

"I am learning new ways here. Useless, but amusing," he said, smiling back.

He stood next to me, accepting a glass of wine from a passing tray. I looked around, still not seeing Angélica. Manuel did not seem to be scanning the room. He looked around sociably, but kept his attention on me.

"Tell me about that lady," he said, indicating Granada with a glance.

"A sharp-tongued beauty, looking for a liaison."

He raised his eyebrow. "And how would one know that?"

"Ladies' talk is vicious," I replied. "She has been married, but she is estranged from her husband. I believe he lives in Spain. It is said she would enjoy a dalliance that came with a city home and a country cottage."

"My. Well, she is beautiful, and that gown is very rich, so he must at least have provided well for her at one time."

I nodded. "She is always very well turned out, though I don't know the source of her funds. She has exquisite taste, and a marksman's aim with her words."

"I would not want a harpy like that."

The nun began to sing, and the room quieted somewhat so that all could enjoy the song. It was a moving spiritual piece, in Latin, about the bounty of God. It also made talking unnecessary for a few minutes.

When the song concluded, the curtains parted and the Marquesa made her grand entrance. In her usual black, she looked only barely festive, with a gold tiara in her black hair, and she served as contrast to Angélica, who entered in her entourage. Angélica was draped in cloth of buttery silk that quivered as she walked, and her golden hair was lifted by a diamond comb, only to fall in a cascade of curls at her shoulders. The room took a collective breath.

The other ladies who attended the Marquesa entered behind them, but were mere shadows of Angélica's overwhelming glory. After we curtsied or bowed to the Marquesa, the group dispersed and I felt Manuel stiffen beside me, as if steeling himself for Angélica's approach. But she stayed by the Marquesa, saying something softly to her, handing her a glass of wine, and attending to her every word.

I understood now. They had not reconciled since the first ball.

"She is beautiful, Manuel," I said.

"Who is?"

I chuckled. "I know and I understand. You are a man. But I am your wife, and my love and devotion to you is timeless."

He looked down at me, and I was stunned to see a hint of a tear in his eye. "And mine to you, Josefina."

I tore my glance away from him, only to catch Angélica's glare before she went back to attending the Marquesa. I allowed myself a moment of triumph.

Luz joined us. Pleasant conversation whiled away the time before we sang our *posada* song. The Marquesa continued to make the rounds, and would soon approach us. Angélica, who had been as if sewn to the Marquesa's hem, stepped away from her as she neared our little group. She moved as if without a care, smiling directly at the nearest gentleman, one of plumage and bright ribbons. His conversation with several others halted as he was pulled into her brilliant aura, and his eyes became riveted upon her. I could not imagine such power.

"Your Highness," said Manuel, bowing to the Marquesa. His eyes strayed to Angélica, who almost had the grandee drooling, but he returned his glance quickly to us.

"Don Manuel, good evening. And Doña Luz. Doña Josefina, a word with you if you would." I could not, of course, decline.

We moved away as much as we could from the rest of the guests. "The Marqués is unwell."

"I am sorry to hear that, Your Highness." My voice was steady. I was indeed sorry to hear that he was merely unwell.

"I wish to discuss his condition with you. Come to my rooms tomorrow, and you will take your midday meal with me."

"I am honored by your invitation. Your Highness. He will not join us for dinner tonight?"

"No."

"It is a pity, but we must pray for his recovery." I felt my appetite return, and the room, the gowns, the ladies—even Angélica—all looked wonderful to me. The lyre sounded the opening bars of the *posada*. With a curtsy, I hurried back to join Manuel and Luz in the petitioning song.

MANUEL DID NOT COME to me that night, nor had my room been disturbed during the dinner. I feared that my plans would fail, but at the very least I had enjoyed my dinner and my evening. I had two more nights to try. I slept well, and woke refreshed.

I took a tray to Sor Inez for breakfast. To my joy, she was able to sit up in bed and take a soft roll dipped in hot chocolate. I watched as a mother would every bite, feeling the sustenance enter her battered body. I, too, ate, and enjoyed my chocolate.

"They have not come," I said, when she had finished.

"I know. But I believe they will. You have done well, and acted bravely in your plan. Were you forced to see the Marqués?"

"The Lord spared me that torment. But I take the midday meal with the Marquesa today. She wants to talk about the Marqués. I will be careful."

"Listen much, speak little. And your husband?"

"He is attentive, but he is still distracted by Angélica."

"You must redouble your efforts." I had correctly guessed that she knew about Angélica. Sor Inez missed little. I wondered if she knew about Father Alonso and suspected what I feared. "Your husband must be fully in your camp if any aspect of this terrible trial becomes known."

I nodded. Whether for her reasons or for mine, I had to lie with Manuel. I sighed. "I will try harder."

"It is frightening, and painful, but you must. It will speed your healing. Are you praying?"

"Yes, Sister."

"Then the Blessed Mother will protect you." I crossed myself as she blessed me. I had faith, but I would welcome a sign of that protection, and soon.

I WAS ESCORTED INTO the Marquesa's private chambers, where I had been the last time, by a lovely girl on the verge of womanhood. Her grace, her smile, everything about her promised a golden future. She curtsied and left, but I could hear her humming as she went through the curtains to the anteroom beyond.

"A charming girl," I said to the Marquesa, after greeting her.

"Certainly. She is the daughter of the Honorable Mateo Espinoza Domínguez, who, I am sure you know, is a powerful Hidalgo in the North."

Indeed I knew of him. "He sets the cattle prices, his herds are so large, and his hacienda and lands are so vast that he alone could feed the army of our King."

"I forget, you are a hacienda wife, and you manage the estate as well."

"Yes, Your Highness. Numbers are easy for me, far more so than words."

"I hope that your studies here improved your mind for poetry and reading, as those studies are drawing to a close."

I was surprised by her statement but I hoped I did not show it. "They certainly have. I leave here greatly educated."

She arched a thin eyebrow. "You have also grown bold."

"I find no benefit in denying the truth."

"Excellent, Doña Josefina. Tell me, then, are you the cause of my husband's current infirmity?"

This time I was unable to mask my surprise, or harness my tongue. "Infirmity? I was unaware of any, other than his moral weakness."

The Marquesa actually laughed aloud. The sound resembled a crow's caw. "That weakness should be subjugated now. He has been rendered incapable of his favorite sins, and blames you. I dare not think how he was in a position to have his most cherished possessions damaged so thoroughly, and he will not tell me how you managed it. But you deny it?"

I could feel myself blushing, though my dark skin could hide the color well. Anger and shame had been battling within me for a week, and as my physical pain subsided my shame had diminished with it, leaving cold anger to possess the field.

"I do not deny that he accosted me, and I do not deny that he deserved any pain he suffers, but I do not concede that I am the author of his pain. If he will not tell you the circumstances of his undoing, then I shall not, either."

"Well, you are as stubborn as I always suspected." She rang a bell, and the lovely girl returned. "Summon the Marqués to me," the Marquesa said.

My heart tightened. I was not prepared to confront the man who had so horribly violated me. Although if he, too, was damaged somehow, he might not wish to see me, either. "Please tell him that I am here as well," I said to the girl.

The girl curtsied again and left. "You order my *menina*?" the Marquesa asked.

"She is too old to be a *menina*. And I do not want the Marqués to be surprised by my presence."

"Kind of you to be so considerate of him, after what you did to him."

I prayed. I begged the Blessed Virgin that he not taunt me, shame me, or even utter what he had done. I prayed that no one would ever know. And if my presence did not deter him, I did not want the Marqués, under the shock of surprise, to say anything that was unplanned. Nevertheless, if he spoke the truth, I would do the same. Let him suffer the shame I felt.

"He is long in coming," I said as the moments passed in tense silence.

"You will see why when he arrives," the Marquesa replied.

At last the curtain parted, and the *menina* reappeared. She looked flushed, her fair skin pink and dampened with perspiration. On her arm, his own face beyond flushed to red, breathing through his open mouth, limped the Marqués. When he saw me, his eyes narrowed in anger.

"Witch! Harpy!" he said.

The Marquesa indicated a chair, and he sat. "You may tell the servants to serve luncheon," she said, dismissing the girl.

"Margarita, I will not dine with her!" the Marqués hissed.

"Nor I with you," I said to him, my voice cold.

"You will both do exactly as I say," the Marquesa intervened. "This is my home, and you, Doña Josefina, are my guest, at least for three more days. And you, Porfirio, know damned well why you will obey me."

I had never thought to wonder how the Marquesa and the Marqués addressed each other. But the momentary distraction faded when the Marqués answered.

"Do not speak to me like that in front of this whore."

"Do not call me a whore, or any other vulgar name, for I am none of the things you have named me. I am an honorable woman, whom you tried to shame. May you rot in Hell." I heard my own voice cursing him, over the ringing in my ears. It was level and icy, belying the fire of my words.

"Oh, you are honorable! Squirming under my cock you are honorable?"

"You lie, Marqués, and you know it."

The Marquesa cawed again. "I knew it, Porfirio. You thought you could get her, didn't you? At last, someone stood up to you! Tell her of your injury, Porfirio. Show her that prick of yours!" His crudeness had not shocked me, but hers was stunning. They sounded like two villagers screaming at each other in a hovel at the end of a dusty street, not like a *marqués* and a *marquesa* in a castle.

"May you both rot in Hell!" he spat.

"Your prick will rot first, right here on earth!" she snarled. Turning to me she added, "I want to know how you did it. It was so swollen that the Court physician could not untie the rope that bound it, nor cut it for fear of snipping the testicles, and had to treat the whole area for two days with cold water until the swelling diminished. One ball remains terribly engorged. He screamed and cursed you continuously. I cannot imagine that you did not hear him, he was so loud!"

The Marqués tried to rise, but the Marquesa pushed him back down into his chair. He cried out when he landed.

"We may have to geld you," she added.

I could not help myself. I laughed. "Your Highness, you seem most pained."

"I'll bet you felt some pretty pain when you sat down," he taunted. But my fear had passed.

"Had you succeeded in your horrid scheme, I no doubt would have felt pain. But though the beating you inflicted left bruises"—and I moved my dress bodice to show the Marquesa the remaining marks on my bosom—"you failed to achieve your sinful aim."

"My dear, I am sorry that you suffered," the Marquesa said, and it seemed that she meant it. "I had no idea that he had gotten violent with you. He usually prefers seduction. I had never heard of him using force. Idiot," she added to him, "if she shows those bruises to her husband, he will call you out for a duel. Not one you would win, I am sure, having seen him. You deserve the punishment she gave you."

A servant entered, bearing covered dishes. "At last," the Marquesa said. "Please lay them there, we will eat alone."

When the three of us were alone again, the Marquesa spoke. "Attend. Porfirio, you will not speak a word of this to anyone, or I will disclose the shame of your rotting balls and useless manhood. Josefina, you will not speak a word, or," she added, "write a word, either. I imagine you would not, in any event, for your reputation would be tarnished beyond repair. Many women, and every man alive, will blame you in some measure. This secret, like so many others in our family, shall remain here. Is that clear?"

"Yes, Your Highness," I said. For of course she was right.

"Harpy," the Marqués muttered, and whether he meant me or his wife mattered little. "I will see you publicly whipped if you speak of this," he added directly to me. I did not deign to reply.

"Please serve yourself, Doña Josefina. The tortillas will get cold," the Marquesa said, in a polite social voice.

"I am not hungry, Your Highness, and beg to be excused."

"I grant you permission," she replied. I curtsied to her, but not to the Marqués.

The girl waited outside in the hall, humming a sweet tune. "Shall I accompany you back to your room?" she asked. I sensed a desire to speak to me, and I nodded.

"What is your name?" I asked.

"Felicitas Espinoza Domínguez, at your service."

I gave her mine.

"Oh, I know who you are. The Marquesa speaks most highly of you. And so, I want to ask you something." She looked down shyly.

"Yes?"

"I want, I mean, I am not worthy of it, but I would like to, I mean . . . ," she stammered.

"Out with it, dear," I said, as if speaking to Joaquín.

She looked relieved, and I realized that she was only months beyond childhood. "I want to write poetry. Will you teach me?"

I smiled. "My sweet girl, I cannot teach you! I leave here in three days! But if you want to learn, tell the Marquesa. She has a wonderful library, and she will let you read anything you want. And when you read, you will learn."

"But I am afraid. Will the heir be unwilling to have a wife who reads?"

"The heir? What has he to do with this?"

"Oh! I was not to tell anyone! Well, it is too late now. It will be announced formally at the last *posada,* on Christmas Eve. I am betrothed to the heir. I wait upon the Marquesa to learn the family ways. We are to be married in three months, when he returns. Can you not say anything until then, please?"

I nodded. It explained why Angélica had been allowed to visit, and why the Marquesa was permitting her to wait upon her before the last dinner. She was raising Angélica's hopes, for the pleasure of dashing them publicly at the final *posada.* I learned more daily.

"Have you met the heir?" I asked.

"No, but I hear he is handsome. My father made the marriage contract, and the heir accepted it. I sent a portrait of myself, but nothing more."

"Felicitas, let me tell you something. I met the heir once. He loves beauty in a woman, and you are beautiful. But he also admires learning. It will please him beyond words to have a wife who is both learned and beautiful."

"You think so? Oh, I am so happy!" And with the exuberance of a fifteen-year-old girl, she threw her arms around me.

Tears sprang to my eyes.

"Why do you cry?" she asked.

I smiled through the tears that now ran openly down my cheeks. "I am happy for your joy, and for your innocence. And you make me miss my children."

"Thank you, Doña Josefina. You have lightened my heart!"

IT WAS THE NIGHT of the last *posada.* Luz and I napped during the day, as the night would wear on until dawn, and we were both unsure we could last the entire time. With her condition becoming noticeable, Luz could retire early. But I could not.

I struggled with my conscience, trying to decide whether to tell Angélica about the impending announcement or not. She had suffered already from the Marquesa's vengeance, and I did not feel she should suffer more. But she had taken my husband. I weighed taking Luz into my confidence, and though I had told her far more intimate truths, I withheld this one. The secret belonged to the Marquesa, not to me. Finally I concluded that Angélica was far tougher than I had first imagined, and would survive the blow. Nonetheless, before I dressed, I stopped in her room.

My first visit returned to my memory afresh when I entered Angélica's room. Her scents and her enormous wardrobe were reminders of the first, innocent time. I almost felt the uncertainty and wonder that I had experienced.

"I cannot believe it was only eight months ago that I was here the first time," I said to her.

"Indeed, a few months have changed everything," she answered.

"And everyone. What will you wear tonight?"

Angélica took out a gorgeous gown and laid the dress out on her bed. It was spectacular, with silver and gold ribbons of silk running the length of the skirt, and a bodice of gold silk embroidered in silver. There was no lace trim, but a filigree of silver thread adorning the edges of the neckline and sleeves. "That is the most beautiful dress I have ever seen, Angélica," I said.

She smiled. "You are always kind. I feel that tonight will be special, more than just Christmas Eve. Something magical will happen."

I bit my tongue to keep from replying. Angélica did not notice my silence. "What will you wear?" she asked.

"I have a burgundy velvet dress, commissioned for this visit, which I am adorning with a white lace collar and sleeves. It is in Luz's room, but you will see it soon."

"I hope it is festive enough for tonight, Josefina," she said, in her old way. "You do not want to look shabby."

I felt somewhat better about holding my peace now. "I assure you it will not embarrass me or Manuel."

"Good," she said, without acknowledging the mention of Manuel. She brushed an invisible speck from her gown. "I think the Marquesa has something special planned for tonight." She smiled a self-satisfied smile.

"Are you attending her tonight before the *posada*?"

"I have been so honored."

"I hope the surprise is wonderful," I murmured. Could the Marquesa have misled the lovely young Felicitas? No, for her father would not ever have stood for such a trick. The Marquesa must have this terrible snare set for Angélica.

"Do you know what the surprise is about?" I asked.

Angélica hummed to herself. "Oh, perhaps the heir will be joining us in a surprise visit."

I had not considered that. "I recall that the Marquesa was not eager for you to be the object of the heir's attentions," I said softly.

Angélica narrowed her eyes. "That was a misunderstanding. Clearly she has reconsidered, keeping me as close as she has since my return. And recall, it was she personally who issued the invitation for me, and for Manuel, to visit."

I flinched when she said his name, and without a title—an unbearable familiarity. She noticed. "Don't fret, Josefina. Your husband is safe. If you spent less time ruining your eyesight with books, and more time attending to his needs, his lusts would wander less, I suppose."

I swallowed sand. "You would know," I said, and walked out. Let her discover the Marquesa's surprise on her own.

I DRESSED WITH Luz, but my mind was in the Marquesa's parlor, and in Angélica's room. "Put your mind to my hair, dear," said Luz, "or you will stick me like a pincushion!"

I apologized, and went back to pinning Luz's dark braids in an elaborate coil. "You are going to turn all the men's heads, even in your blessed condition," I said to her. "Luz," I went on, "if we are to be sisters, you must tell me something. I have told you of the Marqués' shameful treatment of me, and of my sorrows with Angélica, but you have told me only of the idyllic life you live in the North—winter weather excepted. Do you ever suffer as I do, from jealousy, or frustration?"

Luz furrowed her brow. "No," she said after a minute. "I have led a very placid life. Though I do wish I could read more than my name. Other than that, I have few sorrows or regrets. And fewer adventures."

"Adventures are not as pleasant in life as they are in stories," I replied. I, too, had led a placid and unexciting life until I came to the Court this past spring. Until then I had not suffered beatings, rape, adultery, jealousy, or the unbearable scheming of the Court ladies. I had not been tormented with headaches, muteness, or miscarriages. "The adventures I have had since coming to Court have brought me the deepest sorrows of my life. I wonder if I would do it over to gain the knowledge I now have."

"If I had suffered what you have, I would not," Luz said. "And I cannot measure the joy you have gotten from your studies to balance the pain, but I doubt it was worth it."

"I must admit, I have felt deeper, and learned the words to express those deeper emotions, since coming here." I shrugged. "Let me finish dressing so you can arrange my hair. Tonight, I believe something truly special will happen. And I hope that it will be wonderful."

TWENTY-FOUR

HE BALL WAS EVERYTHING I had imagined, and more. It was far more crowded than the heir's welcome ball in the summer, and more festive and colorful than any of the preceding *posadas*. The Marquesa's entrance on the Marqués' arm, attended by Angélica, Felicitas, and several other very beautiful women, caused a collective gasp of appreciation from the room. And a few titters as well, as the Marqués hobbled to a cushioned chair and gingerly lowered himself to sit.

"Rumor has it that he has the pox," Luz said.

"A terrible case of it, then." I smiled at her.

Complicitously, she took my arm. "Let us have some more of those creamy sweets," she said. "I cannot get enough of them!"

"Your baby will be sweet-tempered, then," I replied, for we all knew that a pregnancy that craved sweets made for a sweet baby. Neto, who had caused me to eat sugarcane directly from the field at one point, was living proof of the theory. I smiled, thinking of him. I would be leaving the day after Christmas, and would be with my boys that night.

"You are happy for once," Luz said.

"I cannot wait to go home." I looked across the room for Manuel, who could be found by his height. He and I had greeted one another warmly, and had gone on to circulate. I had not seen his face when the Marquesa and her train entered, but I imagined that he had been as bedazzled by Angélica as every other man. Now I saw that he was looking at her, but she had kept her place near the Marquesa. There were gentlemen and ladies who orbited the noble group, and I could see Angélica talking vivaciously with a few people, but she did not leave the Marquesa's side.

"I wonder if my husband is jealous," I said to Luz softly.

She looked over to where I had been staring. "He is very taken with her. Why does he not approach her, then?"

"I do not know. Perhaps he doesn't feel adequate to the conversation. Although at home he lets others do the talking." I took a few steps toward him.

"No," Luz said. "Let us not go to him yet. I sense that he is not content with our friend Angélica, and perhaps we should see what develops."

I nodded. "At the first *posada,* as you know, they quarreled. But he did not come to my room, as he had promised, so I thought at first that they had reconciled. Yet he did not approach her at dinner, and from what I have gleaned, he has not since. When I visited her this afternoon, she assured me he was safe from her clutches. I did not scratch her eyes out for it, either."

"You are to be commended for your self-control, then," Luz said, with her silver-bell laugh.

I agreed. "But I fear that she will go running back to Manuel after tonight, and perhaps he will welcome her. I cannot tell you why, but it is what I feel."

"He may have the strength to reject her, if she does go to him. Look at his mouth. He does not look pleased."

She was right, though I feared it was jealousy and not disdain that tightened his full lips. In any event, the final *posada* song would begin momentarily, and after that, if there was any announcement to be made, it would be done then. We made ourselves welcome in a small grouping of chairs and awaited the music.

At last Angélica detached herself from the Marquesa and walked over to the musicians. The lead man nodded, and strummed a chord. We all turned our attention to them. A shuffle and rumble began as the party divided into the Pilgrims and the Hosts, but Angélica stayed with the musicians. Then the guitars strummed a set of chords, and with her voice of an angel, Angélica sang out the first line of the *posada* song.

"En el nombre del cielo, os pido posada . . ."

Tears came to my eyes, my emotions wrung by the beauty of her voice, the timelessness of the story. She sang as if the heavenly choir resided in her throat. I saw Manuel's lips part, and my vision blurred. A stab of pain tore through my head and I clutched Luz's arm with an icy hand. She put her hand over mine, but sang with the rest.

The headache subsided as quickly as it had come on, and as we concluded the ritual song with its final welcome, *"Entren, santos peregrinos, peregrinos . . . ,"* I could see again. I wiped my face with a small linen square. "It was beautiful," Luz said, as if my tears had been occasioned only by the beauty of the moment. I nodded silently.

Then the Marquesa rose. Would she be so cruel as to tear down Angélica right after her lovely singing, by announcing the heir's betrothal? I saw Felicitas, nervous and flushed, next to her. Behind Felicitas were a man and woman, clearly her father and mother. She had inherited her beauty from her mother, who held tightly to her husband's arm. I could feel the battle that must be raging in that woman's heart: it was a glorious match, but her baby daughter was about to be betrothed.

"I have the honor of announcing the betrothal of my son, Miguel Ángel Porfirio San Geronimo, to Felicitas Espinoza Domínguez, daughter of the Honorable Mateo Espinoza Domínguez. They are to be married in March, upon my son's return from Salamanca."

Cheers and applause broke out in the room. Glasses were lifted. Little Felicitas clung to her mother, smiling, blushing, and crying at once, and her father, red-faced, shook hands all around. But standing rigid, pale and shaking, Angélica remained by the musicians, who, disregarding her completely, struck up a joyful song.

"Look at her," I said to Luz.

"The child is lovely," Luz replied, looking at Felicitas.

"No! Angélica!" I whispered.

She looked over. "Oh, my! We must go to her! She must be unwell!"

"No. Let her suffer. Remember the story I told you about her disgrace? She was invited back here by the Marquesa just so she could be punished this way."

"You knew?"

I nodded. "But I dared not say. I feared that it would somehow not happen if I said anything. Can you forgive me for not telling you?"

"Of course. But you should know, I keep all of your confidences."

I was so fortunate to have found her.

In this colloquy, I had kept my eyes on Angélica, for though I was unchristian enough to enjoy her being brought low, I was not so unchari-table as to deny her my help if she were to collapse. I also kept an eye on Manuel, who to my surprise did not rush to her side, but raised a glass to the father of the bride. He strode to him confidently, and I watched him drink to the daughter's health, and clasp the man heartily.

"Manuel knows him?"

"I would suppose so, they are both cattle ranchers, though we are not as large—no one in all of New Spain is as large—as the Honorable Espinoza Domínguez."

"Then I can hope for an invitation to the wedding!" Luz said.

"I had not considered that! As we will certainly be Don Mateo's guests, we will bring you along. And if we are her father's guests, perhaps we will someday be young Felicitas's guests. The heir is a lovely young man."

"You are much more highly placed than you told me," Luz teased.

"I learn daily," I replied.

I continued to watch Manuel, as he joined toast after toast. I glanced at Angélica, who had regained a bit of composure as she stood sipping a glass of brandy. The Marquesa, thoroughly engaged in conversation on all sides, spared not a glance for Angélica. Her cruel scheme complete, she could ignore the poor widow.

"Did you notice that not only did the Marqués not make the announce-ment, but the Marquesa referred to the heir as 'my son,' not 'our son'?" I asked Luz.

"I did notice, but the Marquesa is such a headstrong, unusual woman that nothing she does surprises me."

"When I witnessed their argument in the library, she implied that the Marqués was not the heir's father. She said all of the Marqués' children were stillborn."

"How horrible!"

"Both horrible to have your children stillborn, and horrible to say so in front of me. And I paid for his humiliation with my own."

"A man who is brought down in front of a woman will always seek vengeance."

"True. But I wreaked my own. Come, let us congratulate the bride. She is a sweet child, and she wants to study poetry."

"The Blessed Mother protect her!"

"Come, you superstitious girl." Luz and I walked arm in arm to the group. As we passed Angélica, I held out my hand. "We come to toast the bride. Join us."

Angélica did not spit at me, but only barely. She did not join us. We reached the group and I took Manuel's arm. He looked down at me, startled, and I saw that he was slightly flushed. He handed me and Luz glasses of wine. "To Señorita Felicitas!" he said, and we raised our glasses.

He exchanged his empty glass for a full one. "To the Hidalgo, and his señora, many grandchildren!" he said, and drank. I sipped. Manuel was getting drunk. I hoped they would serve dinner soon.

"To my friend and neighboring landowner!" said Don Mateo. They drank up. Don Mateo clapped Manuel on the shoulder. "To my friends!" he said, and they drank again.

I looked at Don Mateo's wife. She shrugged. "I am Maria Magdalena Espinoza de Domínguez," she said. I introduced myself and Doña Luz. "My daughter speaks highly of you, Doña Josefina."

"She is a lovely girl. And as I told her, the heir, whom I have met, will appreciate her and all of her virtues." I did not mention her daughter's desire to learn, as one could not be sure where Doña Magdalena stood on such matters.

"Thank you. I am deeply honored by the match."

"As the Marqués and the Marquesa must be." Don Mateo and Manuel drank another toast. "It appears that our husbands will be toasting the night through," I remarked.

"And snoring through Midnight Mass," Doña Magdalena replied. "But it is a joyous occasion, so we must allow it."

To my relief, dinner platters were being carried in. We would be called to dine shortly, and perhaps, with some food, Manuel would keep from getting completely drunk. Angélica still stood alone, and no one even approached her.

When we finally sat down, I placed myself next to Manuel, but Luz chose the seat beside me before I could steer her to the other side of Manuel. I could not prevent Angélica from sitting on Manuel's other side.

"Ah, the viper sits beside me," Manuel muttered. I had never, in seven years of marriage, heard him say something so nasty.

"Don't you dare speak of me like that!" Angélica hissed back at him.

"Oh, I understand you now," he said. "You wanted me to idle the time, and to get you back here. But you also wanted a second strike at the heir."

"Jealous? You old fool."

"Well, you see who's the fool now, do you not?"

"Manuel," I intervened. "You sound like some of the ladies in the Court. Do not sully your tongue so."

"As you wish, my beautiful wife," he said, and put his arm around me. Though I had longed for his touch, his return to me, this drunken, sloppy embrace, done to spite Angélica, disgusted me. I concealed my feelings, though, and took a spoonful of soup. A second hug from him caused my soup to spill on the tablecloth.

"Enough, my husband. We will cause a scandal, and I will spill the rest of my soup." I smiled as I said it, and he took it in jest.

"You have caused enough scandal, my dear," he replied. "I will let you eat." I felt a chill. But he rose. "I am not very hungry, and must answer nature's call." He took his glass of wine and drained it. I was relieved that he did not stagger as he left the room.

Angélica, too, did not eat. She sipped her wine, but said nothing. At last the gentleman on her right engaged her in conversation, and she managed a dutiful social patter. I confess that I felt sorry for her, but did not aid her. I kept watch for my husband's return.

When he finally came back, Manuel did eat a bit of meat, and took some tortillas, which I hoped would absorb some of the wine, but he declined the sweets. He was silent, but as he was frequently quiet at home, I determined that he was merely ruminating, and no longer drunk. At dinner's end, the music for dancing started up. Manuel rose and joined some gentlemen playing cards in a corner. I watched him as he played, not appearing to venture much in the game, and keeping a steadily refilled glass of wine at his side. Angélica disappeared.

The bells began to ring. Midnight Mass was approaching. It was time to go to the Court's chapel and hear the words of Our Lord on Christmas Eve. Luz bade me good night, kissed me, and wished me joy at Our Savior's birth. I wished her the same, and thanked her for her love and sisterhood. She would retire for the night, for there was not a pregnant woman in Christendom, other than our Holy Mother, who would be expected to be up past midnight.

Taking Manuel's arm, I turned toward the chapel. I was amazed that he could still walk. We were crowded into a pew, and we waited for the priest's entrance. At long last, the sacristan waved his incense censer, and the crowd hushed. Preceded by acolytes, the Bishop of Puebla entered the church.

I felt my heart stop, then pound in my ears. I had not known; it had not occurred to me that he would be here. I had not seen Father Alonso since that fateful night. I knew he had fled with Sor Juana, and that he was another target of the Holy Office the night the paid henchmen had searched my room, beaten Sor Inez, and arranged my defiling. He surely knew what had happened to me. In some ways it was his fault that I had suffered so. As he crossed himself, and the crowd followed suit, I feared I would run screaming from the church. I tasted my share of Angélica's bread of sorrow, for my own Christmas Eve surprise.

"*In nomine Patris, et Filii, et Spiritus Sancti,*" he intoned. "*Amen.*"

My wild thoughts drowned out the prayers. How could he stand there and say Mass? Would not the Inquisition burst in and arrest him? Or was that all a ruse, designed by the Marqués? Was the Bishop absolved, leaving me with the entire burden of our sin? I was ten days late, and he stood easily before the people, unscathed. He began the story of Christ's birth, with the Annunciation, the angel telling Mary she was with child, and her shock. Joseph, too, was stunned by the news, and angry. Manuel would kill me.

As if on cue, Manuel snored softly. I nudged him hard with my elbow. He startled, looking as if he had been caught stealing. He nodded to me and leaned back in the pew. We rose, and I pulled him up with me. We knelt, and I pulled him down. As Father Alonso, the Bishop of Puebla, sang the Creed, I formed a plan.

At last, the dismissal was proclaimed: "*Ite, missa est.*"

Thanks be to God. I would not see the Bishop.

"Come, Manuel. Let us get you back to your room." I took his arm. He did not protest.

We walked in silence toward the gentlemen's wing, the dark corridors barely lit by the occasional candle. A post-Mass breakfast was being served in the dining rooms. Afterward, servants would light the grand lamps, and the halls would be lit for the guests to return to their rooms, but for now they were in shadows and gloom. We reached the stairs.

"You can't come up here," Manuel slurred.

"Of course I can," I said. "I am your wife, and must see you safely to bed."

"That harpy wanted the heir."

"I know, Manuel. Let us not speak of her, she is in the past. I am your wife."

"You are," he said, and pulled me close. And stumbled. I held his arm more tightly, and walked down the hall with him.

"Which is your room, Manuel?"

Fortunately, though drunk to a stupor, he could still identify his room, and those were indeed his effects in the armoire. It was set up with a small parlor and three tiny bedrooms. I followed Manuel into his sleeping room, and turned the key in the lock. Then, brazenly, as I had now experienced more brazen acts in one year than in my previous lifetime, I undressed him.

"My goodness, Josefina, you are not the modest wife," he muttered.

"I am, Manuel, but you must be put to bed."

At last he was only in his undergarment. With effort I leaned into him until he fell on the bed. "Come, wife," he slurred. Then he rolled over, and snored.

I watched him by the light of the single candle. It was but a few hours until dawn. I undressed carefully and pulled on a soft, thin woolen shirt that he often wore under his riding jacket. I inhaled his scent. Then, in the little space that he left, I climbed into the bed next to him, and fell into a sound, untroubled sleep.

WHEN THE MORNING BELLS rang, I opened my eyes, wondering where I was. My heart leaped with happiness at the sight of Manuel, sound asleep next to me. It had been the better part of a year since I had slept with my own husband.

Weak light came in the window, and I heard footsteps outside the door. Servants walked about quietly, leaving pitchers of hot water outside the doors for washing. Snores from Manuel's neighbors made the walls vibrate. It was Christmas.

Manuel must have felt me stirring, for he rolled over and opened an eye. Then another, wide with surprise. "Josefina! What on earth are you doing here?"

"Good morning, Manuel. It is Christmas."

"It is, my wife." He started to sit up, then lay back down with a groan. "My head."

"Yes, well, you drank a great deal of wine last night. I had to put you to bed."

"And you stayed?"

"As you requested."

Manuel looked embarrassed—something else I had never seen. This was a fortnight of many revelations.

"I hope that I did not behave in an ungentlemanly way toward you," he stammered.

"You are my husband, and within your rights."

He smiled. "You'd best creep out before the other gentlemen awake. There is a stair in the back of the hall, leading to the main floor, where you will not be observed."

I did not ask how he knew that. "I will not need it. I may cause minor scandal by being seen, but again, recall, I am your wife, and it is your right to lie with me at your will."

I dressed quickly. I kissed him lightly on the lips, again bade him a blessed Christmas, and left. I walked through the parlor to the hall, and down the main stairs. Though I saw no one, I knew I was seen. It was, of course, part of my plan.

When I returned to my room in the nuns' wing, I was not surprised, either. The papers I had crafted in Sor Juana's style, but giving reverent honor to the Church and the Holy Office, were gone from their hiding place in my bedstead. I took out a clean piece of foolscap, and my pen and ink. I sat at my little desk as the sunlight grew stronger, turning the words over in my mind. Finally, I put pen to paper.

My heart cannot beat timely,
its solemn cadence broken

when love's hot tears would douse
the fervor of the drummer's call
to battle.
Yet your disdain will calm me
and end my long devotion
to your shadow, not your essence,
to which I gave my all,
and lost.

The Bishop was merely a shadow, and my love for him had been but a love for an idea of a man, not a man himself. The man I loved was sleeping in the gentlemen's wing. I would return home and await him, praying that Angélica's claws would be too dulled by shame to stick into him. I addressed the poem to the Bishop, put it on my desk. Later I would have Toño deliver it. I undressed for the second time, and went back to sleep.

*T*WENTY-FIVE

*I*T WAS A LONG ride home, with only Cayetana's husband, Ygnacio, to keep me company. We left very early in the morning, to make the journey in a single day. Sitting on the high seat above the horses, he drove the carriage, and I shared the small interior with a number of parcels from the marquessate to the people of the area. We conversed only briefly during our stops to ease the horses or take care of obvious needs. As the Marqués' valet he must have known something of my plight, and the awkwardness strained what little conversation we could have. Instead I looked at the countryside and thought over my past year.

What struck me most was the cyclical repetition of my two sojourns at Court. I had gone innocently, loved the Bishop, been attacked by the Marqués, and returned pregnant. I had jeopardized my marriage to Manuel, and Angélica had profited from it. She had risen to great social heights and had been reduced by scandal or the Marquesa's design. Throughout this time, I had read perhaps fifty books, and written as many poems. To answer the question Luz had asked me, if I and my baby could survive, it would all have been worth it.

The lassitude of early pregnancy was starting to wear on me, and incipient nausea made the ride interminable. I could not complain or even show any symptoms, for under my plan these would not manifest themselves for another month. I prayed for an easy pregnancy such as Neto's had been, without the headaches and horrors of the most recent one. Merely thinking of that pain made my head hurt.

This baby, if it went full term, would be born in August. A harvest baby, the fruit of my sin. I must not think that way, I reminded myself.

Henceforth, this was Manuel's baby, and I would think only this way. Perhaps we could name it for him. But then, my internal sense of decency would be too offended. Instead, I would let Manuel name it.

We arrived after dark. It was cold, and I huddled in my thickest shawl, in the corner of the carriage. Only when I saw the light of the hacienda did I dare to feel relief. I was really coming home, and home I would stay.

Cayetana came out to meet us. She was dressed in her Mexico City clothing, and I realized that she was really greeting her husband. I was almost an afterthought. I climbed down from the carriage and she broke her embrace to come to me.

"*Bienvenida, señora,*" she said. I hugged her warmly. Her tortilla smell was home to me. "The boys are inside."

I entered my home, where one fire blazed in the sitting room hearth and another in the kitchen stove, and realized how cold it always was at Court. With so many rooms, it would cost a fortune in wood to keep the place warm.

"Where are they?" I asked.

"Surprise!" came the shrieks, and two dark-haired lads bounded out from behind the furniture. Joaquín almost knocked me down, and Neto, second to arrive, collided with him.

"Watch out, stupid!" said Joaquín, pushing Neto.

"You're stupid. I'm not," Neto answered.

"Stop it right now, both of you," Cayetana barked, "and greet your mother properly. This was not how we planned it," she added to me.

"I'm sorry, Mama. Welcome back," Neto said.

I reached down and picked him up. "I am glad to be back," I said to him. "Oof, you've gotten heavy." I kissed him and put him back down.

"He's a fat butterball," Joaquín said, extending his hand to me.

"Come, don't be mean," I said, and took his hand. I shook it as if he were a young landowner. "Don Joaquín." He tightened his lips to keep from laughing. I pulled him into my arms and hugged him. "You have gotten taller." He was up to my elbow now. He permitted the hug for a count of five, then wriggled away.

"Did you break the bad man's nose again?" he asked.

Cayetana turned away, embarrassed. "He heard that story from Anaya, who heard it from that woman's maid. I am sorry, señora."

I knew "that woman" was Angélica. I hadn't realized that the stories would follow me home. "I am sure your husband will tell you even more scandalous tales," I said. Heavens, he was the Marqués' valet. His knowledge would only be from the Marqués' side, and unless he was unnaturally discreet, all would be grist for the gossip between the reunited husband and wife. The story would grow, and twist, until some version even more degrading than the truth would reach Manuel's ears. I swayed on my feet.

"Your mama is tired, boys. Why don't you go get ready for bed, and then you can have chocolate with her." Neto clung to my leg for a moment; then, looking up at me with his large, dark brown eyes so much like my own, he nodded. Cayetana took him by the hand, leading him out of the room. "You refresh yourself, señora, and your boys will be back soon." Joaquín was already gone.

When they came back, I had composed myself. We drank our hot chocolate, ate our sweet bread pastries, and the boys talked over each other trying to get my attention for their stories. Joaquín, less talkative than his brother, had the advantages of a louder voice and a firm belief in the importance of his stories. He was done in a few tales. "You did well, Joaquín. You are a real man now."

"So I can go with Father on the next cattle run?"

I thought about how his roping skills had saved my body and my spirit. "You can if your father will permit it. You are growing up just right!" His eyes sparkled, the flecks of green even more pronounced than those in Manuel's.

"And when does Father return?" Joaquín asked.

"Five more weeks," I said. "He will ride to the North to see a very, very big cattle ranch, even bigger than ours, and then he will be back." Joaquín shrugged. He missed his father, that was clear. "It's sooner than you think," I added.

Neto held my hand. "I can read now, Mama," he said solemnly.

I glanced at Cayetana. She nodded. "What do you read, my love?"

"The book you gave me with the letters, and some others."

"Tomorrow you must show me," I said. "I have many new books that you may like to look at, too."

Finally the boys went off to bed, and Cayetana and I sat in the kitchen, near the stove. "Go to your husband," I said. They would have but the one night, as Ygnacio would return to the castle tomorrow.

"Thank you, señora. Thank God for your safe return."

The next morning, Cayetana took the first opportunity to draw me aside. "Ygnacio tells me terrible things. I have told him not to speak such vicious lies, but he insists. What happened?"

"Tell me what he said."

"You were arrested by the Holy Office, you were beaten by them, the Marqués rescued you, and after you repaid him with your body, you gave him the pox and tied his member to the bed!"

"Good God protect us from such stories. But I *was* beaten by the Holy Office, and I *did* tie the Marqués to a bed." That wrested a small smile from Cayetana. "How did he get loose, I wonder?"

"Ah, that I know. He had craftily kept his wrists away from his body when you tied him, and so as soon as you left he was able to get loose."

"Not all of him," I replied. Cayetana's eyebrows rose. I nodded.

"So that portion is true. That is the best part of the story, although I would not want your husband to hear any portion. But the Inquisition. What could they want with you? Or was it that studying and writing that brought you sorrow, as many said it would?"

"It was, but not the way that ignorant gossips would surmise. They were looking for writings by a holy nun and a bishop, and they beat one elderly nun senseless. They beat me, too, because they thought I knew where the important papers were. But of course I did not, and so they left me alone. It was there that the Marqués came to take advantage of my weakened state, not to rescue me."

"Men. They will brag of nonexistent conquests and lie about a woman's virtue, but stop at nothing to get what they want."

We were quiet. Then I asked, "And while I was gone, were there any visitors?" Cayetana looked at me sideways. "Did Doña Angélica stay here often?"

She looked at the ground. "It is one thing for a man to satisfy his lusts, that is normal. But to allow her to stay here in your absence, it was simply wrong."

I felt the knife twist in my heart, but I asked some more. "How long?"

"Well, señora, you were gone for two months. Doña Angélica was here for two fortnights. Twenty-seven days more than she should have been."

"There is nothing we can do about it."

"No. Now that you are home, we shall not have that problem."

I thought about Manuel, the night he walked past my room to Angélica's, and felt my eyes tear. "No, we shall not. Come, let us plan for the winter."

AFTER THREE WEEKS, I told Cayetana I was with child. Her relief likely equaled mine. I could no longer hide the thickening of my waist, and she would know that my monthly courses were not coming. But I had been free of headaches, and I hoped that I would survive this pregnancy with my baby.

"I will pray to the Virgin a rosary of thanks," she said. "I feared you were ill."

"I did not know I was acting ill," I said. My subterfuge had then been less successful than I had thought.

"When is the baby due, August?"

"August? Oh, no. By my count, middle of September." She shrugged. She would not argue, and she would be right. I would simply have to ensure that Manuel thought the baby was early.

"Neto wants a reading lesson. Shall I fetch him?"

Our reading continued apace, and he was a fantastically good learner. I felt peace when we read together, and I marveled that a child not yet four could sound out some of the words in the Bible.

Alone, I read the books I had brought from the Court, and some of Sor Juana's old poems. I never took out the sheaf of papers I had hidden in my bag of monthly cloths, but shoved them deep into my closet, away from any eyes.

THE FIRST SIGNS OF spring came, and my pregnancy began to show. Manuel would be home in a few days, and to him, I was not yet two months pregnant. It was doubtful that he would consider any female symptom too closely. He had divined my previous pregnancy, he even had known it was to be a daughter, but this time his attention had been elsewhere. Nevertheless, as the day got closer, I began to feel the return of the pains in my head. Cayetana gave me *manzanilla* and other herbs to keep the pain at bay, but we dared not try the strong herbs of my last pregnancy, lest they trigger the strokes or the miscarriage that I had suffered.

He rode up at midday, with several of his trusted men, and, to my surprise, with Ygnacio, Cayetana's husband. I came out to meet him. He dismounted and took me into his arms. "My," he said, letting me go, "you've gotten quite plump!" He smiled and took my hand, as the others saw to the care of the horses and bags. The valet smiled at me, bowed, and proceeded to the kitchen to greet his wife.

"I will give you my good news, then, since you have already noticed. I am with child again. Though I had not yet noticed much roundness. You are too discerning." I smiled into his eyes, my heart pounding. But my fear was misplaced.

"Perhaps it is because we have been apart so long," he said, "that I would welcome any womanly softness. Are you well?" He frowned in concern.

"I am, though my headaches have returned."

Manuel's full lips tightened to a line. "Then we must be careful that we not endanger our son's life."

My heart fell, for I knew that he would now keep his distance, and when he had not me, he would want another. "I believe I am healthy this time," I said. But the stabbing pain immediately shot through my head. I wavered on my feet.

"Come, sit," Manuel said. "You are pale, and we will not risk it."

"So, it will be a son this time?" I asked. He had been right every time, though for this one, he lacked the blood connection, so his predictive accuracy could be faulty.

"It will. We must name him for Christmas." He smiled, his green-brown eyes crinkling.

"You shall choose his name, then," I said, smiling back. Silently I prayed that if I played the charade long enough, I would come to believe it. "How did you come to be traveling with the Marqués' valet?" Had I known of *that* danger, I would have worried more while Manuel was gone.

"He offered to accompany us on this final leg of the journey. We were eight men, and we had need of some assistance from someone like him.

And I believe he is hinting that he would like to join our household, as Cayetana will not leave you."

"I am sure he bored you with endless tales of the Court," I said. My God, what had he said? Manuel's greeting to me had been warm and genuine, so Ignacio had clearly not spoken of the Marqués' grotesque behavior.

"He did. His master is a dissolute wastrel, and his mistress has no heart. But we shall speak of this later. I worried about you constantly. I feared I would find you injured or ill, and I am thankful that you are well, and bringing me another son."

Oh, that he would not talk of this son.

"Was your business good with Don Mateo?"

"Most successful. I will go over the plans with you tomorrow. But will those figures and numbers hurt your head?"

I laughed out loud. "Heavens no! I long to go back to your books. Will we be running our cattle with his?"

"I hope so, my wonderful wife! I am blessed. But we will not do anything that will bring on the attacks you had last time, and if one single figure causes you pain, you will not keep the books until our son is born."

I kissed him. "Let me see to your dinner," I said, and I rose. The moment I stood, a lightning strike of pain shot through me, followed by another. I gripped the edge of the table until it passed. "I am fine," I said shakily. I could not meet Manuel's eyes, but I managed to make my way to the kitchen.

Cayetana and her husband sat companionably at the little table as she diced onions. Anaya stirred a soup filled with chicken, rice, and vegetables that had spent the winter drying in the pantry. The onions, fried in maíz oil, would be folded into tortillas and fried again, to accompany the soup.

"Please put some of the cilantro herb I gave you in the soup," I told Anaya.

"That herb is bad. It stinks," she said.

"I like it, Anaya. Please put it in." She shrugged. She had grown since I had left, and she was taller than Cayetana or I. She was blossoming into a woman. "How old are you now, Anaya?" I asked.

She shrugged again. "I don't know. My mother says I am fourteen, but my father says I am fifteen. Why would that matter?"

"It doesn't. But you are marriageable."

"I am. There are plenty of boys who would want me to warm their hammock." I wondered why we kept this coarse girl in our household still. "If you are with child, señora, you shouldn't eat such nasty herbs."

"This herb is good for her!" said Cayetana sharply. "Now shut up and finish the soup."

Anaya shrugged again. "Neto is seeing things again, you know," she added.

"Seeing things? Like what?" I asked.

"Spirits. Saints. He's afraid that the birds will come back and steal the new baby's spirit like they did your daughter's."

"Anaya, I have told you that I don't want you filling the child's head with that nonsense. You must stop. It is superstitious, and unbecoming of a young, marriageable girl like you." She shrugged. I fought the urge to dismiss her.

"Señora, Ygnacio would like a word with you, if he could," Cayetana intervened.

"Certainly. Come, Ygnacio, we will converse in my office."

We went into the little room off the kitchen. Cayetana came in with a taper from the stove to light the lamp on my desk and the smaller one in the sconce. I sat in the only chair and Ygnacio stood by the door. Cayetana quietly left the room.

"Señora," he started, then shuffled his feet. Such behavior was unexpected from the suave, experienced valet of the Marqués. At Court, he was in the highest level of servants, almost a gentleman. He must have felt very uncomfortable.

"Ygnacio, what is it?"

He looked at the ground. "Señora. I wish to tell you something, and I wish to ask you something. Yet by telling you, I am likely ensuring that you will deny my request."

"Out with it, Ygnacio," I said. My hands were shaking, but my voice was firm.

"I heard the truth, señora. I tended to my master, the Marqués, when he came to his room, his pants barely up, in agony. He said that you did that to him, and that the Holy Office was punishing you. And yet, he bragged of his conquest."

"You are telling me a story that you should not be repeating," I said.

"I did not tell anyone except my wife. Some stories circulated throughout the castle, as servants will talk, especially after the Marqués could not stand at the final *posada*. Your name was not directly associated with those. But that first story, the one he told me that night, or morning as it was, was not the last story." I stared at Ygnacio. "I must tell you, for only then can you understand my predicament."

"Go on."

"Although there was gossip, the words were mostly speculation. The Marquesa told me the truth. The Marqués had sent the Holy Office after you, on information from his wife's cousin, and when they had finished questioning you, he made a violent attempt upon your virtue. This I know from the Marquesa, and my wife, and, well, from others. Mercifully, he was unsuccessful, and your bravery and country skills have exacted revenge. The Marquesa forbade our mentioning the Marqués' incapacity, or anything about it, or you, or the Holy Office, on pain of dismissal. She told the upper servants that the Holy Office was bent upon destroying her and the Bishop of Puebla, and if we valued our positions we would keep silent. But on the first day of the New Year, there was a scene."

"What do you mean, a scene?"

"I generally go in the morning to dress the Marqués. I entered, but he was still in bed. A foul odor assailed my nostrils. I pulled the curtain aside, and he was lying on his back—forgive me, señora—naked. He had thrown off the covers, and he was wet with sweat. His member—I apologize—and his balls were black. They stank. The whole alcove stank. He was putrefying. And he was muttering.

"I did not wish to lean close to hear what he said, but a few words were clear. Your name, señora, was being cursed. Your virtue insulted, your soul damned. As were those of the sister Sor Juana, and His Grace the Bishop, and the Marquesa, but mostly yours. I was frightened. I went to the Marquesa, for as you know, it is she who rules the castle, and she sent for the physicians.

"Though they all came, they could do nothing for him. His fever raged, and his member rotted. At last, it seemed that he would not live through the night. I was sent to fetch a priest. But when the Father entered—and he was just one of those who serve the castle church—the Marqués began to scream.

"He blasphemed, and called the priest a whoremonger, a lecher, a pimp. He accused him of filthy crimes unfit for a lady's ear. And he accused the poor Father of lying with you. At that point, the Marquesa ordered the priest to leave, and the bewildered man gave the Marqués a blessing from a distance and fled. Unfortunately, servants throughout the hall heard the screams, and stories began to swirl."

I sighed. I had not intended such horrors to be visited upon the Marqués, but the horrors he had visited upon me still haunted my nights. "Go on."

"The Marquesa called for Sor Carmen, whose potions and ointments are known for their powers, in the hope that she could do what the physicians could not. The Lord had mercy, for she was in part successful. She was able to break the fever, and stop the rot, but not before the Marqués' male powers had been brought to an end."

"The Lord is merciful," I said, and Ygnacio, who had served in the Court long enough, knew not to ask my meaning.

"The priest returned and offered an exorcism. The Marquesa told him, in my presence, that the only demon to be cast out had left. But by now, the entire Court was buzzing with stories. Your name came up, numerous times. At last, the gossip reached your husband's ear. He is not much of a talker, is he?"

"No, although the Court seems to have loosened his tongue."

"Then he must have been silent as the tomb before he came. For on his last day, at the feast of the Epiphany, he was summoned to the Marqués. You know, señora, that I have always been loyal to my master, and have helped him in many of his entertainments, but be sure I had no idea about his accosting of you, or of his terrible designs upon you."

"What did he say to Don Manuel?"

Ygnacio looked abashed. "He accused your husband of playing with Doña Angélica's affections. Don Manuel said something like 'Nonsense.' I am sure the Marqués wanted something more, since he added that you had sullied your husband's name by your behavior, and that you were unworthy of him, and that Doña Angélica was far more worthy of him than you were. The Marqués went on to say that your studying had unsexed you, that it had angered the Holy Office, and that your writings were the work of the Devil. Your good husband laughed out loud. And finally, the Marqués said—and I beg your pardon—that the Bishop of Puebla had used you like a priest uses a boy."

I felt the bile rise in my throat. "He lies."

"Of course, señora. Your husband, I might add, said exactly that. He rose from the seat where he had attended the Marqués, and he said, 'Liar. If you were still a man, I would kill you.' Without another word he walked out. He packed his bag, and left that evening. I do not know where he spent the night. I do know that he intended to leave in the morning for the North, with a group of gentlemen, including Don Mateo, the father of the heir's betrothed. The gentlemen did indeed leave the following day. Your husband met up with them, and the journey proceeded. But it was that last conversation that led me to join your husband's group. I cannot go on serving the Marqués."

I could not answer. I knew that Ygnacio was asking to join my household, but at the moment I could think of no one but myself. I needed time to absorb the report. I looked up and saw that Ygnacio was waiting for me to speak. "Ygnacio, you have been very honest. But you have served the Marqués for twenty or more years, judging from your age and position. If I take you on, how can I be sure of your loyalty?"

"I will swear it, take a blood oath! No gentleman should speak of a lady the way he did, and especially not to her husband to avenge his own failure. I cannot serve him, and if I cannot serve your household, I will find another."

"Let me think on it. It is Manuel's first day back with me. I am not ready to discuss this now. I will inform you, after consulting with Manuel."

"Thank you, señora." He bowed.

"Do not bow, Ygnacio. We are but landowners, not nobility. We do not have the same elaborate habits that you are used to from the Court."

"My people are from here, and I am happy to return to my land."

I sat quietly for a while after he left. I would have to consult Manuel, and that meant I would have to speak to him about this painful matter. At least, I reflected, the grotesque speech the Marqués had made to Manuel in no way implied that anyone other than Manuel had gotten me with child. For that, for now, I would be grateful.

DINNER WAS SPENT QUIETLY. Manuel was considerate of my condition, and I did not dare raise the issue that pressed upon my mind. The soup, with its cilantro, was delicious, and it soothed my stomach. Cayetana brought me additional herbs in a tea that night. I slept fitfully, but at least I slept.

In the morning, I took chocolate to Manuel, who was already out at the stables. He smiled when he took the cup, and went on with his review of the horses.

"We will need more feed, if we are to increase the cattle this year," he said. I nodded. I would rather talk about cattle than Court. But the terrible job could be put off no longer.

As soon as our midday meal was finished, I said, "Manuel, we must speak of this terrible business at the Court."

"Who said anything to you?" he asked, his eyes narrowing.

"Ygnacio. But don't get angry," I said as he half rose, as if he would go throttle him on the spot. "He wants to join our household, and so he had to tell me what had happened at Court. He heard your interview with the Marqués."

"I will kill him."

"Don't. It is only right for Ygnacio to tell me."

"I do not want you hurt, and I do not want our son to be damaged. You are delicate enough with the pregnancy and the headaches. I would not have told you."

"I know, Manuel."

He looked into my eyes.

I was the one to end the silence. "I know what the Marqués said, and it is not true. But you must know, the Holy Office did interrogate me, and none too gently. They blackened my eye, cut my lip." Just as I could not explain the false Inquisitors to Cayetana, I could not tell Manuel the details of their attack. "And the Marqués did assault me, though you know that I was able to thwart his advances."

"If I had escorted you back to your room, as I had intended, none of this would have happened." He stared at the ground. I thanked the Blessed Virgin that he only knew a quarter of the truth.

"But you have heard, no doubt, of the terrible thing I did to him," I added.

"I did, and I am proud of you. Though I cannot be happy that you were in such intimate quarters with him."

"It was not my doing that got me there."

"I believe it. Why did you not tell me that the Inquisition had taken you to question?"

"Because of what followed. No man ever believes a woman is blameless when she is assaulted." He did not reply. We both knew that was true. "But I did nothing to entice the Marqués, and it is his terrible lust that drove him to involve the Holy Office as well. I did not deserve it."

"I believe it," he said again. I wished he would say more.

"Can you forgive me?" I asked. It rankled that I must beg forgiveness for the nightmare that haunted me, but I knew in my soul that another sin needed forgiving. I substituted one for the other.

"I do," he said. "You are my wife."

"And you are my husband," I answered.

"Bring this child to light," he said.

I nodded. I would do everything in my power to keep this babe alive. And I would pray, with every waking breath, that he did not have red hair.

SEVERAL DAYS LATER CAYETANA informed me that Anaya had run off. "Good," I said. "I am tired of her superstitions and her bad influence on the children."

"And I thank you for letting Ygnacio join our household," she replied.

"Will he miss the finery of the Court?" I asked. He had been the valet of the Marqués, and now he was simply a manservant in a landowner's household.

"Yes, I am sure he will. But he is teaching me many fine things. Did you enjoy the dinner last night?"

I nodded. The meat had a sauce that was light and delicate, and the vegetables were coated in sweet butter. "Was that Ygnacio's contribution?"

"It was. With Anaya gone, Ygnacio offered to help in the kitchen. Your husband is with the cattle and does not require much service, and Ygnacio is not an outdoor man, even if he does come from our people. And, of course, he can read."

"Of course. Perhaps he will teach you."

"He has offered. I suppose it is very modern to teach women to read."

"You may move with the times, Cayetana. You are not too old to be a newlywed, so you are not too old to learn to read." We both smiled at the thought.

"Are you feeling well today?"

"I am. What herbs are you giving me, that keep me from the tortures of the headaches?"

"Chamomile and *yerba buena,* by day, for the headaches. And the leaf of maguey at night, for the nightmares."

"And for that, especially, I bless you."

I had been waking up almost nightly since Manuel's return, sick with fear. In my dreams, I was naked, bound, and men were approaching me, ready to tear into my body. It was no mystery what brought these horrible visions. I had forced them from my mind for weeks, but they would bubble up like mire in the night. The herbs calmed me.

"But I cannot give you maguey in your last three months, señora. So be sure to tell me when you are six months past your last courses." The implication was clear. She did not believe my count.

"I will." I would suffer my nightmares rather than endanger the child. "I was not as regular as usual with the move to the Court, so there is some doubt about the last course." She nodded. Any excuse would do, and there was no way for her to know that Manuel had absented himself from my bed for the first two weeks of his visit.

"There are new flowers on the squash plants," she said. "Would you like those fried with cheese for dinner tonight?"

SPRING CAME AND WENT, and I grew round with child. By June, I was having trouble walking, and my ankles were swollen. The headaches had been mild, but with the increasing heat I could feel the pressure in my head build. All the chamomile in the world would not help me. And the time had come for me to give up the maguey.

The first night, I lay awake waiting for the nightmares. But they did not come. Nor did they appear the second night. The third day, Neto came into the sitting room screaming. I caught him in my arms.

"The birds are back. They're back!" He sobbed in my arms, his plump face red from hysteria.

"Hush," I said. "They're only birds. They like to come in out of the heat. Hush." But Neto would not quiet.

"It's the spirits. They're coming back! They're going to take my baby brother!" He shook with terror.

I silently cursed Anaya. Her bad influence lingered after her departure. "Neto, listen to me. You know how you can read?" He nodded, and hiccupped. "So you know some things that others don't. Well, some people think that the birds take spirits. But those of us who can read know that they don't."

He took some shaky breaths.

"Do you understand, Neto?"

"No."

I stroked his back. "Hush, sweetie. They're only birds. They will not take your spirit. And they will not take the baby's spirit. Hush." He curled into my arms, still unbelieving, but soothed by my crooning.

THAT NIGHT, THE NIGHTMARES came back in force.

I woke up, screaming. Anaya was at my side. "Here, drink," she said, and she held a cup of warm water with maguey.

"No! I cannot. It will kill the baby!"

"Drink," she said again. "You will kill the baby with your screaming otherwise."

I could not kill this child. It was the only thing that would save Manuel's love for me. I sipped, and spat it out. It was bitter. It was not maguey. It was poison. The men were at the door. They would tear my clothes, then they would tear my body as they entered it. I screamed again.

This time my screams awakened me for real. I sat up in bed, panting. Cayetana was not there, Anaya was not there, and the scream had been in my throat only. I shivered and sobbed. But the baby was safe.

SOON THE HEADACHES WERE back during the day, and I could barely rise. I prayed constantly for deliverance and hoped that I would not cry out in any way that would bring to light the truth.

As I sat on the veranda in the oppressive heat of July, a man rode up on horseback. I could not get up to greet him, but he dismounted and approached me.

"Doña Josefina?" I nodded.

"I bring you letters." He handed me a pair of letters, sealed with wax.

"Please, go into the kitchen. A man named Ygnacio will see to your refreshment." He nodded and thanked me. I looked at the seals.

It was customary for messengers to collect letters, then bring them all at once on a circuit, unless they were paid additional sums for immediate attention. I was therefore not surprised to see that the first one, from Doña Luz, was written in early June.

"My dearest sister," she started, bringing a smile to my face. Since I knew she could not read or write more than her name, my letters to her had been short and clear, so that whoever read to her could do so without mistake. It was often a cousin, who also penned her answers. *"I write to tell you that I have been delivered of a daughter, to my husband's delight. After four boys, he was ready for a girl. I have named her for you, in the hope that she will be learned and beautiful. María de los Pilares Josefina is a wonderful baby, and she eats and sleeps well. I miss our days at Court, and I hope that you will join me in November this year. My love and kisses to you. Luz."*

I felt tears, for pregnancy makes criers out of stoics, but I was happy for the birth of her daughter. I would write again when I had my own news.

The second was sealed with a convent seal. I opened it carefully, for it was written on very thin parchment, in a spidery hand. It began with most formal salutations. And then came the news. Sor Inez had retired to the Convent of the Carmelites, not an hour's ride from the hacienda. Sor Inez, for it was she who was my correspondent, had recovered her health, though she no longer sang or played the lyre, and was dedicating her remaining days to the tending of the sick. Sor Juana was said to have abandoned her writing and would do good works instead. Sor Inez beseeched me to "preserve the works that had embellished the good sister's fame," and asked to be commended to my husband.

I reread it several times before I understood. I must keep the letters that I had hidden away so long ago, for Sor Juana was still in danger from the Holy Office. How far away that all seemed now. I tore Sor Inez's letter into little pieces. When I could, I would toss them on the kitchen flames.

I had never gotten an answer from the Bishop of Puebla to my poem of good-bye. I would bear his child, and he would never know. Again I prayed for dark hair.

AUGUST BURNED AND I lay despondent on a chaise on the veranda. I could not sleep at night. Neto clung to me constantly, and the pain in my head made me come close to vomiting every time I rose. I no longer took my meals with Manuel. Joaquín came by once a day and shook my hand. It was as if I had lost my family, except for Neto, whose sticky embrace made me restless and sharp.

There was lightning in the sky that day, and Neto was again crying. We were sitting on the covered veranda, waiting out the stifling heat. I decided that I must go and shut his windows, to keep both the rain and the birds from the nursery. I hauled myself to my feet and wobbled inside. The room was spinning, and the flashes of lightning made crazy shadows on the walls. They seemed to dance like demons, fiery one moment, black the next, as I held Neto's hand for the journey across the house.

We entered the nursery. The large windows were wide open, and gusts of humid wind blew through the room. A shutter banged, and Neto squeezed my hand. The sky outside was darkening, a greenish purple bruise of clouds massed at the horizon. Then a swallow swooped in. Neto screamed.

"Hush!" I said. It was not a soothing sound, but the cry of a startled mother. I loosened my grip on his little hand and grabbed a blanket. I swatted at the bird, which now flew crazily around the room. Then another joined it, and Neto began to sob louder. "Hush!" I said again, loud and sharp. Lightning ran a jagged ray across the clouds. The birds were calling, and the low rumble of thunder started.

Then a crack sounded, and a fork of lightning lit the room. Another crack, and then the birds screeched as the sky exploded in a roar of thunder. Lightning tore the sky asunder.

I DID NOT LOSE consciousness. I lay upon the floor, and I could hear the rain pound, and Neto crying. I could feel the deep, rhythmic pain begin. But when I opened my eyes, the pain was overwhelming, and my head could not stand the horror of the flashing light. I shut them again.

"Mama," Neto cried. "Get up, Mama!"

I tried to answer him, but words would not come. I could think the words, but they would not travel to my mouth. I could not find my legs. When the next contraction came, I tried to curl into it, but my legs were no longer a part of me. I could not cry out; only an animal grunting noise issued from my throat. *Get Cayetana,* I wanted to say. *Get your father. Get someone!* But I had lost my speech.

I put my hand up, and Neto took it. I held him to me, stroking his back, and he quieted. Then he leaned back to look at me with his deep brown eyes. "I will get help, Mama. Don't be afraid." My angel. With a look back at me, he left, running on his chubby little legs, while I lay on the floor of the nursery and listened to the rain.

*T*WENTY-SIX

*L*ABOR WAS SHORT AND brutal. I could not walk or move. I lay in tearing agony, unable even to moan, but feeling every rip as my son arrived. Broken and spent, I allowed Cayetana to place him in my arm. I beheld his pink face, lighter than that of either of my two other boys. I tried to hold him, but I found that my left arm was as dead as my legs. Holding him gingerly with one hand as Cayetana hovered anxiously, I examined him but saw no sign of red hair, only a fair down on his perfect, pale little head. Manuel took him, held him close.

"My son," he said. "My Juan Carlos."

So that was what we named him. I could not speak, and I could not walk. My mind was less than clear, and I could not tell Manuel how grateful I was. Cayetana kept me calm, but when I signaled for paper and pen, and ink to write with, she shook her head. "No writing. Your husband has forbidden it. He wants you to recover."

I pounded the bed in frustration, but exhaustion set in and I slept.

The sky was clear and black outside my window when I woke. I did not know how long I had slept. I needed to use the chamber pot. I tried to push myself up, though only my right arm worked. I tried to call for Cayetana, but my mouth was still silent. The pain between my legs was pounding now that the afterglow of birth had worn off, and I was thirsty. Helpless, I felt tears form. I forced them back. I had been helpless and in intimate pain before and had not cried, and I would not cry now. I fumbled for the pot, finding it beneath my bed.

When Cayetana returned, I was lying in a pool of my own water, blood, and, at last, tears. I could not hold the chamber pot upright, I could not lift myself over it, and I could no longer bear the pain and the misery.

"We will get a nurse for your son," she said. I was unable to object.

Manuel visited me. "I must put you where you will be cared for," he said, looking at me sadly. "Your sickness may pass to the children."

It will not! But I could not speak.

"And you must not read, or write, or do anything that will tax you, until you are well," he added. "I will make the arrangements." I shook my head, but he looked at me with pity and walked away.

I thought that I had suffered, but I knew nothing of suffering until the next morning, when my door opened and behind a stone-faced Cayetana stood the beautiful Angélica. What was she doing in my sickroom?

"Oh, you poor, poor thing," she crooned. "We must see to it that you recover quickly. Now, not to worry. I am going to take care of everything. Today you will be going to the Carmelite convent, where they will care for you. I will visit you daily, make sure that you are getting the best of care. Cayetana," she commanded, "send a girl to help me."

"There is no girl, señora. I will take care of Doña Josefina."

Cayetana changed my cloths, bathed me, and arranged my hair before obeying Angélica. She lifted me and wrapped me in a shawl. "I will have your husband and Ygnacio bring you to the cart," she said. I shook my head hard, but she just nodded.

After Angélica left, Cayetana embraced me. "I am sorry, señora. She arrived this morning, early. That Anaya, who left, had gone into her service. They are well matched, I believe. As Anaya has family here, she heard of your illness right away." Cayetana was upset, and was rattling on heedlessly, trying to fill the sorrowful air with words.

"The people share information quickly," she went on, "and Doña Angélica arrived full of plans. Your husband is bewildered by his fear of losing you. He knows that you will die if you are not cared for. He has no will to stop her. Angélica insists that your sons will catch your sickness if you are here. I must care for the baby. The boys are in need of much less care, and I can get another girl, and we will get a wet nurse for the baby, but someone needs to manage the household. Angélica has made her point to him very strongly."

I clenched my fist in protest, and reached for pen and ink. "No. There

I agree with your husband. All of this reading and writing has harmed you. Remember your first two pregnancies? How easy they were? No strokes, no palsies? I want you to get better, señora. No writing."

Manuel and Angélica rode with me in the cart for the hour's drive to the Carmelite convent. The nuns received me kindly and placed me in a cell of a room, with a bed, a crucifix, and a washstand. Manuel kissed me gently. Angélica smiled, radiant, and assured me she would return on the morrow. Then, taking Manuel's arm, as the knife of pain drove deep into my head, she turned and left.

PART THREE

TWENTY-SEVEN

ANGÉLICA VISITS ME ALMOST daily. From her cruel chatter I discern that Manuel has accepted her claim that she can best assist the nuns with my care. Angélica paints herself as a ministering angel, with the added pleasures of tormenting me and warming my husband's bed.

On the eleventh day, when the little nun comes in with my herbal tea, I signal her with my right hand. "No," she says, "it is forbidden." Manuel has held firm in prohibiting reading and writing, worried that these unwomanly activities have exacerbated my ailments and will delay my recovery.

I grab her hand. I trace on it the letters *INEZ*. "Sor Inez?" she asks. I nod. She smiles, for this is something she can do. "I will send for her."

An hour later, Sor Inez comes in. I look at her tired face. She has recovered from her beating, but the light is gone from her eyes, until she realizes who I am. "Josefina!" She embraces me. With my good arm, I hug her back. She and Luz are the only ones who know what happened at Court, and she understands even more. She holds me as only a fellow sufferer can.

I signal that I wish to write. "Of course," she says. I feel my heart soar as she rustles out, returning with a quill and ink. "I understand that this has been prohibited to you." I nod. "Fools." She hands me the implements, and I am stymied. After all of the frustration, I cannot think of what to say.

Sor Inez smiles. "You must heal. You are young and strong. But the only way you can heal is to tell your story. Write, and do not hold back. I will burn the papers after you write them, but you must exorcise the devil that abides in you, and no priest can do this. Write your full confession, and you will set yourself free. I will bring you paper and ink as you need them."

She makes the sign of the cross over me, and leaves. Carefully propped up on pillows, I dip the quill in the inkwell. I begin to write.

WHEN ANGÉLICA APPEARS THE next morning, her insufferable smirk on her face, I can wiggle my left big toe. I am beside myself with joy, but I keep my face impassive. "You are looking so tired, Josefina. Poor thing. Alone, no husband, no sons. But don't fear. I am taking good care of them all. Manuel sees my care of you as penance for my sins. Men are such fools, aren't they? Now, let us see how you are doing."

She lifts my blanket and my sleeping gown. She parts my legs and removes the cloths. They are no longer staining as furiously; I am almost past the worst of the afterbirth bleeding. She shuts my legs.

"There, there, useless, aren't you?" she says. She pours warm water on a cloth and applies it to my breasts. The cloth soothes as her words cut. "Well, I will report to Manuel how peaked you look. The baby is quite cute, you know?" I try not to react, but I bite my lip and Angélica notices. "Perhaps I will bring him to you tomorrow. Let us see how you are feeling then."

I hate Angélica. She comes to gloat over my misery. I wish that Manuel would send Cayetana. Not only would Cayetana nurse me better, but she would not be a daily reminder of all that I have lost.

As soon as Angélica is gone, I pull the papers from under the pillow, and the pen from beneath my hair, and begin writing again. It is my solace. Manuel has come to see me only once. I must heal. The little nun enters. She is carrying a steaming cup of sweet-smelling tea. I hide my writing, but not quickly enough.

"Oh, no! You mustn't! Oh, dear, what shall I do?" She wrings her hands, desperate, for she fears punishment from her own superior far more than she cares about the harm writing could do me. I harden my heart to her. Though the pen falls from my hand, I will not relinquish my papers. The nun is young, but she is small and cannot win. We tug at the papers like little boys with a rope. At last she gives up. "I will get Sor Inez," she sighs. "Meanwhile, drink your tea."

I take a sip. It is wonderfully sweet and delicious. I take another sip. "I told your dear friend who looks after you, Doña Angélica, how sad you had been. Her maid, a girl of the people, suggested this herbal for you. This will help you heal." I spit out the tea.

"Oh! That writing is making you unstable! I must find Sor Inez!"

The little nun rushes out, and I pour the rest of the tea on the floor. When the sister returns with Sor Inez, she points out the tea on the floor as further evidence of the madness that the writing is causing. My tongue, meanwhile, has gone numb.

"Leave us to pray," says Sor Inez. As soon as the little nun is gone, she hands me back my pen. "What is it?"

"Poison, or slow death of some sort," I write. She sniffs the cup.

"I will attend to you from now on. There is trouble everywhere."

I nod, and pat the bed. Sor Inez sits down. "Sor Juana has confessed to the Archbishop of Mexico. He has ordered her to stop writing. She is in despair. She is coming here." I feel my entire body grow rigid. "Will you receive her?"

Sor Inez knows that I blame part of my sorrow on Sor Juana, for her letters brought me the horrors of the Inquisition. In some inchoate way I blame her for teaching me to write. I am like Adam blaming Eve, who only offered the apple he already craved. Even such heretical thoughts come from Sor Juana. Yes, for all that I blame her. But it is only part, for mostly it was jealousy that made me angry with her. Jealousy over the love of Father Alonso, a love that has come close to destroying me.

I nod. I will see her.

"Good. She will be here in a few days. Have you written anything?"

I hand her a sheaf of papers from under my pillow. My writing is sloppy, for I can barely hold the paper still by placing my left hand on it with my right. "You have been busy," she says.

I look at her, pleading.

"Don't worry. I will burn them for you without reading them. Your confession is to heal your soul, not to entertain me. I will burn them when you have finished. Meanwhile they are safe with me."

Burn them now, I scrawl.

She nods and I smile my thanks.

"Now there is something I wish to try. I have read that at times, when God takes a person's speech with a stroke of His hand, He allows the person to retain the gift of song. Has He left that song with you?"

I shake my head, for I have never had that gift, and can see no reason I would have it now.

"Let us try anyway. Let us sing a hymn you know, something that you would never hesitate to sing. The Litany? *'Sancta Maria,'*" she sings.

Before I can hesitate, my voice croaks out, *"Ora pro nobis."* Pray for us. I gasp. Chills run down my arms.

She continues the Litany. I am responding, and becoming giddy with joy. Tears run down my face, as my voice becomes stronger with each "pray for us."

"You will recover," Sor Inez says. "And soon, when you receive Sor Juana, you may be able to sing to her."

I take up my quill and quickly write a note. I hand it to Sor Inez, as I cannot fold it with one hand. Then I scratch another quick line, for Sor Inez herself. *Thank you, blessed Sister,* I write. *Can you have the note sent to my friend María Luz?*

Sor Inez nods, blesses me.

"Ora pro nobis," I sing back to her.

THE DAYS PROCEED APACE. Each day I write secretly, madly, and each day I feel lighter and stronger. But my heart is still plagued. I have borne the child, and yet Manuel has still banished me. Angélica has taken my place.

When sorrow overtakes me, I cannot sing the Litany back to Sor Inez. "You must keep writing," she says. "Purge your soul."

I try. When I come to the most painful night, the first night of the *posada,* the page is wet with my tears.

The next day, I am awake before the little nun comes to wash me. "You will have visitors today," she tells me. "Let us fix you up a bit." She combs my thick, dark hair.

I make no sound, for I am afraid to show my new skill of singing the response to the Litany. I am even more afraid that the miracle has been fleeting, and will be denied to me. Soon after she leaves me with a cup of chocolate, I hear a tapping at my door. I cannot call for the visitor to enter, so the door opens without my invitation.

Sor Juana's beauty returns to me like a shock. She is thinner, paler than she was at Court, but that makes her large, dark eyes even more overpowering. She is still wearing that huge brooch under her chin, and her wimple is starched and spotless, but she looks to have suffered.

"Good morning, Josefina," she says, her low voice taking me back to the first days at Court.

"*Ora pro nobis,*" I sing back, and the joy of my continued miracle makes me smile.

"Well, Sor Inez has been at you, then," she says, and I nod. Sor Juana seats herself by my bed, taking a rosary in her hands. I have never seen her pray the rosary before. Her hands had a pen, and did not need the busyness of beads.

"Our separation has been painful to me, Josefina," she begins, and I hear exhaustion in her voice. She passes a "Hail Mary" bead through her fingers, moving to the next one without looking. "There is much to tell you, much you will not understand. But listen, and hear me."

I nod, for I am powerless under her spell, and in any event I cannot interrupt.

"I have thought long and hard about where to begin. I must begin in the distant past, and I pray that the pain my story will cause you will cauterize your wounded soul. You know, of course, that I came to the convent to study. I was not jilted by a lover, or spurned by a husband, but rather I longed for the quiet life where I could write. I could read before I was four, and you know yourself how much a girl suffers if she is intellectual. The convent was my answer.

"But I was not meant to be a saint, and when I met our beloved Father Alonso, he and I knew that we were destined for each other. He brought out in me the fire, the beauty, and the soul of poetry. I knew, from the instant our eyes met, that had neither of us taken vows, he would have been the man who would wed me. And he knew, too, that I was the woman to complete him. But we had taken vows, and vows are not lightly broken.

"It was after we met, he and I, that I was able to write my plays, my sonnets, and all of the poems of love that were commissioned, for earthly love is far different from the love of the Eternal Father. Our passions were spent in words, words that at times were so heated and charged that we left one another spent and shaking as if we were lovers. But we were not.

"When you came to the Court, I recognized in you a sister, one who would absorb for me the carnal love of Father Alonso, and allow me the purity of spiritual love. For I knew that Father Alonso, for all of his virtues, was still a man. And it was more difficult for him to live up to his vows than mine were for me. Or so I thought. While I taught you to write, I allowed, no, I led him to your body."

I hold up my hand to stop her. I cannot bear her words.

"No, you have no choice. You shall hear the tale. Father Alonso loved you, yes, but he loved your body in place of mine as well. And I loved him through you. Your passion was my release." I feel my face heat. "Yes, Josefina, I witnessed every move, every moan and cry from both of you, both times. And though you burn from shame, I burned with lust. A sin in one so devoted to God.

"And so, I wrote. And I watched you suffer the torments of the love-lorn. But my love for Father Alonso was safe, for you are married, and you cannot undo the chains of matrimony to live with a priest. And you had loved Father Alonso since you were a girl entering womanhood, so your dream was fulfilled while I stayed chaste. The only deterrent to my full satisfaction came in the form of the Marqués. He is dead, you know."

I shake my head. I had not known. Sor Juana understands.

"Yes, he died of his infection. In terrible pain, and without sympathy from his wife. I suppose you are now both a murderess and an adulteress." I move my right hand as if to strike her. She holds up her own hand and catches mine. "Don't. I would not waste much grief on the state of your soul for that murder. I know what he did to you." She lets go of my hand. "Yes, I do. And I am truly sorry, for it is in part for me that you suffered.

"The Inquisition was alerted by the damned fool Marqués that I had written some letters to Sor Filotea, who of course is actually the Bishop of Puebla. How he knew, I am not sure, but I am certain that the information was brokered by Eustacia. Remember her?" How could I forget? "Her only stock in trade was information, and she obviously sold enough of it to land in the Marqués' bed, and then for him to set her up, albeit temporarily, in a little house. She is now traveling to another cousin's, where she will hope to reside for a bit. Needless to say, the Marquesa will have nothing to do with her.

"It was the Marqués who made the deal: through you he could

provide the letters to Fernándo, that worthless pander of a priest, who could deliver them to the Inquisition for his own aggrandizement. Fernándo, in turn, would provide you. But with your quick thinking, you hid the papers. And paid the price. I have seen the room where you were brought, and I know the uses of the shackles and other instruments of torture. A woman is so vulnerable under those circumstances, isn't she?"

Something in her tone frightens me beyond measure. *"Ora pro nobis,"* I sing softly.

"You can sing other things, you know. Try. Anything you want to say, sing it."

I shake my head. *Pray for us* was what I wanted to say.

"But you were brave, and you got more than revenge. So I say, Josefina, that you prevailed. And the papers the Inquisition found, they were very well written. My style was perfectly imitated, if the sentiments were more piously expressed. You have learned well, Josefina, and you have saved my life. I owe you a deep debt of gratitude. I have confessed the sins of pride and overweening knowledge to the Archbishop of Mexico, and my penance is to cease all writing and devote myself to the care of the sick. And so I will devote myself to you, and to helping you regain your rightful place. And you, Josefina, will tell me what became of the letters I wrote."

I have never before this moment thought to keep the letters, and have always intended to return them. But now, with these revelations, I wonder. I briefly taste power over Sor Juana, whom I had seen as invincible.

"They are nothing to you, and if you have not destroyed them, they could someday destroy you. I am sorry, Josefina. You were not a toy to be played with, and I was not playing. You wanted to love Father Alonso, I wanted to love him, and he loved us both. He is gone now, he has gone back to Salamanca, to the university, where he will be safe and free. The child you bore, of course, is the fruit of all of this. I long to see the boy, as he is the only heir that Father Alonso has, and in a sense, I feel that he is mine, too."

I feel tremors of fear and anger. Is she blackmailing me? That moment of power has been illusory; she still, and always, has the upper hand. I reach for paper and pen, but she pulls them out of my reach. "Sing, Josefina. You can, you know. And you must try, so you can heal."

"*Ora pro nobis,*" I start. She shakes her head. "*En el nombre del cielo,*" I sing, the first line of the *posada* song. In the name of Heaven. I could do it.

"Are you buying the papers with threats?" I sing.

Pain shoots through my head and I cry out. Tears run down my face, and I hug and hold Sor Juana as the fog clears. She may be blackmailing me, but she has unleashed my voice. "Are you threatening to tell Manuel?" I am not tuneful, but I am singing. And I can speak this way. I cry with the joy of it.

She embraces me back. "You did it! You broke through the barrier." Though I would never have believed it, she, too, is crying. "I am not blackmailing you, Josefina. If you still have the letters, I implore you to give them to me. They are my children, the children I will never bear. I would never tell your husband the true father of his child. Has he accepted the boy, then?"

I nod. "But he has sent me away. Angélica is living with him now," I sing.

"I know. But he loves you. After the heir's engagement, she was vicious to Manuel. Now, with your illness, she sees a second chance at him. Manuel feels your absence deeply, but Angélica sees only opportunity in his loneliness and fear. The sooner you heal, the sooner you will cast her from your home."

It is a lot to absorb. "How does he know?" I croak.

"I saw him at Court. He was infatuated with Angélica until he saw her true colors. She was only using him to regain access to the Court, and to try to see the heir. You heard that the heir's wedding was postponed?" I hadn't. "Miguel Ángel's return from Spain was delayed by the defeats of the King's army, and so he will not be able to return until the fall. But Angélica will not have another chance at nobility."

I have had a lot of time to think, lying silent and motionless in my bed. The fortnight in my convent cell has given me the time to reflect. I feel sorry, somehow, for Angélica. Widowed at eighteen, though left considerably wealthy, she is no doubt lonely. But she cannot find solace with my husband, or my babies.

"Your papers are safe," I sing.

Singing is too exhausting, and I lie back on my pillows. "Get me the letters," Sor Juana says. "And I will see to it that what you lost is returned to you." I cannot reply, and she leaves me to sleep, but her words chase each other like echoes through my mind.

In the evening, I receive a message from Luz, written in her cousin's hand. As she is generous with her funds, her reply to my message is delivered right away. She and her cousin will be traveling through here, and will come to me tomorrow. For the first time since I succumbed to Father Alonso, I feel the surge of hope in my breast.

LUZ ARRIVES AFTER THE midday meal. I am in my room, but I can hear her silver-bell laugh well before she gets to my door. Still only using my one good hand, I hide my papers under my pillow. I lie back, eagerly awaiting her.

She enters, and we embrace with joy. I motion her to shut the door. After she does, I sing a line to her.

Her face lights up. "Sweet one! You have recovered."

"Not quite," I sing back.

"Nor are you very melodious," she adds, smiling. "You sing like a dying cow."

It takes tremendous effort, and at times the words do not come, or the wrong ones come out. I am drenched with sweat when I have finished a much-shortened version of my story. Luz has tears in her eyes.

"Go to Manuel. Bring my bag."

"I will do what I can," Luz says. "I will go tonight to your home. My cousin has business in your area, and surely we will be invited to stay. I will rejoin you tomorrow."

The night is spent tossing as best I can, with my leaden legs still immobile, as I plan the steps to my liberation. The first step is to get back the letters, hidden in my cloths so long ago. Success depends not just on me, but on every cog in the wheel being correctly aligned. I love the image, and I think of how it could be put into poetry. I am dreaming of poetry again.

The next morning, I am awake early. The little nun is excited. "We will take you to the visiting room soon. You must look nice for your husband." I start. Is Manuel coming? I suppose he must be, since I am being moved into the visiting room. No men can come into the inner sanctum of the convent, so the one time that Manuel came I was carried into a large parlor outside the main gate to the nunnery. Today is no exception, as two strapping young novices, Indian girls, come to gather me up.

It is strange, since I expected Luz, not Manuel, but I have no choice but to comply. Luz was to bring the letters here so I could barter them with Sor Juana. I cannot do so in Manuel's presence, and Luz would give them over to Sor Juana just by being asked. I did not think to tell her not to. And who knows how long Sor Juana will stay once she gets what she wants?

I fear my plan will be undone, but I must try. My mind spins, thinking of alternatives. The confluence of people present—Luz, Angélica, Sor Juana, and Manuel, all nearby—will not easily be repeated. I may not have another chance before my baby starts calling Angélica "Mama."

The visiting room is gracefully appointed, designed to elicit large dowries from the fathers of girls entering the convent. The walls are painted a deep green, and paintings of the Stations of the Cross, framed in rich woods, lead the eye around the room, chronicling Our Savior's suffering. Wall hangings of woven tapestry warm the room, and the floor's red paving tiles are covered in rugs of vermilion and green. A fire burns in the hearth; well-upholstered chairs are grouped around it.

The novices put me down on a settee, prop my legs up on the long seat, and cover me with blankets. I nod and make the sign of the cross to them in thanks, still wondering how I can make the plan work with Manuel in attendance. I do not wait long before the door opens.

It is not Manuel who enters, but another, most unwelcome, visitor: Angélica. Her golden hair is drawn away from her face in a simple twist, and her golden eyes glitter. She is wearing a plain dress in subdued ochre, with a lace collar. The simplicity of her coiffure and clothing only serves to enhance her beauty, until I look at her mouth. Her lovely lips are pursed, as I saw once before so long ago, giving me a hint of how she will look in ten years. Those of fair skin lose their looks so quickly, I think, irrelevantly. It is her current look that is stealing my husband, not how she will be at thirty.

Angélica glares at me and takes a seat wordlessly. I think to greet her, but I fear that my voice will prove yet another weapon in her arsenal. So I nod, and we sit in uncompanionable silence. I cannot imagine what has gone wrong, to have Angélica, and potentially Manuel, rather than Luz and Sor Juana.

At last the door opens again, and one of the novices enters with chocolate. I am grateful for the distraction, and the bitter brew warms me as I sip. Angélica's cup remains on the table beside her. I pray that she will speak, inform me of the reason for her presence. But my prayer, so insignificant in the face of my many other unanswered prayers, is denied.

When the door opens again, it is with pomp and flair. My husband enters, glances at Angélica but registers nothing on his face, and comes straight to me. He kneels at my side and lifts my hand to his lips. I grunt, most unmelodiously, in shock.

"Josefina," he says softly. "I am sorry. I did not know the depth of my fault."

My hand is cold. He did not know so much that I do not want him to know. Luz was charged with a simple errand, complex only in its execution. In her innocence has Luz been indiscreet? But then, if she has, Manuel would not be here by my side. I grunt again.

Still on one knee, he puts his hand to my face. "No one shall ever mistreat you again, as long as I live." He rises and takes a seat. The novice pours him chocolate, and he takes the cup, engulfing the delicate Holland china in his brown hand. Looking at him, I know that I am still ignorant of what he has been told, though I suspect from his tone that the messenger was not Luz. More, I know that his hand is the hand I love and long for.

I cannot imagine how this tableau will resolve, for Manuel has returned to his characteristic silence, and Angélica seems not inclined to talk. My croaking and supposed singing cannot make for social pastime, and too much of grave importance needs to be said.

I hear the sound of many footsteps, and the cry of a baby. My nipples tingle with the entry of the milk that has been drying up, as my breasts ache with the primordial need to feed the wailing infant. My eyes meet Manuel's and he smiles.

"Our son is healthy," he says, the pleasure on his face clear.

He is coming here. I have not seen my child since he was taken from me, before Manuel sent me here. *"Ora pro nobis,"* I sing, and they both gasp.

Manuel rises partway in his chair, but the door opens then, and a procession of visitors enters. First is Luz with, of all things, my bag of monthly cloths. I would have thought that she would conceal the bag in some discreet basket or other. She is followed by a chubby young native woman, her black plait reaching her knees, who bears in her arms the white-skinned, blond-haired baby I birthed. He is howling, and she is gently jostling him. Her face shows nothing, but her hold on my son is tender. I reach with my one good arm for Juan Carlos. The Indian woman looks at Manuel, who nods. My son, my baby boy, is placed in my arm.

Tears are running freely down my face as I bury it in his baby hair, in his sweet scent, the milk of the wet nurse still fresh on his lips. I want to inhale him, absorb him back inside me. My nose and eyes stream, and I do not try to wipe them, as my only good hand is devoted to my angel. He howls.

The wet nurse gently takes him from me, though I cling to him. "He wants to eat," she says in her own tongue. I must relinquish him, and I do, but only with my hand.

I look up, and sentimental Luz is crying, too. In my absorption with my baby I have not seen the others enter, but now I see that in addition to Luz and Angélica, the wet nurse, the baby, and Manuel, we have also Sor Juana, Sor Inez, and a tall, elegant young man of about twenty-five, whom I have never seen.

"My cousin, Gerardo de la Peña," Luz says, and he bows, Continental style, from the waist.

The nuns nod to Manuel, and Sor Inez introduces herself. "And this is Sor Juana de la Cruz," she adds.

"I am honored to meet you, Sor Inez," Manuel says. "Sor Juana and I have already met."

Sor Inez raises her faint eyebrows, but says nothing. My suspicions about Manuel's acknowledgment of his role in my suffering are confirmed.

Novices come in with trays, and sweets and more chocolate are served. I take a square of linen that Luz hands me, and clean my face. I am having a party without planning it. My deficiencies as a hostess could not be more evident. Sor Juana has no such deficiency, and is clearly prepared to take over the orchestration of this event.

"Your Mercies," she says, and her cool voice draws all eyes. "You are

kind to come and attend Doña Josefina in her troubles. I have no doubt
that now that she is mending, she will return home soon. To heal, she
must see her husband and her children often. Don Manuel, you must
visit at least once a day. And kind Angélica," she says, turning her gray
gaze upon her, "you have tended her with mercy. You must not neglect
your duties at your own home. I will undertake to care for Doña Josefina from here forward." Angélica does not meet anyone's eye. What has
passed between Sor Juana and Angélica can only be imagined.

"I will entertain you with a poem suitable to the occasion, to speed
Josefina's recovery," Sor Juana continues. "The convent invites you to
enjoy these chocolates and sweets, in honor of this wonderful miracle
that the Lord has wrought, in giving back a voice, through song, to
Josefina."

"Though not a harmonious one." Luz laughs, the sound of bells
tinkling.

Sor Juana holds a thick sheaf of poems before her, glancing lightly
down at her own writings. She chooses one and, placing it on the top of
the stack, she clears her throat lightly.

> *"Son by your slave conceived*
> *Owns the rights by rights assigned*
> *To master of the slave aligned—*
> *She serves by son relieved.*
> *He comes from battle in elation—*
> *his fruit in obedience offered,*
> *his fruit, potently fathered,*
> *and grown in careful generation.*
> *Thus are our stained errors*
> *The sons of our souls, the birth of our hearts,*
> *And only our minds will demand redress.*
> *Their perfect souls will newly mirror*
> *The rights of yours, for all their parts,*
> *By yours conceived and birth address."*

Sor Juana looks back down at her papers. She does not assess the
room for a reaction. I breathe hard, unbelieving. How dare she read

such a poem? Had she accused me of adultery, and called my son a bastard, she could not have been clearer. I steal a glance at Manuel. He has a small, bored smile, and he gazes off into the middle of the room. Luz sits with her hands folded in her lap, looking placid, and Angélica and Gerardo are exchanging not terribly covert glances. They have probably heard nothing.

I seek Sor Inez's eyes. She looks at me sagely, and nods. Not one person seems to understand the barbed, insinuating words that have been read. I sigh. The importance of poetry outside of the Court and the Church is obviously vastly exaggerated.

Sor Inez breaks the spell. She rises and offers the chocolate pot around again. Luz comes to my chair-side and strokes my hand.

"It went perfectly," she says quietly. I see that my private bag was stowed in the corner of the room, but its shape shows it no longer contains Sor Juana's papers. I realize that the sheaf Sor Juana was holding includes her letters, so carefully hidden many months before. Papers for which there had been so much suffering.

What was the power of those words, that they could damn her, doom me, and yet wash over the room without leaving a trace?

I nod to Luz, grateful that at least part of my scheme worked. In the guise of getting the cloths for me, she has retrieved the fateful bag, but I have lost the bargaining power of the letters. The papers have been returned. I wonder how Sor Juana knew. And more, who has gotten Manuel to come? It seems I am not the only one with a plan, and I guess that Sor Juana has preempted the bargain. Luz is not capable of such subtlety.

"Don Manuel," Luz says sweetly, "tell us how you came to name your son Juan Carlos." I stiffen, not willing to draw attention to the blanched-looking child of this dark-haired man. Though Manuel's eyes are green and brown, and his hair is brown, not black, this child the color of masa might surely raise a question.

"My aunt," he says, smiling. "As I told you. My aunt Juana Carlotta was also born in a lightning storm, just as my son was. And the lightning took all the color out of her, too. She had even whiter hair, and her eyes, they were almost as pink as a rabbit's!"

"And here I thought you had named him for our King!" Luz laughs.

"Of course, for His Majesty as well," Manuel replies. *Of course.* Those were powerful words.

"Angélica, your voice is truly in your name; perhaps you will sing for us today," Luz says. Angélica's fair skin flushes, but not with pleasure. Once again, she cannot avoid performing at the party for her defeat.

She stands. Staring straight ahead, she takes a deep breath. Once again, I feel pity for her. Once again, she suffers humiliation that she has brought upon herself, but is made to bear so publicly. I glance at Manuel, and my pity vanishes as he looks upon her magnificent form. She opens her mouth, and a choir of angels bursts forth. Her song, a simple ode to the harvest moon, soars to the rafters of the room, fills the corners with silvery light. No, nothing in my voice will ever sound like that.

Although I realize that Luz has invited Angélica to sing at Sor Juana's request, I still deeply resent the contrast it sets up between us. Manuel stares at Angélica, his normally impassive face a war of disgust and desire. Her face is full of secrets.

Sor Juana hands me a paper, and I read as Angélica sings.

Josefina,

Your husband now understands his errors. He left his treasure un-guarded as his eyes strayed.

Imagine, Josefina, your salon, with the fire blazing. Luz and the household have discreetly withdrawn. I am sitting in your chair. Angélica has presided over the evening meal, but my continued presence and my in-sistence on a private interview with your husband have driven her to retire.

He sips his sherry. "Your wife, you must now know, is a beauty." He nods but does not speak. "She is virtuous, but a woman can be lured by the stronger sex." His hand grips his sherry glass. I hope it shatters. "When a husband chases fool's gold, the deep value of the true one may tarnish." I am goading him to speak, and he does at last.

"True gold does not tarnish."

"But a wounded scorpion can iron defame, and the heel that crushes it will be stained."

"Don't speak to me in riddles."

I have his attention. "The man who would defile her is dead. The man who has rights to her has condemned her to death." He stares. "Yes, she will die if you do not reclaim her. Are Angélica's easily obtained favors worth it?"

"Easily obtained?"

"Oh, you are not the only pretender to that golden throne. Unlike your wife, she does not guard her virtue zealously." He knows. And a man, as you have learned, will fog the mirror, then condemn its lack of clarity.

He rises. "I will reclaim what is rightfully mine."

"Protect her, too, for she has suffered grievously to return to you."

And so the interview is over.

Josefina, this I owed you and more. Angélica sings at my command, for though she is vicious, I will not leave her without a future.

Thank you for safeguarding my letters, and for saving my life. Your husband, your voice, and yes, your books, will be given back to you. I have kept my word, as you have kept yours.

> *In Christ,*
> *Juana Inés de la Cruz*

When Angélica is finished, she looks at each in turn. Her usual pride returns to her amber eyes, and she licks her pink lips with pleasure at the transfixed faces before her. And then Angélica turns to Gerardo de la Peña, and smiles that brilliant, blinding smile.

Sor Juana allows a small smile of her own to play briefly upon her lips before she takes up her papers.

Luz stands, too, and comes to me. She kisses my cheek softly. She is my sister. "I will visit again," Luz says, "but my cousin Gerardo has business to attend to, and so I must return to the North, to my husband's home."

"And I, too, will depart," Angélica adds quietly. Sor Juana catches my eye. Heaven only knows what Manuel said to Angélica, but nothing will keep Angélica near me any longer than she has to be.

"You must not travel alone," Gerardo says to Angélica with another courtly bow. "Allow me to accompany you home."

"I will come for you in another week," Manuel says to me. I hold my hand out to him and he takes it. He leans down and strokes my hair. "Our home and our sons await you." I hold his arm to me, afraid to let him go. In my mind, I count out the days. My forty-day birth-Lent will be over in twenty days. We have many words to exchange, and a new life to build.

The past two years of my life have been circular, repeating the themes like a rondo in a poem, with variations each time to surprise the reader. I lost the child of virtue, and saved the child of sin. I have loved in sin, and returned home in love. This time, I vow, I will read the whole poem before I leap into the stanza alive. I will finish my story, and hand the pages to Sor Inez to burn.

$\mathcal{N}$OTE

$\mathcal{S}$OR JUANA INÉS DE la Cruz was born Juana Inés de Asbaje y Ramirez, in 1651. She learned to read by the age of four, and despite her humble birth she became a lady-in-waiting in the Court of the viceroy of Mexico. Her beauty and erudition brought her suitors and probably lovers. She emphatically refused to marry, and entered the convent in 1669.

She remained at court, at times at the Court of the Marqués and Marquesa de Mancera, and later that of the Conde (Count) and Condesa (Countess) Paredes. I have merged the two families into that of the Marquesa de Condera. Sor Juana wrote poems, sonnets, and plays, commissioned and for publication. She argued, in a very unreceptive time, that women had the right to be educated and the right to pursue intellectual lives. In a time when writings, including poetry, were scrutinized by the Inquisition, and could be considered subversive or dangerous to believers, she took grave risks in her insistence on those rights, but she also garnered fame and admiration from many at the court and throughout Mexico.

Her extremely close friendship with the Bishop of Puebla (whose real name was Manuel Fernández de Santa Cruz) gave rise to rumors of a love affair, but those rumors were never proven. What is known is that her relationship with him resulted in the *Carta atenagórica*. This was the culmination of an exchange of letters between her and the Bishop, who wrote under the pen name Sor Filotea de la Cruz to protect Sor Juana from censure for openly debating theological questions with a man, and with a bishop, no less. The Bishop had the letters published in 1690.

Sor Juana was censured nonetheless, and the Archbishop of Mexico ordered her to cease writing. She did so for a short time, but returned to her passion once again. At last she succumbed to the Archbishop's continued demand, and signed her confession with her own blood.

She spent the rest of her life nursing the sick. She died in 1695. She is known in Mexico as *la décima musa,* or the Tenth Muse, and her work is considered a national treasure.

The poems attributed to her in this story are indeed hers, though the translations are mine. The prose poem in chapter 14 is a fabrication, using some of Sor Juana's images. The quotations from the other poets and playwrights of her day are theirs, and the translations are mine. The poems that Josefina wrote are strictly my own invention.

$\mathcal{A}$CKNOWLEDGMENTS

$\mathcal{S}$EEING THIS BOOK IN print is a dream come true for me. I am grateful to so many who helped make this a reality. My parents, Ron and Maria Hagadus, gave me my optimism, drive, and preternatural energy, as well as my love of books, grammar, and poetry, and the opportunities to explore it all. A quirk of fate and my parents' optimistic decisions brought us to Mexico, and their confidence sent me to Harvard for my education. My senior advisor at Harvard helped me write my senior thesis, "The Feminism of Sor Juana Inés de la Cruz," and the beloved and long-gone Professor Juan Marichal suggested the thesis topic.

In Spanish, to give birth is *dar a luz,* or "to bring into the light." In the present, I am deeply grateful to Tom Parker, author and writing teacher extraordinaire; April Eberhardt, my tireless and dedicated agent; my editor, Amy Tannenbaum; and my publisher, Judith Curr. You gave this book light. You are the midwives of this dream.

Although I did large amounts of research with many sources, the two books that readily stand out are *Obras selectas / Juana Inés de la Cruz,* selected and annotated by Georgina Sabát de Rivers and Elías L. Rivers (Barcelona: Editorial Noguer, 1976); and *The Dream of the Poem,* translated and edited by Peter Cole (Princeton, N.J.: Princeton University Press, 2007). The Jew's poems in the first chapter are reprinted by permission from this fabulous book. Errors of fact and translation are all mine.

My children, Julia and Will, inspired the grace, the beauty, and the better charms of the book's youthful characters.

A dedication is not enough to thank my husband, Clyde Long, for reading every draft, encouraging me, believing in the book, and giving me the initial idea for the story. Thank you.

JOSEFINA'S SIN

CLAUDIA H. LONG

A Readers Club Guide

INTRODUCTION

*J*OSEFINA, A SHELTERED LANDOWNER'S wife living a quiet life in seventeenth-century Mexico, receives an invitation from the Marquesa de Condera to act as a lady-in-waiting in the elite viceroyal Court. She is reluctant to leave her family, but the desire to move beyond her small sphere and expose herself to the intellectual and cultural pursuits she has always longed for cannot be denied. Accompanied by the beautiful, cunning Angélica, Josefina finds herself stepping into a complicated world of political and personal rivalries and deceptive, licentious behavior.

Unexpectedly, Josefina finds kinship with the nuns who study the arts at the Court, writing literature and poetry at the risk of persecution by the Spanish Inquisition. Sor Juana Inés de la Cruz opens Josefina's eyes to the evocative power of words and, through them, to the nature and consequences of love, and the dangerous threat of the Holy Office. Josefina begins a tumultuous journey, from a secure wife and loving mother to a woman seeking to understand her desires and dreams while trying to avoid the treacherous pitfalls of the Court. Eventually, she triumphs, managing to find herself in this difficult, confusing, and ultimately fulfilling world.

QUESTIONS AND TOPICS FOR DISCUSSION

1. The title of the novel is *Josefina's Sin*. In the end, what did you feel Josefina's sin truly was? Did you feel that what happened to her was just, or was she the victim of the sins of those around her?

2. *Josefina's Sin* has a cast of female characters who are strong and independent. However, each is motivated by her own ambitions to the point of betrayal. Do you feel these woman would have been stronger had they attempted to form real friendships—as Luz does—instead of turning on or using one another?

3. Think about all the different women who influence Josefina's life. What does she learn from each of these women at various points throughout the novel?

4. Early in the novel, there is a very powerful scene in which a Jewish poet recites a verse, the first poem that touches Josefina in a way she can't understand. Discuss the juxtaposition of love and hate, clarity and uncertainty, art and religion, as evoked by this scene.

5. Power, and the balance of power, plays an important role in every relationship throughout the novel. Angélica's power lies in her beauty and ability to dazzle. What do you think Josefina's power was? Sor Juana's? Discuss how each character, at one point or another, manipulates or abuses power to achieve a particular end. In your opinion, do many of them succeed?

6. How do you view the various examples of marriage, romance, and sexual relationships in this novel? Consider Josefina and Manuel, Josefina and Alonso, Juana and Alonso, the Marqués and the Marquesa, and Angélica and Manuel. Based on your reading, what do you make of attitudes toward marriage during this time? What about attitudes regarding fidelity, sex, or love?

7. What one adjective do you think best captures the character of Josefina? Were you surprised by how others in your group perceived her? What are her strengths and her weaknesses? How was your perception of Josefina altered during the story? How do you think she herself changed throughout the story?

8. The novel is full of examples of blighted ambition and characters trapped by circumstance. Do you feel that unhappiness excuses the scheming behavior or betrayals of some of the more antagonistic characters (consider Angélica, the Marqués, the Marquesa, Granada, and Eustacia)? Or did you find them entirely unsympathetic?

9. It might be said that Josefina's take on religion is much simpler at the beginning of the novel than it is at the end. What did you think about the portrayals of religion versus spirituality and the relationship between passion and faith? Do you think that her exposure to the complexities of faith changed her for the better?

10. The triangle of Juana, Alonso, and Josefina is one of the most intricate plot points of the novel. Do you believe that Alonso truly loved them both? What did you think of Juana's final confession that, in a way, Josefina was no more than an instrument to complete the passion she and Alonso could never share? Do you feel that Josefina was unwittingly used, or did she willingly place herself in the middle of their passion?

11. Josefina reflects, "The Bishop was merely a shadow, and my love for him had been but a love for an idea of a man, not a man himself" (page 286). Do you feel this realization is entirely true? Do you think it is possible to love people for what they represent and what they have given you, without ever truly loving the actual person?

12. Did Josefina's decision to return to Court surprise you? Why do you think she went back? Do you think it was the right choice?

13. Josefina easily forgives Manuel's relationship with Angélica. Do you feel she let the betrayal go too passively, or that she behaved in the only way she could to keep her husband's love? Do you think she would have been as forgiving had she not carried the guilt (and proof) of her own infidelity?

14. At the end, Josefina is stunned by her realization that no one understands Juana's final poem except her. Do you believe that words contain only as much power as we project into them, based on our emotions and desires? Do you agree with Alonso, who believes we understand only what we wish to understand, and that every poem contains a different meaning for each person who hears it?

15. How did you react to Josefina's vow at the conclusion of the novel: "I will read the whole poem before I leap into the stanza alive" (page 327). What do you think the words mean to Josefina? What do they mean to you?

ENHANCE YOUR BOOK CLUB

1. From cooling *jamaica* (hibiscus water), to refreshing tamarind water, to green chiles with cream filling and buttered tortillas, the novel is filled with descriptions of food. Have everyone prepare a traditional Spanish or Mexican dish to bring to the meeting.

2. Do some research on the real Sor Juana, and have every member present a fact or two. Are you surprised by what you learn? How does the real-life figure compare with her portrayal in the book?

3. Compare this novel to other historical fiction depicting court life such as *The Other Boleyn Girl,* by Philippa Gregory, or *Captive Queen,* by Alison Weir. How are they similar? How are they different? If *Josefina's Sin* was made into a movie, whom would you cast?

4. Poetry and the power of words are vital to the novel. Have each member read a favorite poem and compare interpretations. Or discuss Sor Juana's poems (both those in the book and others). Do you have a favorite?

A CONVERSATION WITH CLAUDIA H. LONG

Sor Juana was the focus of your thesis in college and plays a very important role in the novel. What drew you to her in the first place?

The 1970s were tumultuous years, and feminism in literature was a hot topic. I loved Sor Juana's *Carta atenagórica,* in which she dared to challenge a bishop and proclaim a woman's right to study and learn. She did this at great personal risk, and in the end she was forced to renounce her beliefs and sign her confession in her own blood. These were powerful images in an undergraduate's mind!

Though Juana's words and actions greatly influence Josefina's life, this is very much Josefina's story. What was your inspiration, not only in writing this tale but in writing it from Josefina's point of view?

I didn't set out to write Sor Juana's story, but rather the story of a woman whose life Sor Juana touched. Like me, Josefina is drawn by the secret greatness and power of Sor Juana. It was never clear historically why Sor Juana recanted the first time. It was only as Josefina came to life on the page that I realized that Josefina would write Sor Juana's first "recanting" of the *Carta.* It was a way for me to be part of Sor Juana's mystery.

The title of the novel is such an interesting, provocative one. What does it mean to you?

Well, it was meant to catch your eye! And make you want to know what the sin is. Then I lay it out on the first page, so you realize that there's more to sin than the common, almost banal one of adultery.

The novel is rich in sense of place and atmosphere. Is a lot of this historical texture created through heavy research? Which characters, aside from Sor Juana, are based on real-life figures? How did you make the determination whether an imagined

event, dialogue, or action was authentic? Did you come across anything that surprised you while delving into the history of this time period?

Unlike many historical novelists, I am primarily a student of literature. I get most of my historical sense of time and place from the plays and poetry of the time. I am looking for texture and flavor, how people ate, dressed, traveled, married, and mourned. How was love expressed in a poem? Death or desire in a play?

I wasn't looking for actual events. I even fictionalized the Marqués and the Marquesa de Condera, merging two families into one. There is no reason at all to think that the Marqués de Mancera or the Conde Paredes was as licentious as our Marqués, though if you look at a portrait of the Marqués de Mancera, it isn't hard to imagine him behaving reprehensibly!

But the way the viceroyal Court functioned, the way that the Inquisition operated, was all historically researched.

You describe many of the lovely gowns worn at Court in great detail. Do you have a particular interest in the fashions of the age in which Josefina lives? Was it fun writing about the details of the styles and fabrics of the time?

I'm more of a food person than a clothes person, but I looked at the art of the era for ideas about clothing. Again, I did most of my research through the creative arts. I looked at paintings to see how a woman dressed for a portrait if she was a landowner's wife, or if she was a courtier.

Josefina struggles to master the art of turning her thoughts into poems in the novel. Describe your writing process. Are you also a poet? Or was Josefina's poetry in this book your first venture?

I love poetry. I love to read it because it is the distillation of the most complex human emotions into a single, intense image. The poet takes the enormity of the human experience and compresses it into a stanza of words bound together by energy. The reader takes that tiny poem bundle and releases the explosion of force to re-create the multifaceted and overwhelming experience. How great is that?

As to writing poetry, every undergraduate writes poetry! So I have been writing poetry since the seventies, but I have never achieved that perfect intensity. I prefer the full range of the novel.

Many authors find that their characters are extensions of themselves, in one way or another. Do you find that to be true? Which character do you identify with most? Do any of the characters in *Josefina's Sin* carry a resemblance to people you know?

Every character in *Josefina's Sin* has a small part of me, even the Marqués. But they are all fictional creations. Each owns a bit of my heart. I did steal Angélica's voice from a friend, because I most definitely can't sing!

Do you plan to revisit Josefina's world in your next novel? Or are you moving on to an entirely different time, place, and cast of characters?

In my next book, we do return to Josefina's world, twenty years later. In 1711, Consuelo, the Mayor's daughter, is fighting for her family's safety, while the Inquisition, in its waning moments, seeks to expose her family secret. Josefina's son Juan Carlos has grown into a very interesting young man with secrets of his own.

Who are your writing influences and what are you currently reading? Did you look to other popular historical novels such as *The Other Boleyn Girl,* by Philippa Gregory, for guidance?

My absolute favorites are Arturo Perez-Reverte's Captain Alatriste series, especially *Purity of Blood*. I read them in English and Spanish, some of them twice! I was also influenced by *The Coffee Trader,* by David Liss, and *Lucrezia Borgia and the Mother of Poisons,* by Roberta Gellis. They plunge you into the personal dramas of another world and provide you with an understanding of your own reality all at once.